Bayard and Martin:

A Historical Novel About Friendship and

the Civil Rights Movement

To Chris
Thank you for all your support.(
Frederick Will

Inquiries should be addressed to:
Jaed Publications
2504 N. Casitas
Altadena, California 91001
www.jaedpublications.com

ISBN 978-0-997-6552-2-3

Interior Text Design by TWA Solutions and Services

Cover Design by Avista Products

Printed in the United States of America
at One Touch Point-Southwest In Austin, Texas

Bayard and Martin

A Historical Novel About Friendship and

the Civil Rights Movement

by

Frederick J. Williams
Lane Denton
G. Sterling Zinsmeyer

Jaed Publications LLC

Los Angeles, California

Dedication

To all humanity seeking a more perfect world.

Acknowledgments

Contributor/Author Frederick Williams first and foremost acknowledges God for the gift creating and writing given to him. He acknowledges Angelika Rocha and Dr. Theresa Bailey for their outstanding editing of this work. Also, a special thank you to Jessica Tilles of TWA Solutions and Services for her excellent work in laying out the inside text for this work and Carl Booker of Avista Products for the book cover. Also, a thank you to Walter Naegle, Bayard Rustin's partner for life for helping him obtain a better understanding of the talent and genius of Mr. Rustin. An additional thank you to Theresa Williams-Scott for accepting this work for publication with Jaed Publications. Finally, a very special thank you to his wife Venetta Williams for always being there as the greatest supporter of all his writings.

Contributor/Author Lane Denton sends a huge thank you and appreciation to his daughter DeeAnn Denton and his grandson, Denton Ryan Boatner, who make him proud to be their dad and grandad. A special thank you to the individuals that stand committed to the human rights, justice, and freedom of all people worldwide and have been wonderful friends: Christian F. Brunner, former Texas State Representative Betty Denton, Curtis Johnson, Christopher Hammet, Lloyd Walsh, Bud Robinson, Kevin Elms, Robin Early, Emily Oliver, Robert Millar, Mario Guariso, Keith Sanford, Hope Reese, John Chrestia, Tom Green, Jesse Amato, Robert Antenucci, Bob Esterl, Jamie Flores, Michael Hyatt, Ray Chavez, Paul Boskin, Nick Rodriguez, Linda Lewis, and Patrick Small, Blair Davis, Tony Rogers, Paul Carter, Thomas Nylan, Kevine Parman, Cris Houston, Elizabeth Fauerso, David Harris, David Hurtado, Karlos Anzoategu, Gay Hundere, Chris Forbrich, John Tanner, Madyline Proctor, Oliver Muller, Steve Badrich, Chris Marshall, Leigh Marshall, Luis Garcia, and Jon O'Neal. His greatest gift was to work on this project with two dedicated individuals, authors Frederick Williams and G. Sterling Zinsmeyer.

Contributor/Author G. Sterling Zinsmeyer acknowledges his co-authors, Frederick Williams from whom he has learned so much about the contributions of African Americans to this country. Without Fred's amazing and extensive research this book simply would not exist and Lane Denton, a Texas hero, who keeps progressive politics alive and thriving. Lane helped to convince him how important this story needed to be told. He is grateful to his extended family who have encouraged him in this and other endeavors to include, Fred Moreno, Robert Callely, Maria and Edward Gale, Dick Erdman, Derek Simon, Rich Rickaby, Antonia Castaneda and Arturo Madrid. Mostly to his husband of 40 years, Louis Bixenman who grounds and supports him unconditionally in trying to live a life of contribution and curiosity!

PROLOGUE

April 4, 1968

Shock reverberates throughout my body as I hold the phone and listen to James Lawson shout, "They killed him, Bayard. The bastards shot and killed Martin"

My legs suddenly feel limp as I fall back into a big lounge chair in the living room of my apartment in New York City. I feel sick. This can't be happening and if I pinch my arm, I know I will wake up. But dreams or rather nightmares are only for the moment, and you can rise and know it was not real. But that is not the case. An old-time civil rights worker has just informed me that Dr. Martin Luther King, Jr. has been killed.

"Bayard, are you there?" James shouts.

I need to compose myself, "Yes, I'm here. What happened and when did it happen?" I finally ask, not knowing if those are relevant questions at this point in the conversation. But what else is there to say without having enough time to think it out.

"In Memphis," James replies. "You know he's here and it happened at the Lorraine Motel while he was on the balcony smoking a cigarette. Shot came from a building across the street. Bayard, it was terrible. I made it to the hospital moments after they announced he had passed."

Tears well up in my eyes as my sight is blurred. I glare at the time on my watch. It is a little after eight o'clock. I had planned to go out for a while with a friend but would now cancel and be alone. I need time to internalize what James just told me.

"Bayard, we're going to need you down here right away," James says in a calmer tone. "You are the one person that Martin would trust to continue organizing the proposed march on Washington in June. You can be a calming influence on the sanitation workers who, when they hear the news, will be ready to revolt. We have to stop this from becoming an all-out war on the streets in Memphis."

Not only Memphis, I thought, as I listen to James ramble on about why I must get down there right away, but all over the country.

"Your outspoken support for the right of the workers to unionize has served you well with them, and you more than any other leader in the country can help move their cause forward," Lawson continues.

I know I must go, even though my duties here in New York are very pressing. The Institute's major project is the Freedom Budget that occupies most of my time. But this is one of those situations that takes precedence over all others. How can such a magnanimous man just be shot down like some animal? How can this be happening now when we still need him so much. First Malcolm and now Martin.

"Bayard are you listening to me, man." James is practically screaming into the phone.

"Yes, my friend, I'm sorry," I say. "I'm sorry, but I have to give this time to register and of course I will be there for you and the workers." I pause to catch my breath. I find it hard to breathe. "I will make arrangements to fly out of here in the morning and be there by noon."

"Good, I'll let the others know that we can count on you."

"How is Coretta holding up?" I ask.

"I understand that she is taking it quite hard and now is under a doctor's care."

"Has it gone public yet?"

"It is breaking right now, and all hell is going to break loose. We must get a handle on this situation. We have the makings of a race war. We don't know if the shooter was white, but heaven help us if he was."

"Last year we had Newark and Detroit and under a lot less provocation than this," I say with a deep sigh. "Negroes been in a rioting mood since Watts and this might trigger the culmination of all of them."

"Just get down here Bayard and let's get a handle on this situation before it gets beyond our control. I'll look for you in the morning."

"I'll be there." With my assurance, we hang up.

I sit there for a moment and do nothing. I lay my head back on the lounge chair, close my eyes and feel the wetness of the tears. But this is not a moment to feel sorry for Martin or for me; there will be time for that in the future. I get a grip on my emotions, grab the phone and dial Paul's number. He answers on the third ring.

"I just saw it on the news and know that is why you're calling," he says.

"It's a tragedy larger than life. This will be the biggest crisis since the assassination of President Kennedy in '63," I say, voice quite choked.

"I guess our plans for this evening are canceled?" Paul assumes and he is right.

"Yes, I would be terrible company. They have just called and asked that I head out in the morning for Memphis. I have a lot I must do tonight so I can be out of here in the morning."

"I understand and if there is anything I can do for you, please let me know."

"Thank you, Paul. You're a wonderful friend. I'll make it up to you once this all calms down sometime in the next few weeks.

"Be careful and be safe, Bayard."

We finish and hang up. I place the phone down, get up and stroll into my bedroom and flop down on the bed, with legs straddling over the side. I don't know if I want to get undressed and crawl into bed or lay there and just reflect on some of the memories I have of this man and my relationship with him. I choose the latter.

PART ONE
Montgomery, Alabama

1.

February 1956

"You can't do that Phil," Norman Thomas, the elderly Socialist warrior from the past, spoke up adamantly.

He stared directly at me sitting next to A. Phillip Randolph in the second story office of the Brotherhood of Sleeping Car Porters, located in Harlem. James Farmer from CORE sat on the other side of Randolph, with A. J. Muste from the Fellowship of Reconciliation, Bill Worthy, a free-lance journalist for the black press and Jerry Wurf, a union head, all sat around the small conference table listening intently while Norman explained why I shouldn't be the person to go South and represent the pacifist, non-violent approach to change the escalating confrontation in Montgomery.

Thomas continued. "Bayard carries too much baggage that can be harmful to the movement."

"I'm not so sure I agree with you," Randolph said. "I talked with E. D. Nixon earlier this morning, and he expressed his support for Bayard, regardless of that baggage. He told me they need the help that he can bring to the boycott and assured me that Dr. King would agree that Bayard should come down there."

Without spelling it out, everyone at the table knew exactly what Norman was alluding to in his comments. I especially knew that he referred primarily to my arrest in January 1953 in Pasadena, California. My initial thought, as I listened to a man I considered a mentor and an old-time friend, was how and when could I ever recover from the enormous mistake I made then. A mistake within the context of a human one, but because it involved two other men, it received much more attention and repercussions for me. But it did not define me, and no way would I allow my attributes as a dedicated apostle of non-violence be upended in this way. I had to speak up.

"Norman, keep in mind the suggestion that I would be very useful to the movement in Montgomery emanated from a white woman from the South," I interjected before he could respond to Randolph. "Lillian Smith, someone you know quite well because of her work with you and James at the Congress on Racial Equality." I paused and looked over at Framer. I then pulled a paper from inside my jacket pocket and laid it on the table. "This is the telegram from her encouraging me to go down there immediately. She expresses concern for the escalating violence. The whites have already bombed Dr King's home as well as E. D. Nixon's. A substantial segment of the black population is threatening retaliation and encouraging those participating in the boycott to begin carrying guns. That would be disastrous and possibly lead to another slaughter of Negroes like happened in Tulsa back in 1921."

Norman refused to be distracted from his position. "Bayard, there are others that can go down there and deliver the non-violent message besides you. I love you like a son, but Dr. King is young and might not be able to handle the onslaught of attacks, especially the attacks on your arrest in 1953, your association with the Communist Party and the accusation that you were a draft dodger during World War II. Why add such a burden on Dr. King?"

"Despite my extreme disappointment in Bayard, I believe he is the right man for the job," A. J. Muste finally spoke up. "He more than most others, and especially King and the ministers down there, has the practical experience in self-discipline that is a key essential to Gandhian activism." Muste adjusted his body and leaned forward to make a point. "The boycott down there is an extreme opportunity for those of us who have advocated non-violence as the proper tool to achieve moral victories and can serve as a springboard for a mass movement throughout the South. Montgomery is the starting point, and no one is better equipped to lead that battle than Dr. King, but with Bayard's needed assistance."

I again glanced over at James, expecting him to comment but for some reason he remained quiet. His reticence was probably because he did not support me going down there but didn't want to go public with his opposition. He had committed to building a very strong CORE organization, also built around a non-violent approach to change. Both

James and I had spent time in India in late 1940's studying Gandhian non-violence under the master's disciples. Muste had been instrumental in launching CORE as an arm of the Fellowship of Reconciliation as early as 1940, and both James and I had worked to get the organization up and running. The Fellowship had supported CORE both financially and administratively. Since Muste had now spoken out in favor of me going to Montgomery, James would not oppose his position.

"Taking all factors into consideration, I believe our best bet is to support Bayard," Bill Worthy now chimed in. He had always been a friend and collaborated with me on many projects in the city, to include a new movement just launched by a coalition of leftist groups, called In Freedom. "Let's keep in mind that we all come to the table flawed in some way," he continued. "Warts and all, no one individual has been more involved in the struggle than Bayard." He gave me a hard stare. "He went to jail in 43 because of his commitment to non-violence and war, and then just got out of jail a few years ago, when he participated in CORE's Reconciliation Freedom Bus Ride. How many days were you locked up?"

"A month," I said, quite appreciative of Bill's support. "On a chain gang at the Roxboro Prison Camp in Roxboro, North Carolina. I'll never forget that experience and some of the men I met there."

"The workshops, they're the key," Muste said. "You have to conduct workshops on the philosophy of non-Violence." He spoke up like it was a done deal. His renewed support for me represented a complete turnaround from his attitude only two years ago, when he swore that he would never support me for any position in the pacifist cause due to the embarrassment I had brought on the movement. "You've done it before. You understand that the workshops must stress that non-violence is not just a tactic, but a way of life. It is not temporary but permanent."

"I'm well aware of what needs to be stressed at the workshops," I exclaimed somewhat irritated with Muste's tone. I still hadn't totally forgiven him for the manner that he turned his back on me when I was most in need of friendship, especially from him, someone I often looked upon as a father figure.

"Okay, I'm pretty sure that Bayard knows what has to be done." Randolph intervened as he probably recognized this might be going in the wrong direction. We all had to be on the same page to make this a success.

Past indiscretions and problems had to be set aside. I was willing to do just that and hopefully the others would make the same commitment.

"When can you be ready to leave?" Randolph turned and looked at me.

"How about Monday, the 20th. That'll give me tomorrow to get my house in order and be ready to pull out early Monday morning."

"Okay, that'll work," Randolph said. "Henry Washington and Kenny Jones, two of my porters that I'll arrange to drive you down there, will be at your place by seven."

"Remember, Bayard, while you're down there, stay clean," Muste admonished.

"I think I know how to conduct myself," I shot back at him.

"We're through here men," Randolph interjected, determined to not let the subtleties of the conversation go any further.

I quickly shook hands with the others, headed out of the building and waved down a cab to take me back to my apartment in Manhattan.

Arthur would not be happy with this news, I thought while peering out the backseat window of the cab as the driver swerved in and out of traffic, heading back down Broadway to West 107th Street. It was only last year that I had renewed my relationship with him. We had met over ten years ago, at a Quaker Academy in Upstate New York, but nothing really developed from our initial encounter. Arthur had come down to New York City a couple of years ago, to pursue a graduate degree in English Literature at Columbia University. He came into my life while I still recovered from the trauma in Pasadena and suffered from severe depression. He lifted my spirits and got me off the pity couch.

Arthur instantly set out to move me from my drab "rat hole" of an apartment on Mott Street. He found a place near the university on West 127th Street between Broadway and Amsterdam. We simply integrated the apartment with me being the only black and the two of us the only gay couple. It upset the landlord to no end when he saw me traipsing around the place, and even questioned why I was there. However, Arthur felt no need to explain my presence to him since nothing in the lease restricted him from having a roommate. But to have a black roommate, and one who was gay caused the landlord severe pain. Since I would be gone, I figured it would give him some relief for the next few months. As the cab driver pulled up to the apartment, I got out and paid him. I knew the next few hours would not be very pleasant.

Arthur sat at my old antique desk in the living room as I strolled inside, walked over and leaned down to hug him. He reciprocated and kissed me on my arm.

"Where have you been?" he asked. "Must have been something awfully important for you to stay out this late on a Saturday night." He swung his chair around to face me as I sat on the couch, a cherished antique I had gotten while in India.

"I've been asked to go to Montgomery, Alabama and work with Dr. King and the other folks in the bus boycott down there," I just blurted out. "Seems as though there is some fear that the entire event might turn violent. The white troublemakers are doing every and anything to antagonize the Negroes, hoping to incite them to violence. And if that happens, it'll all be catastrophic for my people."

"You're going down there to be the sheriff to keep the peace?"

"That sounds rather cynical, but yes, black people cannot resort to violence because that is a no-win situation."

"When do you plan to leave?"

"Monday morning and that gives us tonight and all day tomorrow to be together."

"How fortunate I am to have your undivided attention for two whole days."

"And the cynicism continues."

"Bayard, when are you going to think about you and just you alone for a change?" Arthur got up, walked over and sat next to me on the couch.

"You know I just adore you for what you do and stand for, but why walk into that hornet's nest down there."

I ran my hand through his wavy blonde hair and stroked the side of his face. "And I adore you also, but my people need me, and the cause never ends for us dedicated to change. You knew that about me when we first got together."

Arthur drew back away from me resting his body on the back of the couch and stared at the ceiling. "Is this what I can expect if we plan to spend our lives together; these abrupt interruptions whenever there is another crisis between the races?"

I turned to face him. "Arthur, these are fast changing times. Less than two years ago the Supreme Court set the precedent for changing the course of history in this country. The Brown decision was the catalyst to eradicate segregation throughout the entire country. Then a man like the landlord in this building won't have grounds to be upset because a Black man is living in the building."

"He's not upset because you're black, but because we're gay. That's what eats at his crotch."

"Don't matter, they're all the same. You get rid of one kind of prejudice and it's going to help bring down other prejudices. The Negro is setting the standard for what'll happen far into the future and we have a chance to play a part in that change. Can't you see, Arthur, this is our chance to make a difference and I mean a real big difference."

"If you're looking for my blessing on you leaving me for God knows how long, I'm just not in the mood to do that, but I'll accept your need to do this."

"I'll be back by the middle of March, promise." I said somewhat pleading with him. "And just think you'll have plenty of time to study without being disturbed. That'll work out fine for you, don't you think?"

Arthur softened his rigidity and hugged me. "I guess that'll work. But let's just enjoy each other and head down to the Village before it's too late."

"You got it," I said. We both got up and prepared to go out into New York night life for a few hours of entertainment.

2.

Driving into Montgomery you couldn't help but to be impressed with the clean streets and the low hanging trees, that I imagine in the summer were quite striking filled with leaves. It was shameful, I thought, that such a pretty city had such an ugly past and present history.

Before leaving New York on Monday morning I was informed that Dr. King would be at a meeting in Nashville, Tennessee when I arrived, and that my initial contact would be with his assistant, Reverend Ralph Abernathy. Once in the city, we drove directly to the parsonage right next to First Baptist Church where Abernathy resided. A crowd had gathered in front of the church as well as on the porch to his home. Four men with rifles at the ready position gave the crowd a menacing look as if to say, "we'll shoot you if we have too."

Henry Washington, who happened to be driving at that time, crept along the street behind a train of cars. I wasn't sure if most of these were gawkers or adversaries ready to do harm and up the ante for violence. We finally pulled up to the curb half a block from the house, parked the car and the two men stayed inside while I hurriedly walked down to the house.

One of the four guards gave me a hard stare and then stepped in front of my path as I was about to walk up the porch steps.

"I ain't ever seen you around here," he said. "Who are you and what you want with Reverend Abernathy.

"I'm down here from New York. Just arrived and I'm here to lend my assistance to the boycott," I replied.

The guard kept his position as he looked me up and down as if to determine should he let me by. He finally stepped aside and motioned with his rifle for me to go on by.

A crowd of men and women, some young and others older, sauntered in and out of the house so the door remained open. I strolled inside and spotted Abernathy sitting on the couch in the living room looking over some papers. He didn't bother to look up as I approached.

"Morning, Reverend Abernathy," I said. "I'm Bayard Rustin and just got down here from New York."

He didn't look up. Just kept going over his papers.

"Dr. King is expecting me as is Mr. Dixon. I'm an associate of A. Philip Randolph and like I said, Dr. King is expecting me."

The second time I mentioned Dr. King's name, Abernathy finally looked up.

"Sorry, didn't mean to ignore you but we're awfully busy. Just got word that the Grand Jury has returned indictments against one hundred of us for breaking some bogus law from way back in 1921, that says it's unlawful to conspire to interfere with lawful business in the state of Alabama." He paused, got up and finally shook my hand. "Have you ever heard of anything so ridiculous? It is definitely not what we're doing."

"No, can't say I have," I said. "Sounds like one of those laws these folks are always conjuring up to use against us. Don't matter where, the same thing happens up North, too."

"Who'd you say sent you down here?" He now sounded apprehensive.

"Mrs. Lillian Smith first suggested to me that I might want to come down here and assist in educating the people in non-violence. You do know Mrs. Smith, don't you?"

"Yes, of course. One of the more decent white folks. But didn't you also say A. Phillip Randolph?"

"Sure did."

"Listen, I don't mean to be short with you, but all hell is breaking loose this morning with these indictments and I just don't have time to talk. Maybe later in the day if you come on back, we can have some time."

I could only hope that this was not an indication of how things would go, but maybe it might be different once I met with E. D. "I understand, and certainly don't want to be in your way."

"Good, good," Abernathy gasped. "Where you staying?"

"They got me over at Ben Moore Hotel. Told me it's the only place that Negroes can stay in Montgomery."

"That's about right," Abernathy chuckled. "Kind of ridiculous when you think about it. All these hotels in the city and Negroes can only stay at a small motel off the Highway 65."

"Well, that's what this is all about. This is the beginning to bringing an end to all this foolishness." I agreed. "These white folks are trying to hold on to a way of life that will soon come to an end. The country is changing, and the South is going to have to stay up with those changes."

"Why don't you get on over and meet with E. D. at Holt Street Baptist Church on Holt and Bullock. That's where he spends a lot of his time during the day. You know they bombed his house just a few weeks ago, and he's moved his family to temporarily live with some friends."

"You have the address?" I asked.

"No, not the exact address, just know it's on the corner. Are you driving?"

"Right now, yes. But in the morning, the men who drove me down here will head back to New York."

"No problem, I'll get one of my church members to take you all over there. Pull your car up front and he'll meet you there." We shook hands and he continued, "Oh, and by the way, when these rednecks find out you're here from New York, they'll be out to get you. Make sure you don't wander out too far after dark unless you're with us, and by all means close your curtains tight when you go to bed."

A large crowd had gathered right out front of Holt Street Baptist Church and the parking lot was full. Evidently, Montgomery Improvement Agency planned some kind of event for that afternoon. The church marquee had glaring letters that read, "Holt Street Baptist Church, Dr. A. W. Wilson, Pastor. Church Founded in 1909, Reverend I. S. Fountain, Founding Pastor." And right below in large letters, "LORD I JUST CAN'T TURN BACK."

Kenny, my other driver, pulled up in front of the church. "Mr. Rustin, you can get out here and I'll find a parking place down the street. We'll see you when you come back out."

"Good, then we can go check into the hotel for the night," I said as I hesitated before getting out of the car.

Suddenly Henry raised his head from against the window where he had been napping since we left Abernathy's place. "Beg your pardon Mr.

Rustin, but Kenny and I done discussed this situation and we feel rested well enough so that we can head on back to New York this evening after you get situated at your hotel."

I sat back in the seat. "What do you mean, you men haven't been in a bed since we left New York yesterday morning. We been on the road for almost twenty-four hours."

Henry turned to face me. "Now that's true but remember we're porters and used to going with just a little bit of sleep. And truth be told, neither one of us is too anxious to spend no more time in this racist city than is necessary."

"Mr. Rustin, I got a cousin who was lynched right outside Selma, Alabama back in 1948, and just because they thought he was getting out of line," Kenny exclaimed without looking back at me. "And they lynched him in his uniform. He'd been sent to Japan to fight them Japs and came back home and got killed by these rednecks. My family left from down here in '49 and ain't none of us been back. Now I took this job 'cause Mr. Randolph asked me too but believe me I didn't want to and the sooner I can get out of here the better."

I sat momentarily frozen in my seat. How could I possibly challenge Kenny's reason for wanting to get out of Alabama as soon as he could.

"I been nervous ever since we crossed the Mason/Dixon Line back in Maryland and came through all these Southern states with New York State license plate. Just knew we'd get pulled over," Henry said. "We sure don't want to be doing a whole lot of driving around in this city with these license plates and we know this place is about to explode."

"Ever since they murdered my cousin, I swore I'd never take any shit off these peckerwoods." Kenny took the palm of both hands and slammed them against the steering wheel. "We know you believe in this non-violent stuff and so does Mr. Randolph. And I respect you for that, but if one these sons of bitches stops us and tries to do any kind of bodily harm, they going to have to kill me, 'cause I'm sure going to kill them." Kenny reached down under the seat and when he rose, he waved a pistol in the car.

"What? You've had a gun on this trip?" I practically shouted.

"Yes sir, Mr. Rustin," he said. "I don't mean to disrespect you, but not all us Negroes believe in letting these folks bomb our homes, rape our women, and kill our boys without fighting back."

"Put that gun down," I demanded. "As long as we're in this car together, don't ever display it again." I paused to catch my breath. "I think it's best that you men do head back to New York. When I get settled in this evening, you should leave."

"Like Kenny said, Mr. Rustin," Henry spoke up. "We don't mean to disrespect you or Mr. Randolph but some of us just believe we got to fight back. Negroes been getting beat up all my life and maybe they'll take that stuff down here, but we from up North and believe if you hit me, I got to hit you back, especially if you're white."

I leaned forward and opened the door. "I don't know how long I'll be, but I'll try to make it as short as possible. And please don't be sitting in this car with New York plates flashing that gun." I got out of the car, walked up the front steps and into the church.

As I strolled through the foyer and into the sanctuary, a tall, balding man shouted, "You must be Bayard Rustin." He waved me down to the front of the church. "I'm E. D. Nixon, and I'm sure glad to see you."

He broke away from two young people he had been talking with and approached me, with right hand extended. We shook hands and he continued, "We have one thing in common and that is we both have the same hero and that's Mr. Randolph. I been a follower of his ever since I met him in St. Louis three years ago. I been a Pullman Porter for ten years and never felt I had any rights as a man until he organized the porters. After meeting him, I came home and organized a branch right here in Montgomery."

"He is quite a leader, my mentor and half the reason I'm down here right now," I said.

"Just half? What's the other half?"

"The opportunity to make non-violence an intricate part of the battle to break down segregation not only here in Montgomery, but all over the South."

Nixon took a step back from me. "That's something we sure don't have in common," he said. "I talked at length with Mr. Randolph and let him know that there are a lot of Negroes right here in Montgomery who don't agree with this non-violent, don't fight back approach. We are very much aware that our leader, Dr. King, is a strong advocate and you'll be working closely with him on the proper use of that tactic. But I---,"

"Pardon me, Mr. Nixon, but it is not a tactic, it is a way of life. It must be a part of your very existence. Sorry didn't mean to cut you off."

"I was going to say that I will not interfere with that approach, but don't expect me to march with you all and let another person hit me or even try to kill me without retaliating."

I momentarily thought how can this man as well as Kenny and Henry, all members of Randolph's Brotherhood of Sleeping Car Porters, be so opposed to a philosophy that he believes in so strongly?

"But we have a much larger problem right now and that is the fact that the sheriff will anytime begin to arrest the nearly one hundred blacks who have been identified as leaders of the protest."

Now he gave me an opportunity to score points with him on a Gandhian principle, without his knowledge that it was happening.

"If I may offer this tidbit of advice that is if you don't mind?

"Please do, just as long as it doesn't call for me to let another man beat me upside the head."

"It doesn't. In fact, it allows you to score a victory over him."

"This I got to hear. Have at it." He motioned for me to take a seat right in the front row pew. He sat next to me as if to make sure I had his full attention.

"Don't let them come to you," I began. "You, all one hundred, go to them. Tomorrow morning have everyone dress up, like you're going to church and march down to the courthouse and tell the sheriff that you are there to turn yourself in and accept punishment for what is a just and rightful cause." What E. D. didn't know, and I didn't tell him was that such action would be consistent with the Gandhian tactic against oppressive powers. By not resisting you rise above your oppressor, so he no longer has the gratification of exercising power over you. "Don't wait for the sheriff to arrest you as if you're a common criminal," I continued. "In the morning, march right down there and let them know that you are wearing your indictment with pride. That will be your victory."

Nixon smiled. "I like it, I really like it."

"Many people have the idea that being non-violent is equivalent to being passive. Nothing is further from the truth. We are always and at all time activists in our behavior. To take abuse without striking back is a method Gandhi used in India and one I learned while studying under his disciples in that country back in 1948."

"You actually went to India and studied under Gandhi?" Nixon asked

"I didn't study under him because by the time I got over there he had already been murdered. But his disciples were excellent teachers and just as dedicated to the pacifist ideology as was Gandhi. I had many discussions with Nehru. The Indian people have very little respect for Western pacifists because they don't believe the American people have made any sacrifices, but I believe that will change with the battle to eliminate these abusive laws in the South." I stopped to catch my breath.

"You think we should just march up to that courthouse tomorrow and surrender to the authorities," Nixon said using this opportunity to return to the subject at hand.

"Exactly, it will catch them off guard and they probably won't know how to respond."

"Mr. Nixon, you're needed in the other room," a young lady interrupted our conversation. She stood waiting for a response.

"All right, I'll be right there," Nixon said as he stood up.

I also got up.

"Come on with me," he signaled for me to follow him. "The others who have received indictments are gathering in the Pastor's conference room to discuss strategy." He walked just a few steps in front of me and I followed close behind. "Let's find out if the others think your idea is a good one."

It was after eight o'clock when Henry pulled up in front of the four-story red brick building with two white signs above the first floor, right at the corner of High and Jackson Street. The one just above the entrance to the building read, "Majestic Café," and the one directly above it read "Ben Moore Hotel." I climbed out of the backseat and before I could get to the back of the car, Kenny also had gotten out and was taking my luggage out of the trunk.

"We was told to make sure we got you all the way into the hotel," Kenny said as he grabbed both my suitcases and started to the entrance to the hotel. I followed close behind him and Henry stayed in the car. I knew he wanted to hit the road back to New York and as soon as I got checked in, they would hit the highway and leave this city behind them.

I strolled up to the registration desk and before I could speak, the clerk behind the counter said, "You must be Mr. Bayard Rustin from New York?"

"That's a pretty good guess," I said.

"Ain't no guess," the clerk replied. "We been expecting you and I knew it was you by the way you're dressed, all big city, New York like."

Kenny placed my luggage down and stood off to the right patiently waiting for me to hurry up and get checked in so he could get out of there.

"Is that a good thing or a bad thing?" I questioned the clerk

"All depends," he responded. "Pretty good thing for us from down here 'cause we don't ever hardly see no northern folks in here but been quite a few showing up since this mess got started." He paused as if expecting a response from me. He got none and continued. "It's a bad thing for you 'cause this KKK folks gonna know you ain't from around here and they gonna be watching you awfully close." Again, he paused waiting for a response like he just knew his remarks would get a rise out of me. And again, it didn't so he slid a registration form toward me and said, "Please fill this out and I can get you squared away in a room."

I finished the registration and slid the form back toward him. He studied it for a minute and then gave me a key. "Room 202, second floor down the right side of the hall."

Remembering what others had told me about being careful while in my room and to sleep lightly, I asked, "Can't you give me a room on the fourth floor?"

"No sir, all the rooms are on the second and third floor. It's a dance hall up on the fourth floor," he said and then smiled. "On this floor is the Majestic Café with some of the best food in Montgomery, and there is a barber shop in the basement case you might need a haircut in the morning."

I took the key and then turned to face Kenny who stood patiently waiting. "I think I'll be all right now," I said as I bent down to pick up my luggage.

He reached down and grabbed both suitcases before I did. "No way Mr. Rustin," he said as he lifted them off the ground. "Our instructions was to make sure you were all checked in and that's what I plan to do."

I stared at him somewhat in disbelief with his level of thoroughness and commitment to Mr. Randolph. "No problem." We both walked past the registration desk and toward the stairwell to the second floor.

Kenny wasted no time placing the luggage in the closet area of the very small room, with nothing more than a bed, one chair and a very tight bathroom area. We then headed back downstairs and out to the car still parked right in front of the hotel.

Kenny opened the driver's side door and startled Henry who had drifted off to sleep. Made me wonder about the two of them getting back on the road and it was already after nine o'clock. Kenny climbed into the driver's seat.

"I can start off driving," he said. "I know I can make the other side of Atlanta and probably to South Carolina."

"That works for me." Henry stretched and wiped the sleep from his eyes. "Give me time to catch some more sleep and then I'll get us to Virginia by the morning."

"You men sure you're all right to make this drive back to New York?" I had to ask. "You can always get a good night's rest and take off in the morning. Get you there by tomorrow night."

"No way, Mr. Rustin," Kenny said as he started the car, a strong indication that my suggestion was for naught. "We appreciate the concern and the offer, but we're out of here."

"I understand," I stepped back onto the curb. "Be careful and be safe." I said and the car pulled off down the street. I watched as they turned the corner and disappeared. There was no turning back for me as now my safety valve just left. Up until that moment, I could always change my mind, climb into the back seat of the car, and return to the safe environment of New York.

I could feel a chill and wasn't sure if it hit me from the cold wind that blew in from the river or the fact that I had to face up to the reality of being isolated among a lot of strangers, many who resented my presence here, and many who would never accept non-violence as a way to fight racial bigotry.

I pulled my topcoat tighter around my body and finally stared down Jackson Street toward the parish house where Martin and Coretta lived, all lit up with lights that made it a sitting target. I could also make out the figures of two men standing out front. I walked down Jackson and a young Negro boy who couldn't have been no older than eighteen, pointed his rifle right at my midsection.

"That's far enough," he commanded. "Who are you and why you here in front of Dr. King's house?"

I watched as the other young man at the other end of the house now rushed toward me also brandishing a rifle. "Who is he Jessie? And what's he want with Dr. King?"

"Don't know, but I sure mean to find out," Jessie answered. "What you want Mister?" he asked but before I could respond, he continued. "We ain't about to let you near Dr. King's house. It's been bombed once back in January and it ain't about to happen again."

"Trust me, I am not here to do any harm to Dr. King's house or any other house in the neighborhood. For that matter, I don't mean to do any harm to anyone. I'm up here from New York and come to help in the boycott. I'm staying down the street at the Ben Moore Hotel, and just wanted to personally observe the damage done to Dr. King's house."

"We can't let you any closer. Maybe when Dr. King gets back from his trip on Thursday, he'll let you in."

"That's fine with me. Have a good night." I walked back toward the hotel.

Halfway down the block I could detect a car following close behind me with the lights out. I was tempted to stop, turn around and look inside. But my better judgement suggested that wouldn't be too wise, so I picked up my pace and breathed a sigh of relief when I finally reached the hotel, swung the door open and bolted inside.

As I hurried past the registration desk, the same young man who had registered me into the hotel looked up from the book he was reading and said, "Being that you from out of town, it's not too wise for you to be wandering these streets after dark. Best stay in your room and make sure you keep your blinds closed. These white folks notorious for throwing stuff through your window if they know the room you're in."

Thank you," I said and ran up the steps.

3.

It was like magic to my eyes as I watched one man after another, dressed in their Sunday best, march up the courthouse steps and inside to report to the jailer. Nixon was the first one to go inside and proudly announce that he was there to be arrested for fighting a battle for justice. The men had accepted my suggestion made yesterday at the meeting that they voluntarily turn themselves in and make a clear statement that they managed their destination.

A crowd had assembled outside the courthouse and applauded as each man made his way up the steps and inside. Before disappearing behind the doors, they bowed and tipped their hats to the men and women assembled outside. Soon a white crowd also gathered right behind where we stood. They appeared to be in shock at the sight of all those black folks reporting to jail.

Most of the men paid their own bail and the NAACP, through Nixon's efforts, had wired down enough money that morning to cover bail for all the others. By noon, they had been released and we headed over to Dexter Baptist Church for a celebration of unity, even though Dr. King remained out of town.

A rumor had spread that Daddy King tried desperately to keep Martin in Atlanta where he had stopped after his conference in Nashville. Daddy King knew that his son had been named as one of the conspirators under the indictment and argued that the police really didn't want the other hundred, but only his son. Rumblings had started around the church that Martin considered not coming back to Montgomery and staying in Atlanta as assistant pastor to his father at Ebenezer and eventually taking over as pastor.

"Nothing is further from the truth," Reverend Abernathy shouted from the pulpit to a packed church. "Dr. King will be on his way back sometime this afternoon. He just got delayed in Atlanta but has no plans not to come home to us." He spotted me as I had just walked into the sanctuary and stood in the back. He quickly waved me forward.

I reluctantly strolled toward the front, a little apprehensive to be introduced to this crowd that seemed to be angry about the rumor. Hopefully, they wouldn't take it out on me. I stopped right at the front pew and hoped that the Reverend would not invite me up to the pulpit.

"Let me take this opportunity to introduce to you all, a friend we have all the way down here from New York, Mr. Bayard Rustin. He has been involved in civil rights for the past twenty years and is a good friend of the great A. Phillip Randolph, the man who defied the Pullman organization and united the black workers under the Brotherhood of Sleeping Car Porters. He is here at the request of our leader Dr. King with a very special mission and message for us. Let's give him a good Montgomery greeting and get him up here to say a few words." Abernathy extended his arms as an indication for the men and women to clap a greeting.

This was totally unexpected as the crowd applauded and I walked up to the microphone set up on the other side of the pulpit. I had been briefed years ago that unless you are a Baptist preacher you never go to the pulpit microphone. That is reserved only for ordained ministers. Most Baptist churches will always have an alternative microphone for others to use.

"On behalf of the Montgomery Improvement Association, I greet you and welcome you to our city and our struggle," Abernathy said with a smile.

While adjusting the microphone, I wondered just how much these people really knew about me, and when my past surfaced would they still be so cordial. I assumed Abernathy knew about Pasadena and other members of the Montgomery Improvement Association, especially Mr. Nixon. The other lingering thought centered around how they would respond when they knew the primary reason for my presence in their city, and as a part of their cause, was to convince them to put away their guns. If last night was any indication of what to expect then my welcome might be short lived.

"Thank you, Reverend Abernathy," I began. "It's my honor and pleasure to be with you all here in Montgomery and possibly play a small role in making history."

"Ain't you one of them Mahatma Gandhi men who don't believe in fighting back?" someone shouted from the crowd.

I guess my reputation preceded me, I thought, before responding. "I can assure you that I believe, and Mahatma Gandhi believed in fighting back," I replied. This wasn't the direction I wanted this introduction to take but since the man put it out there, I felt compelled to answer.

"You don't believe in using no guns, is that right?" the same man shouted.

"Please let's be cordial and polite to our guest," Abernathy said from the pulpit.

"That's perfectly all right Reverend," I said. I did appreciate his intervention but why not face up to the issue now instead of later. Gandhi always told his followers there would be many who doubted pacifism and others who would embrace the concept. Their goal was to influence and convince as many as possible of the positive good of non-violence. That's why I came to Montgomery and might as well get started right then with the task. "You are absolutely correct, my friend, in what you say. We do not believe in the use of destructive weapons of any nature as the way to improve on one's life. We believe that love is the most powerful weapon in man's arsenal. Once you shoot and kill another, you can never make a change in that persons' behavior."

"Yeah, well why don't you tell that to them peckerwoods on the other side of town who just the other night held a rally and you know what their call for unity and action was?"

I was a little reluctant to feed into this man's set-up by responding to his question but did anyway. "No, I don't. I wasn't in town yet." I knew what was probably coming and decided I might as well deal with it now.

"Let me read from this leaflet they passed out to the thousands that gathered for their hateful attack on what we're trying to do on this side of town. He held the leaflet high in the air and repeated the contents which he obviously had memorized. "We hold these truths to be self-evident that all whites are created equal with certain rights, among these are life, liberty and pursuit of dead niggers."

I refrained for the moment and listened as the entire crowd reacted with negative jeers and boos. Men and women raised their outstretched arms and made fists as signs of defiance. There was no way I could counter that kind of hateful rhetoric on the leaflet the man continued to hold high above his head, that set off a negative response from these church-going folks who, at that moment, wanted no part of a non-violent lecture from me.

Suddenly their jeers and boos turned to cheers as Nixon led the men into the sanctuary and up to the front of the church. They provided me with a momentary escape from the onslaught. I moved back from the microphone as Nixon took my place and addressed the audience.

"What a glorious victory we enjoyed this morning," he shouted. "We men, all one-hundred of us, marched into the courthouse and down to the jail and volunteered to be arrested for what we believed in."

The mood in the sanctuary had shifted from anger to joy.

Nixon continued. "When our friend from New York, Mr. Bayard Rustin, first presented this idea to me yesterday, I thought it was crazy. No one voluntarily goes to jail, but when he explained it in detail to me and all these men, we agreed it made sense." He paused, turned and faced me. "Thank you." He then turned back to face the crowd. "He explained that we should refuse to be hunted down like dogs. White folks believe that's the way we supposed to act when they come looking for us. Instead we went to them and they stood there all flabbergasted just like they couldn't believe it was happening."

The crowd continued to cheer and applaud the men who stood stoically in the front row of the church and faced their admirers. Instantly, Reverend Abernathy took to the pulpit and used this opportunity to further fire up the crowd.

"This morning, me and some of the members of the Association adopted a theme song for our movement written by our guest, Mr. Bayard Rustin. It goes like this, 'We are moving on to victory. We shall all stand together till everyone is free. We know love is the watchword for peace and liberty. Black and white all are brothers to live in harmony. We are moving on to victory. With hope and dignity.'"

While Abernathy sang, the piano player picked up the tune of the old spiritual, "Give me that old-time religion," and the entire congregation began to sing along as the verses were repeated four times, building the crowd to a fever pitch. For the next half-hour over a half-dozen ministers took to the pulpit and offered a prayer of deliverance for what they wanted to accomplish, all while the piano player, now joined by the organist, continued to play.

Standing in the background and observing what amounted to a good old-fashion Baptist prayer meeting my thoughts drifted back to home in West Chester, Pennsylvania, growing up in a religiously devout household. On Sundays I spent all day in Bethel A. M. E. Church where Grandpa Janifer was a deacon. During high school, I even preached a couple of sermons and everyone just knew I'd grow up to be a preacher. That possibility was short lived but as I listened to the singing, I also recalled the many times I sang solo for the church.

"Let me assure you, children of the Almighty, God is working His miracles right here in Montgomery," Abernathy exclaimed after the music and prayers ended. "He sent one of his real emissaries to this church to do His work and Dr. King has been ordained to make a difference in this city, all over this state and across this country. His mission was pre-ordained, and you don't have to worry about him coming home because God is directing his actions, and I can assure you, He is sending him back to continue the work of the Lord." He paused and looked over at Nixon who still stood at the other microphone. "Brother, is there anything else you'd like to add?"

"No, I believe pretty much everything that needed to be said has been shared with all these good people. We just have to continue to be diligent and know that the battle has just begun, but it is ours to win." He also paused and turned to look at me. "Brother Rustin, is there anything you'd like to say at this time?"

I didn't bother to get up, but instead shook my head no. I didn't want to give the crowd the opportunity to shift their mood back to anger. I knew if I did approach the microphone, it would cause them to return to the subject of non-violence and that had generated quite a stir earlier before the men marched into the sanctuary. That short exchange convinced me that my work would be restricted to the leaders not the masses. I could effectively train Dr. King and other ministers in the effective use of non-violent methods and they pass it on to the followers who were directly involved in the boycott. This must be done piece meal and I was satisfied with that approach.

Just as I felt that I couldn't be any lonelier and isolated, I caught a glimpse of Bill Worthy coming into the sanctuary. I never expected to see someone from New York in that place. My spirits began to change. I now had an ally from home and his support would make my job that much easier. But it was just like Bill to make it to where the action was happening. As a journalist, he always followed the story having gone to China right after the revolution for a short period of time. If I could have expected anyone from New York to show up, it would be Bill. I couldn't wait to get down from this place up front and brief him to what was going on here in Montgomery.

We made it back to the Majestic Café inside the Ben Moore Hotel, where Bill was also checked in, just before closing time. He had managed to get the very last room available on the third floor. The hotel was completely booked with Negro reporters from across the country. Evidently the **Baltimore African American** had pulled some strings with the owners of the hotel and managed to reserve him a room. We had a table right in front of a big picture window that looked out onto Jackson Street. The restaurant was full to capacity and the two waitresses hurried from one table to the next taking orders and delivering meals. We waited for them to finally get to our table.

"What made you decide to come down here?" I asked as I watched the waitress take an order from the two men and two women at the table next to us.

"Now come on, Bayard, you know there was no way I'd miss out on this history that's happening right in front of us. The **Baltimore African American** had contacted me in New York and asked if I'd make the trip."

"You have no idea how pleased I was to see you walk through that door. Earlier, I'd taken quite a tongue lashing from the people there. Evidently the Citizens Council, which is nothing more than the Ku Klux Klan in suits, put out some leaflets calling for the killing of all the niggers as they put it."

"I guess that could make someone a little angry," Bill said. "Especially if the person they are angry with, is talking about putting down all your weapons and making yourself vulnerable to a group of people who are pledged to shoot you."

"I know you all agreed to support my efforts to come down here and push the whole concept on non-violence as a means to effectuate change, but I can't do it in a large setting like at the church earlier," I said as I watched that same car that followed me back to the hotel last night slowly drive by the hotel. Only this time there were four men inside the car.

Bill also watched the car drive slowly by. "Some of your friends?" he asked.

"Not quite," I said. "They followed me back to the hotel last night after I'd walked down to Dexter Baptist Church and the bombed parish where King lives."

"Yeah, I noticed it when I came in. It was bombed pretty good. I can understand why these folks are a little nervous and tend to reject what you're preaching."

"Problem is, I don't believe the leadership is sold on the idea of non-violence. King must know that his house is being guarded by men carrying weapons."

"I believe Dr. King has taken the position that non-violence is the tactic to be employed in this case," Bill suggested.

"But you see that's the problem. Non-violence is not just a tactic but it's a way of life. You just don't employ it once and then jettison it later. You fully live it as the principle that guides your behavior. If Dr. King had accepted that basic tenant, then there is no way he would allow those men to stand out front of his house with guns."

"It looks like you have your work cut out for you," Bill said. "By the way, where is Dr. King? He wasn't at the meeting."

"He's in Atlanta and will be back first thing in the morning. I plan to be at his house bright and early. You care to join me?"

"I'd love to, but you might have a bigger problem than just teaching the masses to be passive." He paused as the waitress finally approached our table.

"Can I take you gentlemen's orders," she asked.

"Yes, for sure," I said. "I'll have tonight's special of friend pork chops, mashed potatoes and greens, with a Pepsi. And later a piece of sweet potato pie."

She finished writing my order on a note pad and then looked at Bill.

"The same order for me," he said.

She smiled, "I'll get them out to you in no time," she said and turned and walked away.

"Like I was saying," Bill continued. "John Swomley and Charles Lawrence over at the Fellowship of Reconciliation are making rumblings with Randolph and the others who supported you coming down here. They claim that you're too big a risk and that you need to be replaced immediately."

Ever since the incident in Pasadena, Swomley had turned against me and played a key role in getting me dismissed from the organization. Lawrence had just become national chairman and I believe took his lead from Swomley who was the organization's executive secretary.

"They believe you might actually cause an incident and that your background will come to light and that will be the ammunition the whites need to damage the boycott. They're not talking about your failure to go into the draft or your communist affiliation. They are specifically talking about your homosexual activities. They are working hard to get you replaced with Glen Smiley from California."

"I've known Glen since my early days at the Fellowship," I responded showing very little emotion. "He is well versed in Gandhian philosophy and certainly could do an outstanding job teaching it to Dr. King."

"But he's white," Bill blurted out so that some of the other diners looked over at our table. He lowered his voice and continued. "It is important that you be the one who brings the Gandhian methodology to the Negro clergy, not only here but all over the South."

"Glen is a good man, and if necessary, he would be an excellent replacement," I retorted.

"Damnit Bayard, stop being so condescending. The Negro race needs our own people to lead in every aspect of this movement. You have an important role to play and hopefully, Mr. Randolph and the others will not give in to Swomley's efforts to replace you."

"Let's just see what happens," I said in an attempt to calm Bill down. "In the meantime, let's enjoy our meal, get a good night's sleep and be ready to meet with Dr. King in the morning."

"If you say so," Bill replied as the waitress brought our tray of food to the table.

"And remember to close your shades in your room and don't go out walking tonight. These folks will know you're not from around here. That advice was given to me last night by a very wise young man at the desk and I feel compelled to pass it on to you."

4.

"Bayard, I have a pressing emergency back home in New York and need to spend the morning taking care of it," Bill said over the phone a little after seven. "Can I catch up to you later in the day, maybe for lunch if you're free?"

I had already dressed and ready to walk out the door and meet him in the cafeteria. I wondered what could be more important than meeting with the most important Black man in America. "No problem," I said not prepared to query why he had to cancel. "Maybe we can meet back here about noon and take it from there."

"Sounds good to me," he said, and we hung up.

I decided to skip breakfast and head right over to the King residence. I still felt a little stuffed from the heavy dinner last night and this feeling of anxiety to finally meet the new, sensational leader of Black America pushed me past the entrance to the Majestic, despite the excellent aromas of bacon and coffee.

The morning temperature had dropped from yesterday and as I strolled out into the morning air the chill hit me and I instantly pulled my overcoat uptight around my neck. My thoughts turned to the many men and women who would walk this morning from their homes to their jobs in the white neighborhoods. Some of them walked as far as five miles if they missed out on a ride, a common occurrence because of the police order to stop private cars acting as public transportation. Several reports had estimated the number of participants in the boycott at nearly seventeen thousand. That was seventeen thousand men, women and children who had taken abuse from drivers of the buses for years. But they had finally gotten to the point where they would rather confront the freezing cold than continue to confront abusive human beings. As I approached the King residence, I recognized that they were the real heroes in this battle. Not King, Nixon, Abernathy or the other black leaders in the city, but those nameless thousands that followed the lead of others and remained loyal to the cause.

A much larger and older man stopped me just as I reached the porch. This time he had no rifle. I guess he figured his size compensated for the need to carry a weapon.

"Sorry, I can't let you go in," he said.

"But the Dr. King is expecting me." I tried to get around him, but his size served as a deterrent. I had to convince him of my legitimacy. "I'm up here from New York at Dr. King's request and I know he just got back in town. I really need to meet him before the MIA meeting tonight."

"Don't matter to me, my orders is not to let anyone in."

"If you don't let me by, I believe Dr. King's going to be just a bit upset."

"Don't matter I…,"

"Let him up." Coretta Scott King called out standing behind the screen door on the porch.

The man looked up at her, then at me and moved out of the way. I strolled past him and up the steps of the porch. "Mrs. King, it is a pleasure."

"Come on in," she said while holding the screen door open.

As I walked past her into the house I asked, "How did you know me?"

"Yes, you're Mr. Rustin from New York. Years back you spoke to my high school class in Marion, Alabama. You were representing the Fellowship of Reconciliation. You probably don't remember, but I definitely remember you."

"That is a compliment to say the least," I said. She motioned for me to have a seat at the kitchen table.

"Martin had to go to a seven o'clock meeting but told me to let you know he'd be back a little after eight. Would you like a cup of coffee?"

"I'd love a cup of coffee."

"Cream and sugar?"

"No, I'll take it black."

After pouring the cup of coffee and placing it on the table, she then took a seat on the other side. "My baby is sleep right now. Everyone's been nervous about what's happening with all these bombs and violence. Martin was meeting at the church discussing the boycott when the bomb went off. Thank God me and Yuki was in my bedroom and the explosion only shattered the glass in the living room and did some damage on the porch." She paused to take a sip from her cup, and I did the same. "The men from the church went to work right away and practically repaired all the damage in less than a week. God is good. There is still some work left to be done but not as bad as before."

"I really do admire the courage you all have displayed throughout this entire ordeal," I said.

"We have the Lord on our side and if He is with you, who can harm you?"

"Good point," I said, but not quite sure I agreed. No doubt God was just and fair, but sometimes He looked for you to do certain things on your own. I didn't believe in making God a crutch or as some ministers preached "lean on Jesus."

"It is men like you who've paved the way for men like my husband," she said. "The way that you and Mr. Randolph challenged President Roosevelt back in 1941 and then President Truman in '48 opened the door for this movement."

I took another sip from my cup and took it all in. I was willing to accept some of the credit for the advances the race had made over the past fifteen years, but most of it belonged to Mr. Randolph. I was there when he forced President Roosevelt's hand on the employment issue and forced him to sign that executive order. Then he did the same with President Truman and his efforts led to the integration of the military. But those battles were fought up North where men could be more reasonable. There was no reasoning with the white mobs in the South and that's why men like Dr. King and Nixon were much more magnanimous than we in the North. I had to share that with Coretta.

"We did our part but there is no comparison to what you all are doing here in the South where the stakes are so much higher," I said. "I admire what your husband is doing and all the other leaders and of course you also." Looking out the kitchen window I watched as Dr. King pulled his Ford into the driveway, got out and headed inside through the kitchen entrance.

I stood to greet him as he walked through the door. He smiled, walked over to me and extended his arm. We shook vigorously.

"Bayard Rustin, I take it," he said.

"How are you Dr. King?" I asked.

"Please, with you it is Martin and I'm doing quite well." He took off his coat and hung it on a rack just outside the kitchen, quickly returned and poured himself a cup of coffee. He then pulled a pack of cigarettes from inside his shirt pocket, offered me one, which I gladly accepted. We both lit up and that created the right mood for us.

"Pray that your stay here in Montgomery has been pleasant so far," he said.

"You gentlemen excuse me," Coretta said before I could respond. "I need to check on my child and take care some business around the house. Hope to see you again Mr. Rustin."

We all got up as she did and nodded our approval. She then hurried out of the kitchen. Martin and I sat back down.

"My stay so far has been quite interesting," I finally responded. "I met Reverend Abernathy, had a long conversation with E. D. Nixon and attended a very lively rally yesterday that carried over into the night at Dexter."

"Okay then, you've met the key players on our side of the struggle. We need a lot of help down here because there is an incredible amount of work that must be done in order to make this work. You come highly recommended by a number of people that I really respect."

"I appreciate that Martin, but I want to be quite frank and truthful with you," I said as I took another sip of coffee and a long drag on the cigarette. "I sincerely believe that I can be extremely helpful to you in providing your people with a good understanding how a non-violent protest movement is designed to work. But I do come with baggage that could possibly be harmful to the movement."

I placed the cigarette in an ash tray that King had put in front of me and ran my fingers around the top edge of the cup. "Early in my life when I was a young man like you, I made a mistake and joined the Communist

Party believing that they had our interest at heart and wanted to help us achieve our rights in this country. I was very active, recruiting members from across the Northern states but then when Germany invaded the Soviet Union and they became allies with us, I was told to halt my talks about segregation in the South and instead of criticizing this country, begin to praise it. That I would not do and walked away from the Party."

I paused, picked up my cigarette and took another drag from it. I flicked the ash and put it out in the ash tray. King listened while smoking his cigarette and sipping from his coffee cup. All the time he didn't take his eyes off me, staring intently. I knew he was trying to decide if all the good things he'd heard about me seemed to measure up to the man telling him of his weaknesses that could possibly harm his movement.

"Unlike most Negroes I grew up in a Quaker environment in a small town fifty miles north of Philadelphia. My grandmother, who for all intents and purposes, was my mother, at least that's how I looked on her, raised me. A basic tenant, not open for debate is the concept of passivism. Quakers abhor war and violence and that is my background, so when World War II broke out, I refused to sign up for the draft and as a result spent three years in prison and have since been labeled a draft dodger."

Martin put out his cigarette, got up and poured himself another cup of coffee. He then brought the coffee pot over to me and refilled my cup. He sat back down. "Bayard, none of this is necessary. Don't you think a half dozen different people have briefed me about you and your background? I know all about you. I know you were arrested in 1953 on a moral charge in Pasadena, California and I know you are a homosexual."

"But it's important that you know I am not ashamed of who I am. Not the former Communist, not the pacifist and not the homosexual. They all make up who I am."

"You have to know as a Baptist minister, I don't approve of homosexual behavior, but I don't plan to judge you. There are a lot of ministers that will, if and when they find out that you are not only homosexual but have been arrested for having an affair in the backseat of a car."

I didn't expect for him to have the specifics on what happened in Pasadena. I also didn't expect that the incident would ever go away, at least not any time soon. I wasn't embarrassed or ashamed about having an affair with another man, after all, that's who I am. But I was embarrassed that it happened in the back seat of a car and I didn't have enough sense to know that the incident was a set-up by J. Edgar Hoover and the FBI.

"Despite these potential problems, Martin, I do believe I can be of considerable help to you and your cause," I said. "I know you're committed to a non-violent approach for fighting segregation not only here in Montgomery, but all over the South."

"I've been told that there are maybe four people in this country who happen to be well-versed on Gandhi's philosophy as a tactic to bring change," King said. "And one of those four would be you simply because you've put it into action over the years. I need your help to get to where you are in the knowledge of non-violence." He paused as if to collect his thoughts. "Listen, our people here in the South know nothing about such practices but they are good people, decent, hard-working and honest folks who have over the years taken more abuse than any group of people should have to take. How much more they are willing to endure, I don't know. But I do know a resort to armed violence will lead to a massacre down here, simply because we are definitely out-numbered and easily out-gunned."

He stopped and stood up. "I don't care what you've done in the past or what you plan to do in the future in your private life, but I do care that you can help me convince these folks that non-violence is the only choice we have."

I also got up, assuming we were about to leave. "I'll do my best."

"There's a meeting of the Steering Committee for the Association, why don't you join us this morning and we'll see how much opposition we might have to your presence and in taking a lead role in perfecting our use of non-violent tactics."

I followed Martin out the front door and wondered why we didn't go out the back to the car. But it didn't take long to know why. He began walking down Jackson Street toward the hotel. He finally shared our destination with me. "We often have the steering committee meeting at the Majestic. They set up a nice size round table for us and give us a pot of coffee. Sometimes, they'll throw in some donuts and biscuits." He paused long enough to wave at a man driving by in his Chevrolet. "He's going to pick up some of the folks who live a long way from their work and some of them who just can't make the walk."

"You don't get nervous walking down the street all in the open like this?" I asked as it became quite clear that the man in that car could have been an adversary and Martin was an easy moving target.

"I don't walk too far," he said. "Most of the time, I'm in a car. But this was only a block and if I couldn't make just a block I might as well give up."

I shook my head from side to side in amazement just as we walked into the hotel. These men and women involved in this rebellion had to be the bravest I had ever encountered. Living in the shadow of destruction but still carrying on had to be an act of faith. As we approached, Abernathy immediately looked directly at Martin.

"We just got word that the mayor, all three commissioners and the representative from the bus company turned down our demands," he said. "E.D. thinks now we need to get the fed's involved."

"Precisely," Nixon now spoke up as Martin and I took the two remaining seats around the table.

I sat at the table next to a tall, light skinned man, well dressed in a suit and wearing thick horn-rimmed glasses. He immediately extended his hand. "Fred Gray," he said.

I recognized his name and now could put a face with it. He was the attorney representing Rosa Parks and had filed an appeal to her guilty verdict for breaking the segregation law of the state of Alabama.

We shook hands, "Bayard Rustin," I said.

"I know," he said.

"For those of you who don't know Bayard Rustin," King spoke up. "He is one of the most respected advocates for non-violence as the tactic to defeat bigotry and segregation. He has the support of someone we all are familiar with and admire and that is A. Phillip Randolph."

Three other men at the table, Rufus Lewis, director of the transportation pool, Reverend Robert Graetz, a white pastor of Trinity Lutheran Church located in the predominantly black neighborhood with a majority black congregation, and Reverend S. S. Seay one of the most respected of the senior Black ministers in the city all reached over and shook my hand. With the introductions out of the way, they returned to the business at hand.

"We are ready to file with the federal court," Gray said. "But we have one problem and that is with Mrs. Jeanetta Reese, who signed up and now wants to back out as one of the complainants in the suit." Gray picked up his copy of the **Advertiser and** continued. "Here is what's being reported in the newspaper. 'Jeanetta Reese, who works as a maid for Mayor Gayle's sister told the Mayor that she didn't want to have nothing to do with that mess, referring to the lawsuit. She further told him that she was surprised to see her name listed as a plaintiff.' We can't afford to have anyone of the plaintiffs to back out on us now. It shows a sign of weakness and encourages them to get to the others to see if they can break their will."

"Who is her pastor?" Reverend Seay asked.

"Not sure," Abernathy said. "But I understand that they got police cars parked out front of her house to prevent anyone from getting to her. And I doubt if she'll be going to church anytime soon."

"Take her name off and let's get the suit filed right away," King instructed. "I had the opportunity to talk with Roy Wilkins and alerted him to the fact that we might be filing the suit and hopefully could get the aid of the NAACP lawyers, preferably Thurgood Marshall, after the stellar job he did in the Brown case." King paused to let his words resonate with the others. "Now the other matter we need to discuss is changing the nature of the mass meetings at the different churches. We can't hold any more mass protest meetings. Instead from now on, we will only have prayer meetings."

"Why you want to do that?" Lewis asked.

"Because we must begin to stress the moral nature of our struggle. That can best be done through prayer." He paused and pulled out a paper from inside his jacket pocket. "Over the past three days, I came up with five prayers that will meet our goals. They are a prayer for the success of our meetings, a prayer for strength of spirit to carry on nonviolently and of course Bayard will be important in carrying out this prayer." He again paused and looked directly over at me. He continued, "A prayer for our bodies to stay strong in order to continue our walk for freedom, a prayer for those who oppose us and a prayer that all men will become brothers and live with justice and equality throughout the city, the state and the country."

As I listened to King rattle off the prayers it became very clear to me that the Negro church was going through a serious transformation. It was changing from the come to Jesus church for the past fifty years to a much more socially involved one. My thoughts concentrated on Reverend Howard Thurman, who I had met at Howard University years ago when he served on the Board of Fellowship of Reconciliation and a staunch advocate for ministers involved in social change. These ministers were carrying on the work started by the fiery minister who preceded King at Dexter, Vernon Johns who, the story goes, was the grandson of a slave who killed his master. A social revolution against bigotry, racism and hate had been initiated by the ministers and churches in Montgomery and that was the logical place where it should have begun. I felt a chill throughout my body, a chill of joy for being a part of this movement. I knew that I could be the key to making it all work by bringing to the Christian principles the Gandhian tactics. I needed to get with Dr. King and start the rigorous process of applying those tactics used in India, here in Montgomery right away.

5.

Events appeared to be happening at an accelerated speed and it seemed like every hour the steering committee had something new to deal with. King had just gotten back in town and we all knew that the police would be looking to arrest him on the bogus 1921 charge that the others had faced. No doubt he needed to get down to the station, turn himself in as the others had done, before they picked him up and ruined the meaning of what happened yesterday.

From inside the restaurant looking out, we all took a deep breath as we glared out the window and watched a patrol car cruise by. We couldn't tell if the police could actually see us in the restaurant or spot King inside. Fortunately, they kept driving but Abernathy and I looked at each other and knew what had to be done. He spoke out.

"Martin, we can't delay any longer," he said. "You have to turn yourself in and not allow them to make a spectacle of you."

"You know we all did it the other day," E.D. spoke up. "Bayard suggested that we not wait around for the trash to arrest us as in the past. Negroes just sit around and wait for them to come and when they run, they get shot down like dogs. That wasn't gonna happen this time."

"Was a beautiful site, if such a thing can have any beauty," Rufus chimed in. "All those Negroes in suits and ties marching into the police department just like it was an honor to be arrested."

"And it was an honor," Gray added. "Was an honor to be arrested for our own cause and not anyone else's? Those men stood up like men and refused to be treated like boys." He turned and looked directly at me. "Thank you, Bayard, thank you."

There was no need for me to speak up. I remained silent. But I knew Martin, as their leader, had to do the same.

"Gentlemen, if we are finished with our business here, that's exactly what I'm going to do," Martin said. "Mr. Gray, I'll need you to accompany me so that I'll have legal representation."

"No problem," Gray concurred.

We stood from the table. "Let's get out of here before they come barging in any minute," Martin said. "I'll meet you all at First Baptist this evening. Probably take me a couple of hours to get bailed out." He turned to me. "Bayard, what you plan to do?"

"I figured I'd hang around the hotel until later this afternoon and then head on over to First Baptist," I answered. I had other plans but did not want to share them with the others for fear that they would discourage me.

"Reverend, can you lead us in a prayer for those things we must do today?" Martin asked Abernathy.

"Gentlemen, please take your brother's hand," Abernathy instructed. I grasped the hand of Gray to my right and Lewis to my left."

As Abernathy began his prayer, my thoughts wandered. I hadn't participated in this ritual of holding hands during prayer since my last semester as a student at Wilberforce College and we were required to attend morning religious services. Wilberforce College was owned and controlled by the African Methodist Episcopal Church. I lasted there for only one year, leaving abruptly when they insisted that I join the ROTC. As a Quaker raised pacifist, there was no way I could participate in any type military exercises. And there was no way possible I would ever serve in an army trained to kill other people.

It was at Wilberforce that I came to grips with my sexual preference. I fell in love with a young man my age from California. During spring break, he came home to West Chester with me. We shared strong feelings for each other, but after I left Wilberforce, we lost contact and I often wondered what happened to him and did he, like me, allow his true sexual desires to surface in his life.

"Mr. Rustin, would you like to come with me?" Lewis asked as we broke our grip. "You might want to observe the operation of the carpool firsthand."

"As long as my presence won't compromise your operation in any way," I said.

"My operation was compromised the very first day we started this protest," Lewis said.

Rufus' invitation to go with him interrupted the plan I had for that afternoon, but it could wait. I needed to know more about how this operation functioned at the grass roots level, and the carpool was where it all began. We said our good-byes and headed out of the restaurant not knowing whether Martin would be at the church prayer service that evening or locked up in jail.

Walking out into the cold morning air a chill shot through my body. Parked across the street from the hotel was the same black vehicle with the two white men sitting inside that had been following me since I first arrived in Montgomery. I gave them a hard stare and as I did Rufus punched me on the arm.

"Don't look over there," he scowled. "You can't acknowledge them that way. Let it be because they aren't going away."

"Who are they?" I asked even though I had a pretty good idea who they were.

"They either undercover police or members of the White Citizens Council, and often they turn out to be the same." He stopped in front of a large black limousine with lettering on the side that read "LEWIS FUNERAL HOME."

We both climbed into the limo and he pulled out into the street. As he did the black car pulled out with a distance between our two vehicles.

"They don't bother to be discreet about what they're doing," I said as I looked out the side mirror.

"No, they don't, and I'm sure their interest in following me has increased considerably since you're now traveling with me," he paused and briefly looked at me. "They know you're from out of town and probably from New York by the way you dress."

"And not to mention they've associated you with me and that can't be good," I added.

"Nothing to them is good unless a Black man is bowing down and kissing their ass," Rufus said rather emphatically. "Well we're about to get out of the ass kissing business and move into the ass kicking business."

"I pray that you mean that only metaphorically and not literally.

"I don't know what all the metaphoric, whatever means. But I do know that we going to start fighting back and it's way overdue."

I momentarily dismissed the two men in the black car and focused my attention on this man who seemed determined to fight back. "You must have a pretty good business," I said as I shifted my body toward Rufus. "Why are you willing to risk losing what accomplishments you've made on something you don't know what'll happen?"

"I do know the outcome," Rufus shot back at me with no hesitation. "Negroes are going to get off their knees for a change. When they lynched that young Negro boy over in Mississippi last summer that was the last straw. Mrs. Rosa Parks told them folks that she wasn't giving up her seat, 'cause she was still thinking about Emmitt Till. If she took that kind of stand then I'm willing to risk everything, regardless of the outcome, 'cause I'm also still thinking about young Emmitt."

"You know that at some point in this struggle, these white folks are going to pick up guns and begin to shoot. Are you willing to fight off the temptation and shoot back?" I asked.

Again, he looked away from the road and momentarily stared at me. "You're here to teach all of us the tactic of non-violence. And for the most part, I believe you will be successful because the Negro in the South has always been forced to not strike back. When they spit on us, hit us and even kill us, we're supposed to look the other way or as our ministers like to tell us, turn the other cheek. We've been pretty much programed for that kind of response after a hundred years of taking abuse." He paused as if carefully picking his words. "The movement is pretty much divided between those who are willing to remain passive in the wake of considerable violence and then there is the group who will tell you 'hell no.' Right now, I'm willing to put my faith in Dr. King and go along with what he thinks is best. After all, I recommended him to head up the movement and so I'm kind of obligated to follow his lead."

"How did you all happen to select Dr. King to run this movement?"

"Why you ask? You think it was a mistake?"

"No, not at all. It's just that he is new to the city and you have other ministers who've been involved in the movement from its beginning. And then you have E.D. Nixon who got the whole thing started."

"No not him, no way," he practically shouted. "He wanted to be the head person and that's why I hurried and nominated Dr. King."

His response was rather abrupt. "I take it that you and E.D. don't necessarily get along?" I asked.

"We never have."

"Is there a lot of dissension in the movement?"

"Initially there was, but we all have pretty much settled on Dr. King as the leader and since he's taken over, things have calmed down."

"Is E. D. satisfied with Dr. King?'

"I believe he's okay with him, but I do not believe he's going to buy into this whole notion of non-violence and at some point, will make some noise." Rufus pulled into a parking lot in front of a large wooden structure. "You've met the leaders now it's time for you to meet the real folks that make this happen."

I got out and followed him into a building buzzing with conversations and activities inside. As soon as we made it through the doorway a young boy no older than 18 ran up to Rufus.

"Mr. Lewis, we short on vehicles. We got a number of people that need to be picked up and took to work. They just out there waiting. What we gonna do?"

At least ten women, old and young, stood along the side of the building evidently waiting for transportation to take them across town to their jobs. I watched a Cadillac pull up next to the building. The driver, a white lady who looked to be in her early forties, waved at one of the black women standing along the building. She hurried over to the car, jumped in the back seat and the lady drove off.

Before the first car was out of sight, a blue Chevrolet driven by a white woman, pulled up next to the building. The lady blew her horn and another black woman hurried over to the car and also jumped in the back seat. They pulled out into the street and I watched as the car made a turn at the corner and disappeared from sight.

"Mr. Lewis, we can't do this much longer," a heavy-set woman limped up to Rufus. "We been walking for weeks and now we just can't do it any longer. You got to get us some transportation or we gonna have to go back to the buses."

"Don't even consider that," Rufus gasped. "Don't you know that's exactly what they want to see happen."

"Then you need to get us some transportation," a second woman joined in the conversation. "I see you drove up here in a limousine, why don't you use it?"

"I do when I'm not officiating a funeral," Rufus said. "But I understand your concern and we'll bring that up this evening at the prayer meeting."

"In the meantime, how we suppose to get to work this morning?" the heavyset woman asked.

Just as she finished asking the question two cars, a Chevrolet and Buick pulled into the driveway saving Rufus from having to answer her.

"There you go," he said pointing to the cars." There is Mr. Jenkins and Anderson. They just finished one run and can take you all now."

The two women hurried over to the Chevrolet and climbed inside the car. Five other women who'd been waiting along the wall of the building also rushed over to both cars and got inside. The cars pulled out of the driveway on to the main street and disappeared from sight.

"I don't know what we're gonna do," Rufus said as we both watched the two cars pull away. "We've exhausted all the cars available to us. I've hustled just about every car in the city and now some of the drivers are dropping out because of threats from the police and the White Citizens Council."

"I was under the impression that most of the people were walking to their jobs," I said.

Rufus wrapped his arm around my shoulder as we walked back inside the building and to his office. "We have over thirty thousand men and women participating in this strike," he began. "Half of them walk every day, but the other half, for various reasons, need to be transported by car to their jobs. To provide transportation for nearly ten to fifteen thousand people every day, five days a week is a monumental task. Not all Negroes believe in what we're doing here and then some are so afraid that they wouldn't do anything to help out."

We walked into his small office, he took a seat in the chair at his desk and I sat across from him.

He continued. "Dr. King needs to get this thing settled real soon 'cause I just don't know how long we can keep the folks dedicated to the struggle. This boycott been going on now for over a month and them white folks ain't bending in their position. They believe these folks gonna get tired and just go back to riding the buses and take the same old abuse they used to. Rosa Parks will be forgotten about, Dr. King will go back to delivering his sermons on Sunday and it will business as usual.' He paused to take in all he just said. "Yes, I'm afraid these white folks got it all figured out."

I leaned forward in my chair. "You all can't let that happen. You can't quit because if you quit, it'll be years before this will be tried anywhere else in this South."

"These white folks know their Negroes. They have to, in order to keep us oppressed the way they do. They'll just sit tight and wait for it all to fall apart."

"You're not going to quit?" I asked with some exhilaration.

"No, not at all," he quickly replied. "As long as the good Lord gives me the strength to keep doing what he wants me to, I'll keep fighting. But I can't speak for forty thousand other people. We already had one key person quit on us. Ms. Reese backed out on the suit against the bus company."

"But the others didn't and that's what is encouraging," I said.

"I guess we'll get a chance to gauge the mood of the people this evening when we have our first prayer meeting at First Baptist."

"You're right," I added. "And this will be Dr. King's first meeting with the troops since he got back from Nashville. The way he's received will tell us a lot about how we move forward."

"Yes sir, Dr. King is good, but not quite as good as Reverend Vernon Johns." A smile crossed Rufus face. "That man used to love to make white folks turn red in the face. A few years back, he did a sermon titled, 'It is Safe to Murder Negroes in Montgomery.' He was irate because a week before the police had stopped a Negro for speeding and beat him half to death while Negroes stood around and watched. He was upset with both the police who did the beating and with those Negroes who just watched it happen." Rufus leaned across the front of the desk. "And then there was the time that he drove on to the campus of Alabama State with a truckload of watermelons and sold slices to the students." He now leaned back and laughed aloud. "Can you imagine how that went over with the Deacon Board at Dexter's? They were irate as well as embarrassed. Here you had the learned minister of Dexter selling slices of watermelon on the college campus. That was the last straw and I believe it led to the church finally getting rid of him."

I was intrigued with his stories of this well-known minister and his antics. "You're a member of Dexter, aren't you?" I asked.

"Sure am, been there for over ten years."

"How did you feel about them getting rid of Johns?"

"I was against it. In fact, I'd ridden with him onto the campus when he sold the watermelons. He was my hero and I still miss him today."

"But you are willing to give Dr. King a chance?"

"Absolutely. In fact, I don't think they could have found a better replacement for Reverend Johns than King. And what's rather ironic is that he may turn out to be a bigger embarrassment to those stuck-up Negroes at Dexter than Johns was." Rufus checked his watch and then stood up. "Think I'd better get you back over to the hotel."

"Yeah, I think so," I agreed.

We strolled out of his office and out into the cold but fresh air.

"Remember, the prayer meeting starts at seven o'clock. If you need a ride, I can pick you up."

"I can manage." We got into the limousine and he started toward the hotel. I was anxious to get back so I could call New York and report to Mr. Randolph the progress I was making in Montgomery.

6.

First Baptist was packed when I arrived along with Bill Worthy right at seven o'clock that evening. Evidently the movement had attracted the attention of the national media. Television cameras stood hoisted on tripods in the back of the room ready to capture the proceedings inside of the church. Newspaper reporters sat in the back row pew ready to write their stories on the same subject. Just as I walked in, Abernathy waved for me to come to the front of the church. He stood there with the other leaders, absent the presence of King. As I made my way to the front, I noticed both Reverend Graetz and Nixon standing right behind Abernathy. I knew I'd have a difficult time dealing with them because I now knew they did not approve of my lifestyle. I joined them behind Abernathy, reluctantly shook their hands and then concentrated on looking straight ahead. It was not in my nature to be duplicitous.

Abernathy stepped up to the pulpit microphone and began to sing, "We are moving on to victory. We shall stand together until everyone is free. We are moving on to victory. With hope and dignity. Black and white all are brothers. To live in harmony." It didn't take long for the entire crowd to join in. I smiled within because I had written that song on the way down to Montgomery and presented it to Abernathy. The purpose was for the lyrics to represent four important ideas of the movement; militancy, dignity, nonviolence and brotherhood. My influence was now being felt on the movement while I remained inconspicuously in the background.

After a good five minutes of the crowd singing and shouting, it suddenly shifted to a loud cheer as Dr. King walked through the front door of the church, followed by the men who had been arrested the other day at the courthouse. He made his way to the front and stood next to Abernathy at the pulpit.

"Brothers and sisters," Abernathy shouted over the cheering crowd. "Here is our leader, the man the newspapers said would not return to Montgomery but would stay in Atlanta because of the arrest warrant." Abernathy paused and placed his arm around Dr. King's shoulder. "But praise the Lord, he is here with us now. Let's hear it for our leader."

The crowd applauded loudly as Martin stepped up to the mike, held his hand up as a signal for them to quiet down. "Brothers and sisters, let us pray." As he began a prayer, my mind wandered back in time to the many days that Black leaders stayed at my Grandmother's home in Westchester simply because they could not stay at the local hotels. One week it would be Dr. W. E. B. Du Bois sitting at our supper table discussing the problems he perceived with the Booker T. Washington approach to fighting segregation. No doubt, Grandma agreed more with Du Bois than Washington and felt that Negroes had to stand up and fight back for their God-given rights of equality. On another occasion, the great James Weldon Johnson arrived in town to deliver a speech at the local college and he spent the night at our home. Then again, the leading Black woman, Mary McCleod Bethune from Florida stayed with us. As I listened to King's long peroration as a prayer, I recognized that my early years under the tutelage of my Grandmother had prepared me for this position in life. I knew this represented my beginning of dealing at the highest echelon of leadership in the Black world. She did a great job of preparing me.

"Brothers and sisters, the establishment in Montgomery, in the state of Alabama and throughout the South are angered because we dare to challenge their long-established system of segregation. They tell the rest of the world that we are wrong in trying to break a system that has worked well for years. But we say to them that we are not wrong," he paused while the crowd broke out in applause.

Their response energized Dr. King. He continued, "My brothers and sisters, if we are wrong, Jesus of Nazareth was merely a utopian dreamer and never came down to earth. If we are wrong, justice is a lie."

"Preach Brother Martin." In unison, a large number of men and women shouted out and their voices resonated throughout the sanctuary and you could feel the energy level rising.

"If we are wrong then this is not a Christian nation and the devil rules unstoppable by us who believe in the Bible, in Jesus, God and the Holy Spirit."

The sounds of "Hallelujah, hallelujah," drowned out the words of Dr. King and he had to pause and allow the people to shout their reassurances to his words.

I could detect something very important to the entire Black population taking place inside that church. It was a movement that could have profound implications for all future activities to end the sinful system of apartheid. Dr. King was uniting the secular and the sectarian under one umbrella in order to make change. It was exciting to sit and listen to him make a new history. He ended on a high note.

"And we are determined here in Montgomery to work and fight until justice runs down like water, and righteousness like a mighty stream. Justice is love correcting that which would work against love." He raised his arms high in the air as a gesture to reach for Heaven. "We must behave so that the sages of the future would look back at the Negroes of Montgomery and say they were a people who had the moral courage to stand up for their rights. God grant that we will do it before it is too late. God bless you all and onward you mighty people."

While the crowd went wild cheering King, I glared at Bill who stood at the back of the room and I am sure that our thoughts merged regardless of the distance between us. This movement was ideal for the application of Gandhian tactics. I knew I must go to work right away training the leadership on how best to inculcate the followers with the belief that this movement can only be successful if organized and implemented based on the practice of non-violence. As I followed the leadership off the stage and out a side door, I knew that my work for the next month would be right there in Montgomery at the side of this dynamic, young preacher.

"We'll have a leadership meeting right there in the cafeteria at the hotel at nine o'clock in the morning," King said to me as we strolled out into the chilly night air. "We need you there to begin our discussion on tactics."

"I'll be there," I answered.

"Good, I'll see you in the morning." He finished and walked arm and arm with Coretta to a waiting Chevrolet to take him home. After the bombing of his home, he no longer drove himself. The leadership had insisted that he have a driver and someone riding shotgun with a gun. That was the first lesson he would have to learn when we met. He could not have armed guards to protect him. That destroys the value of non-violence and sends a message to his followers that they, also, can be armed.

"Are you heading back to the hotel?" Bill asked as he brought me out of my musing.

"As a matter of fact, no," I said. "I have some business that I must attend to this evening."

"Then I'll see you sometime tomorrow." He turned and walked in the direction of the hotel.

It was already after nine o'clock, the temperature had dropped, and I knew I should have gone back to the hotel, locked myself in the room and waited for the next day. But that had never been my nature. Not that I sought trouble, but I refused to run from it. I needed to confront Jeanetta Reese and convince her to not drop out of the legal suit against the bus company. She had to understand the damage she could possibly do to the cause by doing so. I wasn't sure if I'd get a friendly greeting but what she did could ultimately cause irreparable damage to the movement, I had to try.

"Need a ride somewhere?" The young man driving the Chevrolet that took Dr. King home pulled up next to the curb, rolled down the window and shouted to me.

"Yes, I do," I said and quickly got inside the car.

"Where to?" he asked.

"Jeanetta Reese's home, do you know where she lives?"

"What, you have to be kidding." The young man looked at me with a rather distressed expression. "I know where she lives, but ain't no way you can get in to see her."

"Why not?" I asked

"Because they got police standing out in front of her house, stopping anyone from getting to her to change her mind."

"What's your name, young man?"

"Bobby."

"Well Bobby we have to try. If you're not afraid."

"I ain't afraid Mr. Rustin." He pulled back his coat jacket and put his hand on the butt of a gun tucked inside his pants.

My first thought was to reach over, snatch the gun and toss it out the window. But I resisted the temptation. Instead I relaxed back in the seat and momentarily closed my eyes. As Bobby put the car in drive and started out into the traffic, I knew my job here was going to be a difficult one. I sat up in the passenger seat as we made our way to a side street with very little lighting. Bobby pulled over to the curb. I could see two police cars halfway up the block, parked in front of a wooden framed house.

"That's it, Mr. Rustin," Bobby said. I'm going to stay parked back here out of the way, but I'll be able to see your every move. If something happens with them policemen, remember I got my gun and ain't afraid to use it."

"By all means, no matter what happens to me, you do not attempt to use that gun," I scowled.

"But Mr. Rustin I can't sit here and let them people kill you. We over that period now. Emmitt Till changed the whole mood of people here in the South. Some young folks like me want the fight."

"Do you hear me Bobby, no way do you use that gun." My tone was stern.

"Yes sir, if you say so. But if they come after me, I can't make you no promises."

"Just wait here for me. It'll all be fine." I finished and got out of the car. As I started up the sidewalk, I recognized the magnitude of the task before me. This might take years to accomplish. But, if Gandhi was able to get it done in India, we certainly could do it here in the South. It would only take intense training in self-discipline. That was exactly what Gandhi's activism required. However, my task at that moment was to find a way to get around the two big policemen who got out of their car and stood in the middle of the sidewalk, blocking my passage up to Jeanetta's home.

"Where you think you going, boy?" The larger of the two policemen asked me.

I had conjured up my story for them while we drove from the church to her house. "I'm a reporter for two international newspapers and I want to interview Mrs. Jeanetta Reese as to why she decided to drop out of the suit."

"Ain't no story to be gotten, she just didn't want to get all tied up in that disgrace."

"But do you mind if I ask her?"

"What's your name and what newspapers?" He took out a notepad and a pencil.

"Bayard Rustin and the newspapers are **Le Figaro**, a French paper located in Paris and the other one is a British newspaper, The **Manchester Guardian** out of London. I'm not here to try to persuade Mrs. Reese to change her mind, but only to get her story for my papers."

The officer stared at me as if trying to determine if I was trustworthy or not. Evidently, my story convinced him because he moved aside and waved me by. "Give you fifteen minutes and if you're not out by then, we're coming in to get you. Understand boy?"

I rushed by the policemen on to the porch and knocked on the door.

After a short interval, the porch light went on. "Who is it?" A woman's voice called out.

Not sure how to answer I took a chance. "Name's Bayard Rustin from New York and I'm with a national newspaper. Would just like to talk with you, get your side of the story as to why you dropped out of the lawsuit."

"Don't have much to say on the matter. Sorry I can't really help you."

"Wait Mrs. Reese, please give me no more than ten minutes of your time. It's important that the world understand your side of the story."

"Who am I to go up against the preachers," she said. "They ain't gonna believe me no way."

"At least give me the opportunity to tell your story. You have that coming to you." I felt rather guilty because my explanation wasn't quite true. There would be no way that I'd be sympathetic with her position.

But I needed to get inside to try to persuade her to change her position. My time was running short. I only had ten minutes and I'd already used three minutes trying to persuade her to let me in. I finally heard the lock turn, and the door swung open. An attractive, brown skinned, middle age woman, with graying hair waved me inside. Once inside I glanced across the room at a very large Black man sitting in one of the chairs. He gave me a menacing stare as if to say don't try anything funny. He didn't have to worry; the police right outside had given the same stares.

Jeanetta closed the door and stood near it as if ready to open it up and wave me back out, just as she had waved me in. She did not invite me to sit down.

"What is it you want to know?" she asked in a very dry voice.

"Mrs. Reese, you know you're pulling out of the suit, may jeopardize the chances of winning. The bus company is going to use it as an indication that the Black community is not organized behind the boycott."

"Mr. Rustin, you said you're from up north. Well in that case, I guess you don't know how things really are down here," she said and placed her hand back on the door handle.

I caught the hint. Be careful or I'll open the door, signal to the police and you'll be out of here. "Might I ask you Mrs. Reese, what made you change your mind?"

She took her hand off the door handle and relaxed back against the door. "Mr. Rustin, we Black folks down here don't have no money other than what we make working for the white folks, cleaning up their homes and taking care of their kids. Is it what we prefer to do? Not really, but we just don't have no choice. We all know that the white folks ain't never treated us fairly nowhere in the South. The buses ain't no different." She paused and stared over at the man sitting in the chair.

I detected a slight crack in the defense of her position. "But Mrs. Reese it isn't ever going to change if you don't fight back," I urged.

The hand went back on the door handle. I'd failed to make my point with her.

"Thought you was some kind of reporter from up North," the deep voice of the man sitting in the chair sounded out. "Don't sound like no reporter to me. Sound like someone that Dr. King and his folks sent over here to change Jeanetta's mind."

"No, not at all," I quickly replied. "I do want to know why she felt compelled to no longer be a part of the legal suit."

With hand still firmly gripping the door handle she said. "I'll tell you why and then you got to leave."

"That's fair," I said. No need to argue because I knew the police would probably be knocking at the door any minute.

"I work for the mayor's aunt and they made it known that I couldn't expect to keep working for her if I was going to do something to hurt her nephew. She made it quite clear getting involved in all that mess would hurt him." She paused, took in a deep breath and glared over at the man sitting in the chair as if seeking reassurance.

"She tried to resist their threats, but it wasn't going to work," the man spoke up. "You think they got those two big redneck policemen out front to guard Jeanetta? Hell no. It's to remind her of the constant threat that something could happen to her or one of her family members if she backed down and joined in the threat."

His explanation for the presence of the police caught me off guard. I never thought for a moment that they were there to make sure she didn't get out and do any harm. They made it appear they wanted to prevent anyone from getting in and doing harm. I had just learned a lesson on how the South operates. They never mean any good to Negroes, only bad.

"So, you see I can't change my mind Mr. Rustin. I want to live." She finally turned the knob and swung the door open. Her timing seemed to mesh with the police. When the door swung open, they stood there about to come in and escort me out.

I quickly walked to the door. "Thank you for your time Mrs. Reese." I passed by the police, skipped down the porch steps, and rushed over to the Chevrolet where Bobby waited for me. He started the car and without speaking we sped out of there.

Bobby dropped me off at the hotel. As I jumped out of the car, I noticed that same black vehicle parked across the street, but no one sat inside. Just as I walked into the hotel and started across the lobby to the stairs, the young attendant ran from a back room and stood at the registration desk.

"Mr. Rustin, I need to tell ya---," the attendant stopped before finishing his sentence.

I abruptly stopped and stared at him for a moment. He simply pointed at the stairs and then disappeared to a room in the back. I looked up the stairwell, then stared back at where the young boy had stood with a frightened look all over his face. Was he trying to warn me of a danger that might be lurking at the tops of the stairs? I slowly ascended the stairs until I reached the top. No sign of any danger so I continued down the hall to my room. The door to the room was cracked open and the light on, no doubt a sign someone was inside. I swung the door open and there sat two well-dress white men, both with guns resting in their laps.

"What can I do for you men?" I asked in attempt to remain calm.

"You can get your fucking nigger, gay ass out of Montgomery," one of the men scowled

"Yeah, we just don't like communist faggots in our city causing trouble with our good niggers," the other man chimed in.

I left the door open but stepped right inside. "Haven't the slightest idea of what you men are talking about. Now I'd like for you to get out of my room. Thought you all weren't supposed to frequent Black facilities. Isn't that what your segregated laws demand?"

The first man to talk looked over at the other one. "Yeah, he's one of those smart-ass niggers from up North. Kind that come down here and causes trouble." He jumped up from his chair and before I could make a move grabbed me around my throat and pushed me back against the wall. "We warning you boy," he shrieked with speckles of spit hitting my face, he stood so close.

The other man also jumped to his feet, rushed over to where I was pinned against the wall and placed his gun at the temple area of my head. "I should just go on and blow his fucking brains out. Just be another sick ass faggot going around trying to fuck our kids." He moved in closer. "Is that what you like to do, nigger, fuck kids?"

"Don't shoot his ass Roy. 'Cause the nigger gonna get out of Montgomery in the morning," the other man said.

I had to show these men that I did not fear them with their ignorance and their guns. I pushed the gun away. "As a matter of fact, I plan to hang around and make your lives miserable," I scowled. "Now why don't you get the fuck out of my room. You made your point, but it just floated out that door in the same way you need to."

The blow struck me right above my right eye, I crashed to the floor and the sights all blurred before me. I could hardly make out which of the two men leaned down over me, but I heard him distinctly.

His voice seething with hatred and anger, he said. "I don't know what's worst, a fucking arrogant nigger, a draft dodging communist or a sick ass homosexual. But I know when one person fits all them, he needs to be put away just like a rabid dog. And that's what's going to happen to you, boy, if you don't get the fuck out of Montgomery."

He stood and kicked me once in the ribs, then the two of them left the room, leaving the door open. I managed to crawl on the floor over to the door and push it shut with my leg, then crawl back over to the bed and while in excruciating pain pulled myself up and laid down.

7.

"My God, what happened to you?" Martin asked as I made my way into the restaurant where the leadership team had gathered around the same table, we met at a few days ago. "Are you all right? Do you need to go to the hospital?"

"Let me call Dr. Rodgers," Abernathy spoke up. "That's a terrible bruise."

I strolled into the dining room with a terrible headache and sharp pain on my left side of my body but was determined not to let the others know just how much pain I felt right at that moment.

"I'll be just fine." I lied, as I walked to the same chair I occupied at the last meeting, between Rufus and Fred Gray.

"You had visitors last night, didn't you?" Rufus asked.

"Yeah, they were waiting for me in my room. The young boy on the desk last night tried to warn me, but I think he was too scared to tell me they were in my room."

"We need to report this to the authorities," Gray spoke up for one of the only times he had said anything at all.

"No," I exclaimed loudly. "That is exactly what they want us to do. Every time they resort to violence and we respond with either our own violence or report it to the authorities, they know they still have control. You all know better than I do, that lynch mobs are effective because they can terrorize the people. From this day forward, we respond with a Gandhian tactic and that is to pour out more love and forgiveness to them by not responding to their actions. When we no longer fear their attacks, they lose and we win."

"What the hell are you talking about man?" Nixon exploded. "They just beat the living shit out of you and you want us to thank them?"

"Not thank them Mr. Nixon but find it in our hearts to forgive them. If we, as leaders of this movement, are not capable of that, then the followers never will, and it will slowly deteriorate into nothing but violence."

"I don't think it's going to be safe for you to stay around here," Graetz said.

"No," I gasped. "I came here to do a job and I plan to do just that." I paused and glared at each one of the men around the table. I would not be intimidated, nor would I be pressured to leave. I had taken much worse beatings than what I experienced last night, and they never stopped me. I was on a mission and had to complete it. If Graetz and Nixon believed what happened last night would grant them their desire to see me gone, they were sadly mistaken. "What we need most now is to begin training on the non-violent tactics as soon as possible."

"I don't understand why we need any kind of training," Graetz said. "We have all committed to a non-violent movement. We just need to put it into effect."

I found this man rather irritating. "On three different occasions, I have seen people with guns, and I don't mean the bad guys. I do believe that we have a lot of work to do. But it must be with only the leadership. You all must totally believe in the philosophy and use it as a tactic with the others. If you don't, it will not work."

"I'm telling you right now, I can't accept it as a tactic," Nixon spoke up. "Look at you, a big old bruise on your forehead and you're lucky they didn't shoot you, and you talking about being non-violent. Bet you wish you had a gun last night?"

"No, I don't," I shot back at him with a sharp retort. "As a true believer in the Gandhian approach, you invite struggle because it tests your commitment to the cause and your will power to resist retaliation. Love can be your only response."

"That's very admirable, but I just can't see us sitting around while people are getting beat up and shot and not fight back," Nixon continued. "When you start this training, you can leave me out."

"I'm afraid we can't leave you out. In fact, we can't leave out anyone who is recognized as a leader. You must all take a vow to never raise a fist, carry a gun or any other weapon against someone who is considered an enemy." I was adamant with my words.

King leaned forward on the table. "I am committed to a non-violence philosophy but must draw the line with your friends in New York. You see no just society can exist without a police power. It is absolutely necessary. But for our movement, I can concur that we as leaders must be committed totally, both as a philosophy and as a tactic to non-violence." King leaned back in his chair and stared at me.

I didn't agree but refrained from discussing the matter any further. I had made my most important point, that the civil rights movement in Montgomery and hopefully all over the South, must be a passive non-violent movement. And it must be led by Dr. King.

"Well, gentlemen I think…" Abernathy had begun to speak but was suddenly interrupted.

"Dr. King, you have to know what kind of danger you are in with this man," a tall, slender Negro pointed at me, "as part of your team."

"And who are you?" Abernathy asked with irritation in his voice.

"Names Emory Jackson from the **Birmingham World**, a Negro newspaper out of Birmingham. I know this man quite well. He is nothing but a troublemaker." The man glared at me. "Get rid of him or I'm taking the story to the **Montgomery Advertiser** and give them the story about how Rustin is a Communist and a pervert."

"Sir, this is a private meeting and I'll thank you to leave," Dr. King spoke up.

"I will Dr. King simply because I do respect you a great deal. But if this man is still around here next week, he'll be blasted all over the newspaper and on television as an imposter and Northern troublemaker. Decision is yours." The man finished turned and hurried out of the room and out of the hotel.

"Well," Dr. King started. "Maybe a little more excitement than what we needed this morning."

Aggrieved by this attack I stood and said. "I think I'll excuse myself from the meeting with you all this morning and just see you later in the day."

"You don't have to do that," Dr. King said

"I think it's best," Reverend Graetz interjected. "I believe we need to discuss this man's presence because confusion seems to follow him."

I refused to respond to his comment, but instead said. "Gentlemen, I'll see you either later in the evening or tomorrow at Dr. King's church." I turned and walked away.

I hurried up the stairs into my room and fell out on the bed. My head hurt badly, and my ribs ached excessively and for what? A bunch of Negroes who didn't seem to appreciate what I was determined to do for them. Didn't they realize that this victory could not be won on a violent battlefield but only on a peaceful one? I rubbed my side and the pain shot through me like a piercing arrow. Despite my obstinance when Graetz suggested that I leave, I began to think that it might be best for all involved.

Maybe Randolph and his group needed to replace me with someone who was well schooled in the Gandhian non-violent approach and could fit well as part of this leadership group. The only three that seemed to be satisfied with my involvement were Abernathy and King and Rufus Lewis. For the most part Gray had remained rather reticent. However, I knew that in order to make what I had to teach work, would take the total cooperation of the entire group. There was only one other person trained well enough in the philosophy and the tactics and that was a minister from California. I snatched the phone from its cradle and dialed Randolph's number in New York.

I slept the entire afternoon and by the time I woke up it was night. I needed to go down to the restaurant and grab a bite to eat. But what I needed more than that was some company. With this kind of depression, I craved male companionship. I sat up in the bed and lit a cigarette. I knew there had to be a place where gay men congregated because there were plenty in New York. I was not in New York but probably in one of the most intolerable states and cities to gay activity. It went on, I knew, but behind closed doors and in secret meeting places. I just didn't know where those places might be located, and I couldn't take a chance and go out into the street and ask questions. I certainly wouldn't ask the boy at the desk downstairs. After Pasadena, I just couldn't take another chance. Especially since Mr. Randolph had forgiven me for my indiscretion. I took the last drag off the cigarette, put it out and headed downstairs to get a bite to eat. After my earlier discussion on the phone with Mr. Randolph, my days in Montgomery were numbered and I could get back to my life in New York. I had that much control over my emotions.

On Sunday morning, I met Bill Worthy in the lobby of the hotel and walked the six cold blocks to Dexter Baptist Church. The wound on my forehead was still visible but I no longer suffered from a headache and the pain in my ribs had also subsided. When we reached the church, it was standing room only. But the usher recognized me from the previous meetings as someone rather important. He escorted Bill and me down to the third row where an entire pew had been reserved, I imagine for dignitaries. Having attended a Baptist Church back home, I knew the first row was reserved for the deacons and the second for their wives. It didn't take long for our pew to fill up as the ushers for the next five minutes constantly escorted people to sit with us.

Right at eleven o'clock the doors of the church opened, the musician took his place at the piano and at least fifty men and women dressed in white choir robes started down the two outer aisles toward the front of the church. When they entered, the entire congregation stood and turned to watch them as they strolled to the rhythm of the piano and sang, "When the saints come marching in. When the saints come marching home. Oh Lord I want to be in that number. When the saints come marching home." Simultaneously with the choir rhythmically strolling their way to the front, Dr. King dressed in a black robe with red trimming, with two other ministers, also wearing robes made their way into dais from a side door. The other two men sat down in large high back chairs, leaving the one in the middle empty. Dr. King took his place at the pulpit as the choir still sang, "when those saints go marching in." They finally finished and took their positions at the back of the dais and stood while King began the service.

"Let us pray," King said, and the congregation remained standing while he led them in prayer.

"Eternal God out of whose absolute power and infinite intelligence the whole universe has come into being, we humbly confess that we have not loved thee with our hearts, souls and minds and we have not loved our neighbors as Christ loved."

"Amen, amen, amen," the congregation responded in unison just as if it had been practiced. But then, on second thought, it had been practiced for years, generations, decades and centuries in the Black church.

King continued, "But God we thank you for the inspiration of Jesus."

"Thank you, Jesus, thank you, Jesus, thank you Jesus," the congregation chanted in rhythm.

King paused for a moment then continued. "Grant that we will love you with all our hearts and souls and minds and love our neighbors as we love ourselves and even our enemies. Make us willing to do Your will come what may. Increase the number of followers of good will and moral sensitivity. Give us renewed confidence in non-violence and the way of love as taught by Jesus. Amen."

A smile lit up my face when he mentioned the words non-violence. I looked up at him with admiration. King managed to do something no other minister had successfully done, and that was to interconnect the love for Jesus as spiritual experience with the love for a non-violent peaceful transition in the South. It gave me a very heavy dose of joy to know that I might play an important role in this kind of history making endeavor.

King turned and took his seat between the two other ministers, while a heavyset woman from the choir strolled over to the other podium with a mike. She closed her eyes for a moment as the piano player began a tune. She then opened her eyes, looked up as if searching for Heaven and began to sing.

"Why should I feel discouraged? And why should the shadows come?

"Why should my heart feel lonely. And long for Heaven and home.

"When Jesus is my portion. A constant friend is He.

"His eye is on the sparrow. I know he watches over me."

"Sing sister Evelyn. Sing that song," someone shouted from the congregation. She possessed a beautiful voice and sounded great singing solo, but now the rest of the choir joined in and the sounds resonated throughout the sanctuary and had to touch the souls of everyone listening. I know it touched mine as they sang.

"I sing because I'm happy. I sing because I'm free.

"I know his eye is on the sparrow. I know he watches me."

It felt like the church might just explode with ecstatic joy as members in the pews extended their arms and some of the women stood and began to clap. The response served as a stimulus for the choir as their emotional thrust of the words took us all to a higher level. I wanted to stand and shout and I'm sure Bill wanted to do the same. Dexter was considered the more elite Baptist church where all the doctors, lawyers and schoolteachers attended. They were considered the more reserved Baptists, but at that moment as the choir brought their joy in song to an end, they were simply doing what Black folks did all over this country on a Sunday morning. Rejoice in the Lord and escape from the misery of this life into the beauty of the life promised them. It was the time they escaped into what Dr. Du Bois described as the double consciousness. I felt nothing but great pride and joy to be a part of the Sunday celebration and did not know that in just a few minutes my participation would increase considerably.

The choir sat down as Dr. King returned to the pulpit and announced.

"We here at Dexter are honored and pleased to have an outstanding Negro leader in our presence this morning."

I began to look around to see who he was referring to.

"Yes sir, he is all the way up here from New York and is committed to helping us in our determination to break down segregation in this city."

He wouldn't do this, I thought. But he did.

"I'm going to ask the great spokesperson Bayard Rustin to stand along with Mr. Bill Worthy who is also up here from New York covering our movement for the Black press."

We stood to a standing ovation from the congregation. That was not good enough for Dr. King. He continued, "Now I know that Mr. Rustin is just an outstanding singer. Yes sir, I've been told that he sang first tenor and did a number of solo spirituals while a student at Wilberforce back in the 1930's and that he had a choice between a career that could have made him the next Roland Hayes or Paul Robeson. So, I'm going to ask him to come up here and please share with us one of his many spirituals he enjoys singing. Let me have an Amen from the church to get him up here."

In unison, the congregation shouted, "Amen."

I strolled up to the same podium the lady from the choir had occupied.

"I have to say, I didn't expect this." I turned and looked back at Dr. King who had returned to his seat. "I'm kind of afraid to follow behind that great rendition we just heard of one of the magnificent spirituals. You have an outstanding choir here at Dexter, but that is to be expected." I paused to a few amen responses. But I'll do my best." I adjusted the mike and began.

"Oh, freedom, oh, freedom. Oh, freedom over me."

The congregation exploded with shouts of joy when they recognized the song; a real classical spiritual that they knew as one sang by our ancestors on plantations throughout the South during slavery.

"And before I'll be a slave. I'll be buried in my grave.
And go home to my Lord and be free."

As I sang that stanza, the entire congregation stood up and shouts of joy rang out throughout the sanctuary. I could even hear Dr. King call out words of encouragement. I continued. Instantly, the piano player joined in as he now provided me with the music to support the lyrics. I felt it and the words just rolled out like they did when I sang this same song as a member of the Wilberforce Quartet in 1933.

"No more weeping, no more weeping. No more weeping over me.
And before I'll be a slave, I'll be buried in my grave.
And go home to my Lord and be free."

I sang three more verses of this classic, and the choir joined in with me and finally the congregation did also. We must have gone on for at least ten minutes and when we finished, I was exhausted. I put my entire soul into that song, and it drained my energy. I finally felt a part of the Montgomery community. I was no longer an outsider, but one of my people and it felt great. I returned to my seat to a rousing ovation and Dr. King strolled up to the pulpit to deliver the day's sermon.

I tried to relax and just enjoy the sermon, but I was fired up after that song. I sat erect in the pew, hands folded and perched on my lap. I looked up at the young man who now had the responsibility for an entire movement.

For the next half hour, King intertwined the secular with the sectarian. He began with a passage from Leviticus 19:17, "Do not hate your brother in your heart." He paused for a moment to allow the Biblical passage to have its effect on the parishioners "Our white Southern brothers should not be hated based on the word of the Lord, because the most prejudiced mind in Montgomery or in America could become a mind of goodwill," King explained as he cleverly invoked the secular. But then returned to the Bible, "For Matthew 26:52 also tells us that Jesus said to him, 'put your sword back into its place. For all who take the sword will perish by the sword.'" Like a master magician, he used Biblical verses to justify the non-violent tactic to fight against segregation on the buses in the city. "It is through the blood of Jesus, that the world will be cleansed of its sins and segregation is a sin," he continued.

King's words struck a positive note with me as I listened to him tell his congregation that the church would now change its focus. No longer would it be the old time "Come to Jesus," approach that had ruled since the end of slavery but would now take on a much more social activist role. And I had no doubt that King's mission was to make that happen, not only in Montgomery, but all over the South.

He ended, "We are concerned not merely to win justice in the buses, but rather to behave in a new and different way—to be non-violent so that we may remove injustice itself, both from society and from ourselves. This is a struggle which we cannot lose no matter what the apparent outcome, if we ourselves succeed in becoming better and more loving people."

He closed the service with a departing prayer and then hurried to the back of the church to shake hands with the members as they exited out the doors. Bill and I got in the line and patiently waited as the men shook his hands and all the ladies had to get a hug.

"That was an outstanding message," I said and shook his hand.

"I believe we need to talk about how we proceed to get the message to our people about the importance of remaining non-violent," King said, and I detected some concern in his voice.

"Did something happen?" I asked with the same amount of concern.

"Yes, last night there was an incident over by Holt Baptist Church. You know that's the main headquarters for the Montgomery Improvement Association," King exclaimed as he now shook Bill's hand. "I had actually prepared a different sermon for today, but when I got word that some of our boys confronted some white hoodlums who painted derogatory words on the side of the church, I changed my message."

"Anyone hurt?" I asked.

"No, not yet. But we need to let our people know that we cannot win in a fight with guns. They have too many. I'd like for you to come by the house this evening and let's talk about how we proceed."

"I can do that," I said.

"Bobby will pick you up at seven and…"

"Dr. King I can walk to the parish, it's not that far."

"No, not at all," he said. "You've already been attacked one time and we don't want to take any chances. Bobby will pick you up and bring you to the house where there are armed guards ready to act if there is any trouble."

I frowned listening to him. I knew the first lesson he must learn was no guns and especially not with him or the people guarding him. This would be a very long process and I only hoped that I could hang around to complete the job.

8.

"I'm afraid they don't want you down there anymore," Randolph said even before I could begin to give him a report. "Some of them believe you're going to be a detriment to what they want to accomplish. Evidently, a reporter from a black newspaper in Birmingham recognized you and told the leadership that they need to get you out of there or he'd blow the whistle on you. He knew about the Pasadena incident."

"What the hell," I exploded, paused and took a strong drag on my cigarette. "Was it Dr. King who contacted you?"

"No, but it's not important who did. What's important is that you've been compromised, and we need to send someone down there to replace you."

It had to be E. D. Nixon I thought as I listened to Mr. Randolph. He was the only other person in that leadership group who'd know to call him.

"Is there a Reverend Robert Graetz? I believe he's a white Lutheran Minister who is a part of the leadership team and close to Dr. King. He's expressed concerns about your background."

"He was at the leadership meeting this morning at the hotel when a Negro reporter stormed into the meeting and warned Dr. King to get rid of me."

"Bayard, your reputation precedes you," Randolph shot back. "You'd better get used to people forming their own opinions about you because you live a different lifestyle, one they don't approve of, especially if they're ministers."

"But King has no problem with my background," I offered. "We discussed it in detail, and he feels my value to the movement far outweighs the negatives."

"That's one man," Randolph gasped. "And he is one man who might easily be influenced by the others if they are in the majority. I think everyone up here has decided we need to send a replacement."

"How about you Mr. Randolph?" I asked desperately hoping to hear the right response. "I'm not ashamed of who I am and will not give in to any kind of intimidation. I have a lot to offer this movement but at any time they feel it is not wanted, I'll leave."

"Just keep in mind you're from New York and that is one strike against you down there, and you're a homosexual and that is the second strike. We can't afford for you to get that third strike." He paused and I knew why. He had to make that statement before answering me. "You know I'll always be in your corner. You're like a son to me and I'll never turn my back on you. But this time I'm outnumbered. Even Farmer as well Muste agreed we need to send a replacement."

"There is only one individual that's capable of instructing Dr. King and the others in the Gandhian procedures of non-violence and that is Glen Smiley," I said.

"We know and have already alerted him that he needs to leave tomorrow for Montgomery."

I smiled, very much aware that the decision to send Glen had been made even before Mr. Randolph called me. I instinctively recognized who was behind this desire to get me out of Montgomery. It had to be John Swomley, who had taken over from A. J. Muste in leadership of the Fellowship of Reconciliation. There had always been a fierce rivalry between John and me as far back as the early 1940's. He had originally been assigned as my supervisor, but I never recognized him in that position, and for years I simply went above him right to A.J. Muste when seeking approval of a project. And during those same years, he showed his resentment toward me and probably led the fight to get me expelled from the Fellowship because of Pasadena.

"Are you still there?" Randolph asked and brought me out of my musing. "Reverend Graetz has already made arrangements for someone to pick him up at the airport in the morning and bring him over to the Ben Moore Hotel. He'll be there at ten in the morning so be there to meet him. And just so you'll know, Swomley has advised Glen to stay away from you because of the negative impression you are making on those people down there and it will affect how they feel about us here in New York. Of course, I don't feel that way, but I just thought I'd warn you."

"Any action Swomley takes doesn't surprise me," I said. "Glen will be a perfect fit and I'm sure Dr. King will be quite pleased. I'll be here to meet him, and the timing is perfect because the leadership team has breakfast meetings here in the morning." I did find it rather ironic that a white preacher would replace a black man in assisting black men in the tactic of non-violence to be used against white men. But if they had to replace me, there was no one more qualified than Glen. However, despite their decision in New York to replace me, I decided right at that moment, that I would only leave if Dr. King made the request. I planned to find out that evening if he also wanted me out.

"Be careful Bayard. I don't want anything to happen to you. Remember who you're dealing with down there. Please be careful." Randolph ended and hung up.

Mr. Randolph's warning resonated with me as I hung the phone up and sat on the side of the bed. I wasn't quite sure who represented the real danger to me, the red-neck members of the White Citizens Council, or some of the bigoted preachers in the movement. I needed to give my presence there some serious thought. One bigot was as bad as another and why should I spend my time training the leadership of the movement in the finer points of non-violence, if they ultimately were no better than the people they would target as the enemy.

I stretched out on the bed and gave some thought to Glen replacing me in this assignment. He was a good man and the two of us had been friends for years. In fact, I considered him the only white man that could continue the work I would begin with Dr. King that evening. He was thoroughly acquainted with the concept as practiced in India under Gandhi and his followers. He was committed to non-violence just like me, he spent three years in prison during World War II as a Pacifist. He was courageous rather soft-spoken unless the topic was about segregation. He would do King well as my replacement. I planned to introduce them as soon as he arrived in Montgomery.

King waited at his opened front door as I climbed out of the car and made it up the steps and inside the house.

"Come on in Bayard and let's go into the kitchen," he greeted me. "Coretta has a pot of coffee ready for us."

"Sounds just right for me," I said as I walked into the living room and glared down at a gun resting in a large chair. I stopped right there. "Dr. King, that must go immediately," I scowled as I pointed at the gun. "First lesson is that the leader must have a total commitment to non-violence and that means no guns or weapons. You can't own them because that means you are not totally committed."

King gave me a hard stare and continued walking into the kitchen. I followed close behind and we both took chairs at the kitchen table. The coffee aroma filled the room. He still hadn't spoken after my comments about the gun. Coretta poured coffee and then also sat at the table. He finally broke the silence.

"I need protection for my family," he said rather pensive in his response. "Not for me, but for my family."

"You do know that they bombed the front of our house only a month ago," Coretta interjected. "The MIA insisted that we have armed guards out front, that Martin no longer drive alone and that we stay armed inside the house. Our son is only two months old and I could never forgive myself if I allowed him to be harmed by these racists."

I listened with a sympathetic ear. But I knew that personal tragedies or fears of danger from the oppressor would allow him to win. He wanted to know that the leader of the movement feared him to the point that he had to be armed. That violated the first principle of the Gandhian philosophy. The great Indian leader had always insisted that his followers have no weapons and in order to do that, he had to make that a life commitment. The leadership had scored a major victory when they marched down to the jail and surrendered as a gesture of suggesting they did not fear the white corrupt legal system or the men who ran it. Their next step was to stand up to the guns, clubs, stones and whatever the enemy used to force the movement to fear them. King had to understand this, or the movement was destined to fail.

"What are you thinking Mr. Rustin?" King asked.

"I'm trying to figure out how to share with you the idea that no matter the degree of danger and who faces that danger, you, and especially you cannot be armed," I said emphatically. Coretta adjusted her body in the chair, and I knew she was about to dispute me. "Please, before you all say anything or figure I'm the bad guy, just hear me out." I paused to make sure we were all of one accord. She relaxed back in the chair and I continued. "For all your followers, non-violence does not have to be a way of life, but they must believe in it as a tactic to win this war. And this is a war. But for you, Dr. King, and for Reverend Abernathy and the other leaders, this must become a way of life. A philosophy that dictates your behavior, not only during this crisis but for all crises in the future."

It was now Dr. King's turn to adjust his body in the chair. He grabbed his cup and drank. I did the same. We needed this slight reprieve. I could just imagine what was floating around in his mind. I didn't mean to suggest that he should put the life of his newborn in danger, but there was no other way to make my point. If he had the determination necessary to make this work, he needed to listen intently and follow my lead. I knew what would work and what wouldn't, going forward. I strongly felt that he knew that but still was not very comfortable with the idea. I also knew there was no way Coretta would be pleased with this and probably offer some opposition after I left. But that happened to be the hard decision Martin had to make.

"I wrote my doctorate degree on Gandhi's movement and thought I really had a grasp on how it would work in the real world," King finally said. "I was wrong and now I know I have a lot to learn. I'll need you to teach me. Think you can stick around long enough to do that?"

Instinctively, my thoughts hurled back to the conversation earlier in the day with Mr. Randolph. King just answered my question. He wanted me to stay in Montgomery and continue to work with him. I allowed for a slight smile. King and his followers had no idea as to just how fortunate they were, to have the two most knowledgeable men in the country on the philosophy and tactics of nonviolence with me and Glen Smiley, due to arrive in the morning.

"All the guns must be gone in the morning," I said. "They must be gone from your home, and from the guards out front and from Bobby the driver." I paused to collect my thoughts. "

"Bobby told you he carries a gun?" King smiled. "I told him to be sure and not let you know that, or you just might get out of the car."

"He did when he thought we might run into some trouble when I asked him to drive me over to Mrs. Reese's home the other evening."

"You went to see Jeanetta Reese?" Coretta asked.

"Sure did and the police let me in to see her," I said.

"You have no fear at all, do you?" King suggested as a question.

"Martin, we as a people can no longer fear anything or anyone," I exclaimed. "Fear ruled us for centuries and look what we got for it." I paused and then answered. "Nothing."

"What makes a man like you tick?" Coretta asked.

"The same thing that makes your husband and you tick. A determination to change the condition of our people in this country. No matter what the price we might have to pay, it must happen. We cannot allow another generation to grow up fearing their every step, their every word and their every action because some people have decided what the proper behavior is for Negroes not only here in the South but up North also."

"You know we're going to confront a great deal of opposition not only from the white folks but from our folks also," King said. "We're going to have the Negroes who are still deathly afraid of the white man, then you have the ones who will be jealous of our progress and then those who like things just like they are and don't want us bringing about any kind of change."

"Haven't we always had that kind," I said. "We can be our own worst enemies at times."

"What happened to you growing up that you're willing to come down here and really risk your life for a fight that you can argue is not yours at all?" Coretta asked.

I held my head high for a moment then looked directly at her. "We all share a common dilemma I don't care if you're from Mississippi or

Minnesota and that is, we're black in a country that has never really wanted us here after slavery and still don't want us as their equals. What happens in Montgomery must affect all of us throughout the country. And rightfully so because we can't afford to let the white man divide us. If I can't feel your pain in this battle and join the struggle, then ultimately, he will win by eliminating each group, one at a time.

"This is going to be a very long battle and chances are the both of us might not live to see the final outcome." King again drank from his cup.

"What is life worth if you can't give it up for something worthy of your sacrifice?" I asked.

"Are you prepared to die here in the South when you could be up North free from the turmoil?"

"Let me again repeat that I would never be free of the turmoil."

"You carry many burdens, my friend, and I know God has given you the strength to endure."

"I hope so," I replied.

"You know the beating in your hotel room was just the first warning?"

"I realize that, but I can assure you I've taken much worst over the years, especially in prison during the war and on the chain gang in North Carolina in '49." I watched as Coretta got up and headed back into the bedroom. The baby had begun to cry.

Martin also watched as she disappeared into the bedroom. "She is a mighty strong woman," he said. "When those animals bombed the house last month, I thought she might crack under the stress. She didn't and I'm fortunate to have her with me. Who has been your strength?"

It was now my turn to adjust my body in the chair. I slid it back from the table and crossed my legs. I pulled a cigarette out from the package. "Do you mind?" I asked.

"Not at all, in fact I'll have one myself." I passed the package over to King and he snatched one and pulled a lighter from his pocket and lit it. I did the same.

"My grandmother has always been my inspiration," I said. "She raised me, and the interesting thing is I believed she was my mother until I was thirteen. They finally told me that her oldest daughter, who I all along believed to be my sister, was my mother. Despite that revelation I continued to treat her as my mother and of course my grandfather as my father. But you must know my grandmother. She was a real go getter." I took a deep drag on the cigarette and blew out the smoke. "When I was young," I continued, "I used to attend bible school with her, and she stressed the Old Testament much more than the New. You see, she really believed that Negroes had much more to learn from the Jewish experience in the Old Testament than from Matthew, Mark, Luke and John."

"That's in keeping with Negroes coming out of slavery or born right after it ended. They inherited the beliefs of the slaves that like the Jews they were serving in bondage and just like the Jews had Moses to bring them to the Promised Land, someday a savior would rise up and take them to their promised land."

"I guess you can say that we're still searching for that promise land." I followed King's movement as he got up, strolled over to the stove, picked up the coffee pot and re-filled our cups." It dawned on me that I might have the most important Negro in the entire country serving me coffee. I put out the cigarette in the ash tray on the table and took a sip from the cup.

"Yes, we are," King finally replied after sitting back down at the table. "The first phase was done with the thirteenth amendment and freedom. But we are now in the second phase and that is the fight for equality. We have to make the Declaration of Independence live up to its dictates and prove that Thomas Jefferson was not a liar."

"I hope someday you can meet my grandmother before she goes home to be with the Lord."

"Let me ask you a personal question and feel free not to answer if you think I've overstepped my bounds with you."

I knew precisely what was coming but also felt ready to deal with it. If I and this potentially great leader planned to work together, it was important that we be perfectly honest with each other. "Please ask," I answered and quickly lit another cigarette.

"Isn't it difficult being both a Negro and a homosexual?"

"Not at all," I quickly answered. "Because they both are natural for me. They come quite easy; it is only difficult for those who don't care to understand that being gay is as natural as being straight. Now let me ask you a question, if I might?"

"Certainly," King answered and lit another cigarette.

"Do you pass judgement on men like me?"

King took a sip from his cup and a drag on the cigarette and slowly allowed the smoke to trickle from his mouth. I perceived it to be a delaying tactic to get his thoughts together. He finally said, "My God is not telling me to judge you at all. But instead to use your services in the struggle to finally help His people achieve absolute freedom and equality."

"But shouldn't equality be something afforded to all groups of people regardless of their color, religious beliefs or sexual orientation?"

"Yes, I do believe equality should be universally applied to all groups of people. That's what civil rights is all about."

I probably should have left the conversation right there, but I couldn't. "Do you, as do most ministers believe homosexuality is a sin?"

"Yes," he answered with no hesitation. "But man is prone to a great deal of sins. That's why He sent His son here to suffer and die for our sins. In many ways, I would argue that the Constitution was written knowing that man was not infallible. You must answer to God in the next life but in the meantime you have the right to be treated as any other man or woman according to the dictates of the Constitution." He again drank from his cup and took another drag. "If being a homosexual, you'll have to deal with it in Heaven just like the adulterer, thief, murderer and heaven forbid the non-believer will have to also.

I glanced at the clock on the wall. It read ten-thirty. I needed to get back to the hotel and get some rest. Tomorrow was going to be very busy with Glen coming in from New York.

"You must get rid of the guns in the house and tell your guards not to show up tomorrow with guns. And by all means make sure young Bobby gets rid of his gun." I said.

We both got up from the table. "Right now, I am somewhat of a reluctant student but will carry out my assignment." We both walked through the living room and I noticed that the gun had been removed from the chair evidently by Coretta. That was a good start.

I swung the door open and saw Bobby sitting in the car waiting for me. "Dr. King, I look forward to our continued discussion not only on the tactic but on life in general."

"As do I," he said. "And don't worry about Bobby. I'll make sure he leaves his gun at home from now on."

"You don't want him to just leave his gun at home, but to get rid of it." We finished, shook hands and I hurried to the car knowing I was well protected by the two men standing guard at the home.

9.

The ringing phone on the nightstand startled me out of a deep sleep. Before picking it up I checked my watch. It read six-thirty. It had to be a call from New York and only Arthur would call that early. No doubt he'd be angry since I hadn't talked with him since I left a week ago. I took a deep breath and put the phone to my ear.

"They're saying terrible things about you," Arthur shouted.

I was right. "Good morning Arthur and how have you been."

"You wouldn't know because you haven't taken the time to call me."

"I do apologize, but it has been very hectic down here."

"Understandable, but that's not why I'm calling," he said and hesitated, probably waiting for me to ask why he called. I accommodated him.

"And to what do I owe this call at six-thirty in the morning?"

"Like I said, they are saying terrible things about you up here. Saying that you are putting the entire movement down there in jeopardy with your presence." He paused this time to let his words sink in. "A young man from the War Resisters League, the people I assume are still paying your salary came by yesterday afternoon and asked me to call you and persuade you to come home."

"What are they saying?" I asked even though I pretty much knew the answer.

"That you're a communist and that a Reverend Ralph Abernathy has been trained by you in communistic tactics and you all plan some kind of revolt."

"What? Reverend Abernathy a communist, you're joking. He's a very devout and dedicated Baptist minister. Don't they know communisms and Christianity don't mix?"

"I don't know Bayard. I hear what you're saying. But I'm very much concerned for your safety. I don't want anything to happen to you."

"I know, and I'm going to be very careful."

"Bayard, that's not your fight. Your battle is on the international front, in Africa and other places. Why not let the ministers down there take care of that fight?" Arthur allowed some pleading in his voice.

"Oh, my dear Arthur you cannot separate the struggles and I belong to all of them," I said. "Nonviolence is as important here in Montgomery as it was in India and as it is in Africa. We are all searching for nonviolent answers in a society that accepts an assumption of violence as the only way to resolve problems." It was my turn to pause and allow the words to resonate with my lover. If we planned a future together, he had to understand that this was my life and my dedication just like studying English literature at Columbia University was his.

"Bayard, I don't want to lose you to some racist pig whose life doesn't even start to measure up to yours," Arthur interjected.

"No worry, my days here may be numbered." I perched the phone between the side of my face and shoulder, grabbed a cigarette from the package on the nightstand and lit it. "Glen Smiley will be here today. I'll probably stick around for a few more days and then head on back to New York. There is a lot of work to be done for the movement from New York and I can continue to assist from up there."

"Then I can plan on seeing you within the next week."

"Hopefully, yes."

"I really do love you, Bayard and would be crushed if something happened to you."

"I promise you, I'll be all right and will return to you in one piece."

"Be careful."

"You got it." I finished and hung up the phone.

I took a long drag on the cigarette, blew out the smoke and watched as it circulated around the room.

Arthur had been my first serious relationship since David Platt years ago, and I wanted to make it work with us. After Pasadena, I was determined to break free of the one-night stands with strangers and with nothing of value to the relationship but sex. I needed someone who really did understand that my plight was two-fold. Not only was I black, something that brought a lot of problems, but also gay and that exacerbated the problem. But I was determined to fight on both fronts and that's why Arthur had to understand that I must be in Montgomery at the beginning of what could possibly escalate into a major movement to not only break down prejudice based on color but also on sex.

After laying there for a few more minutes, I put out the cigarette, got up and began to get ready to meet the leaders, downstairs in the restaurant and wait for Glen to arrive. Knowing him as I did, there was no doubt he would ignore Swomley's warning to stay away from me and instead look to me for some guidance during his first days in Montgomery. It was Monday morning; February 27 and I'd been in Montgomery for a little less than a week, yet it seemed like months.

Our timing was impeccable. Just as I walked down the stairs into the lobby of the hotel, Glen, accompanied by Reverend Graetz walked through the door. He immediately answered the question would he ignore me by hurrying over to where I stood.

"Bayard, how wonderful to see you," he said as we hugged.

"Welcome to the war zone," I said, wrapped my arm around his shoulder. "Let me introduce you to the other members of the team." I ignored Graetz and led Glen into the dining room where the others sat around the usual table near the window.

Martin stood up first and held out his arm. "You must be the man they claim is as well versed in nonviolence as Bayard here."

Glen reciprocated and shook Martin's hand. "Believe me, Dr. King no one is as well versed in the Gandhian tactics as Bayard."

"Then we can consider ourselves blessed to have the two best gurus of Gandhi here with us in Montgomery," King said and directed Glen to an empty chair that had been set up at the table in anticipation of his arrival. He first shook the other leader's hands and then sat down next to Martin.

"Bayard, I assume you'll be leaving now that Glen is here to represent the entire delegation supporting our efforts in New York," Nixon spoke up first. "It is my understanding that Mr. Randolph and the others expect you to return real soon."

"I thought I'd leave that decision to Dr. King," I shot back. "If he desires, I can stay here and assist Glen in his efforts."

They all looked at Martin who appeared to be rather uncomfortable with the decision laid squarely on him. Silence engulfed the room as no one wanted to make this a confrontation about my presence.

"As far as I'm concerned Bayard is a great asset to our efforts," Abernathy broke the silence. "He was the person who came up with the strategy to march on the jail and turn ourselves in before being humiliated and arrested. You do remember that don't you all."

"Gentlemen, whatever we do, we can't allow the appearance of division, especially over a white man replacing a black man in the effort," Rufus added. "No offense meant Reverend Smiley, but we must stand united as blacks in this fight."

"Let's be quite frank with each other," Nixon continued. "I called Mr. Randolph and suggested that Bayard be replaced." He paused and looked directly at me. "No offense Bayard, but you bring a lot of baggage that could possibly hurt us in the long haul."

"I'm willing to accept Dr. King's recommendation as to what I should do." Martin probably didn't appreciate me putting the decision squarely on his shoulders, but that's where it belonged. I had bonded with him and now it was his turn to show just how much that meant. He still remained silent. The answer to the dilemma came bolting into the room.

"Dr. King, I warned you about this man," Emory Jackson, the black Birmingham reporter shouted as he pointed his finger at me. "Now he has really created a mess. He had the nerve to go over to Mrs. Reese's house the other night and told the police that he was a reporter for two foreign newspapers and wanted to interview her, but really was there to berate her for dropping out of the legal suit."

"Sir, I believe we told you the last time you interrupted this meeting that you were not invited," Rufus stood and said.

"Don't jump the messenger," Jackson responded. "I'm only here to warn you that if you don't get this man out of here, there's going to be trouble. The authorities are contacting the two newspapers he claims to represent and verifying with them that it's true."

For the first time in the past week I began to feel intimidated. It was apparent that this man did not like me because of my past, and he wouldn't let it go away. If what he said was true and the authorities had contacted the editors at Le Figaro and Manchester Guardian, it could cause serious problems for me.

"Enough of this please gentlemen," I said and stood up for emphasis. "My intentions for coming down here have always been to assist you all as best I could. But it now appears that I may be the center of attention taking well deserved attention from the cause itself, and the thousands of men and women walking for freedom."

"You don't have to do this," Rufus spoke up. He had become my closest ally and I did appreciate his support.

"As a matter of fact, yes I do," I continued. "I have in the past been affiliated with the Communist Party, I did three years in prison because I refused to participate in a war and of course, I am the kind of man that many of you find disgusting. But let me assure you that I am also the kind of man that you need." I paused and looked directly at Martin. "You need me because you understand very little about a tactic you plan to employ to defeat the menace of segregation." I now turned and stared over at Glen. "New York has sent you a replacement for me who is well trained in the tactics. Glen can do a very sufficient job, but the two of us together would be a tremendous asset to you all. But I can only be as useful to you all if you are willing to not dwell on my past and allow me to do what I know best."

"I say you stay," Abernathy spoke up.

"Let's take it one day at a time," Martin finally said. "Sir we appreciate your interest and help but at this time, I believe Bayard is needed and that his past is just that." Martin stood and looked at the black reporter. "Now if you will excuse us, we do have some very important business to discuss."

"That's fine, but remember I warned you ahead of time," Jackson said. "Mr. Rustin, I don't have anything against you as a person, but I do feel it necessary to speak my mind when I suspect anyone or anything that might jeopardize the cause here in Montgomery."

"Then allow me to speak my mind and I'll be finished," I spoke up. "If and when I feel that my presence does more damage to the cause than good, I'll gladly bow out. Until that time, I'll continue to do whatever I can to fight the sin of segregation."

"That settled gentlemen, let's get back to business," Abernathy said. "Sir if you will excuse us, we have some very pressing issues to discuss."

"Good day gentlemen, and I'll undoubtedly see you again." Jackson turned and walked out of the restaurant.

Martin sat back down, and I did the same. "Gentlemen, we are going into our ninth week of the boycott and it is becoming much more difficult…"

My mind drifted and I no longer paid attention to Martin. Practically everyone involved in my presence in Montgomery now opposed my remaining down here. In fact, New York sent a replacement. The whites resented my presence and as amazing as it was, so did many of the blacks. But regardless of the opposition, I was determined to stay until Martin finally asked me to leave. This movement had to be the most important since the actual ending of slavery almost a hundred years ago. We were about to put the final piece together that could possibly bring blacks into full citizenship with all others. That was a cause for which I had been preparing all my life. If I didn't see this fight to the very end, then the months on the chain gang in North Carolina and the three years in prison during the war would be for naught.

"Since the very beginning of this movement, the Negro community has invested over thirty-five thousand dollars of their hard-earned money to make it work," King said. "And we need more but the men and women are beginning to get restless. They want this to end."

"We need more cars," Rufus snuck in a comment.

I needed to concentrate on the issues at hand and not reflect on the past. "I believe we can raise money out of New York," I said. "I'll call Mr. Randolph this evening and ask for some assistance."

"Bayard, I believe at this point we need to have Glen make that call," Nixon intervened.

"Let me clear up a few things," Glen now spoke up. "Bayard Rustin is still one of the most respected men within the two organizations who are major supporters of your efforts and that is the War Resisters League who still have him on their payroll and the Fellowship of Reconciliation. He still has the strong support of Mr. Randolph, so he will be the right person to make that call."

"See what you can do," King said. "They have set March 7 for my court date and I don't think they've set dates for the others involved in the indictments so that means they are going after me."

"Break the leader and the others will follow," I said. "They're hoping that you will offer a deal, so you won't have to go to jail."

"That'll never happen. Jail has to become our second residence for those of us leading this fight," King retorted. "We cannot fear incarceration but to the contrary must welcome it as a commitment as part of the nonviolent philosophy for change."

I smiled knowing that my mentee was learning at a rapid pace the fundamentals of the philosophy he had now adopted. If I were to leave tomorrow, Glen would continue that lesson.

"One other important change is that you must no longer refer to this as a boycott." I said. I was not about to be silenced and would continue to teach if I remained in the city. "It is too limited in scope. It leaves the impression that once the boycott ends the cause is over. And that is not true with what you are doing. This is just the beginning of a protest against an entire way of life."

"Very good, Bayard," Abernathy said. "No one is to use the term boycott going forward and please discourage all our followers to use the term protest in the future."

"Are we about finished for the day," Reverend Graetz who had remained silent throughout the entire ordeal finally spoke up. "I need to get Reverend Smiley over to the Montgomery Inn."

"I'd prefer to stay right here at the Ben Moore, but I understand the law is just as strict about whites integrating Black establishments as they about Blacks going to their hotels."

"With the exception, late at night when white folks show up to go up to the dance floor upstairs. Law seems to look the other way," Rufus said.

"Isn't that how it has always been," I said.

"I believe we're finished here," King said and stood. The others followed suit. "Bayard, if you're not busy, I thought maybe you and your reporter friend would like to drop by to meet the little lady who has caused all this commotion."

"I've been waiting for the opportunity," I said. "Let me get Bill and we'll meet you out front." I hurried out of the dining area and through the hallway. I wanted to get out of there before one of the detractors complained. After all, I couldn't come all the way to Montgomery and not at least meet Rosa Parks.

It was a very short ride over to the apartment complex where Rosa Parks lived. Bill and I rode in the back seat and Martin sat up front with Bobby doing the driving. I wanted to ask him if he had discarded the gun. But instead Martin wanted to talk about help from up North.

"I don't see how we're going to make it if we don't get some serious financial help from the money people up North," he said right after we pulled off from the hotel. "These good people have dug deep into their pockets and come up with most of the cash we've used so far. We've had to pay for the gas for the cars used to drive them to work and often we'd have to compensate a man or woman who would get fired because they were participating in the protest. We've been at this for two months and we just plain need help."

"I'm sure Mr. Randolph's going to approach the unions for help. Have you had the opportunity to talk with Roy Wilkins at the NAACP?" I asked.

"No, I haven't," he tersely replied. "I shouldn't have to go begging other organizations to help us. Haven't heard a thing from the Urban League either. You know both Lester Granger and Roy don't approve of our tactics. Thurgood Marshall has been outspoken in opposition to the whole idea of protest to force change. They seem to believe that everything must come through the courts."

"This is something very different than what they believe in," I said not to be in defense of them but only as an explanation. "NAACP has always taken the position that all change must come through litigation."

"And they are flying high on the Supreme Court victory on school desegregation in '54," Bill said.

"But how successful has it been?" Martin questioned. "Last year they came back with a remedy that simply said with all deliberate speed which we interpreted down here to take as much time as you need."

"Yeah, and unfortunately, the Court does not have any enforcement power," I said. "If the Executive Branch doesn't step up to the plate and force the issue on the states, nothing will get done."

"That gentlemen, is our dilemma," Martin said. "That's why we here in the South must take the approach to disobey what we consider to be unjust laws. And be willing to suffer the consequences for our actions."

Bobby pulled the car up next to the curb. Martin opened his door. "Here we are gentlemen. Let's go meet the bravest woman in the entire country."

Bill and I also got out. "I'm all for that," I concurred.

A petite fair-complexioned woman with her hair pulled back, wearing wire rimmed glasses, smiled once she opened the door and recognized Martin. "Afternoon Reverend," she said in a soft rather melodic voice. "I wasn't expecting you. Raymond just left a few minutes ago. Come in."

She waved us inside. "I do believe I recognize this young man with you," she said and pointed to me. "But I haven't had the pleasure of meeting the other gentleman."

"Bill Worthy down here covering what you began for the northern black press," Bill said.

"Well welcome to Montgomery." Rosa closed the door and signaled for the three of us to take seats in the living room.

Bill and I sat at opposite ends of a couch and Martin sat in an oversized chair.

"Could I offer you men something to drink and I only have coffee?"

"No ma'am," Martin answered for all of us. "I don't plan to take up much of your time, but I just wanted these men to have the opportunity to meet you."

Rosa pulled a chair from the kitchen table and placed it in front of the coffee table. "This man here is Mr. Bayard Rustin from New York," she said. "You been on the local news for the past two days."

I hadn't watched the news or heard a broadcast for the past three days and wasn't aware that I had somewhat become the center of attention. That was not good.

She continued, "They been saying some very nasty things about you and even said that you barged into Jeanetta Reese's house and insisted that she rejoin the legal suit. Said the police had to forcefully get you out and that you're some kind of communist agitator."

"Is that all they said?" I was curious as to whether the more egregious charges had surfaced.

"No, they have said some other things, but I will leave it at that. We welcome you and need your help. And if Dr. King wants you here that's all that counts.

I felt relieved. "As long as I can help in our shared struggle I will be here as long as it takes to make a difference."

"How are you holding up?" Martin asked. "Haven't seen you out to any of the rallies lately?"

"It's been kind of hard, especially on Raymond. But with God's grace we're doing all right."

"Any more threatening telephone calls?" Martin again asked.

"We had the phone disconnected for the time being," she said. "We just couldn't take it anymore. These are really some hateful people. How can one race of people hate another as much as they do us?"

"The devil's always busy," Martin offered. "He never rests and will destroy our very soul if given the opportunity. Many of these folks belong to him and we just have to fight them with love."

"The question everyone up North keeps asking is why, Mrs. Parks?" Bill asked. "You've put your life on the line, and I understand have lost your job. What made you decide not to get up from that seat on the bus?"

Rosa smiled. "Emmitt Till, "she said. "And his mother Mimi Till and what she had to endure and the fact that those folks never considered the anguish and pain their hateful actions caused her. I decided at that point if I had the opportunity to lash out at that kind of hatred, I would take advantage of it and they gave me that chance."

I couldn't help but to think of my grandmother. Over thirty years ago she had the same kind of fire in her bones. Julia Rustin would have done just as Rosa Parks did. She did fight against bigotry and prejudice in West Chester and was one of the very first to join the NAACP when it decided to open a branch there.

"We are very fortunate to have Bayard with us," King said. "He brings the very effective Gandhian tactic of utilizing nonviolence to counter hate and violence. He'll be working with our leadership."

It was rather interesting and somewhat amusing that he gave no consideration to the other leader's assertion that I should depart the city. He did not mention Glen. Evidently, he felt more comfortable expressing his true feelings away from the others. It made me feel good and more determined to continue in the fight.

"You know Reverend King, I never imagined that my one action on that bus would trigger this kind of movement," Rosa said. "I pray every night that I did the right thing and that God will bless what we are doing here in Montgomery."

"Mrs. Parks, what you have done is greater than any action taken by Negroes since emancipation," I chimed in. "Whoever dreamt that it would be a woman that opened the door and insisted that we march right out of the dark ages into the light. What you have done is blessed by God. I want to be one of the first to thank you for what you've started."

Again, she smiled. "Thank you, Mr. Rustin."

"I know you've heard of Harriett Tubman, Sojourner Truth and Ida B. Wells-Barnett," Bill added to the conversation.

"I didn't have much schooling, but in our schools, we certainly did learn about those courageous Black women, especially at the Montgomery School for Colored Girls years ago, I mean many years ago."

"Mrs. Parks someday your name will be associated with them," Bill stated rather emphatically.

"No doubt about it." King concurred.

No need for me to say the same. The point was well made and very truthful.

"Rosa, I just wanted these men to meet you and know the person that started this entire movement," King said and then stood up. "We're going to get out of your way and get on back over to the church."

We all stood up and prepared to leave.

"Thank you, Reverend King." She stood and pushed her chair back over to the kitchen table. "We have a long way to go, but we're going to win this battle."

"And then we're going to win the war," I interjected.

"Have a good and blessed day, gentlemen." Rosa held the door open as we walked out.

"We'll do just that," King replied. "I'll be back in touch with you and please tell Raymond we send our greetings and are sorry we missed him."

She closed the door and the three of us made it back to the car, got in and Bobby started back to the church. We spoke very little on the ride to Dexter. Nothing needed to be said. We had now met the glorious saint like lady who had showed the courage of a Joan of Arc and like the French heroine touched us in such a way that we could only want to stay in the middle of this battle until it was finally won.

10.

"Our nigras were very content until these northern agitators came down here and started to stir up trouble," William Armistead "Tacky" Gayle Jr., Mayor of Montgomery screamed into the mike at the audience watching the Dave Garroway Morning News Broadcast on NBC television. I sat in Dr. King's office at Dexter with Bill, Martin, Reverend Abernathy and the newest member of the team Glen Smiley. We watched as the mayor practically eviscerated our attempts to break down segregation on the buses.

He continued his attack. "Why don't these communists and all these perverts go back to New York where they belong and allow decent white and Nigra citizens of our city to work out any problems that we might have."

"At least he's admitting they might have a problem," I said. "That's some progress." Maybe I was becoming somewhat paranoid, but I felt all eyes turned toward me as he attacked the New York influence on the movement.

"We know there is a left-wing communist reporter from the nigra press and a draft dodger with a prison record who are leading this movement."

Now I didn't feel quite alone. They had thrown Bill into the mix.

"And we just got word that a white nigra-loving minister from out of liberal California just arrived and is involved with them."

This time we all looked over at Glen.

"I guess they must be talking about me since Reverend Graetz is not from California," he said and smiled.

"Don't you believe the Negro citizens of this city have a right to equal treatment on the buses?" The reporter finally asked.

"Yes, they do, and we believe they receive fair and equal treatment and they gladly submit and accept our laws."

"But Mrs. Rosa Parks didn't, and she was arrested?"

"That's true but she was influenced by the NAACP, a radical Nigra organization founded by a communist, years ago."

"He must be referring to Dr. Du Bois," I interjected.

"This is just so much nonsense," Bill added.

Dr. King remained rather reticent as the interview continued.

"Mr. Gayle, you are aware that the NAACP just won an historic decision before the Supreme Court in 1954. And…,"

"That's another bunch of radicals and our Senators have all signed a pledge to fight that decision with all power within their means. Many of our citizens are asking that they be impeached." He interrupted the reporter. "I have nothing more to say on this matter." Gayle abruptly turned and walked away.

A rather surprised reporter hesitated for a moment and then turned to face the camera. "Back to you Dave Garroway in New York."

"We know that under the leadership of Dr. Martin Luther King Jr., the Montgomery Improvement Association has recently filed suit in federal court against the mayor and the bus company." Garroway announced to his listeners. "We will keep you posted as events continue to develop in Montgomery, Alabama."

Martin got up and strolled over to the television and turned it off. "Their strategy is to attack Bayard and Bill as the cause for the movement," he added. "We just can't afford to allow them to distract from the major issue here."

I knew exactly where he was going with his thinking. I wanted to beat him to the punch. "You think it's time for us to leave?" I asked.

"No, not leave but maybe put some distance between us," he said. "You both are a welcomed addition to what we must accomplish, but they will continue to dwell on that outsider claim for as long as they can. What I am suggesting is that maybe you re-locate for a while somewhere else, but close enough so that I can continue to meet and communicate with you all."

"What do you suggest?" Abernathy asked.

"Birmingham, yes Birmingham." King suggested. "It's much larger than Montgomery and you can get lost in the community there. It'll be convenient for me to drive up there to meet with you on occasion."

"What about my involvement," Glen spoke up. "They threw me into the mix."

"No, I'll need you to continue what Bayard started," King said. "Our primary goal is to familiarize our followers with the tactics of non-violence, and we need you to continue in that pursuit. They have no baggage that will stick that they can feed the flock. You're a minister and that helps."

"Let me make it quite clear, I could never replace Bayard because he is the very best and I have learned from him over the years, but I'll do my best."

"When do you think we should leave?" Bill asked.

"Late tonight, it'll take us a couple hours to get up there," Martin said. "I'll call A. G. Gaston and make sure he has room for you at his new motel." He paused and gave us a very hard stare. "And let's make sure no one else other than the four of us know what we're doing."

"What made you change your mind?" I had to ask. "Just yesterday you didn't share the other's determination to get us out of here."

"I didn't agree with their reasons," King quickly answered. "To me, it's not about your past or what you've done. I personally am not concerned with that. But we all sat here and heard the mayor on national broadcast castigate our legitimate efforts to integrate this city based on outside influence. The world must know that it is the efforts and determination of Negroes here in Montgomery and throughout the South to change these laws."

"That's right," Abernathy added. "The movement started right here in Montgomery among the citizens of this city. The men and women who have been walking since December six are residents of the city and not outsiders, so I see your point."

"As long as they have excuses not to change the laws, they will continue to fight," Martin continued. "We have to eliminate all possible excuses so that in the end, the world will know that it is just straight out racism. With you all gone from the city but not the cause, then it is a win situation for us."

I accepted Martin's explanation and the strategy for us to move north to Birmingham, removing me as a target for attack by the mayor or others. But I also wondered, how long these men and women could continue to endure these kinds of vicious lies and attacks against them. I had to ask.

"When does this end? How much abuse can one people take?"

"We don't know the answer to that," Martin said. "But we don't feel no ways tired. We know our Lord hasn't brought us this far and He won't deceive or leave us to the hands of the devil."

What more could I say except. "We need to get back over to the hotel and pack." We got up to leave.

"In the meantime, I'll call A. G. and make sure he has rooms for you all," King said as we walked through the sanctuary to the front of the church and out to the car where Bobby waited to take us back to the hotel. "And I'll pick you all up at ten."

As we drove down Archer Street, I thought how quickly events were happening, and how my time in Montgomery was cut short for all the wrong reasons. I still had so much more work to do, and even though I knew Glen could get it done, I still felt an emptiness that I'd never experienced before. Montgomery was my cause, something I had been groomed to do as early as high school. As a Black man concerned about what happened to my people in Montgomery and all over the country, I felt that for some reason I was being cut out from participating in all the work that needed to be done. Would I ever get another opportunity to be in the middle of the battle as I had been for the past week? And would Dr. King allow me to work closely with him as he moved on to more projects in the future, something he was destined to do. He has charisma leadership written all over him, more so than any other leader I had encountered in my forty-three years on earth, to include my mentor Mr. Randolph.

Bobby pulled up in front of the hotel and we got out. Later that night, I'd leave Montgomery not knowing if I'd ever return. It left a chilling affect on me.

11.

Bobby pulled into the enclosed parking court at the Gaston Motel located on 5th Avenue in the Negro district of Birmingham right at two o'clock in the morning. King had ridden up front, with Bill and me in the backseats, for the two hundred miles from Montgomery. Our departure was like a cloak and dagger event. Bobby had pulled the car into the alley behind the Ben Moore Hotel and we exited out the back way. When he pulled onto the main street, Bill and I ducked our heads so that the ever-present black car with the thugs always sitting inside couldn't see us. We feared that they would notify some of their Klan friends once we got on the darkened roads between the two cities and they would make sure we never made it to Birmingham. They'd probably figure that King was being driven home after a long evening of prolonged strategies with me somewhere in the hotel and I was probably still up in my room preparing the next day's activities. Our plan worked and we all breathed a sigh of relief as we got out of the car and headed to the registration desk at the motel.

"Dr. King, welcome to the Gaston Motel," George Small, the motel manager, met us at the door just as if he had been waiting for us to arrive. He handed Martin two keys. "We have your guests all registered into two suites on the second floor. Mr. Gaston is waiting for you all in Suite 205. Just take the stairs outside at the end of the building up to the second floor and the suite is the last one to your left." He snapped his finger and two much younger men hurried up to where we stood. "Please get these men's luggage and take it up to the suites," he ordered. He did all this before we could respond to his greeting.

Dr. King reached out and shook the man's hand. "Thank you," he said. We followed and shook his hand, then headed back out of the registration office, up the stairs and to the suite. Still holding the keys, Martin unlocked the door and we all strolled into the small living room of a well-furnished suite, with three separate bedrooms. Just as we entered two men, one older than the other got up from the couch and met us in the middle of the room.

"You must be Mr. A. G. Gaston," King said as he shook hands with the older man then turned and did the same with the other man, "because I know this warrior here. How you doing Fred?" he asked Reverend Fred Shuttlesworth. "I've delivered my two freedom fighters from New York, Bayard Rustin and Bill Worthy. Hopefully, they will be here with you for at least the next week."

"Please have a seat," Gaston said as he motioned to the couch and two chairs. I grabbed a chair closest to the desk against the wall. Bill sat on one end of the couch. "You gentlemen got a taste of pure hatred I assume?"

"It was an experience, one like we hadn't experienced up North," I said.

"No doubt for me, it has been different," Bill added.

"But let's not fool ourselves," Shuttlesworth said. "You have many of the same problems up North, it's just subtle."

I watched as the two young men brought my luggage into the room and placed it inside a large closet near the entrance to the bathroom. They then walked back out to deliver Bill's luggage to his suite.

"One thing they don't have is a Theophilus Eugene Bull Connor," Gaston said. "He is undoubtedly going to be elected the next Commissioner over the police in Birmingham and no doubt there will be problems for the Negro."

"That's for certain," Shuttlesworth interjected. "He's already warned that the Negroes in Birmingham better not try to bring any kind of protest or boycott like you all have in Montgomery here to Birmingham. Said the good white folks in his city aren't soft toward their Negroes the way they appear to be in Montgomery."

"How are things going in Montgomery?" Gaston asked. "You know we can't count on getting the truth from the reports in the newspapers here. I know they've been quite critical of you Dr. King. One reporter wrote that when you allow your local Negroes to go up North and get an education, they bring that liberal nonsense back here to the South. He claimed they shouldn't be allowed to come back but instead forced to remain up North where they belong."

"It's going on ninety days and my people are still loyal and determined that we will win this battle," King exclaimed proudly. "They have tried the same tactics in Montgomery as they would here in Birmingham, but we have stood tall and determined not to falter. And Bayard has been instrumental in bringing to the cause the necessary tactic that I believe will ultimately help us achieve our goal."

Shuttlesworth looked directly at me. "Yes, I understand it's the same tactic that Mahatma Gandhi used to cripple and defeat the British back in the late 40's."

"And it will eventually lead to the eradication of segregation all over the South," I added. "Montgomery is only the beginning for us."

"I don't know if it will work here in Birmingham," Gaston suggested. "These Negroes are so sick and tired of the violence and the bombings, that they want some white blood to flow for a change. They just sick and tired of our blood being the only blood that is spilled."

Shuttlesworth moved right to the edge of his chair as if that would help stress his next point. "Yes, we just had a young Negro lynched right outside the city. I had to preach the boy's funeral and it was just sickening watching his parents and his family suffer through that ordeal. Almost made me want to pick up a gun and go out and kill some white folks."

I cringed as I listened to a minister speak of killing. So much work had to be done throughout the South for the non-violent tactic to work as the best instrument to eradicate all the hate.

"This entire movement must be orchestrated by the church and the ministers," Gaston suggested. "Because it will only work, in the long run, if it is ruled by the blood of Jesus and the love of our Lord. Anything short of that will not work."

"I'll say amen to that," Martin said. "But I must get back down to Montgomery. We have a leadership meeting in the morning." He got up as did Bobby the driver who had come inside with us this time.

"Yes, we need to let these gentlemen get some rest." Gaston also got up. "We have an excellent restaurant as part of the motel, and they fix the most amazing breakfast you can ever want. We have some pretty big stars that have to stay here when they come to Birmingham. Duke Ellington, Ella Fitzgerald and Louis Armstrong have lodged here. We must have good food for such distinguished guests and the same is true for you all."

Bill, who had remained rather silent during the exchange also got up as did I.

Bobby opened the door and the cold Birmingham night chill blew inside the heated room. We all walked over to the door and the others walked outside as I remained inside the room.

"Martin, thank you for everything you've done Bill and me," I said as we shook hands.

"No, thank you Bayard and don't think this is the end," Martin rejoined. "We just needed to get you out of Montgomery, but you are definitely still an intricate part of whatever we do. And that includes you too, Bill."

I watched as the others either made their way down the stairs or in the case of Bill down the balcony to his suite. Once they were all gone, I closed my door, quickly made it to my bedroom and fell out on the bed totally exhausted from the long day and night.

"What do you mean you're in Birmingham," Arthur once again shouted at me through the telephone. I had awakened a little after seven and knew I had to let him know I wasn't on my way back to New York but had decided to hang around, close to Montgomery for a few more days.

"Arthur, you have to understand, this is just not something I can come into for a week and then disappear when so much work has to be done."

"Maybe you just don't understand the facts of life, Bayard. They don't want you down there because you are a homosexual, had communist leanings and a draft dodger. Why is that so difficult for you to comprehend? You are not like them. You are different, that is, unless you've decided to change your lifestyle. Which in case you have, please let me know so I can get all your things out of the apartment."

His rather acerbic tone irritated me, but I had to understand he felt left out of what I was doing and probably harbored some jealousy. He might even imagine me with another man. Under different circumstances I wouldn't tolerate his arrogance. But I did.

"That's ridiculous Arthur," I said maintaining a cordial tone. "I am a homosexual and have no problems with that aspect of my life. I will always be gay. I am not a communist and was not a draft dodger but a conscientious objector to the war. The one person who matters the most in this entire endeavor is Dr. King and he wants me close by for just a little longer. I owe him that much and I owe my people as much because besides all the other designations, I am still a Negro.

"Bayard, let me ask you what is more important to you, being a Negro or being gay?"

"They are equally as important, Arthur, because they both constitute who I am."

"They can't be both equal and you be in my life."

His words hit me like a bomb exploding all around me. This was a subject I didn't want to deal with over the phone and separated by nearly a thousand miles. "I'm afraid they have to be equally important to me. You're fortunate Arthur because you don't have the double burden of being gay and black. But what you're telling me is that the Negro's cause is not your cause and you want me to give that up and only be one of the two. Let's discuss this when I get back to New York."

"And when will that be? I get rather lonely here by myself."

"Promise you, it won't be long, and we can work out these problems."

"Have you been with anyone since you've been down there?"

"No Arthur, I haven't, and I won't." How thoughtless for him to imagine I would take such a chance, given the nature of my visit down here and with Pasadena still strong on my conscience.

"You better not," he shot back. "I can take you being down there selling them on the non-violence tactic, but I can't take you being with another man."

"We understand each other, and I will let you know when I plan to leave." I needed to get off the phone because Arthur was irritating me.

"That's fine Bayard but make it sooner than later." He said and we both hung up.

I needed a cigarette and reached over to the bedside table, pulled one from the pack and lit it. I seriously viewed the problems of the world from a humanitarian perspective. The Negro and gay oppression in this country were one in the same that is human beings persecuted because of who they happened to be. Most of my relationships had been with white men not because of the skin color but because of their mind set. I always believed that Arthur thought about these issues in the same manner as I did, but now that I was totally involved in the color problem in the South, I began to understand that he never did share the same sentiments and that had become a problem for us. I could only hope that he would come around and we would be able to work it out because I was committed to both fights and didn't plan to relinquish one because my partner failed to comprehend the importance of both.

Bill sat at a table in the restaurant sipping on a cup of coffee when I strolled inside and joined him.

"Those suites are outstanding," he said. "Now I know how royalty feels when they stay in luxury suites."

"Really comfortable," I agreed and signaled for the waitress to come over to our table. She did and I asked for a cup of coffee. "I guess we have to figure out something to do until we hear from Martin."

'I tell you what, let's go over to Mississippi and visit the place where Emmitt Till was brutalized."

"What? Are you serious?"

"Definitely am serious. Talked with Amzie Moore, who said we could hang out at his place in Cleveland for a couple days and see the Delta where real hatred resides."

What an intriguing idea I thought. We were so close and probably I wouldn't hear from Martin for a couple days and if necessary, could get back to Birmingham in a half day. If there was anything that could firm up my commitment to the cause and reject Arthur's notion that it wasn't my battle, it would be visiting Money, Mississippi.

"Would we be able to make it to Money, Mississippi, and visit the store where it all happened?"

"No doubt, Amzie said he'd be happy to take us there. He's closely followed the work you've been doing in Montgomery and wants to meet you. We might have to spend a couple days, but what the heck, we're not doing anything here in Birmingham."

The waitress brought my coffee and asked. "Can I take your orders for breakfast?"

"A waffle with grits and fried chicken," Bill said.

"Same for me," I said. "You sure we can do this?" I asked returning to the subject of traveling over to Mississippi.

"Leave it to me," he proudly replied. "I called the Greyhound Bus Depot; they have a bus that leaves at three-thirty this afternoon and we can be on it." He hesitated, and a broad smile crossed his face. "That is, if you can refrain from getting arrested because you have to ride in the back of the bus."

"For this journey, I believe I can. Let's do it."

12.

George Small volunteered to drive us over to the Greyhound Bus Depot and we arrived there right at two-thirty. We thanked him, got out of the car and headed into the terminal. He promised to pick us up when we got back and provided me with the number to call when we arrived back in Birmingham.

"The White Only" sign stared us directly in the face as we walked up to the entrance to the terminal. With a confused expression covering my face, I asked the porter standing out front.

"Where are we supposed to buy our tickets if this is a white only terminal?"

The elderly man smiled. "It's all right to go in there just to buy your tickets. Then you go around to the side near the back for the colored only waiting lounge."

"We can go in here without getting beat and thrown in jail?" Bill asked sarcastically.

"Yeah, just don't sit down and let any white folks get their tickets before you, even if they get in line after you," the porter replied.

"Are these people familiar with the 1946 United States Supreme Court decision in the Irene Morgan verse the Commonwealth of Virginia decision?" I asked rhetorically.

"What's that?" The porter asked with a rather confused look.

"Never mind. Thanks for the information," I said and the two of us walked into the terminal.

An oversized white security guard with pistol and club visibly in sight watched as we approached the ticket counter. He didn't really have to worry about us. We just wanted to get our tickets and get out of there before the Klan showed up and beat the hell out of us. We purchased our tickets, strolled back out of the terminal to the back where the sign read "Colored Only."

We walked into a very small, cramped area that possibly had been a back room sometime in the past. Two benches with no back rest were placed along the walls. An older man sat at one end of the bench, a young girl with a baby snuggled in her arms sat at the other end of the same bench. A middle-aged woman occupied the middle of the other bench, so Bill and I sat at opposite ends. Unlike the main terminal, there was no heat and a cold chill encompassed the room. The room was dark and dreary, and gave off a feeling of pious dejection, a sense of defeat that all was lost. You could feel it in the three others sitting in the room.

After sitting in that room for over a half hour we finally saw the bus pass by and go to the front of the terminal. We all got up, walked outside and to the back of the line as the white passengers got on first. Bill and I stood behind the elderly man, the middle-aged woman and the young girl with the baby. Finally, when we got to the front, the man and woman boarded the bus, but the driver taking the tickets stopped the young girl who had handed her ticket to him.

"Where's the ticket for the nigger baby?" he asked.

"They told me I didn't have to get a ticket for her as long as she sat in my lap," the young girl answered.

"I don't care what they told ya, the baby got to have a ticket."

At least he didn't say nigger this time, I thought.

"Sir, I don't have no more money to pay for a ticket and won't be able to get any until we get to Cleveland."

"Well, you ain't gonna get to Cleveland unless you can give me the money for the other nigger."

Clearly, I gave him too much credit for some decency. It was time for me to intervene. "How much?" I asked.

The driver looked at me. "Fifty cent children's fare from here to Cleveland, Mississippi." He scowled.

I gave him the fifty cents and the young girl turned and looked at me. "Thank you, sir."

I nodded to her, gave the driver my ticket and followed Bill onto the bus. We made our way to the last two seats in the back. He took the window and I sat in the aisle seat. After another fifteen-minute delay, the driver climbed into the driver's seat and the bus pulled out of the station and within another ten minutes sped down Highway 80 on our way to Mississippi.

I tried to relax and just enjoy the ride but to no avail. Bill had fallen off to sleep with his head propped against the window. I stared out along the highway and just as I did, we passed a chain gang of Black men dressed in orange prison suits with picks and shovels busy moving dirt from one place to another. Riding in the back of the bus and glancing out at those men took me back seven years to a time I'd rather forget but never could.

Try as I may, I couldn't forget March 21, 1949 when I surrendered to the Orange County Court in Hillsboro, North Carolina to begin a sentence for thirty days on the chain gang. My offense was for sitting in a bus seat out of the Jim Crow Section, even though the United Supreme Court had ruled segregation on interstate travel unconstitutional. As part of the Journey of Reconciliation organized by James Farmer of CORE, I was one of nineteen men and women who tested the strength of the law by integrating the buses in the upper South. I thought that my conviction would be over-turned if we could just get it to the Supreme Court. But the NAACP decided to drop the case and advised me against petitioning the Higher Court. Roy Wilkins personally called me in New York and told me that I would undoubtedly have to go to jail because the black lawyer who had the ticket stub that proved I was an interstate passenger had lost them. However, Wilkins also admitted that the lawyer probably was paid to destroy it after I had trusted them and gave the stub to them.

For the next thirty days, I lived in a two-room facility with over a hundred men cramped together. We slept on double beds that were so close together you had to turn sideways to pass between them. I could still smell the stench in that room even though I knew after seven years it had to be my imagination working overtime. I still had visions of the bright lights that remained on all night and the fact that the men had to get permission to get out of the bunks at night. I can still hear them hollering out to the guards "Getting' up Captain," or "Closing the window Captain," and "Going to the toilet Captain." This went on all night long and even though I was usually dead tired after being out on the road all day, I still couldn't sleep.

The wasted lives of the men caught up in that madness was the most disturbing. There was Easy Life who befriended me, Purple on my chain gang crew who made the most profound statement, "Man born of Black woman is born to see black days." I still had images of the old man who the guards hung from the bars facing the cell with arms chained to two vertical bars. After a few hours, his feet and glands swelled, and he stopped breathing. The guard rushed in and took him down and to the infirmary. But he was expected to be back out on the chain gang the next day. And I remembered Softshoe, called that name because of his corns and bunions. He told me that if I didn't want to tip my cap they gave me, then don't wear it at all. "If you ain't got no hat on, you ain't got to doff it."

I did my twenty-two days and they released me, but I often wondered what happened to those men. How many got out and found a way to stay out, and how many returned time and time again simply because they had no desire to make it on the outside. The psychological emasculation of these men destroyed their confidence that they could do anything other than serve time on a chain gang and I knew this was true all over the South.

"Cleveland, Mississippi," the driver shouted as he pulled next to a small building that had a sign that read "Greyhound Bus Depot." Just as he opened the door, a couple of white women, a white man with two children walked out of the building and lined up to board the bus. From the back three black men and one woman approached the bus and lined up behind the whites.

"All white passengers off first," the driver said as he swung the door open. "Niggers wait in the back until the white folks get aboard."

I began to feel that this trip should have been averted. I didn't know how many of these insults I could tolerate. Bill must have picked up my passion.

"Just remain relaxed," he said. "We'll be out of this stupidity once Amzie picks us up. It's something we needed to experience. It's what our people put up with every day in this rat hole."

"I don't know how they do it and keep their sanity," I whispered.

"Many of them don't and the others I imagine just escape into their own reality," he said. "It's what Dr. Du Bois has termed the veil and double consciousness surrounding the Negro. This world and then our world without them. It's necessary for survival."

After all the white folks got off and the others got on, it was finally our turn. We followed the older man, the middle-aged woman and the young girl with the baby off the bus. We walked to the front of the building and spotted the only black man standing across the street in front of a Chevrolet. We figured it had to be Amzie. He removed all doubt.

"Bill Worthy and Bayard Rustin, I assume," he said as he waved us across the street. We retrieved our suitcases and hurried over to him.

"You have to be that man who's raising all this hell with these white folks down here," Bill said as he shook Amzie's hand.

"That's me," he said and then shook my hand. He then grabbed our suitcases. "Get on in the car and let's get out of here." He tossed the suitcases in the trunk, jumped in the driver's seat and pulled off. I sat in the back and Bill up front.

Driving down the two-lane road I stared out at the fields that lay bare now but would soon be filled with cotton. Rows of shacks sat back off the road and occasionally, a large mansion-sized house also sat further back from the road.

"Those are sharecroppers' houses," Amzie said as he noticed both Bill and I had our heads turned staring out the window at a sight we really had never seen up close in our lives. Coming from the city, this was all new to us. "And you know who the big houses belong to," he added. "They are called shot gun houses 'cause you can shoot a shotgun right through the front door and out the back and that's the whole house."

Amzie drove about another mile and took one hand off the steering wheel and pointed to a house much bigger than the shacks but not nearly as large as the mansions. "That house used to belong to a successful farmer who put his trust in a white man. The man promised to make sure he could keep his property, but by the time he finished his manipulations the man owed him over forty thousand dollars with no way to pay. The white man foreclosed on him and took the property and the poor man ended up shooting himself, his wife and three children. The biggest tragedy to ever hit our little city. White man didn't even attend the funeral."

Bill and I sat silently listening to Amzie as he pointed to another medium-sized house surrounded by fields for crops. "That farm belongs to a good church-going man named Ted Keenan. He's a good friend of mine and a real brave man. Last year he signed an affidavit that Negro votes had been destroyed and that went straight to the FBI in Washington, D.C. I convinced him to join the local NAACP. I'm the president here in Cleveland and sure ain't easy. Well now he comes by my house after church and tells me that his minister warns him to watch the kind of praying he does in the church. He just prayed that God would remove all segregation and discrimination from the land." He paused and then asked, "Now ain't nothing wrong with that prayer is there?"

"No," Bill and I said almost in unison.

"Now Ted Keenan got one of the biggest farms owned by a Negro, over 240 acres with three tenant farmers and their families working for him," Amzie continued. "The other two Negro farmers that are not quite as large as Keenan but still very successful warned him that he'd better steer clear of all that integration nonsense and just stick to farming or the White Citizens Council going to destroy him economically. After putting considerable pressure on poor Keenan, they finally got their message across to him and he dropped all his activity with the NAACP." Again, he paused as if to let it all sink in with us. "If that weren't enough, they then sent the Negro President of Mississippi Vocational College in Itta Bena to see Keenan. He told my friend that the Council wanted him to become a spy on the NAACP and the other radical Negro in the same manner as many of the ministers do around here. But he refused and for some reason they decided to leave him alone and he's doing just fine now."

I leaned forward so that I was almost in the front of the car. "Wait a minute you just said like a lot of ministers do down here. Is that correct?"

"You go to most of these churches on Sunday and you'll see the people in the congregation either walking or driving old cars. But there will be one that always sticks out and that'll be the minister's Cadillac. Now you don't think those poor members of the church can tithe enough money so that they can drive one of the most expensive cars on the road?" He asked but didn't wait for a response. "No sir, the White Citizens Council pays for those Negroes cars with the understanding that they'll preach one specific sermon all the time and that is, 'God alone in His own good time, could lead the Negro to freedom.' I can guarantee you before tomorrow evening half dozen of them will have headed over to Indianola to Robert Patterson's office to report to him that you two are here looking around and causing trouble."

"And who is Robert Patterson?" Bill asked.

"He's the secretary of the Citizens Council of Mississippi and it's his job to keep all the Negroes in line and make sure nothing happens in Mississippi like what is going on in Montgomery, Alabama right now."

I sat back in the seat already exhausted and we'd only been there less than hour.

We finally pulled into Amzie's driveway. He parked the car, we got out and headed inside. As we strolled into the living room, we were met by four men and two ladies who evidently had been waiting for us to arrive. Even before we could get settled in, we listened to some harrowing stories about what these poor people had suffered at the hands of the Klan and the Citizen's Council. By the time they finished it was well after nine o'clock. We had a light dinner and finally made it to bed, with the understanding there would be a lot more tomorrow of what we had heard that night.

13.

The back room of Amzie's home was not quite as comfortable as the suite at the Gaston Motel and the bed much smaller, but I managed to get a decent night's sleep and woke that morning ready for what I felt would be one of the most enlightening ventures of the last three weeks. After lying there for an extra ten minutes thinking about what I might see that day in the rural areas of Mississippi, I managed to get up, dress and make my way to the front of the house and into the kitchen. The smell of fresh coffee and fried bacon tickled my senses as I smiled at Amzie and Bill already seated at the kitchen table.

"Good morning," I greeted the two and took a seat at the table.

"Ready for some breakfast?" Amzie asked

"Sure am, but could use some coffee," I said as I pulled a cigarette out the package and lit it. I assumed it was okay because there was an ashtray on the table.

"Good, 'cause we have a very long day ahead of us." Amzie got up and before he could get to the coffee pot, his wife Ruth, who had been in the living room, came in and poured me a cup.

"You finally up and about," she said as she placed the cup on the table in front of me. "Been waiting on you before I served you all breakfast."

"I apologize. If I'd known you had taken the time to prepare what I know will be an outstanding breakfast, I'd been down here hours ago."

"You're all right," Amzie added. "Ruth's just teasing. We all only got down here a few minutes ago. And I'm glad you got all your rest because you're gonna need it for what you're gonna see today."

"It's that bad," Bill chimed in.

"It's not bad, it's depressing," Ruth said as she brought a tray with bacon, eggs, potatoes, and toast and sat it down on the table. "From here to Money, Mississippi is nothing but share cropping farms, and the level of living is not of the highest quality. That any people have to live the way those folks do and there's not much we can do to change it is just darn depressing."

"It's not just the sharecroppers, it's all of us," Amzie said. "God knows that Ruth and I have done battle with these people over the years, especially since I decided to head up the NAACP here."

"I guess down here the word NAACP is as bad as communist," Bill said.

"You got that right," Amzie answered. "These folks don't give us enough credit to organize and run an effective organization, so it has to be some outside source like the communist."

"I guess a white communist is smarter than anyone black," I added with a chuckle. "Right again." Amzie tossed a forkful of eggs into his mouth.

"Maybe we might be better if this country was ruled by a communist system, because this so-called democracy hasn't done much for us over the years," Bill said.

"No, don't ever think that," I shot back as visions of how the communist party had turned against the entire black struggle once they became an ally with the United States during World War II. "That's when I became disillusioned with them and quit the party in New York City back in 1939. When it was no longer in their self-interest to support our efforts in this country, Stalin instantly turned against us and allied with the South. So please don't ever think those people are our friends."

"I guess we have very few friends anywhere in this world," Amzie gasped. "We're alone in our struggle."

"No, we're not," Ruth interjected. "We have God and Jesus and that's all we need. Someday we will prevail. Someday we'll win."

"I hope so," Amzie said. "I sure hope you're right. One thing about the Negro race, we have the patience of Job waiting for the time when God will lift the evil from our backs and deliver as He did in the Bible."

"Hallelujah," I added. Not much needed to be said as we finished our breakfast, loaded into Amzie's Chevrolet and headed down the two-lane road to observe some of the people that had the patience of Job.

The further Amzie drove down this small two-lane highway the more desolate the land became. Nothing lies before us but field and every mile or so we saw a large white house surrounded by several shanties. After driving for over a half hour, Amzie pulled off to the side of the road. He pointed to a large billboard and said. "Read that and you'll know exactly what it's like down here.

Bill and I both peered out the window at the billboard in astonishment. It read.

"YOU NIGGERS CAN'T LIVE UNLESS WE LET YOU. YOUR FOOD, YOUR WORK AND YOUR VERY LIVES DEPEND ON GOOD-HEARTED WHITE PEOPLE. WHEN THE LIKES OF YOU LEARN YOUR PLACE AND STAY AWAY FROM ORGANIZATIONS LIKE THE NAACP RACE RELATIONS CAN BE CORDIAL. TROUBLE COMES WHEN YOU DON'T RESPECT YOUR OWN RACE AND STAY IN YOUR ASSIGNED PLACE IN SOCIETY!"

I reared back in the seat and closed my eyes for a minute. I just knew this couldn't be real. But because I had just read it, I knew it was. For a minute, I just listened as Amzie and Bill conversed in the front seats.

"How do they allow a billboard like that to remain up?" Bill asked.

"You have to know that the White Citizens Council runs everything down here. The local political officers, the police, the courts, everybody. And they are all of one accord and that billboard says it all. They mean it and most of the Negroes comply." Amzie pulled back out onto the road and we continued the journey.

"But you don't give in to that bull shit," Bill said.

"No way, because I ain't nobody's nigger, boy, or whatever choice words these folks want to use to define us."

"Why don't the others have your kind of courage?" Bill continued.

Amzie turned off the main road onto what was nothing more than a dirt trail. In front of us sat a shack. "You can ask these folks that question," he said as he pulled up to the shack, turned off the engine and waved us to get out of the car and join him.

We walked up the three steps to the rickety porch and he knocked on the door. It flew open from the force of Amzie's fist. The stench from inside was suffocating but we peered through the door.

"Can we come in?" Amzie asked a young girl who sat on a wooden chair with a baby in her arms.

"Mr. Amzie, come on in sir," she said. "Wilbur's outside at the toilet. He'll be back in directly."

We stepped inside to a practically bare room with only three chairs and an old table. Off to the right was a room with a mattress on the floor and pallets where three young kids still slept. The only other room was a kitchen with a stove and an old ice box. The back door was swung open. You could see the outhouse through the opened door.

"How are you doing, Mae?" Amzie asked.

"Doin' fine and bein' blessed everyday by the good Lord." She shifted the baby from one side of her body to the other and adjusted her position in the chair.

"These men here are from Birmingham. I'm taking them up to Money, so they can see where that young boy was lynched last summer."

"Oh Lord, have mercy. That sure was shameful the way they did that boy. But ain't nothing we can do about it but pray that his soul was saved and went on home to be with Jesus."

I turned and looked at Bill. Our thoughts merged without having to speak. How could we allow this to happen in this country? How could we, as Negroes, allow this to continue to happen to our people? I didn't know who was more at blame; the white power structure that kept these poor folks oppressed or the Negroes who allowed it to happen. My mind thought back on what Amie had said yesterday. The preachers drive the Cadillacs and the congregation walks.

"Mr. Amzie, what brings you out to the country this time of morning?" A man who looked to be much older than the girl strolled through the back door and closed it behind him.

"Morning Wilbur," Amzie said. "On my way to take these two men from Birmingham up to Money for a view. How you feel this morning?"

"I'm doing fair as can be expected. Got to get out in the field this morning and already running a little late." Wilbur walked over to the bedroom opening and shouted. "Boy, get on up, we got to get out of here."

One of the boys who appeared to be just about five jumped up rubbing his eyes. He ran past all of us and out the back door.

"You got some city men come down here to cause trouble?" Wilbur scowled. He looked directly at me. "What you all think you can do down here but make it harder for us than what it already is?"

"They didn't come down here to cause no trouble Wilbur," Mae spoke up. "Just kinder want to see what's going on. Ain't that right Mr. Azzie?"

"You right Mae, they didn't come here to make trouble," Amie replied then looked at Wilbur. "These are good men, want to try to do something to make things right just like me."

"Yeah, you and all that NAACP, all you do is make things hard for us who got to live with this white man for our survival."

As I listened to Wilbur, I better understood the writing on the billboard back on the road. It wasn't for Negroes like me and Bill or even Azzie. It was for men like Wilbur as a reminder to always remember your place in this part of the country. I wanted to ask him why he stayed here and lived like this, but my better judgement stopped me. I just listened.

"How are things ever going to get better, Wilbur, if we don't have the NAACP or what the Negroes are doing up in Montgomery, Alabama?" Amie asked.

"What they don' up in Montgomery?" Wilbur watched as his son ran back into the house, went to the bedroom and put something in his pockets.

"You don't know about the bus protest movement and Dr. Martin Luther King?" I now asked.

"Naw, never heard of him. We don't get much of anything happening outside of this county." Wilbur hurried into the one room, grabbed a coat and headed for the front door, with his son right behind him.

I watched his movement. It was a wonder that he'd heard about the Emmitt Till lynching. Wilbur wasn't the most informed person. I felt compelled to be respectful of his lifestyle but just as compelled to ask one more question. "Your boy doesn't go to school?"

"Hell no, why should he go to school? Ain't nothin' out here for a nigguh but the dirt and grind of the cotton."

"I want my boy to go to school but…"

"Well he ain't." Wilbur cut Mae off. "He got to help me out in that field make enough crop to pay for this shack we live in and give you enough food to feed these young'uns Ain't got no time for no school and won't do no good no way."

"How do you get your mail out here?" I asked.

"Sometimes the mailman will drop it off in that box out front by the road, and sometimes we goes into the post office in town to pick it up," Wilbur said.

"If you allow me, I'm going to send you a radio through the mail so you can at least listen to what's happening outside this county. Will you allow that?"

"Oh, please sir, we'd love to get a radio," Mae answered before Wilbur could speak. He remained silent so I took that as a yes from him, also.

I gave Wilbur the writing pad I'd brought with me into the house and handed him a pen. "Write your address and I'll mail it to you as soon as I get back to New York."

Instead of writing the address, he thrust the pad and pencil to Mae. She took it, handed the baby to him and wrote the address. He then dropped the baby back in her lap and gave her a disdainful look.

"Well, me and my boy got to get to work. You all enjoy your stay here in the Delta and don't do or say nothing to these white folks 'cause they'll wait until you leave and take it out on us left here after you all go back to your big cities." He pushed his son out in front of him and followed behind and out the door.

"Thank you, Mae for letting us take up some of your time," Amzie said. "We need to get on down the road so we can be in Money by noon."

"Thank you for comin' by. We don't get no company out here and it gets real lonely being here all day with nothin' to do but keep these babies quiet."

"At least you'll be able to listen to music when I get this radio to you in the next week," I said.

"Thank you, sir. God certainly sent you to us. I'll praise Him all day long for the blessing."

"You take care of yourself," Bill finally spoke up.

I found it rather interesting that Bill remained quiet throughout the time we spent in there. I knew he was processing this tragedy, assessing it from the perspective that maybe a communist and socialist system would serve people like Wilbur and Mae better than a democracy and capitalism. I knew for sure that socialism was far superior to this form of an economic system that allowed such a large disparity between those who have and those who have not.

We got back on the road and I remained quiet for the first ten minutes. I heard Bill and Amzie talking but what they said didn't register with me. My head remained back there in that shack of a home not fit for human beings. I couldn't get beyond the lifestyle that forced all the children and parents to sleep in one room with no beds. For the first time, the thought occurred to me that the protest concentrated on the wrong issues. It wasn't so much social issues like segregation that was critical for Negroes, but instead economic issues. What good did it do for the race to be able to sit anywhere on a bus or eat in any restaurant when it did nothing to eradicate the plight of Wilbur and Mae.

After an hour of the same scenery from the back seat of the car, Amzie finally said.

"This is it, Money, Mississippi. Straight ahead is the store where it all happened."

Amzie pulled over next to the railroad track and we peered across the street at a two story-building with an extended roof out over the sidewalk and a headboard that read "Bryant's Grocery Meat Market," and two Coca-Cola advertising signs on each end. I watched as a couple Negroes strolled inside the store. A large white man stepped outside and peered over at us.

"That's where Till supposedly said something to Roy Bryant's wife and later that night, he and his half-brother J. W. Milan drove over to Emmitt's great Uncle Moses Wright's home and grabbed the boy."

Yeah, I read about it in **Look Magazine** back in January," I said. "They admitted to their guilt and got paid about four thousand dollars for the story by the magazine."

"Only in this country can you lynch a young black and get paid for your story," Bill added with sarcasm.

"What's so ironic is that most of their customers are Negroes from the fields," Amzie said. "But they've been boycotting the place and word is out they might have to close down."

"Protest pays off," I added.

"Seen enough of this place?" Amzie asked.

"More than enough," I said.

"Then let me take you over to the barn where they actually murdered him." Amzie pulled off and we started down the two-lane road, with the man watching us as we drove away.

As soon as we pulled off a squad car got behind us. I started to turn around and look back at them, but Amzie, shrieked, "Don't do that. Don't look back or they sure will pull us over." He looked in the rear view and then straight ahead.

"They know we're not from around here?" I asked

"You better believe it," Amzie said. "They know their Negroes and who belongs to them. And they get very suspicious of any others poking around."

"Damn, how can people live like this?" Bill scoffed.

"How can Wilbur and Mae live the way they do?" Amzie asked but didn't wait for an answer. "After years and years of this treatment, you begin to believe the lie."

"The lie being that you really do believe you are an inferior being," I suggested. "And the treatment you receive is acceptable to you."

"And if you don't like it, you pack up and go north or move to one of the cities." Bill added.

"You all got it right." Amzie again peered out the mirror. "They turned off."

My initial thought as we continued up the road was that black people in this country have been psychologically emasculated. I couldn't think of any time in the history of civilization when a people had been psychologically tormented to believe they were an inferior human being to all others. That's what has happened to the Negro in the country and the damage has been devastating.

Amzie pulled up on the side of the road. "Look across the street to your left and that's the barn where they tortured and killed that poor boy last August."

I stared across the street at a wooden structure with a roof slanting down from the top and an open entry area. But instantly my attention was diverted from the barn over to a heavy-set white man who walked out to the driveway with a shot gun snuggled between his body and right arm. He glared over as if daring us to make a move toward his property.

"Is that one of the men who did the killing?" I asked.

"No, that's J. W. Milan's brother in law and he don't let no one come on that property. I heard that the white folks run J. W. and Roy out of town, they moved somewhere north of here," Amzie explained.

While listening to Amzie I watched as a tall, lanky black boy ran from around the back of the barn and stood next to the white man. He also caught Amzie's attention.

"That young boy just run from around the barn, actually saw the killing. He was milking the cows when J. W. and Roy brought Emmitt to the barn. When he looked inside and saw what was happening, he ran up the street to a neighbor's house, but they was too scared to do anything about it."

"You mean there was the chance that black folks might have been able to save that boy's life?" I asked.

"I guess if they'd gotten together and hurried over to the barn with their guns, but that just wasn't going to happen down here," Amzie explained. "Maybe up North or even in a city like Birmingham, but not down here."

All a part of the psychological emasculation I mused.

"Did the boy testify at the trial?" Bill inquired.

"No, too scared." Amzie turned and looked back at me. "You know how you can train a dog to certain behavior and if he doesn't follow it, he knows he gonna get whipped. Well that's the same down here. Wasn't no way that boy was gonna testify in front of all those white folks, and especially after he witnessed what happened to the Till boy."

The white man started up the driveway toward us.

"Think we probably overstayed our welcome," Amzie said. He started the car and we pulled off. "Let's go see what was supposed to be that boy's final resting place."

After another fifteen minutes, the terrain began to change. Instead of barren fields we began to see trees on both sides of the road. When we reached a narrow bridge that extended across the river, he stopped. I instantly looked behind to make sure no cars were behind us. I then peered down the river that stretched as far as the eye can see but bent to the left after a while. Trees lined both sides of the riverbank. I momentarily closed my eyes and a vision of two white men throwing the limp, young, black body, weighted down with irons, into the river and the boy disappearing beneath the water.

"This river been the enemy of Negroes for a long time," Amzie said and I detected the sadness in his voice. "Old man who lived here all his life claims that over one thousand bodies been thrown into this river since 1900. It's got all those black ghosts down the bottom and he claims every once in a while, you can hear them moan in agony."

I felt the blood rushing to the top of my head and the anger seeping through. Water, a sign of life meant death for so many Negroes and only because they were Black. I could only imagine the terror they felt while being brutalized by an animal more vicious than any in the woods. I could only imagine the pain their families suffered not knowing for sure if their loved one was trapped in the muddy bottom of the river.

"Had enough?" Amzie asked. "Have you all seen what you came down here to experience?"

"Yes, I think we have," Bill replied.

"Ready to head back to a safer and more secure environment?"

"I think so." It was my turn to respond.

We made it back to Amzie's house, packed our bags and he took us to the Greyhound Depot where we boarded a six-thirty bus back to Birmingham, and I never imagined that I would be happy to get back to a place as racist and ugly as that city. But I was ready to go.

14.

"Mr. Randolph, you have been right all along," I said to Mr. Randolph on the phone the next morning in my suite at the Gaston Motel back in Birmingham. "The issue is economics and not civil rights as defined by King's movement in Montgomery. And if it's economics then the real battle has to be for the ballot down here."

"That's been my position as far back as 1920 when Negroes in places like Harlem were arguing about how we survive in this country," Randolph said.

"You think there's poverty in Harlem, you have to see what it's like down here." I snatched a cigarette out of the pack and lit it while holding the phone between my cheek and shoulder. "Bill and I went down to Cleveland, Mississippi yesterday and Amzie Moore took us over to Money where Emmitt was killed. But the most startling aspect of that trip was when we stopped and spent a few minutes with a share cropping family."

"That'll never end unless we can secure the vote, but more important is there must be a re-distribution of the wealth in this country," Randolph explained. "In the meantime, you need to plan your return to New York. I understand that Glen is doing an admirable job with Dr. King and they all are happy with his presence."

His words hit hard, but I refused to entertain their meaning. Being in Birmingham made it impossible for me to be very effective in what would happen in Montgomery. I guess I could plan to leave. I knew that would make Arthur awfully happy.

"I guess I could get out of here sometime tomorrow," I said. "Later I'll call the airlines and see what time I can leave."

"Good, then we can continue this conversation as we discuss how best we can assist in the movement that probably is going to spread all over the South."

"Arthur will pick me up and I'll try to get over to the office before day's end." We finished and hung up.

Last night when we got in, I was so dead tired I went straight to bed, dirty body and all. After I finally climbed out of bed, I poured a steaming tub of hot water, soaked for a good fifteen minutes and when I finally got out, I dressed and made it downstairs to the restaurant. Bill was already down there sitting at a table sipping on a cup of coffee.

"A big difference this morning from where we were yesterday," I said as I sat across from him at the table.

"I'll say," Bill said. "Bayard, I'm leaving for New York later this afternoon. I have a four o'clock flight out of here. I've seen enough."

"Maybe I'll do the same," I said. I'd figured I'd hang around until tomorrow, but I had no real reason to do so." Just as I finished, I felt a tap on my shoulder.

"Mr. Rustin, a call for you at the receptionist counter," George Small the manager said.

Thank you." I got up and followed George to the receptionist counter. The receptionist handed me the phone.

"Bayard, I need to see you this evening," Martin said.

"Where are you Martin?"

"In Montgomery, but I plan to have Bobby drive me up there. I think I need for you to come back here for a couple days."

"You can't be serious?"

"I don't joke too much during these trying times."

There goes my getting back to New York later today with Bill. "What time do you think you'll be up here?"

"Probably after ten. We'll pick you up and get you back here. We have to do it at night because we can't let the others know you're back, that is, but Ralph and Rufus. They're safe."

I reluctantly said, "I'll be ready." We finished and hung up. I stood there momentarily trying to internalize exactly what was happening. Why did he need me back in Montgomery when I'd just gotten out of there a couple days ago, in a hurry? But I agreed, not so much out of curiosity or because I wanted to go back, but only because of the respect that was growing within me for this man.

"You're going to stay here with Deacon Smith," Martin explained as we made our way up the steps and onto to the porch of a man whom I had seen at Dexter but never met. Like many deacons in Baptists Church, he sat in the first row and passed the collection plate when it was time for the congregation to either tithe or make an offering. He had also stood up front after the service, when Martin made the call to join the church.

Martin knocked and instantly the front door swung open. A stocky dark-skinned man with a full crop of gray hair waved us inside.

"Deacon Smith, I know you've seen Mr. Rustin at our church and probably at many of the prayer rallies we've held at the church," Martin said.

"Yes, I did, Reverend." Deacon Smith stuck his hand out to me, and we shook hands.

"My pleasure, Deacon," I said.

"We can't afford to have you stay at the Ben Moore Hotel or at any of the residents of the men involved in the movement," Martin explained as we all took seats in the parlor. "Because all our houses are being watched. And as you found out, the Ben Moore is constantly under surveillance because they know whoever comes to town to get involved will probably stay there. Fortunately, Deacon Smith has kept a low profile and I figured you wouldn't be spotted here."

"It's not the Ben Moore, but hopefully you'll be comfortable," Deacon Smith said. "I have you set up in the guest bedroom."

My state of being was just short of shock so I just sat there and took it all in. I couldn't believe I was back in Montgomery, the city I had been run out of just a few days ago.

"I appreciate the hospitality," I said.

"We have quite a struggle in front of us and if I can play a small part by opening my home to a leader like you, it is a pleasure," Deacon Smith said.

"Speaking of the struggle, we need to talk first thing in the morning, before I meet with the others. Is six o'clock too early for you?" Dr. King asked.

"If the Deacon will be so kind as to wake me about five?" I looked over at Deacon Smith and smiled.

"I usually get up about four thirty, so no problem."

"Good, then we're set." Martin rose out of his chair. "It's been a very long day and night for me. I need to get on home and get some rest."

Deacon Smith got up with Martin and walked him to the door. I was so dead tired; I couldn't move from my position in the chair.

"Be ready in the morning," Martin said and looked back at me. He then walked out, and the Deacon closed the door.

"You want to come with me," Deacon said. "I'll show you to your room."

"Nothing would give me greater pleasure." I got up and followed the Deacon down the hallway to the room. It was already after midnight and I had to be up by five. I needed to get to bed and rest for what could prove to be a very busy day in just a few hours.

King arrived right on time and I was up and ready to meet with him at exactly six o'clock. In fact, I'd already had a cup of coffee prepared by Martha Smith, the Deacon's wife. She was busy preparing some bacon and eggs when Martin strolled into the kitchen.

"My Lord, Reverend, would you like some breakfast?" She asked him.

"No Sister Martha, I had an early breakfast before I left this morning," Martin said as he took a seat across from me at the table.

Deacon Smith also took a seat at the table.

"I need your help," Martin blurted out with no delay. "We are in so deep that I'm not sure the protest can continue. If we don't get some help from up North, we'll run out of funds to keep this going."

Martha placed a plate of eggs, bacon and toast in front of me.

"I can have Mr. Randolph talk with the labor leaders." I suggested while digging into my breakfast. "Has Roy Wilkins volunteered to send any money?"

"Neither he nor Lester Granger over at the Urban league have offered any support," Martin answered. "I don't believe either one of them or their organizations believe in what we are doing down here. They are still stuck on the idea that all gains that Negroes make in this country should go through the courts, which of course means they will be in control."

"I need to talk with Mr. Randolph about getting the labor leaders to commit to your approach," I said. 'But you have to understand that you must expand the scope of your movement from just social integration to economic growth. This movement has to become bigger than just integrating buses and restaurants, but to integrating the workplace and breaking down economic exploitation against not only Negroes but all people."

"We are open to new approaches and ideas," King exclaimed. "But you know that whatever new finances and ideas must appear to come from right here in Montgomery. The MIA must be out front on everything that's happening. But we will be more than happy to receive outside assistance at this point."

"I know, I got a taste of that outsider accusation last time I was here."

"I've concluded that once this is resolved in Montgomery, we must move on to cities like Birmingham and even Jackson, Mississippi and it has to be based on the Christian principle of non-violence. We must teach all our followers throughout the south that it is admirable to turn to the other cheek."

I had a very strong inclination to remind Martin that Gandhi was not a Christian and the impetus for this approach began with him. But I refrained. He was after all a Baptist minister and all things positive and good had to emanate from Jesus and the Christian faith.

Instead I said, "You probably need to set up a school just like the Highlander one in Tennessee. I'd participate and I'm sure Glen Smiley would also."

"Glen Smiley has been just wonderful carrying on where you left off," Martin said.

"It's men like Glen who make us recognize that this entire movement is not race specific, it belongs to all humanity."

Martin leaned half across the table. "We can't lose, Bayard. If we lose here, it might be years before we get another chance to destroy this wicked and evil system."

"Martin, we're not going to lose." I reassured him. I put my fork down and concentrated on him and not the eggs. "This movement is signaling the beginning of a New Negro just like the Harlem Renaissance did back in the 1920's. We are witnessing a revolutionary change in the Negro's evaluation of himself and he is beginning to like what he sees."

"Yes, I get that feeling every night we hold a prayer meeting and I look out at my people who have congregated in the church to celebrate our new attitude about life. The look in their collective faces reflects a positive attitude about what we are all about. Maybe Negroes will begin to love each other."

"Martin, do you realize that you are re-defining the role of the church in our lives," I said, feeling very enthusiastic about the direction of this conversation. "It's been almost one-hundred years since our folks walked off those plantations into a life of freedom. But they didn't know how to make it work for themselves, so they turned to the church and asked their ministers to deliver for them."

"No doubt the church was their foundation and solace oftentimes from the evil all around them. But it didn't bring about equality. They were free but not equal."

"That's because our ministers put all their faith in the next world and not this one. They promised them salvation but not equality and then you come along with a different approach."

"I'm not quite sure I follow your meaning," King said.

"You're changing the church from a tool solely for salvation to a tool to help achieve social equality. Don't you see, this all had to begin within the church because you all are the only institution with enough independence to make this work."

King reared back in his chair. "This is what Howard Thurman has been doing for years and what my predecessor at Dexter was doing," he said.

"But theirs were basically individual efforts lacking the entire community support. They weren't able to reach out to the masses the way you have," I explained. "You are a pioneer and your destiny is to use your charismatic energy to take this movement much further than just here in Montgomery." Momentarily, visions of Wilbur and Mae shot through my mental vision. "The people I saw yesterday in Mississippi are going to need you and it can only be you as a minister and a social gadfly to eradicate some of their suffering."

"This is going to be a monumental task and it's going to take more than just me to make it work."

"You're going to have a whole race behind you. Do you think that might be enough support?"

"Will you be with me?" He asked with humility.

"As long as you want me with you, I'll be right there."

"Would you take on the organizing effort in the North and especially New York?"

"Will my past be a hindrance to you?"

"Only if you allow it to be."

"I guess you can say that I've suffered through the slings and arrows of outrageous attacks over the past ten years and have become somewhat immune to it. My concern is that you will also be capable to withstand the attacks?"

"I mentioned to you before, your private life is of no concern to me. If God considers your actions immoral, then He will do what He sees fit for your sins."

"I'd rather take my chances with God than with men who want to play God. What I do is not a sin but natural and nothing that is natural can be sinful. Sins consists of doing things outside the natural realm of universal laws." I finished my breakfast and asked. "What's next?"

Martin pulled out an envelope from his inside pocket and handed it to me.

"Since I asked you to stay over an additional day, thought it only right that we pay for your ticket back to New York."

I gave him a very hard stare, opened the envelope and gazed on a ticket leaving at two p.m. From Montgomery, Alabama back to New York.

"Thank you."

Martin reached across the table and we shook hands. "Welcome to my team Bayard Rustin. I will be in touch with you as soon as you get back to New York. We still have a long way to go in this battle to integrate the bus system here, but we're going to win. And after that victory is when I'm really going to need you. We have the entire South that must be broken down and changed."

"You're right and there is only one way to make that happen and that is through the non-violent approach to change."

"Gotta run," Martin said and got up from the table. "Bobby will be here to pick you up about noon and get you to the airport. Have a nice trip back and we'll be in touch."

I sat there and watched as Martin hurried out the front door. My time in Montgomery had come to an end, but my involvement in what could be the greatest social movement in this country's history had just begun. I was thrilled and excited about the prospects for what we would accomplish in the months and years before us.

PART TWO
New York City

15.

I sat at the harpsicord in the living room of my apartment playing a classical Bach tune. At a little past midnight, the beautiful string sounds of the harpsicord filled the room as I tried to concentrate on the music. Arthur had already retired to the bedroom and waited patiently for me to join him. But visions of the South interfered. I wanted to hold him in my arms and make love, but my body was still tense from the trip back home. I just needed the music to calm me and put me in the mood. How could I give Arthur what he needed, and I wanted, with Wilbur and Mae and that little boy in that nasty shack so visible to me. My last meeting with Martin also added to my dilemma.

Martin asked me to establish a base for him in New York and all points north of the Mason Dixon Line. What he needed most was money, and moral support never hurt. I could think of no better place to raise cash than in New York. The Jewish community, Wall Street, the labor unions, even the Black churches were potential sources that we could tap. The only problem would be Roy Wilkins at the NAACP and Lester Grange at the Urban League. They believed all those sources belonged to them and would not look on approvingly as we challenged what they considered their exclusive right to New York. But now the time had come for them to move over and make room for the new boy on the block. Social activism and taking to the streets would soon replace the legal approach to eradicating segregation. If the Montgomery boycott is a success a new phase in constant battle for equality for the Negro will begin. Prior to leaving for Montgomery, I had joined with an active few who shared my desire to help raise money for Southern Black activists being targeted by white supremacist. Tomorrow I would call Stanley Levinson and Ella Baker, and accelerate the group's activities.

"Bayard, how long do I have to wait, another two weeks or more?" Arthur called from the bedroom.

"Sorry, just needed to wind down a little," I said. I closed the harpsicord, turned out the lights and strolled to the bedroom.

Yesterday late in the afternoon right after my plane landed at La Guardia, I called both Stan and Ella and asked if they could meet me in Mr. Randolph's office in Harlem at nine in the morning. They agreed so when I walked into the office a little after nine, they both were there. Mr. Randolph hadn't yet arrived, so I invited them into his office. I sat in one of the chairs across from his desk and turned it to face Stan and Ella who sat in opposite corners of the couch against the wall decorated with plagues and pictures of Mr. Randolph dating back to the Harlem Renaissance.

"I take it you had a successful two weeks in Montgomery, given the excitement in your voice yesterday when we talked," Stan said.

"Successful from one perspective, disappointing from another," I answered as I leaned forward in the chair.

"Explain that," Ella chimed in.

"I am convinced that Dr. King has begun a movement that is going to reverberate throughout the south and all over this country. With non-violence as the tool for the battle, Montgomery is going to be the catalyst that destroys segregation. But the poverty I also witnessed led me to believe that this battle is not just about breaking down segregation on buses and at restaurants and hotels, but more importantly about overcoming the debilitating effects of poverty on all people."

"I think I know how you believe we fit in," Stan said.

"We need to raise vast amounts of money to support Dr. King's efforts," I said with great emphasis. "And that responsibility is going to be placed directly on us."

"We don't have access to a lot of money, how is it going to be our responsibility?" Ella now asked.

"We don't personally have access, but we know where the money is here in New York. All of us sometime or other have worked on money raising projects. It's like knowing where the bodies are buried. We have to go dig them up and convince them that this is a just cause that affects the entire country."

"I don't think your traditional civil rights organizations are going to be too pleased with you treading on their sacred territory," Stan quipped.

"That's too damn bad," Ella shot back. "They have dominated the scene for far too long and serve as some kind of gate keepers to control the ebb and flow of the civil rights movement.

Ella had strong feelings about the country's oldest civil rights organization. She had worked with the organization for some years back in the 1940's and had built up some very good contacts throughout the South that eventually would be useful to us.

"It's time for some new blood and a different approach," she continued. "Don't get me wrong, I respect the organization and Mr. Wilkins but there's nothing wrong with moving over and inviting new and innovative ideas and leaders. That's exactly what Dr. King represents in 1956."

"In Friendship is the organizational structure we'll use to launch this effort," I suggested. "We already have Mr. Randolph, James Farmer and A. J. Muste on board."

"How about Congressman Powell, will he cooperate?" Stan asked.

"Only if he feels no threat to his turf and if he gets a large degree of credit if our efforts are successful."

"When can you get King up here?" It was Ella's turn to ask.

"Don't know. I don't believe he's ever given a fund-raising speech outside of the South," I said.

"He has to know he must come up here if the fund-raising efforts are going to be successful," Stan suggested. He looked around Randolph's office and said. "We need some office space for ourselves. I have some extra space over on East Fifty-Seventh Street and I'll put up the first five hundred dollars to kick it off. Consider that my contribution to the cause of freedom in the South."

"Good, that'll pay Ella's salary since she's going to be the Executive Secretary of this endeavor," I said.

"I am?" Ella scowled. "That's news to me."

"Right now, this minute, we're a three-person operation. All decisions are in our hands," I said. "How do you vote, Stan?"

"For Ella to be the Executive Secretary."

"Then, it's done," I said. "We have a major challenge before us, but no doubt we can make this happen. But we are not going to be relegated to only raising money. We will begin to develop strategies for expanding this movement out of Montgomery and into other Southern cities. We need to begin preparing working papers to present to King and the other key ministers involved with him." I paused so that the other two could consider what I was suggesting. "I'll call King later this afternoon and tell him of our plans."

"Seems that we're finished for this morning," Stan said. We all got up and walked back into the reception area.

"Can Ella get into the new office by the morning?" I asked.

"Sure can," Stan replied. "Has a desk and a few chairs. Not as fancy as Mr. Randolph's but sufficient for its purpose."

"Let's meet there in the morning," I suggested.

"We need to open a checking account sometime tomorrow so I can make the first deposit into the cause," Stan said.

"You and Ella go on the account." I opened the door and we all walked out into the reception area and into a new adventure.

I hurried out of the building and up 125th street toward a pawn shop on the corner of Lennox Avenue. Just before I reached the shop, I pulled a crumbled piece of paper from my pocket and looked at the address in Ruleville, Mississippi, where I had promised to send a small radio for Mae. I strolled inside EZ Pawn and up to the counter.

"Yeah, can I help you?" A bald head, heavy set white man asked.

"Looking for a radio that works," I said.

"All my merchandise is in workable condition," the man replied some indignation in his tone. He reached inside the counter and pulled out a small radio that I had spotted just before he grabbed it. "This one is in great shape."

"How much?" I asked.

"Forty-five dollars. It retails for seventy."

"I'll give you twenty."

The man gave me a rather curious look as if to say are you crazy. "Forty is as low as I will go."

My inclination was to explain to this man that my reason for purchasing this radio had to do with a poor family in the Mississippi

Delta, living in a shack with only three rooms, very few windows. But from the look on his face, I didn't think he would even care.

"Twenty-five," I said.

A deep frown spread across the man's forehead. For a minute, I thought maybe he would explode and come across that counter in an attack mode.

"Thirty-five and that is the bottom line," he shouted. "Either you take it, or I'll stick it back in the glass display counter."

I pulled the money out of my pocket and placed it on the counter. "You got it, now can you put it in a box for me? I need to mail it to some people in Mississippi."

"I'll see if I can find something for you," he said as he stuffed the money in his pocket and disappeared behind a curtain. After less than a minute, he returned with a box, placed the radio inside and handed it to me.

"Thanks." I reached over to shake his hand, but he refused. That was my warning that I needed to get out of there. I turned and hurried outside and toward the subway to go back downtown to Greenwich Village. Mr. Randolph was over in New Jersey and didn't plan on returning until late that evening. That gave me a chance to do something I hadn't done in a very long time. I would hang out with some of my socialist friends and talk politics for the rest of the afternoon.

The White Horse Tavern was already crowded with professors and students from Columbia University when I arrived. I spotted Michael Harrington sitting with what appeared to be some students at a table near the back of the place. It had been months since I'd talked with Michael and with the political conventions only months away, I figured this would be a real treat. I made my way through many of the customers standing in the aisle with beers or wine glasses and smiled as I finally got to his table.

"Well, if this isn't a real treat for sore eyes," Michael blurted out and reached up to shake my hand. "Bayard Rustin, the new savior of the South, welcome back to New York."

"Where did you get this idea that I'm the new savior of the South," I said as we released our handshake and I took the only empty seat at the table. "That's a real oxymoron calling me some kind of savior."

"We've been following your activities down there," he said. "Heard that you almost got arrested in Montgomery and had to escape to Birmingham. What did you do, try to talk some sense into those Klan members?"

"As a matter for fact, I was rather low key all the time. White folks down there just looking for the folks from up north coming down there and talking crazy to their Nigras." I looked at the two young people sitting at the table.

"Oh, yes these are two very bright students who attend Brooklyn College and are real loyal socialists, Rachelle Horowitz and Tom Kahn."

I nodded at the two young students and then turned my attention back to Michael.

"It's a real mess down there," I said.

"You didn't know that before you went down there?"

"I guess I did but not quite to the extent that I observed, especially over in the Delta in Mississippi."

The waitress sauntered up to our table. "Can I get you a drink?" she asked

"Yes, a scotch and soda," I said. "Ready for another?" I looked at Michael.

"A beer for me and bring my young friends some cokes."

The waitress took the order and moved over to another table.

"What you observed, my friend, was pure unadulterated poverty and I mean at its most pure form."

'It's disgraceful and a sin."

"What you have to understand is that capitalism needs poverty."

"What is your point?" I asked just as I caught the eye of a very handsome young man who no doubt was checking me out. Probably wondering about my availability for an afternoon of ecstasy.

"Whenever you allow select individuals like the Rockefellers and the Carnegies to accumulate vast fortunes and horde the resources, there will be another select group of individuals who will go without. That is what you observed in the Delta and you can see the same kind of poverty in every major city in this country. And that is why I am committed to a socialist agenda for this country."

"Socialism is the wave of the future," Tom interjected. "My generation will be committed to revolutionary change in this country so that the rich will no longer be able to horde the money from everyone else. After all, money is the property of all the people and should be treated as such."

I was impressed with this young man who couldn't be any older than twenty. He articulated quite well. And the energy I picked up from him was so strong I also knew he must be gay.

"I find it rather curious that your people are probably some of the most loyal capitalists in this country," Michael suggested.

"And why is that?" I asked even though I knew the answer.

The waitress finally worked her way to our table and placed all the drinks on the table. I took the tab to pay for them, but Michael snatched it out of my hand.

"Just add these to my tab," he said.

"Sure will." The waitress took the tab, turned and walked to the next table.

"Because of all the races that have come to this country, the one race that has been most abused by a capitalist system is the Negro," Michael finally responded to my question while also watching the waitress as she turned and walked away. "All other races, especially from Europe came here to get rich, but your ancestors were brought here as machines to help make the Europeans rich." He finished.

"That's part of the story," I said. "And since they no longer need that machine, they have tried to get rid of us, but we just keep multiplying and won't go away."

"There seems to be a nexus between Christianity and capitalism in this country. Wasn't it Marx who said Christianity is the opiate of the people and helps keep them subservient to a capitalist system?" Tom quipped.

This young boy's deep analysis of the economic condition of Negroes was very impressive. I had to ask him, "How old are you?'

"I'm seventeen and I'll turn eighteen on September 15. Why do you ask?"

"You're very erudite for your age," I said. "You had to be raised in a radical leftist family."

"Right Bayard," Michael interjected. "His father, Thomas David Kahn, has been an active member of the Communist Party here in New York for a while."

"I can appreciate your concern for age Mr. Rustin but trust me I can handle myself in most conversations," Tom exclaimed.

"What's the last book you've read?" I had to challenge this brash young man.

"Trotsky's **Revolution**," Tom said.

"Bayard, I believe you can use these young people to do busy work around your office," Michael suggested. He looked at Tom and Rachelle. "You all think you might be interested in working with Bayard on the civil rights issues?"

"Yes, definitely," Rachelle spoke up. "When can we start?"

"How about you, young man," I now looked at Tom, "You think you might be interested in helping bring down the segregated system in the South?"

"Just like General Sherman went through and burnt down everything from Atlanta to the ocean during the Civil War, yes let's go in there and give those Southerners a second beating."

"Your enthusiasm and energy are encouraging," I said. "But violence is not our method of operation in 1956, we're going to use a new approach, it's the Gandhian approach."

"That's right, Mr. Harrington told us you're one of those non-violent guys who believes in loving your enemy until they come over to your side," Tom chuckled.

I chose to ignore Tom's cynicism. "When are you all available?"

"We both have classes until noon during the week but can probably get to wherever your office is located by one," Rachelle said.

"But Saturdays we're available all day," Tom added.

"Office address is 870 East 57th Street. Can you start tomorrow? We have to begin planning a major fundraiser for Dr. King and the bus boycott in Montgomery, Alabama."

"Does that mean we'll get the opportunity to meet Dr. King?" Rachelle asked.

"More than likely, at some point when he's up here raising funds."

"Mr. Harrington, what do you think?" Rachelle turned to look at Michael.

"Great idea, that's why I suggested it," Michael answered.

"Then we're set," I added. I swallowed the last of my drink, got up to leave and as I did, the man at the bar smiled at me. I smiled back at him but kept walking toward the exit. Years back I would have given into the temptation because he was a good-looking man. But after Pasadena, I swore that I would fight off temptation for stray one-night affairs. The price you pay if compromised was much too great. In the past, I embarrassed the men who put confidence in me at the Fellowship for Reconciliation. I wouldn't do the same with Dr. King and the entire movement underway in the south.

16.

Tom and Rachelle were dedicated workaholics. They never missed a day and probably would have been there on Sundays, but I insisted they not come but rest from the monotony of the work I had them doing. The organization In Friendship had laid plans for a major fundraiser for Dr. King and the Montgomery Movement for May 22. We planned to send out over fifty thousand invitations, and it was their job to stuff them into envelopes for mailing.

The afternoon of March 22, they made it into the office a little after one o'clock. However, I didn't really notice them coming in because I was glued to the television waiting for the verdict in Dr. King's trial for violating the state's law against boycotting. The trial grew out of the indictments back in February, when over one hundred presumed leaders of the boycott were arrested, and I convinced them to march down to the courthouse and surrender. None of the others had been brought to trial, just Dr. King. The plan was to convict King and hopefully that would break the back of the boycott and bring it to an end.

Tom and Rachelle joined me in my office where I had placed a small black and white television. Just as they hurried inside and took a couple chairs in front of my desk, the report came on the news. From behind the news desk at WBAL, the reporter read a statement.

"Dr. Martin Luther King, Jr. has been found guilty of violating the Alabama State Law against boycotting and has been fined five hundred dollars or given the option to spend 386 days in jail. Dr. King's attorney, Arthur Shore, immediately announced that they would appeal the decision to the higher state courts with optimism that the lower court decision will be overturned. It would possibly be another year before the appeal will be heard. Because of the appeal, the other cases involving other protestors who were also indicted in February will be delayed pending the outcome of the King case."

"And you want to preach a love thy neighbor sermon for those racist pigs," Tom scowled.

Tom's impudence could be annoying, but his spirit was in the right place. "When you react in the same manner that they acted, then you become just like them," I said.

"But when you don't react with some strength, then they continue to walk all over you," Rachelle joined in.

"Yeah, there's no way that white people would have stood for their children to be lynched the way the Negro does. Their son gets lynched and then they go to church and pray over it." Tom's face turned red and his temples pulsated.

I got up, walked over and turned off the television, then returned to sit behind my desk. These young folks reminded me of Kenny, my young driver who had driven me from New York to Montgomery and Bobby, Dr. King's driver. It was important that I keep in mind that they represented a much younger generation and their thinking differed from the way I looked at situations. I needed to respond to his attempt to make a virtue out of violence, but the phone rang before I could.

"Bayard, this is Martin," Dr. King said. 'I imagine you heard the court decision?"

"Yes, I did."

"No doubt we will appeal to the next level. It is important that we find ways to get these cases out of the hands of state judges and to the national level in Washington, which means to the Supreme Court."

"Well, Martin we didn't expect any other outcome than what they delivered."

The mention of Martin caught the attention of Tom and Rachelle. Their heads shot straight up.

"Is that Dr. King?" Tom whispered to me.

I removed the phone from my ear, put my hand over the receiver and whispered back. "Yes."

"I'm calling to let you know I'll be in New York next weekend," Martin said.

"What? When did this come about?" I asked.

"Reverend Gardner C. Taylor at Concord Baptist Church in Brooklyn has extended the invitation to me right at the last minute. Said he could easily fill the church and raise money for the movement. He has the second largest Baptist congregation in the entire country."

"How can I help out?"

"Thought maybe you could arrange a meeting between me and some of the New York leadership that can help us out down here in Montgomery," King explained. "Money is a problem for us. We have pretty much drained our resources here in Alabama. The Negroes throughout the state have been very helpful, but we can go to that well only so often. It's time for us to look outside the South for support."

"I'll see what I can do and get back to you. Not much time to get it together," I said.

"I know but if anyone can pull it off, it's you my friend. And also, I'd like for you to accompany me to the church on Sunday."

"Are you sure of that. You know the problem we've already had with some of the ministers?" I asked.

"Let's leave what happened in Montgomery behind us," King shot back with no hesitation. "You are my point man in New York and all points south of the Mason Dixon line; that is if you agree to take on that kind of responsibility."

"Martin, you have to know that you're taking on the greater risk, but if you are willing to deal with the criticism, then I'm on board. I'll check back with your secretary about all the details for next weekend."

"That's exactly what I'm willing to do because your expertise far exceeds the negatives as other people perceive them. Let's get this country moving forward in a progressive manner and eradicate all prejudices. See you this weekend." He finished, and we hung up.

Tom and Rachelle both had this curious look on their faces anxious for me to share my conversation with them.

"Dr. King will be here next weekend and it'll be his first trip north since he's received all this press coverage," I shared with them.

"What can we do to help?" Rachelle asked.

"Will we get a chance to meet him?" Tom spoke up before I could respond to Rachelle.

"You all must keep your eyes on the prize and that is the fund raiser we're planning for May. This is very short notice and cannot interfere with all the work that must be done. If you can make it to the church and find a way inside, I'll see to it that you get a chance to meet him."

I felt rather devious in my answer, but I just couldn't plan for them to meet Martin given the short notice of his schedule and given the fact that he wanted a meeting with some of the leadership that same weekend. I felt bad for them, but knew eventually given all the work before us, they would have ample opportunities to meet the new leader of the Negro movement in the country.

Concord Baptist Church was in the Bedford/Stuyvesant neighborhood in Brooklyn and by the time I arrived at the church, there was standing room only. Martin had left instructions for me to tell the ushers to escort me to Reverend Taylor's office in the back of the church. He'd flown in late last evening and the Reverend picked him up at the airport and took him to a meeting of the local Baptist Association, a meeting that I obviously would not attend. He'd spent the night at the Reverend's home and so I still hadn't talked with him.

I did arrange a meeting later Sunday afternoon at 4:00 p.m. at Mr. Randolph's office in Harlem. Roy Wilkins, James Farmer and A. J. Muste promised to attend. He planned to spend a couple hours with us and then Reverend Taylor would take him out to dinner and his plane was to leave at nine o'clock that evening from La Guardia Airport. Already at this point in his leadership position, his schedule was quite hectic, and I could only imagine in the next few years that it would escalate. The price he had to pay for leadership.

As I followed the usher down the side aisle, I searched around the church looking for Tom and Rachelle but didn't see them. They probably never imagined the church to be packed an hour before the service and now when they did arrive, they would only be able to stand outside, with thousands of others jammed on the street to listen to a loud speaker set up to blast King's sermon all over Bedford Stuyvesant.

I had never met Reverend Taylor but heard of the good things he did in the Brooklyn area. From what I could gather, he was a minister of the Vernon Johns and Howard Thurman cloth. Young like Martin, he was undoubtedly destined to carry out the same kind of protest up North that King had started in Montgomery. We finally made it to the side door that the minister used to enter the sanctuary. We went out into a hall and finally he knocked at Reverend Taylor's office door.

"Yes, come on in," a voice from inside instructed.

He swung the door open and as I walked inside, I saw Martin sitting in a lounge chair near the wall of the office. He immediately got up, hurried over and we hugged.

"Bayard, it's so good to see you," he said with a smile. He then turned and with his arm around my shoulder said. "Dr. Taylor, this is the man who has brought the tactic of non-violence to the movement in the South, Bayard Rustin."

Reverend Taylor also stood up behind his desk but did not come around to shake my hand. "Mr. Rustin, yes I've heard about you," he said. "You've been working with A. Phillip Randolph a great deal of the time, haven't you?"

"Yes, I have," I answered and stood my ground. "Been associated with Mr. Randolph since 1941 when he first organized the proposed march on Washington, D.C., the march that forced President Roosevelt to issue an executive order integrating the defense industry in this country."

"My predecessor here at Concord, the late great Reverend Doctor James Adams, thought highly of Mr. Randolph, at least that's what I've heard. I didn't have the pleasure of meeting Reverend Adams. He died and that's how I got up here from Baton Rouge, the congregation selected me. I am so blessed to be here in the New York vicinity.

"Bayard will be heading up my out-reach here in the North," Dr. King finally spoke up. "He is a child of God who brings a very special knowledge to our mission in the South. Even though he was only in Montgomery for a couple weeks, he shared valuable advice with all of us on how best to proceed."

Reverend Taylor stared across the desk at me with a rather curious expression. Instantly, my suspicions set in. Did he know I was gay, and did he read about Pasadena because the story hit all the national newspapers, or was I just being paranoid? I didn't waver or give a hint of nervousness. Instead I stared right back at him. The silence was broken as we heard the melodic sounds of the choir from the sanctuary.

"If you can use anything Lord, You can use me
Take my hands, Lord and my feet
Touch my heart, Lord and speak through Me
If You can use anything Lord, You can use me,"

"Choirs marching in," Reverend Taylor said. "In just a few minutes, the usher will come in and let me know it's time for us to march out."

"It was pretty packed when I came in," I said.

"Yes, the people will be lined up outside for this sermon. Word had it last night that we could possibly expect at least two thousand people," Reverend Taylor added.

"Pray I am worthy of their trust to deliver a message with God's meaning," Martin said.

"You do know that many of us support your effort, Martin, but there are a lot of ministers who have begun to speak out against you."

"I know that's the case right in Montgomery." Dr. King twisted his body in the chair indicating his discomfort with the subject.

"You're going to have major problems at the National Baptist Convention this summer, because Reverend Jackson does not support you at all."

Martin twisted his body to look at me. "Reverend John Jackson is the President of the Convention. His church is in Chicago."

"The enemy is not only in white skin," Dr. Taylor said. "He wears black skin also. I believe Reverend Jackson is probably envious of Martin and believes he should be leading any movement that affects the race."

"Unfortunately, that has always been the case with our people," I said. "It was just fortunate that Harriett Tubman was never betrayed by the slaves that she risked her life to take out of bondage."

"She was a blessed lady," Reverend Taylor said. "Mrs. Tubman did the Lord's work, so she operated with a veil of protection around her."

"Martin also needs that veil of protection as he does the Lord's work," I suggested and just as I finished the door swung open.

"It's time Reverend," a man dressed in all black and wearing white gloves said and then quickly closed the door.

"I always reserve one seat to the far right in the first row for special guests," Reverend said to me. "When we enter the sanctuary, you can take that seat and Dr. King will follow me up to the podium." He came from behind the desk and we followed him to the door and out of the office.

The organist had the church rocking to the tune of "I'll Fly Away," as we strolled into the sanctuary and I took the seat that the Reverend had suggested. Martin sat in a chair behind the pulpit and Reverend Taylor spoke into the microphone.

"We are privileged this morning here at Concord to have the preacher who has set this entire country on fire with his fire from the pulpit and from the streets of Montgomery, Alabama. It was only a few years ago that the student Martin Luther King Jr., preached a sermon from this pulpit on his way to graduate school in Boston. Now he has returned to us as Dr. Martin Luther King, Jr., and again he will share with you all the important work that God has called upon him to do down South where our people still face so much oppression. With no further ado, let me call to the pulpit, my friend and fellow preacher of the gospel of Jesus Christ, Dr. Reverend Martin Luther King, Jr."

I could feel the extraordinary energy flowing from the church as the entire congregation jumped to their feet and began to clap while Martin made his way to the pulpit, hugging Dr. Taylor as they passed each other. This would be his first speech outside the South since he became involved in the Montgomery boycott. And his first speech that I would hear since coaching him on the more important aspects of Gandhian philosophy. I was anxious to listen to how he had incorporated it into his sermons.

Martin began in his slow deliberate pace, beginning with a short prayer and giving thanks to Reverend Taylor for extending an invitation to speak in his pulpit. He warmed up and began to talk about the struggle for equality in the South for his people and then he turned specifically to Montgomery and the bus protest. What Martin had perfected since I last heard him speak, was to tie the love thy neighbor concept of Christianity with the non-violent approach to effectuate change. He touched on the difference between non-resistance and non-violence, something I had stressed with him. He told the audience that non-resistance leaves one in a state of stagnant passivity and complacency. Whereas non-violence means you resist the evil forces you are confronting in a strong and determined manner, you engage in direct action.

He then moved on to the necessity of love as a critical component of non-violent action. Love, as he explained it, transforms into a powerful force of direct action and since it is non-violent it arouses the sense of guilt in the opponent. Elevating to that very smooth, rhythmic cadence, Martin now introduced the white man in the South into the sermon. Love, with non-violence and forgiveness makes the white man in the South quite uncomfortable. It contradicts his false and misleading concept of the black man and woman. It makes him quite uncomfortable and disturbs his sense of contentment with his mis-perceived idea of a race he feels he knows quite well.

After only fifteen minutes of his sermon, Martin had the congregation fired up. I felt fired up also and like many, wanted to jump up and shout hallelujah. I was engrossed in every word he preached when an usher tapped me on my shoulder. I turned and he handed me a note.

"I was told to give this to you, Mr. Rustin," he said and quickly turned and walked away.

I watched him as he headed toward the back of the church and then stared at the note he handed me, curious as to who would contact me in the church. It could only be one person. I quickly opened it up and I was right. It read, "Meeting place for this afternoon has been changed from my office to Adam's church at Abyssinian in Harlem. Another one of his insecurities. He's probably upset that Martin is speaking at Concord and not at his church. He has to be in control of everything happening in Black New York and this is just another example. Please bring Martin there. Phil."

Damnit, if this egomaniac hadn't broken my attentiveness to Martin and his speech. My concentration was interrupted as I now had to deal with Powell and his nonsense. He always had to find a way to take control and probably felt threatened by Dr. Taylor's success, as he branched out into civil rights issues in New York. He also refused to pay deference to Powell and anyone who did that, he considered a threat. And now, the new recognized young leader of the movement in the South, had made his first appearance in New York at another church, taking the spotlight away from Powell. Why Mr. Randolph felt compelled to give into that man's behavior, I never would understand. Especially after he managed to sabotage a voter registration drive a couple years ago that Mr. Randolph planned for Harlem. He had put me in charge of finding the people to work with us in registering Harlemites to vote. Despite his popularity, Powell had managed to make several enemies who would jump at any opportunity to defeat him in the next Congressional election.

Powell knew that Mr. Randolph wanted to spend the entire summer registering voters, so he announced that he was going to put on a birthday party for himself that would last throughout the summer, all of June, July and August. He used church money to offer the very volunteers I had gathered for the voter registration to help in his celebration. Of course, those young people jumped at that opportunity. As a result, we were forced to cancel our voter registration drive. He called Mr. Randolph and apologized, claiming he had no idea what we had planned to do.

Now here he was doing the same kind of devious manipulation again. But I had no choice but to comply with Mr. Randolph's request. When Martin finally finished his sermon, he stood at the front entrance to the church and must have shook hands with every member who was in attendance. At three-thirty, we finally wrapped up his visit at the church and Dr. Taylor agreed to drive us over to Abyssinian. Martin extended an invitation to him to join us at Powell's church, but he told us that would probably not be a good idea and turned down the invitation. I was burning up with anger when we finally pulled up in front of the church, said our goodbyes and headed inside.

17.

Abyssinian was a beautifully built church, both on the outside and inside. It was a Gothic style structure taking most of one side of 138th Street between Lennox Avenue and Seventh Avenue. I was very familiar with the church. When I first moved to Harlem back in 1936, I lived with my aunt, whom most of my young life I assumed to be my sister, on St. Nicholas Street near 138th Street. That was just before Adam took the reins of the church from his father Adam Sr. who had been there through the 1920's and most of the 30's.

As soon as we entered the vestibule an attendant approached us.

"Please gentlemen, follow me. Reverend Powell is waiting for you in his conference room."

We followed the usher through the large sanctuary and out a side door at the front of the church. We continued behind him down a long hallway with numerous offices on both sides. This area of the church could easily rival a major Lower Manhattan Building somewhere around Wall Street. We finally reached the conference room where Mr. Randolph and Roy Wilkins, from the NAACP, were already seated around a long shining conference table with high back leather chairs. At the very front of the table was an extremely large leather chair, obviously reserved for Powell, who hadn't yet arrived in the room.

Martin preceded me inside the room, and immediately both Mr. Randolph and Wilkins got up from where they sat and reached out to shake his hand.

"Dr. King, welcome to New York," Wilkins said.

"What an excellent job you are doing for our people there in Montgomery," Mr. Randolph quipped. "My pleasure to finally meet you after talking with you on so many occasions on the phone."

"Gentlemen, thank you for so many warm welcomes I've received here in New York," Dr. King responded to their warm salutations. "Whoever said New Yorkers were not friendly people."

"They aren't all so friendly," Powell interjected as he rushed into the room and shook Martin's hand. "Gentlemen, please have a seat and we can get started. I have a very important meeting that I have delayed so I could meet with you all."

In his usual take charge manner, Adam strolled to the front of the table and sat in his chair. We took chairs closer to where he sat, all on one side of the table.

"Dr. King what you are doing in Montgomery is admirable and you are to be complemented for your courage and determination," Adam said. "When the boycott first began, me and some of the other ministers here in New York reached out to your organization and planned a work stoppage for one day right here in the city in support of you, but for some reason, you and your people did not seem to support our effort."

It didn't take long for Adam to throw a bombshell and only Dr. King was surprised that he did so. Dr. King had a rather sheepish expression as though he didn't expect that kind of reception, at least not right away, especially after what he experienced over at Concord only a few hours ago. I could read the disgust all over Dr. Randolph's face, but I knew he would not intervene but leave it to Dr. King to respond.

"I'm sorry Reverend Powell if you all took it that way. It was not meant to slight you all and we do appreciate all the assistance we can get from all over the country," Dr. King started with his very slow, but deliberate delivery. "But we must be very careful in the early months of this revolution that we not allow our opponents to make the charge that this movement is being orchestrated by people not from the South."

Adam shifted in his chair and then dropped another bombshell. "Why is it that you allowed Mr. Rustin to get involved?" He refused to look at me.

There was no doubt that Adam held some animus against me, because he knew I was gay and he had spoken out many times against homosexuals, often referring to us as sexual degenerates who stalked young children. Hopefully he wouldn't make that an issue.

Mr. Randolph wouldn't stand for anymore of this nonsense. "Let me inform you Adam that it was a group decision, of which I was one of the decision makers, who decided to send Bayard to Montgomery to assist in instructing the boycotters and their leaders in the proper use of non-violent tactics. And I must say, his trip was a success."

"That's very interesting Phil. I talked with Emory Jackson of the Birmingham black newspaper who told me that Mr. Rustin had been quite ineffectual and, in fact, did some damage to the movement. Something about his past that was plaguing the movement."

Powell brought it right out in the open, Pasadena 1953. The man was heartless I thought but felt Mr. Randolph's hand pressing down on my arm as an indication to remain silent. All over New York it was known that Powell got a great deal of satisfaction when he caused another to react emotionally to his attacks.

Finally, Dr. King spoke up. "I can assure you Mr. Rustin's past had nothing to do with his leaving Montgomery. If anything, it was because he made a very positive impact on the movement and the whites began to claim that the movement was being led by outsiders, and that explains why he left and why we refused your assistance."

The tension in the room was building and evidently Roy Wilkins picked up on it.

"Gentlemen let's get back to why we are here this afternoon," he said. "Dr. King you have effectively fired the first salvo of a new day coming to this country. We up here in the North know that you are about to begin breaking down the barriers of oppression of our people where you live."

"Please do not misunderstand my position or the position of the MIA," King spoke up. "We need a great deal of support and especially financial support. The cost to maintain the carpools alone has reached over three thousand dollars a week and that doesn't include the need for two hired staff people, and also to cover the costs of tickets that the Montgomery authorities hand out to our drivers like its candy. I don't know how much longer we can last if we don't get some financial support."

"I imagine that's going to be rather tough here in New York," Adam quipped. "You see, the NAACP, Urban League and CORE all have their hands out to the Wall Street community and the Jewish people. You willing to give up your cut of the money, Roy?" He asked and stared directly at Wilkins. "And how about you Phil? Don't you get most of your funding from the unions, you willing to cut back?"

It was no secret around New York and especially Harlem that Powell, a sneaky, conniving, manipulator, managed to keep power by dividing groups against each other. He attempted to do that now with Dr. King. I expected him to convince the man that his only friend was Powell himself. But Mr. Randolph also recognized what the congressman was doing and quickly moved to put an end to his manipulations.

"Yes, I am, if necessary," Randolph said emphatically. "You make this sound like what we do is try to outmaneuver each other for money, with no regard for the bigger issue and that is the need to fight the enemy of our people. No one in the room is my enemy nor my competitor, but my partner in this battle to eradicate segregation and the biggest need for that effort is in the South. That makes Dr. King's struggle all our struggle and trumps our individual organizational needs." Mr. Randolph paused to allow his words to sink in. "And to demonstrate that we are not competing with each other, I suggest a major fund raiser sponsored by all our organizations to be held right in Madison Square Garden."

"That's an excellent idea," Wilkins said. "I believe the Urban League will join us as well as CORE."

"The Unions will come along. They always want to be a part of a united front," Mr. Randolph added.

King remained reticent, I'm sure very pleased with what he heard.

"How long will it take you to plan it, Bayard?" Randolph turned and looked at me.

Expecting Powell to raise opposition, I hesitated before answering. But then I realized he wouldn't state his opposition right in the open at the meeting. No doubt he'd contact the others, except for Mr. Randolph, and complain of my involvement later.

I felt compelled to respond. "Can be done by sometime in May depending on an open date at the Garden."

"May then it is," Wilkins said. "If you need help with staff let me know and we'll get some of our people to help you."

I immediately thought of Tom and Rachelle and answered, "I don't think I will. I have two crackerjack workers from Brooklyn College who'll be all over this."

"Then it's settled. All we must do now is make it happen," Randolph said. "I believe this might be the very first time when all the major Negro organizations came together under one roof to raise money for one cause. This is good progress."

A broad smile spread across Powell's face. "Now you see good things happen when you gather at Abyssinian Baptist Church." He rose out of his chair. "Have another meeting on the other side of the church, but you are welcome to stay here and meet as long as necessary."

"I believe we are finished here," I said. "I need to get Dr. King back over to Concord. He's having dinner with Reverend Taylor and leaves later this evening." I got a big kick describing Dr. King's final hours in New York. Knowing that he would ultimately be in the company of Reverend Taylor burnt Powell up. A frown spread across his face.

"Next time you visit New York, if it happens to be in May, you must visit Abyssinian as a guest preacher." Powell said. "Everyone in the ministry preaches from this pulpit. Kind of establishes their importance in the ministry."

We walked back out and into the sanctuary.

"It would be an extreme pleasure," King said.

"Have a safe trip back to Montgomery and I look forward to playing an important role in the movement." Powell said, turned and headed in a different direction.

"He's going to be a problem," Mr. Randolph said, as we walked outside and settled inside the black limousine that waited for us there to take King back over to Concord.

"It's all about power and ego to him," I said. "If we play his game and make sure he's included in anything we do in New York, he'll be all right."

"It's not my intention to cause political turmoil up here," King added.

"We are not going to be subservient to the Congressman," Mr. Randolph scowled. "My God, I worked with his father when he was minister at Abyssinian, and he was just a small child running around the church. We're going to build a coalition and he's welcomed be a part of it, but he is not welcomed to play dictator."

"It is important that we expand our movement to the North," King said. "We can't do it without your help and especially Bayard's organizational skills."

After Powell's subtle attack on me, I felt good hearing King's reassurance that, regardless of what many might perceive as my sexual problems, he stood with me. The Congressman might cause some problems, but nothing that couldn't be overcome by our determination to move forward with a national civil rights agenda led by the preacher from Montgomery.

18.

Mr. Randolph stuck to his commitment and managed to put together a coalition of organizations, both business, unions and civil rights, and scheduled a major fundraiser for the Montgomery operation for May 10 at Madison Square Garden. His influence in the New York Community was exceptional as every important figure, to include Powell, agreed to participate.

Our team worked diligently to make the event a success. We knew the movement's continued operation depended on a healthy injection of funds into the till of MIA. Dr. King had called me the first week in April and bemoaned the lack of money, and the fact that the marchers were getting discouraged with the movement. We both agreed that just couldn't happen, because the movement's failure in Montgomery would kill the larger picture of spreading the fight throughout the South.

The movement received its first major break late in April. King called me at the In-Friendship Office in a very enthusiastic mood.

"Good news Bayard," he shouted into the phone. "We just got word that the Supreme Court affirmed a federal appellate court ruling striking down segregated seating on Municipal Buses in Columbia, South Carolina." Martin paused to catch his breath and obviously allowing this valuable information to register with me. "This will undoubtedly set the precedent to end segregated bus systems all over the South and right here in Montgomery," he continued with extreme enthusiasm.

"This might convince the Montgomery City Lines to integrate their buses which would be a victory for us," I suggested.

"We got word that they did tell the drivers to no longer enforce the segregated seating, but…"

"That means the boycott can now end," I interrupted rejoicing at the news.

"Not so fast," Martin's tone was solemn. "Mayor Gayle made a public announcement that the segregated laws would continue to be enforced, and any bus driver who failed to do so would be arrested and thrown in jail."

"I guess that changed the bus company's position?"

"No, not really. They came back and announced that their legal department would defend any driver who refused to comply with the segregation ordinance. We now have the bus company and city at odds, which means it is all falling apart for them."

"That's a good thing for us," I exclaimed with joy. "The courts will inevitably rule that ordinance unlawful, and that'll be the end of our first battle. We can't slow down our efforts after Montgomery, but must move on to other battles and, from what I understand, Birmingham is going to be a real challenge if you decide to take it on."

"Yes, our friend Fred Shuttlesworth is anxious to get going. It'll only be a matter of time before the battle moves on to his city."

"He made that quite clear in Birmingham," I reminded Martin.

"Tomorrow night at the mass meeting at Holt, I'll make it quite clear that the protest will continue despite the warfare taking place at city hall," he said and then chuckled. "We have a few more tough months in front of us Bayard, but soon we'll be able to put this behind us and proclaim what a glorious victory for not just Negroes, but for the country. Got to get back to work now and I'll talk with you soon." Martin finished, and we hung up.

Standing and looking down from inside a private suite at Madison Square Garden, I was extremely pleased because you couldn't see an empty seat in the arena. Two weeks before the actual fund raiser we knew our hard work would pay off, and our team pulled off the first major successful collective effort to raise money for the Montgomery boycott. We had lined up a stellar collection of super stars to include Eleanor Roosevelt whom we figured would be the best person to close out the event. Before she went on, we scheduled to hear from Congressman Powell, whom we knew was not happy that he could not close out the program.

It was a little before eleven o'clock when I finally began to feel just a little bit nervous. The problem being that no one had heard from Congressman Powell, scheduled to speak for fifteen minutes right at eleven o'clock. Then Ms. Roosevelt would close out the program and we knew we had to be out of the arena by midnight or pay an additional fee for the help and guards. The evening had progressed with no glitches and we had raised over twenty-five thousand dollars. It would be a shame if we had to sacrifice some of the proceeds because the program ran over the time limit.

The Blues singer and guitarist Josh White was on the stage singing, "Can't we hear that train whistle blow. Lord I wish that train wasn't Jim Crow." He had been up there over a half-hour stalling while we waited for Powell. "Stop Jim Crow so I can ride. Black and White riding side by side," Josh continued to entertain. Finally, Mr. Randolph burst into the suite.

"Bayard, where is Powell? You gotta find Adam or we have to move on without him."

"No, no, you can't do that," I gasped. The thought of finishing the program without the Congressman having his say on the big stage would ruin the entire evening. He would carry on the next day so that no one would ever know it had been a success. "Just relax, stay here and I'll find him." I rushed out of the suite and headed down to the main stage.

I fought my way through the crowd and up to the stage. Josh White had just finished singing, "I'm marching, I'm marching. I'm marching down freedom road," which was very appropriate for the occasion. I caught him as he came down the steps. If anyone knew where Adam was, he would know.

"I need you to help me find the Congressman," I said with urgency in my tone.

"Ain't no problem," Josh replied. "Adams just across the street sitting at the bar in that restaurant."

"Can you please send someone over there to get him?" I asked with still the same amount of urgency.

"Relax," Josh said. "I'll send my brother over there and he'll get him."

"Hurry please. We have the late President Roosevelt's wife waiting to speak and she can't do it until after Powell does. If she speaks and we close it down, you know what'll happen."

I watched nervously as Josh strutted over to where his brother stood, whispered something to him and he took off out of the arena. Mr. Randolph made his way over next to me and said.

"Where is this man? Leave it to Adam to cause problems."

Suddenly all the lights in the arena went out. "Oh my God, now what?" Randolph scowled.

"I don't know but I'll…"

"Ladies and Gentlemen turn your attention to the entrance to the arena" a voice over the loudspeaker interrupted me and a spotlight came on providing a stream of light at the back of the arena.

Powell stood there with the light beaming down on him.

"I present to you our most honorable Congressman Adam Clayton Powell," the announcer blurted out.

I couldn't believe this man. He began his walk down the aisle toward the center stage. The crowd erupted in cheers, calling out "Powell, Powell, Powell, he's our man."

Mr. Randolph placed his hand on my shoulder. "I've been around New York and Harlem for over thirty years, and not even Marcus Garvey could showboat as well as this man. Will you just look at this?"

That's exactly what I did, I looked at Powell as he continued his stroll to the stage and walked up to the microphone.

"They told me it was getting late and I needed to get over here," he said. "Well, my friends it is never too late for equality, never too late for justice and never too late for the rights of my people."

Again, the crowd burst out shouting "Adam, Adam, Adam," while all the time applauding. I had to make sure this didn't get out of control and turn into a long diatribe. I scribbled a note on paper and hurried onto the stage, to hand the note to Powell. He looked at the contents, **Dear Adam, Mr. Randolph asked me to ask you to cut your speech short. For every five minutes we are in here after twelve, it costs us a thousand dollars, money we don't have. Mrs. Roosevelt has not spoken yet and she has been promised to speak last. Will you please hurry.**

Adam finished and waved me off and the crowd applauded his gesture toward me. "I've got a note here," he shouted out, "from somebody, a Bayard Rust-in. Anybody ever heard of him?"

"No, who's he?" the crowd responded.

The louder and more enthusiastic the crowd responded to his ranting the more it seemed to energize him. He continued, "He told me if we're not out of here by midnight, it's going to cost us a thousand dollars. Can I ask you a question?" He paused for the audience response.

"Yes."

"Does anyone think we should stop having this important meeting because it's going to cost us something?" Pause.

"No."

"Well I will tell this Bay-ard Rust-in, whoever he is, I will stand here and we will stand here all night if necessary to tell the world, and to tell the government, and to tell the President of the United States, we want freedom and we're willing to pay for it."

I wasn't surprised nor angered when he called out my name in a rather sarcastic manner. He needed a scape goat, someone to attack to build up his credibility with the audience. I thought not much different than what the mayor did on television in Montgomery, when they blamed outsiders from up North for the problems with the Negroes. Different location and different accuser, but the same tactic.

He had the crowd at a fever pitch and held his arm in the air to quiet them down so he could continue his diatribe.

"Let me tell this Bay-ard Rust-in when the check comes, he can send it to Abyssinian Baptist Church in Harlem, and we'll pay for the freedom we are enjoying tonight."

He now totally controlled the crowd and therefore controlled the proceedings. No way we could cut him off without exciting a riot. We stood and listened to him for another fifteen minutes. When he finally finished, Mr. Randolph introduced Eleanor Roosevelt who spoke for less than five minutes and we closed out the night. Instead of the evening being about the Montgomery protest and what was happening in the South, it was about Adam Clayton Powell, because that's the way he wanted it and in New York what Adam wanted he usually got. I knew, that as we moved forward trying to connect the Southern movement with the North, especially New York, Powell would be a hindrance in the future.

"Martin, we raised twenty-five thousand dollars for you last night," I said, talking with him by phone from the living room of my apartment. "Sorry you couldn't make it, but next time you have to be here."

"I understand and raising that kind of money, you know I'll be there next time," King said. "But I had to be here because of the ruling coming out of the three-panel federal court that segregated busing was unconstitutional."

"Yes, we heard this morning," I said. "It's just a matter of time and you'll be able to have your first major victory."

"I heard from E. D. Nixon that Adam caused some problems at the Madison Square Garden last night," King said obviously not yet ready to claim a victory. "What's wrong with that man?

"Hubris, my friend, is a terrible disease and Adam suffers from it more than any other person I know. He just can't share the limelight with no one else. He had to make it about him and not about the movement, and especially not about you."

"That's fine with me as long as we keep bringing in the money because we really do need it. Victory is not ours yet and we have to keep the movement going."

"How are the troops holding up?" I asked.

"The people's enthusiasm has not waned at all," he replied. "They are determined never to return to Jim Crow buses. The mass meetings are still packed, and those who had wanted to use guns in the beginning are gradually coming to see the futility in that approach, and that is thanks to you."

With victory practically knocking on the door, it was clear to me that winning in Montgomery would have no permanent meaning in the overall racial struggle, unless it leads to the achievement of dozens of similar victories all over the South. In order to achieve that kind of success, the movement needed a sustaining structure that could translate what we were learning, into a broad strategy of success. I needed to share that vision with Martin. I couldn't make it happen, I could only be the visionary or dreamer.

"Martin, you must begin to think beyond Montgomery and to a much larger movement," I suggested. "From Montgomery, we must begin to establish a power base. And that can only be accomplished through voting." I paused to allow this new train of thought to register with Martin. Momentarily I thought of Mae holding that baby in that shack back in the Mississippi Delta. "We have to begin looking to the future and how we not only break down segregation, but how we gain political and economic power."

"Bayard, I didn't ask for this kind of responsibility," Martin bemoaned. "Once Montgomery is over, I want to get back to pastoring my church and just preaching."

"That'll never happen," I shot back. "Your future and your destiny have been set. I know you don't necessarily believe in manifest destiny, but you'd better because your work has just begun." I waited momentarily because I knew he was processing my words. "What we need to begin doing is laying out a plan for the future. Once Montgomery is finished, we need to move right away into the next phase."

"Can you share with me your thoughts in the next few weeks?" Martin conceded.

"Yes, I can do that," I said with a smile.

"Good, now I need to get over to Bell Street Baptist Church. The minister there has created some problems for us, and they need to be resolved before it gets out of hand."

"I'll begin immediately to formulate a foundation for moving forward. Congratulations on the federal court decision and the twenty-five thousand dollars I plan to get to you within the next few days."

"Thank you, Bayard for all that you are doing," Martin said with humility. "You are a great man and I promise you will always be with me as we do move on from Montgomery."

"You sure of that?" I asked, and he knew exactly what I meant.

"You, my friend, are fighting two battles. One is that you are a Negro and the other is that you are gay. I admire you for your fighting spirit. If we in the country solve one of the two, it will only be a matter of time before we solve the other. And you will go down as a leader in eradicating prejudice on two fronts. Let's keep up the good work together."

"Let's do that," I said, and we hung up.

19.

Martin had provided me with the greatest opportunity of my life. He told me to put together the foundation for a national movement to end segregation throughout the South, and to initiate a program aimed at achieving economic and political power for the Negro, also in the South. During our discussion, however, what had struck me most was his acknowledging that my struggle was two-fold and of comparable importance. The victory in one would ultimately lead to a victory in the other. We both agreed that the success of the Negro movement to eradicate segregation would open the doors to other minorities to include women, the disabled and the gay community. All movements would hitch-hike on the back of the Negroes and that's another reason it could not fail. I accepted the challenge to conceptualize an organizational structure, different in approach from the NAACP and Urban League, to be led by Martin.

The challenge was overwhelming, and I knew I'd need help, others whom I could share ideas and they could do the same with me. Like minded activists who would challenge my assertions and bring their ideas to the table for consideration. No two individuals could fill that bill better than Stanley and Ella. We met in the office of In Friendship to begin a discussion on how to proceed. Tom and Rachelle joined us. I began the discussion.

"Montgomery is coming to an end and Dr. King has asked that I work on a larger plan to continue the work in the South," I said.

Without hesitation, Ella spoke up. "What is needed is an alternative to the NAACP and Urban League. I love Roy Wilkins and especially Thurgood Marshall, but they are convinced that all our gains must come through the legal system. Their thinking is stuck in the courts."

"No doubt direct action is necessary," Stanley added.

"But it has to be a non-violent nature," I said. "And what group better situated to carry that message than the Negro preachers."

"Let me get this straight," Ella sat straight up in her chair on the other side of my desk. "You plan to organize the Negro preachers in the South as a collective body?" She paused and smiled. "Good luck."

"What's that for?" I asked.

"You got the Baptists, the Methodists and the non-denominational holy rollers and they have never come together for any cause. Now, suddenly you're going to make that happen."

"Not me," I corrected her. "Dr. King will do that. He has emerged as a national leader for the Negro in the South, and his credibility will triple once the buses are integrated in Montgomery."

"I understand he really turned them out at Concord when he spoke there," Stanley added. "His message resonates all over the country."

"Yes, and it is our job to give it some structure," I said. I finally glanced over at Tom and Rachelle. I was somewhat surprised that Tom hadn't added to the conversation. It wasn't like him to sit quietly by during a discussion of substance. I turned my attention back to Stanley and Ella. "Is it possible for us to develop some concept papers based around the theme that there is a New Negro emerging and that he and she will not be denied their proper place in this society?"

"It's like an evolutionary process," Tom finally chimed in.

"Exactly," I concurred. "We have passed through stages of the evolution of the race. The first change occurred during the 1920's when the Negro jettisoned the slave mentality and claimed an independence of thinking." I paused as I recalled a lecture by Alan Locke, godfather of the Harlem Renaissance to a group of us assembled at Langston Hughes' apartment on 132ⁿᵈ Street. "Professor Locke from Howard University called it the movement of the New Negro, that was the first time I heard that term. He went on to explain that we had, after forty years of emancipation, finally thrown off the chains of mental slavery. Writers like Hughes and Wallace Thurman refused to accept limitations to their creativity. Our purpose is to outline a position paper that stresses the Negroes progress beyond that point, to one of refusing to accept limitations to our freedoms."

"Yes, that's it," Stanley said very excited. "It has taken another forty years for those chains to finally be removed in the South just as they were removed in Harlem, Chicago and Detroit and other places outside the South. What an outstanding concept."

"They're not quite removed yet," I suggested. "But Montgomery is a start. What's happening there is critically important for two reasons. The first is that it represents the first mass protest that was completely controlled by the Negro, fearless of what could happen to them as a result. The second critically important accomplishment is the psychological emancipation of the Negro, no longer dependent on the laws and economics of the Southern white man. Once the Negro refuses to accept his position of subservience then the entire system in the South will crumble. And that begins with Montgomery." I felt exhausted but quite satisfied. "The foundation for this cataclysmic upheaval in this country is now in our hands in this very small office in New York. We have no choice but to get the job done."

"That all sounds great and quite inspiring," Ella quipped. "But how do you convince those thousands of preachers, you will need to buy off, on this concept?"

"That, again, will be in the hands of Dr. King. And if there is any one preacher in this country that can get the job done, I believe it is him. His charisma is overwhelming, and his delivery of a sermon is untouchable. We just need to get to work and present him with the ammunition necessary to get the job done."

They all laughed. "To hear you use ammunition in any way as an analogy to something bigger is funny," Tom said.

"All right, now that you all got a good laugh let's get to work and help change history," I said.

For years, I had struggled with my homosexuality. I recognized early in life that something was different about me from the other boys in high school. I fought it by doing those things that prove you are normal as measured by society in the 1920's. I played on the football team, ran track and tried to be tough all along knowing that really wasn't me. That's why the more I interacted with young Tom, I picked up the same struggles within him. I knew I had to help him confront that battle.

Tom found any excuse to visit me at my apartment, separate from Rachelle and that alone was unusual. He desperately needed to reach out to me but just didn't know how. That also was unusual for him. One evening after he left the apartment, I raised the issue with Arthur.

"I believe Tom is at a place in his life that he's not comfortable," I said as we both sat on the couch.

"It's obvious that he's gay," Arthur blurted out. "And he's at that age when it is most difficult to deal with, especially in a country built around a false concept of the macho man. This is especially hard on white boys. We grow up on John Wayne, the ultimate cowboy, who whips all the bad men and all the Indians by himself. And then you have Cary Grant, the ultimate smooth and handsome man who all the women want to be with. He can only be that way as long as the women want him, but if he happened to desire to be with men, then he loses all that attention. There is no way Clark Gable could be gay and get the media attention he does. Even if he was, he'd have to stay in the closet. Every father wants his son to emulate those kinds of men." He paused, took my hand and caressed it. I squeezed his hand in response.

"You have a point," I said. "Probably the difference between a Negro who is gay and a white man, is that the society expects nothing more from the Negro. But a white boy who grows to be homosexual has disappointed the white race, because they are not supposed to possess such abnormal behavior. Sometimes, I imagine their father is more ashamed and embarrassed than he is of anything else."

"Outstanding observation, Mr. Rustin, but with that said, how do you propose to help young Tom?"

"That young man is one of the brightest and best this country has to offer. He has to know that his preferences sexually, does not diminish that fact," I said. "Right now, he is at the stage when he is ashamed to love a man because of John Wayne and Cary Grant."

"Like I said, it is a hell of a battle for young white men. Especially if you want your father to be proud of who you are, when usually, he'll kick you out of the house or dis-own you when he finds out his little Johnny is not going to grow up to be the next big John."

"What is most disgusting is those people who will argue that a gay man and a lesbian woman have a choice and, therefore, they get just what they deserve and that is harassment and rejection from society."

Arthur straightened up and pulled away from me. "If you had a choice, what would you have chosen?" he asked.

"I guess not to be gay because it would have made life much easier, but since that wasn't a choice for me, I am content with who I am."

"Were you ever attracted to women and did you ever date any?" he continued his questioning.

Why, suddenly, this inquiry after we had been together for over a year? I thought maybe Arthur was struggling himself.

"I did on a couple occasions but did not pursue any kind of relationship with them. In fact, a number of young ladies found me quite attractive and didn't understand why I refused their flirtation."

"Would you ever go back?"

I felt a touch of irritation. "Why are you asking these questions?" I scowled. "There is no going back because there is nothing to go back to and second, I am satisfied with who I am. I have no regrets about my life."

Arthur slid over next to me on the couch. "Sorry Bayard, I didn't mean to upset you."

I pushed him away. "Are you struggling with your sexuality, Arthur? Are you having problems being a homosexual?"

He stiffened. "No," he shot back quickly which told me that he was struggling with our relationship.

"When I get the opportunity, I will discuss Tom's hesitancy to deal with who he is," I said deliberately changing the subject.

"Please be careful how you do it," Arthur whispered. "Are you coming to bed?" he asked.

"No, I don't think so at least not right now. I have some more work that must be done tonight for our meeting in the morning. I'll be in later."

Arthur stood and walked toward the bedroom. He stopped before going in and turned to look back at me. "Bayard, I do love you."

"Thank you, I love you also," I said. "Are you all right?"

"Yes, I'm fine. I'll see you when you come to bed." Arthur disappeared into the bedroom.

I sat staring at the bedroom door and conjuring memories of David Platt. He had been my first real serious lover whom I stayed with for years. In fact, he remained loyal to me while I served a three-year prison sentence for refusing to report to the draft in 1944. But soon after getting out of prison, we began to drift away from each other. I felt a distance growing between us and it was the same feeling I had right at this moment with Arthur. But just like David, what we had in common was our affinity to be with men. That, in and of itself, was not strong enough to sustain a relationship. As I turned away from the bedroom and concentrated on the papers that Tom had brought earlier, I knew my time with Arthur might be growing short.

20.

The joyous news of the Supreme Court decision came clear and loud through the television on November 13, almost nine months after I became totally engrossed in the Montgomery Bus Boycott. I sat sipping a cup of coffee, smoking a cigarette, and listening intently to the reporter.

"The United Supreme Court affirmed the lower court decision that the Montgomery Bus Company and the City must end segregation."

Arthur had already left the apartment for an early morning class on British Literature at Columbia University. He was nearing the end of the course work and would, in January, begin study for his examinations. I felt rather relieved that he was not there at that moment. Sharing it with him just didn't seem right.

"When the Court delivers the finding to the lower court and then to the city, all segregation must end," the reporter continued. "Let's go to Montgomery where James Reddick, our reporter down there has a statement from Dr. Martin Luther King, Jr. James come on in."

I moved right to the end of my chair, took a heavy sip of coffee and listened.

"Dr. King," the reporter began, "you have successfully struck a blow against prejudice and segregation here in Montgomery, Alabama. How does it feel?"

"Well, I haven't done a thing. God has struck a blow against evil in this city. All praise and glory go to Him." King paused for a moment then continued, a tactic that he employed quite successfully. "The men and women of Montgomery are to be commended for their stalwart effort, their determination, and their never give up attitude that made this all possible."

A sense of humility total engulfed this man, I thought as I listened to him. He certainly wasn't plagued with the disease of hubris. Would he remain a humble man as his stature grew throughout the world and more reporters fought for interviews with him?

"Now that you have broken segregation here in Montgomery, what's your next move?" the reporter asked.

"I have no idea," King responded. "I guess I'll just wait and see where God directs me and the movement. But we still have work to do here in Montgomery. I am sure the bus company will not actually eradicate segregation until the order is received down here."

"Will you continue with the boycott?"

"No, I think the leadership team will call off the boycott, thank God."

"I am sure the entire world will be anxiously awaiting your next move if you plan to continue attacking segregation after this monumental victory. Thank you and now back to our studio in New York."

A chill shot through my entire body as I contemplated the task that I had taken on and was in the middle of completing with the help of Stanley and Ella. Dr. King's next move would depend on the credibility of our suggestions for a comprehensive plan based on a solid foundation moving forward. I squashed my cigarette in the ash tray, downed the rest of my coffee and headed for the shower. I needed to get dressed and down to the office. My energy surged and I could think of only one goal, putting the finishing touches on our report and getting it to Dr. King in Montgomery as soon as possible.

"Bayard, events are happening awfully fast down here, and I need you to come to Montgomery and let's strategize," Martin exclaimed. "We are preparing for that day in December when we'll board the buses and sit wherever we please. But what then?"

"We're working on the last phase of a plan for you to consider," I answered with some reluctance. I wasn't sure I wanted to return to Montgomery yet.

Martin detected my reluctance. "I only need you for a day. I'll get you in and out as quickly as possible, but I just need to know what our plans are going to be. If you heard the interview with the reporter on national television, you know I wasn't prepared to answer his question where do we go from here."

"Martin, we've been working on a proposed plan for you to present to all the ministers, but we're not quite finished yet. Can you give me a couple more weeks?"

"I don't believe we have a couple more weeks. Just bring me what you have, and we'll take it from there."

The determination in his voice told me there was no need to object. "I can make arrangements to be down there in a week," I suggested.

"No, tonight and I'll have a ticket waiting for you at La Guardia Airport. I want you to fly into Birmingham and Bobby will be there to pick you up. Your presence here would set off a firebomb of protest, not only by the white media but by the Negroes who feel you are a detriment to our cause." He paused as if expecting some objection from me. None coming he continued. "Bobby will bring you straight to the parsonage and you'll spend the night here and we'll have you out the next evening. In the meantime, be prepared for an all-day session of discussion. I need you to convince me that we are prepared and that we must take this movement to a much higher level."

My initial thought was just how Arthur would respond to me returning to Montgomery so soon after my last experience there. Our relationship seemed to be teetering much like the one with David Platt that ultimately ended with us going our separate ways. I wasn't quite ready to part company with Arthur but knew I must respond to this higher calling. I had to go.

"I'll be there with the working papers that David Levinson, Ella Baker and I have been working on for the past two months."

"David Levinson, I've heard of him," King said but did not mention Ella. No doubt he knew her because of the work she had done over the years organizing NAACP offices, throughout the South. What he thought of Ella was another matter and maybe that's why he made no mention of her.

"We have outlined a very comprehensive plan that expands your operation into a number of key functions and takes you outside of Montgomery and into other areas that need penetration."

"Sounds good to me, now will you get yourself ready and be down here this evening."

"Do I have a choice?" I asked rhetorically.

"No," he answered emphatically.

TWA Flight 1055 began its descent into Birmingham and as it did, I peered out the window at the beautiful landscape of the city. I smiled just thinking how such beauty could hide such ugliness. I wondered why Negroes stayed in a place where the people really did dislike them to the point of hatred. Martin promised I'd only be here for a day and that was enough for me.

It was a little after nine when we landed, and I finally climbed into the car waiting for me and we headed for Montgomery. Bobby had instructed me to sit in the backseat, which I found rather unusual since there was only the two of us in the car. When we approached Montgomery, I found out the reason for sitting back there.

"Mr. Rustin, if you don't mind, Dr. King wants you to duck down from this point until we reach the parsonage. Don't want nobody to know you're coming."

"But it's dark outside. Nobody can see me in the car."

"I understand, sir but Dr. King don't want to take no chances. So please duck down if you don't mind."

I did mind, but still stretched out on the back seat with my head below window level. I felt like I had a disease that everyone feared they might catch. I laid still for what seemed like another half-hour. Finally, Bobby turned into what I assumed was the driveway of the parsonage and turned off the engine.

"Mr. Rustin, thank you sir for cooperating," Bobby said as he opened the back door and allowed me to get out.

Soon as I reached the top step to the porch, the front door swung open and Martin stood there smiling. "Come on in," he said and moved to the side to allow me to pass by into the living room.

I glanced at the chair where the gun had been the last time I visited him in his home. No gun now and I considered that to be progress. I also looked at the well-decorated Christmas tree in front of the window. A pile of nicely wrapped gifts lay neatly placed under the tree and it was obvious the King family had prepared well for the most important holiday in the Christian faith. I followed Martin into the kitchen and took a chair across from him at the table.

"Thank you for coming down here on such short notice," Martin said as he extended his arm across the table and we shook hands.

"I really do get the feeling that I am not liked at all in this city. Having to duck my head down in the back seat of the car was a bit much," I said.

"I got a fresh pot of coffee." Martin got up, walked over to the stove where the coffee pot and two cups were in place to be used. He poured two cups and returned to the table, placing one cup in front of me. "I like you, I trust you and I respect you," he said emphatically. "And that's why I needed you to get down here right away.

"Why the rush, we won the battle. God has given you Christians one tremendous gift with the Supreme Court decision," I said.

"But you have said in the past, we just won the battle and now must prepare for the war. God's gift will come when all segregation is gone. These people are not going to give up that easily. Just look how they resisted the Supreme Court decision in the Brown case. Schools are nowhere near being integrated in the South and for that matter not even in many parts of the North."

I sipped from the cup, took a package of cigarettes out of my pocket and lit one. I offered one to Martin which he took and also lit. The smoke circulated around the table and into parts of the kitchen.

"I'll be quite honest with you," Martin continued. "I need to pick your brain as to what is the best strategy and how do we proceed. You must know that these Southerners are going to be planning on how to counter our future moves. We caught them off guard with the Montgomery boycott and furthermore, they never dreamt that Negroes would stick together for over a year the way we did. Now they have to go back and regroup. They must recognize they are dealing with a different Negro than before. We need to anticipate what they will do, just as they are anticipating our next move."

"I anticipate two problems," I said. "You just articulated the first one and the second is that some Negroes are going to be envious of the notoriety that will come your way as the movement continues to grow, and experience successes in other parts of the South. And then you're going to have the problem of other Baptists, especially ministers, who will want to bring you down. There are a lot of ministers, as well as, other Negroes who will not support what you are doing."

A broad smile crossed Martin's face. "I'm smiling because last summer we had just that kind of problem. Back in June just after we had gone on vacation with the Abernathy's, a young minister working with MIA accused us of mis-appropriating money or lining our pockets with donations for the movement. He was the minister over at Bell Street Baptist and his congregation was so upset with him that they immediately dismissed him. He eventually recanted but it was too late. The entire Black community condemned him because he was the first person to publicly show a weakness in our team. All because he was envious of the kind of publicity I was receiving." Martin sipped from his cup, then put out the cigarette and relaxed back in his chair.

"Do you believe you're going to get the support of the National Baptist Convention when they meet in 57?" I asked but didn't wait for an answer. "Reverend Jackson, President of the Convention, is known as a strong-willed, dictatorial leader of the preachers. How is he going to view you as a young rather new member of the convention, but someone who might become more recognized than Jackson?"

"That could be a problem."

"And how about all the university presidents, like your mentor Dr. Mays at Morehouse? Will these men have the nerve to stand up to the white establishment that support these colleges, and have historically made certain that the Negro they put in charge will not rock the boat as you are doing?"

"They also could be a problem. No doubt there are going to be a lot of Negroes so accustomed to accepting this way of life in the South, that they'll put a fight against what we plan to do. But because they oppose us, does that mean we don't keep moving ahead?"

I finished off my coffee and put out the cigarette that had burnt down, then also relaxed in the chair. "We have a number of position papers outlining how you should move forward after Montgomery. I'll leave them with you, and you can read through them and let me know how you feel about our suggestions." I deliberately did not respond to his question but instead got right to the point as to why he had summoned me down there.

"Bayard, I'm so busy and consumed with other matters, chances are I probably won't read them," Martin quipped. "So tomorrow, why don't you just brief me on your suggestions, and we'll take it from there."

"I can do that, but I'd better get a good night's sleep because to be quite honest with you, I'm worn out."

"Let's pray that we won't have another disturbance like the other night," King scoffed. "They shot out a window in the living room. We just got it replaced earlier today."

"Now you tell me," I replied jokingly.

"You'll be all right. They won't be back."

"How do you know that?" I had to ask.

"Prayer, my friend, strong and deep prayer." He answered and opened the door to the room where I would spend the night.

I immediately glanced over at the window. It was intact. "I do believe God's got your back, so I feel quite confident that nothing's going to come flying through that window."

"Be assured," King said and then closed the door.

I had gotten up just a little after seven and felt relieved that a brick didn't come flying through the window during the night. After a refreshing shower, I joined Martin in the kitchen for breakfast. That's when he told me that Coretta and the baby had gone to stay with her family in Marion, Alabama eighty miles west of Montgomery. He insisted that she go to a safe place after the window smashing disturbance the other day. One of the many loyal members of the church had come in about eight, fixed breakfast for us, and then we retired into the dining room where our serious conversation began.

"One of my most vivid memories, when I was about maybe ten or eleven, was listening to all the fuss being made about this Negro woman playing in a major movie," King reminisced as we sat in the dining room at the table.

"Of course, I didn't know what all the fuss was about," he continued. "Hattie McDaniel made the entire race proud, even though she was cast as a maid with a very stereotypical name, Mammy. But that wasn't the worst part, when the show first premiered in Atlanta, no Negroes were allowed in the theater. It wasn't until the movie played at theaters that had segregated seating for Negroes in the balcony that we could see it."

He paused in deep thought and I allowed him that space, as I knew he was organizing his thoughts in order to assess his position in the movement. He glared at me as though he wanted to penetrate right to my soul with a very important message. "You were raised up North Bayard, so you escaped a great deal of this humiliation that we confronted daily down here. They tried their best to make us feel that we were dirt beneath their feet. And as kids we never understood why, until we got a little older and they made it quite clear that's how they felt."

Apparently, he was very much misinformed. I had to clear up his misunderstanding as to how we lived in the North.

"Contrary to what you may have believed about our situation up North, I can assure you that our theaters were also segregated. And we also had to sit in the balcony, a place they termed as Nigger Heaven," I said. "In high school, I played on the football team and when we won a game, all the players celebrated at a local restaurant except the three Negroes on the team. They didn't serve us and yes that was in West Chester Pennsylvania."

"I guess as Negroes we all share the same burden," King quipped.

"And that's why it's so important that we expand from Montgomery to all over the South and into the North," I added. "And why it's important that the structural nature of how we do this is a necessity."

"That's why I have you down here." King leaned forward and placed his hands halfway across the table. "Bayard, you are without doubt one of the wisest and most talented men in this country, and I really do need to lean on you so let's get busy and make sure we use this day to advance our mission. Where do we start?"

"We have seven position papers we developed over the past three months," I began. I didn't bother to share the actual papers with him since he told me that he probably wouldn't read them.

"The we, being you, Levinson and Baker I assume?"

"Exactly, this was done by three people with the administrative help of two bright college students."

"Hopefully, someday in the future, I'll be able to personally thank them, but share with me what you have."

"Martin, it is imperative that you maintain the psychological momentum that'll come with your success here in Montgomery. Your people here understood that they had a shared grievance and that was mistreatment on the buses in the city. They all experienced that abuse at one time or another, and you probably have thousands of Negroes who could have done exactly what Rosa Parks did," I began. "There is also the important economic component to what happened here in Montgomery and probably can be applied throughout the South, and into the North for that matter. The protest hurt the bus company to the point that they wanted to settle the dispute, but the city wouldn't allow it."

"Negroes, probably more than any other one race depends on buses to get where they are going," Martin interjected. "If you drive through the wealthier communities in any city, you will always find bus stops. Now they're not out there for the residents of the area, but for the maids and butlers who live in the Negro areas of the city and must find transportation to the homes where they do the work. It is an economic interest for all parties involved."

"Yes, and the mobilization of the people was because they recognized the necessity to band together for a common cause, and that is the message you must spread throughout the South. Negroes have a common cause and it all stems back to an economic interest."

"Our protests are directly linked to our economic survival and that has always been the case in this country, especially after slavery."

Martin's tone reflected his enthusiasm in the subject. We were making progress and touching on the main points we developed back in New York. "Shared grievances vital to the masses of Negroes are the ones that can trigger organized action, and that action going forward will be non-violent protest in the streets."

"Yes, yes, yes," King proclaimed. "We will be deviating from what has been the standard method for Negroes to express their displeasure with their condition, and that has been through the courts."

"I don't think Roy Wilkins is going to be too pleased with this new approach," I said. "The NAACP has always been out front on these issues and you are about to change that starting with your victory here in Montgomery."

"I know and that's where you and Phil come into the picture. I need you to be my emissary in New York and for you to smooth it all over with Roy. Rather have him be my friend and not my opponent."

"We can do that for you Martin, but what is really critical is that you have a united front of ministers and other organizational leaders here in the South under one umbrella with you," I suggested. I pulled out a cigarette, offered one to him. He took it and we both lit up. I continued. "We need an institutional base and that base has to be the foundation for the protest movement, to be grounded in our churches. The most stable institution within our culture and the one that demands the attention of the Negro masses, is the church." I paused, took a very deep drag on my cigarette and blew the smoke out. I watched it as it circulated around the room. "Aggressive non-violent, and I mean aggressive and not passive, direct action must be organized under a united effort of the churches and their leaders. We need only one organization, and Martin, you must be the leader. Are you ready for that heavy responsibility?"

"No, he isn't," an older Black man standing in the entrance to the dining room shouted. I recognized him as Martin's father. He marched into the room and stood right at the head of the table.

"Martin, what do you think you're doing?" He asked but didn't wait for an answer. "Whatever it is, it has endangered your wife and baby and chased them out of their home. You have been found guilty of breaking a city law and could possibly end up in jail, and most important you are neglecting your duties as a pastor to Dexter. Shame on you and it is now time to put this all to an end."

It was common knowledge all over the country that the pastor of Ebenezer Baptist Church in Atlanta, the senior Martin King was a hard-nosed no-nonsense minister who ruled his church with an iron hand and, evidently, he applied that same method to his children and family. As I sat there, I got a heavy dose of that application.

"As soon as I heard of the shooting, I headed down here from Atlanta and I plan to take you and your family back there with me. You can resign your pastor ship with Dexter and become assistant pastor at Ebenezer." He stared directly at his son and ignored me as if I wasn't in the room.

"I think I need to retire to the kitchen," I said, put out my cigarette and started to get up.

"No, Bayard, stay right where you are," Martin brusquely said as he also squashed his cigarette in the ash tray. "I'm sorry you drove all the way down here without first communicating your intention," Martin shot back at his father. "But I do not plan to give up my church nor do I plan to give up the movement."

"Martin, have you taken leave of your senses. This is no game you're playing with down here. These white folks are serious, and they will kill you, your family, me, your brother and your mother if necessary. They don't have a heart. They're like animals when it comes to dealing with us. Is that what you want to happen?" Martin Sr. allowed a little pleading in the tone of his words.

"No, I haven't, and I know exactly what I'm doing and all the danger that accompanies this cause. But I can't abandon what is taking place right now in this city and eventually all over the South." Martin's tone, unlike his father, was stern and determined.

"They ran Vernon Johns right out of Dexter because he was a rebel just like you," Martin Sr. continued, obviously determined not to lose this battle. "Is that what you want the members at Dexter to do to you?"

"I don't think that's going to happen," Martin said. "In fact, many of the members are very sorry that they didn't back Reverend Johns when he was taking on all the evil in this city, and will not make that same mistake with me. They are all in my corner."

"Lunch is ready," the lady from the church who had fixed our breakfast said while standing just outside the dining room. Because of the heated discussion no one had noticed her there.

"No, absolutely not," Martin Sr. scowled. "We don't need food. What we need is prayer."

"Thank you, Martha," Martin said. "We'll eat later."

I watched as Martha hurried back into the kitchen. I wanted to follow her in there and escape this minor war between a father and a son and, most important, two powerful ministers.

"Martin, I didn't raise you and send you to Morehouse to end up as some kind of fool," Martin Sr. said. "How long are you going to continue down this sure path of destruction?"

"Until God tells me to stop and right now, I'm not getting that kind of message from Him, so I guess I'll just keep doing what I'm doing and with the help of this man here, make a major difference in the condition of our people." Martin pointed his finger at me.

His father shot a glance my way and I prepared for the onslaught. I knew it was coming because at this point, I'd make a good scape goat for his failure to convince his son to give up and go to Atlanta with him. Fortunately, he spared me his wrath.

"Martin, I am very upset with you, but I'm going to pray that you come to your senses," he said. "I'm going over to Holt Baptist before heading back to Atlanta. If you change your mind and realize that what I am offering to you is the best, give me a call." He turned and looked at me. "If you care about my son and his family, you will stop encouraging this mis-guided disturbance and convince Martin to concentrate on being a good minister."

I felt relieved as I watched this man turn and head out of the room. His wrath on me had been minor. I noticed that Martin's head was bowed, and a very somber expression filled his face. No doubt he did not want to disappoint his father, but he had no choice. A grander movement was calling him.

"Let's have lunch and continue," he finally said. "We need to finish within the next three hours so Bobby can get you back up to Birmingham for your flight back to New York tonight."

I followed him into the kitchen where Martha had set up two places at the table. We both sat on different sides as she poured lemonade into two glasses and then went to the stove.

"Do you think he'll eventually come around and support what you're doing?" I asked.

"Yes, once he knows I'm serious and will not give up until this is done or I am killed," Martin said.

I felt a chill. But what he suggested was a possibility. He could be killed as could any of us. I knew that accounted for some of the aggressive behavior from his father.

"The latter is not an option," I countered. "You are much too important for the work that must be done to die."

"Only God makes that decision and how does the joke go, if you want to make God laugh just tell him about your plans for the future."

"Right now, let's just assume that God agrees with the path you are taking and will protect you with His grace."

Martha placed the two plates in front of us. We ate and afterwards spent the next three hours laying out plans for a major meeting of all the ministers in the South, who would like to be a part of the movement to meet in Atlanta, Georgia on January 10 and 11. I promised to have the working documents outlining the rationale and institutional structure for the new organization at the meeting. I questioned if it made sense for me to personally be there, since this would be a meeting primarily of ministers who were anti-homosexual and my presence may deter from the purpose. Martin insisted and explained how he needed and counted on me to make this happen, regardless of any distractions.

We finished a little after four o'clock and exchanged Christmas greetings, even though as a Quaker I did not celebrate that holiday, Bobby drove me back up to Birmingham, again while ducking down in the back seat. I boarded an eight thirty flight back to New York and returned home to put the final touches on a project that would have profound implications for the future of race relationships in this country.

21.

I watched the television screen from my living room with mixed emotions, as Martin and Glenn Smiley boarded a municipal bus at a major bus stop in Montgomery. Arthur sat next to me on the couch. It was a history making moment. The order from the Supreme Court had finally arrived and the city gave up its attempt to block integrating the buses. Martin had called me last night, excited about what would be happening that morning and expressed his one regret that I couldn't be there to step on that bus and sit wherever we chose. Instead, Glenn would have the pleasure of making history with him. He and Glenn had grown close over the past year, but still I was the one who first showed up to assist him and felt it should be me there with him.

We listened as the reporter for NBC reported the event. "The bus has pulled up to the stop only a block away from the home of Dr. King and the first person to board is Reverend Ralph Abernathy, followed by a woman whose name we do not have." He hesitated while Reverend Abernathy boarded and the camera followed him to the very first seat in the front of the bus. He sat there, and the woman sat next to him. The reporter continued. "Now Dr. King and his very close commandant, the man who has taught him the Gandhi tactic of non-violence, Reverend Glenn Smiley, are taking the seat right behind Reverend Abernathy."

A tinge of envy shot through my body as I watched them board the bus. Arthur must have detected my frustration. He took my hand and squeezed it tightly.

"How dare they give Glenn credit for introducing non-violence to Dr. King," he scowled. "It was you and you deserve the credit. The success of this movement is due to you, Bayard, and no one else."

I could appreciate Arthur's anger because deep inside I felt the same. But something also deep inside would not allow me the pleasure of expressing that feeling. My role in the movement going forward would be relegated to the back burner, even though many of the ideas were mine. No doubt when the mass meeting in Atlanta next month occurred, I again would be pushed to the back. I had to always be prepared to play that role.

"When are you going to stop allowing these people to take advantage of you?" Arthur asked. "It happens time and time again, no matter who it is, they drain your brain and take credit for your accomplishments."

"We all have a cross to bear," I shot back. "You haven't confronted yours yet, but it is coming someday. If you continue in this lifestyle that we both enjoy, you too will face that day when it becomes a burden and you will have to make a decision."

Arthur pulled back away from me. "What are you getting at?"

"My cross to bear happened in January three years ago next month, and it won't let me go," I explained. "The reason why, is because small thinking people won't let it go. I made a serious mistake getting caught in a car with two others and that is my cross to bear. When that happened, the people I thought were my friends abandoned me. And the most hurtful was when A. J. Muste turned his back on me. I'd been working on the cause of peace for the organization and they terminated my position. Thank God for the War Resisters League, because they were willing to overlook that mistake and give me a job. Otherwise, I don't know how I would have made it out here. And of course, Mr. Randolph also helped. He has never turned his back on me, and I'll always be grateful to him for that."

"I guess image is more important than knowledge these days, especially since all the damage done by Eugene McCarthy," Arthur said. "Someday I'll be up for a dean's position at the university, and I imagine that the board at Columbia University will be concerned with the image I portray to the students in the English Department."

"Probably so," I replied not knowing what else to say.

"Something I was thinking about lately is we met at a Quaker retreat years ago," Arthur reminisced changing the direction of the conversation. "Have you ever considered it wrong to be a Quaker and homosexual?

"Not at all, because I've never considered it sinful to be a homosexual," I said wondering where he was going with this line of questions.

"All my life I've had to hide my attraction to men from my family," he said sounding somewhat contrite. "They are of the Quaker sect that believes homosexuality is sinful and abhorrent."

"Arthur, do you consider it to be a sin and do you find sleeping with me every night an abhorrent experience?" I noticed that lately our conversations drifted to our relationship as two men living together. Maybe Arthur was struggling with his sexual identity in the same way as young Tom Kahn. But there was no reason for him, at his age, to question who he really was. I wanted to tell him that he either accepts his life as a gay man or make some changes.

"No, not at all, I love sleeping with you and I love how we make love together," he smiled and reached over once again and took my hand. "Nothing gives me more joy than to be in your arms."

"Before you accept that position someday as dean, do you feel an obligation to let the administration know that you share a life with a gay man, and a Black one at that?" I felt compelled to ask him.

"Wait just a minute now Bayard, you know damn well race has nothing to do with this," he loudly proclaimed.

"Well then there is only one answer, being gay has something to do with it," I shot back. "I don't think that you're a free man within yourself. You struggle with your identity."

"Tell me why we should have to feel queer for enjoying the company of someone of the same sex?" Arthur finally opened up and shared with me a concern he'd never expressed before.

I had to be careful with my response. I needed to make it right. "Arthur, sexual expression is possible between any two people, and their particular gender is not the deciding factor, unless their goal is procreation. Sex for enjoyment alone with a woman is no different than having sex with a man. It is simply for enjoyment."

Arthur slid over close to me. "You always make me feel better with who I am," he said and kissed me. "I need to get dressed and get over to the university."

"You do that, because I have a lot of work to do in preparation for the meeting next month in Atlanta."

"Again, you're going to do all the work and get none of the credit." Arthur stood up and strolled to the bedroom. "Don't allow them to continue treating you this way. Tell Dr. King that you must be acknowledged for your work." Not waiting for a response, he disappeared into the bedroom, closing the door behind him.

On Christmas morning Arthur was already up when I finally awakened sometime after seven in the morning. I could hear him on the telephone in the living room talking with his family in West Chester. He had made a commitment to catch the train to his home, and spend the next two days with them. Obviously, I would not accompany him, so I decided to catch the train to Syracuse, New York to spend the day with my close and dearest friends, Norman Whitney and his sister Mildred. I had to rush to get dressed because my train left Union Station at ten in the morning, only fifteen minutes after the one Arthur would catch.

We had a very light breakfast that he prepared, while I dressed for the day. We caught a cab to the train station and arrived just fifteen minutes before Arthur would board. I watched as his train pulled off, then hurried to the gate and found a seat on the ten o'clock train to Syracuse. I felt relaxed and free of all worries, as I closed my eyes and reflected on my relationship with Norman and Mildred.

As much as anyone who had been in my life, to include my grandmother, Norman understood that being a homosexual was not a choice for me. I just didn't decide one day that I liked boys and later men. He really served as my spiritual guide and like a father. He and Mildred stood by me after the terrible Pasadena incident. In fact, once they released me from prison, instead of returning directly to New York to face the wrath of Muste and the members of FOR, I spent a few days in Syracuse in the very same house I would stay with them this Christmas. What I appreciated most about them was that the two refused to censure me because of my awful behavior. The time I spent with them after Pasadena saved me from myself because I felt so self-destructive. I had been to prison two other times, once during the war and the other on the chain gang in North Carolina. I never felt ashamed for those periods of incarnation because the cause was right, but I did feel shameful for the thirty days of imprisonment.

I will always remember the words Whitney shared with me in correspondence. "I hope that my faith and trust may surround you." I memorized the words studying them each night after lockup. "I know nothing of the particular circumstances, but I think I know something of the agony of your body and soul. Remember you are called upon to minister to your fellow men and to use your time uniquely. You are therefore, called upon to bear the burden of the world's suffering uniquely, even this pain. I am confident that out of this experience you will become still further refined and enriched to be the instrument of God's way of love, His will of peace, His witness to truth." In times of despair and of joy, I called upon my two friends in Syracuse for encouragement. These next few days would serve that purpose, as I knew I must energize for what lie in front of me beginning with the meeting in January. Knowing that I was in for a joyful experience and looking at the beautiful countryside out the train window, I drifted off to sleep.

A light snow had just begun to fall when the train pulled into the station a little after three o'clock in the afternoon. I grabbed my overnight bag and exited onto the platform, and saw both Norman and Mildred waving at me as I made my way to the lobby.

"How was the ride?" Norman asked as I hugged him and then Mildred.

"Peaceful and restful." I smiled as we headed out of the station and to the car.

"You sit up front with Norman and I'll grab the back seat," Mildred said as Norman tossed my bag in the trunk.

I climbed into the front seat and we headed to their home in the suburbs of the city.

"From the reports coming out of New York from the Quakers, you have been a very busy man these past months," Norman began the conversation as he merged onto the highway, got in the left lane, and picked up his speed.

"I wasn't aware the society was following my activities," I said somewhat surprised at the source of his information, regarding my activities. "I haven't really been attending any of the meetings."

"But they know what you're up to because you are one of us," Mildred spoke up from the backseat.

"Speaking of one of us how is your grandmother?" Norman asked. "She certainly has been one of the leaders in the movement in Pennsylvania."

"Still leading," I answered. "I've been so busy I've neglected to talk with her."

"I'm sure she understands," Mildred said. "But she's always been so good to you, and most importantly understanding. You must call her."

Mildred always assumed the motherly role, reminding me of those things that I neglected to do but knew must be done. She was right most of the time and especially on this occasion. My grandmother, whom I had believed to be my mother until the age of 13, was the pillar that lifted me up when I needed help. She was the first person I told about my desire to be with boys, and she simply responded, "if that is your preference then do what your heart dictates."

"I'm anxious to hear about your plans for the future with Dr. King," Norman interrupted my musing. "This is a very interesting situation, a Baptist minister and a homosexual working together to solve the problems of the Negro in a racist and sexist country," he suggested as he turned into his driveway and up to the front of the house.

"What is more important than the religion, the sex and the color is that I view life from a humanitarian perspective," I said. "I don't look at Dr. King as a minister, and I view all the racists lined up against the Negro in the South and for that matter here in New York, as human beings, all spiritually endowed with the ability to get beyond the surface of who we are here on earth, but what we all are as spiritual beings."

"Well said," Mildred commented as we exited the car and headed inside the house.

Sitting in the large recliner in the den my eyes were riveted on the flames dancing toward the chimney opening in the fireplace. With the snow falling outside the window and the warmth created by the fire, I felt more relaxed than I had experienced in quite a while. Probably the last time I felt this comfortable was years ago when I first returned to New

York after being released from the California prison, and stayed with these beautiful souls before going on to New York. This was just like home to me and Mildred and Norman, my extended family. I felt no pressure as I did everyday with Arthur. I didn't have to be anyone special, not a lover to anyone, or teacher, just friend with two individuals who put no expectations on me. It couldn't get much better than that.

Norman finally strolled into the den with a glass partially filled with wine. He handed it to me.

"As I recall you do appreciate a good glass of wine," he said.

"I certainly do," I said. "As well as a good cigarette." I placed the glass on the table next to the recliner, pulled a cigarette from the package and lit it. There was an ash tray conveniently placed on the table next to the glass of wine.

Norman sat in the large cushioned chair to the left of the recliner. He lit his pipe and reared back for a moment as in deep thought. "I take it you haven't been singing or playing the lute lately," he said.

"I've been so wrapped up in what's happening down South that I haven't done anything else," I sighed. "It's been overwhelming to say the least."

"I take it that Pasadena is now behind you," Norman said.

I stared straight ahead at the flame from the fire and thought for a moment. Was Pasadena behind me? "I don't think it will ever be behind me," I quipped. "But can I deal with the consequences that will follow me because of that situation, hopefully yes."

"Don't you think you may be mixing water and oil, if you get involved with all those ministers in the South who seem to be in charge of the movement down there?"

"I'm not so sure it will make much of a difference, as long as they can see some value in what I have to offer," I replied.

"And if the value is not equivalent to their unreasonable dislike for your lifestyle, then what happens?"

"I don't know," I said honestly because I really didn't. I could probably resume my international peace initiatives, fighting against the cold war

196 | Williams-Denton-Zinsmeyer

concept and the spread of nuclear arms. That was the direction my life was going before I received the call to get involved in Montgomery. Africa was another option. The countries over there were in the middle of a similar fight we had going on in the South. It always seems to boil down to a struggle of people of color against the white minority, who somehow had managed to amass all the collective power over the past centuries. "I didn't begin my journey as an advocate for civil rights," I continued. "When I first met you and Mildred back in, I believe 1937, we united against the pending wars we saw on the horizon. Our advocacy was against any form of violence, be it by individuals or the state."

"Yes, and I do remember warning you against your involvement with the Communist Party, but you joined anyway."

"A major mistake on my part and one I'll regret for the rest of my life," I admitted my error. "That's a tag I'm not sure I'll be able to overcome, that along with being a homosexual." I paused to reflect on the morning that the Black reporter from Birmingham charged into the meeting at the restaurant at the Ben Moore Hotel and accused me of being a Communist. "That could become a problem if I do continue working with Dr. King."

"Whatever you decide to do, you know Mildred and I will always be in your corner," Norman exclaimed.

"In the meantime, I want you to rest and enjoy the next two days here with us," Mildred said as she walked into the den. "Dinner will be served in the next ten minutes so if you want to freshen up, now is the time to do it." She finished and walked back out.

"Bayard, two years ago we worked with a Quaker committee out of New York City in an attempt to develop a paradigm as an alternative to violence," Norman said.

I finished off the wine in my glass and put out the cigarette that had burned down in the ashtray. I prepared to get up and follow Mildred's instruction but when he mentioned our work back in 1954, I settled back in the chair to listen.

"I absolutely do recall what we wanted to do then," I said. "It was very convenient for me because it gave me the opportunity to divert from what had happened in Pasadena."

"Our mantra became speaking truth to power, and we wrote a seventy-page tract based on that." He paused as if to allow me to recall. "One of the major points we made was that the militarism not only caused wars but also devastated a democracy. Well, that is the same principle you must apply to your work in the South, only replace militarism with racism." He stood and prepared to go into the dining room. I also got up. "As you get deeply involved in the struggle in the South just remember that you cannot take a stand for truth and justice without causing some suffering, and that suffering might be inflicted on you."

"I believe I'm ready," I said as we made our way to the table that was beautifully set with a white laced tablecloth, porcelain plates, cloth napkins and deliciously smelling entrees.

22.

The Belleview Hotel had been built at the corner of Auburn and Piedmont, right in the middle of the Negro community in Atlanta. It was only a few blocks from Ebenezer Baptist Church, the location for the coming together of Negro ministers from nine different states in the South. Ella Baker and I checked into the hotel on Wednesday, January 9 and planned to meet Reverend King and Abernathy later that evening to go over the agenda for the conference the next day. The King's along with Abernathy decided to stay at Reverend King Sr.'s parish.

Evidently, he had gotten over his anger with his son and insisted that the meeting take place at his church. Probably so he could make sure he maintained some control. He was one of the most respected ministers in the country and a close ally to Reverend Jackson from Chicago, the President of the National Baptist Conference. Stanley Levinson didn't make the trip because the ministers had made it quite clear to Martin that the session was for Negroes only. One of the three architects of the proposed organizations, that would unite Negroes throughout the South, had been black balled and I found that disheartening and quite ironic. Martin had agreed but that was a battle that he lost overwhelmingly. Naturally, I thought when would it be my turn.

An air of excitement filled the lobby of the hotel as many of the ministers were also staying there. The talk was exactly about what they might accomplish for the next two days and could this seriously be the beginning of the end of segregation.

We had scheduled to meet at seven o'clock in a private room at the hotel. Just before seven, my phone rang in the room.

"Bayard, there have been several bombings back in Montgomery," Martin said while breathing heavily. "Ralph's church has been bombed as has Reverend Graetz. Thank God no one was injured, but it looks as though Ralph and I will have to go back to Montgomery this evening."

"How about our agenda for tomorrow?" I asked.

"Give it to Reverend Fred Shuttlesworth and to Coretta in the morning. They'll just have to do the best they can in running the session until I can get back."

"Do you have any idea when you might get back?" My confidence that we might be able to pull this off began to wane. All along, it was my belief that only Martin could make this happen, and now he would be absent at the beginning of the session. We'd be fortunate if many of the ministers just wouldn't pack up and take off back to their cities, believing this entire plan was a farce.

"I'll be back just as soon as I can, but make sure you give all the information to Reverend Shuttlesworth and Coretta and, by all means, don't you and Ella try to run the session."

"You sure you just don't want to cancel it until you get back?"

"No way, Fred Shuttlesworth is quite capable and the ministers respect Coretta enough to follow her lead."

"Martin, you have to know that we put a lot of time and effort into this project and I'd hate to see it fall flat because you're gone."

"I promise you that it won't. Just follow what I'm saying, and we'll be all right. I'll be there just as soon as I can. But you have to know, I must go back to Montgomery for the moral support my people will need at this time."

"I can understand."

"Good, I'll see you sometime tomorrow or maybe on Friday. God is with us and it'll all work out," he said and then hung up.

"I sure hope so," I said as I held the phone for a few seconds before finally hanging it up.

Ella and I took a cab to the church and when we arrived there a large crowd of reporters stood blocking the entrance. There were also a large number of policemen parked in cars and on foot up and down the boulevard. We had just gotten out of the cab, when a plain-clothes-policemen approached me.

"You, Mr. Rustin?" he asked.

"Yes, I am, what's the problem?"

"We just got word that a carload of troublemakers out of Florida have just arrived in the city and plan to disrupt your meeting," he said. "You'd better get everyone inside the church as fast as possible and we'll handle it out here if they show up. We would like to have the front of the church clear just in case these men show up and just start shooting."

"I'm not in charge, but I'll do the best I can," I said.

"We'll help you out." The detective waved for some uniformed officers to join us.

I turned to Ella, "Why don't you go inside, and I'll help these officers to get everybody inside."

"Let me have the resolutions and the organizational charter we prepared for the session," she said. "I'll make sure they get distributed and also give our outline for conducting the session to Reverend Shuttlesworth. He's probably already inside with Mrs. King."

I handed Ella the large brown envelope with all the paperwork inside. She quickly made her way inside. I stood on the steps waving the ministers inside. My thoughts momentarily concentrated on Norman's final words at his home in Syracuse. "You cannot take a stand for truth and justice without causing some suffering." I was ready if the men from Florida showed up.

I had finally gotten all the ministers in the church and turned to go inside, when a Ford Truck with Florida plates came flying down Auburn Street in the direction of the church. I quickly opened the door and started inside, but stopped and watched as the action unfolded on Auburn Avenue. Two police cruisers got behind the truck and two others blocked the street before the truck reached the front of the church. I watched as the detective who had warned me, jumped out of one of the cruisers with gun drawn and walked toward the truck that had come to an abrupt stop. The detective was followed by at least ten policemen, who all got out of the vehicles and converged on the truck.

Evidently, the city of Atlanta wanted no trouble in their city, while so much national attention was concentrated on the gathering of high-profile

Negro ministers from all over the South. The press was there outside the church and able to capture what happened. Atlanta would look good as the news spread throughout the country of how they protected a gathering of Negroes from a truck load of racists there to do harm. One of the reasons for holding the meeting in Atlanta, besides King Sr. insisting on it being there, was because we knew Mayor William Hartsfield had made it clear that his city would not become known as a city of violence and bombing such as Birmingham. In fact, he'd run for election on the motto "Atlanta, a city too busy to hate." I watched as his police force enforced that belief on the rabble rousers from Florida. The police finally led the truck down the street and away from the church, and probably all the way to the outskirts of town with a strong warning to get out and don't come back.

I felt good, as I finally made it into the church and took a seat near the back. Reverend Shuttlesworth had just begun to read the provisions for establishing the organization.

"Our first assignment is to officially adopt a name for our new organization," Shuttlesworth exclaimed.

A minister dressed in a purple suit immediately jumped to his feet. "I think before we agree on a name, we need to know exactly what we plan to accomplish with this new organization. We all have profound confidence in Dr. Martin Luther King and know that he was called away on an emergency and will pray for the people in Montgomery as they continue to struggle with racism, but we need to get down to business here and know just what we are agreeing to do."

"According to the resolutions prepared by Dr. King the first thing on our agenda would be the total integration of all bus systems throughout the South."

I smiled as Reverend Shuttlesworth spoke as though Dr. King had prepared the plan. But that was all right, if the ministers in the church knew that a communist, a homosexual and a woman prepared their total plan for action, they'd probably walk out.

"We must use Montgomery as a prototype as we move into other cities in a united front," Shuttlesworth continued. "The protests must all be local, organized and led by local leaders, but coached by our new national organization with Dr. King at the head." Shuttlesworth paused and looked down on the paper we prepared for him. Evidently, he was studying something we had written. He finally read from it. "We must recognize in this new period that direct action is our most potent political weapon. We must understand that our refusal to accept Jim Crow in specific areas challenges the entire social, political and economic order that has kept us second class citizens since 1876."

"Well-written, well-spoken," the ministers responded in unison.

Again, I smiled and looked over at Ella Baker who was sitting in the row to my right. Those lines were written by Stanley Levinson, the communist.

Reverend Shuttlesworth continued, "An additional resolution states that these campaigns must be based on the most stable institution in the Negro culture and that is the church. That was the case in Montgomery. The bus boycott started at Holt Baptist Church and prayer meetings were held at First Baptist Church and at Dexter Baptist Church. That will be the case as the movement grows in activities."

When Shuttlesworth finished, all the ministers in the sanctuary jumped to their feet and began to applaud. "Praise the Lord, praise Jesus, His work is finally being recognized," the ministers shouted.

This time Ella smiled as we both recognized her work. She had concentrated much of her writing on the importance of the church in the movement. She pointed out that the church in the South would replace the NAACP as the go to institution, because the latter had been outlawed in most Southern cities. The Negro church was economically independent and protected from government intrusion into its actives by the First Amendment to the Constitution. It was only logical that the churches be out front in the new wave of activities to eradicate segregation, and the ministers in lead roles with Dr. King at the head.

Shuttlesworth held his hand in the air and shouted over the hand clapping and the Amens. "Let me continue." He again looked down on the paper. "An additional resolution states that the bus protest clearly revealed certain economic facts. One, the Negro's dollar as a factor in the economic organization of the community. Two, his refusal to ride had a catastrophic effect on the economics of the bus companies and three, the unintended but nonetheless direct effect of the protest on downtown merchants was real."

Now it was my turn to gloat. He read my exact words as I prepared them as it had been my responsibility to write on the economic impact of the protest and how it would be the same throughout the South. The Negro had strong buying power that often was taken for granted by the white world. The Negro must make the supporters of an economically unequal system pay dearly.

He continued to read from my writings, "While there is still much legal work to be done, there is ample and convincing evidence that the center of gravity has shifted from the courts to community action. The job before us now is to demonstrate that our cause is basic to the welfare of the community, and we must challenge our white fellow citizens and win them over to believe in and to practice democracy. We must recognize that in this new period, direct action through non-violent means is our most potent political weapon."

The ministers clapped their approval of the resolution. The thought that they had no idea they were giving approval to the writing and ideas of a person whom they preached was a sinner and an abomination to God, brought a smile to my face once again.

By noon all the resolutions drafted in an office in Manhattan in New York City had been approved by a contingent of ministers, whose churches were scattered throughout the South. The irony of this entire situation did not escape me. If this gathering turns out to be a history making event, one man will receive credit and that will be Dr. King and the three of us who spent endless nights and long days trying to figure this out would be lost in history.

After a two-hour lunch break, we all gathered back in the sanctuary of the church to conduct the business on the agenda for the afternoon.

Shuttlesworth again took control. "Now that we have adopted all the resolutions and acknowledge what our mission will be, can we finally get to naming the organization? Our temporary name has been the Southern Christian Leadership Conference on Transportation and that is rather restrictive, because it indicates that we will only deal with transportation issues.

"It is a Christian gathering and we are all leaders from the South, so why don't we just drop the word transportation and called in The Southern Christian Leadership Conference," a minister who had been very active in shouting Amens and clapping his hands suggested.

"Let me see a show of hands of those who are in favor of the name Southern Christian Leadership Conference." Coretta finally got involved in the proceedings.

Every minister raised their hand.

"Good. Then it is done." Shuttlesworth proclaimed. "We now need only to choose a president of the organization and I do believe I know who everyone has in mind."

Three ministers immediately jumped to their feet.

"Dr. Martin Luther King, Jr.," one of the ministers said.

"I second the nomination," the second minister who had gotten to his feet said.

"Good it has been moved and seconded, how did you all vote," Shuttlesworth said without recognizing the third minister who had gotten up.

It was unanimous. "I guess we know who our leader will be as we step out on this very dangerous adventure. Let the record reflect that Dr. Martin Luther King, Jr., Pastor of Dexter Baptist Church in Montgomery, Alabama has been elected President of the Southern Christian Leadership Conference."

Again, applause and shouts, "God is Good, God is Good."

"I have a statement here we just got from Brother Martin. He is asking for our understanding and forgiveness for missing this day's business but will be driving back to Atlanta first thing in the morning along with Reverend Abernathy and will join us as soon as he arrives back in town. I believe our business is complete for today and Reverend Steele will you close this session out with prayer?"

Like all the others, I bowed my head out of respect for the prayer but my mind drifted and I heard very little of Reverend Steele's closing. I had just experienced the making of history, the creation of an organization that would take the lead in the battle to eradicate segregation in our country. I thought that much of the same process took place back in 1909 when a small group of concerned citizens gathered to create the NAACP. Only time will tell if this movement can be just as effective as the NAACP had been over the past fifty years.

It was mid-day Friday that Martin finally made an appearance at the conference. I had taken my seat at the back of the church and didn't have the opportunity to greet him when he entered sanctuary. He came in from a side door and immediately addressed the other ministers.

"I apologize to this distinguished gathering of my fellow men of the cloth," he began. "But as you all know by now, we had considerable damage done to a number of our houses of worship just the other night. There were six bombings and the parish of Reverend Graetz was the most damaged. But I am here to report to you all that not one person was injured in all the destruction." He paused to allow his words to resonate. "Do you all hear me, not one hair on one person was harmed. God is good."

"Amen, God is good," the ministers responded in unison.

"Let this be a sign unto you. God is truly our protector. He permits men the freedom to do evil. He also has His way to protect His children."

Another chorus of Amens accompanied Martin's testimony to the goodness of God. What he said next touched me deeply.

"Despite the violent actions of our white brethren, we must continue to adhere to the principles of non-violence as we move from this place to confront evil wherever it exists. We must call upon our people to accept Christian Love in full knowledge of its power to defy evil. Non-violence is not a symbol of weakness or cowardice, but, as Jesus and Gandhi demonstrated, nonviolent resistance transforms weakness into strength and breeds courage in the face of danger."

In less than a year, Martin had become a complete and thorough disciple of the non- violent philosophy not just as a tactic but as a way life.

It was now deeply embedded in his heart and he could not turn back now. His approach as a leader of the most important movement at the time was Gandhian-like, and I felt good knowing that I had planted that initial seed with him that night I told him to remove the gun from the chair and to instruct his body guards to no longer come to his home armed.

Martin continued, "The first action of the Southern Christian Leadership Conference will be three telegrams to be sent off this afternoon by Reverend Steele. The first will go to President Dwight Eisenhower from all sixty members urging him to make a public speech advocating compliance with the 1954 Brown Supreme Court decision, and pledging the support of his office for total desegregation of the schools throughout the South. We shall also send a second telegram to Vice President Richard Nixon to take a tour of the South and view firsthand the violence against Negroes. And finally, a third telegram will be directed to the United States Attorney General Herbert Brownell, urging him to meet with acknowledged Negro leaders to discuss ways that the Federal Government can take action to prevent the ongoing violence against the Negro."

Martin paused as the sanctuary exploded with applause and Amens. "We will give our government officials one month from today to respond and when we meet next month in New Orleans, if we don't receive the answer that we deserve, then we will plan to take further action."

Martin hurried down from the podium and positioned himself right in front of the first pew where many of the leaders of the new organization were sitting. As he began to speak, his delivery took on that very special ability of a Baptist preacher to allow the words to roll out with a slow and deliberate melodic tone. "Let it be known to the entire world that a new day is dawning in the South, and a determined people will not tolerate the abuses of the past one hundred years not another day. Montgomery was a good start. But that's all it was, a good start." He again paused took in a deep breath and continued. "My brothers of the cloth, God has given us direct instructions to use our commitment to Christian love and our dedication to peaceful non-violent change to make a difference. We will show so much strength to our adversary, that they can do nothing else but surrender. We are on the road to great and beautiful things and we must remain focused until the job is done."

As I listened to Martin close out the two-day session, it occurred to me that I had just participated in the most important meeting taking place in the country at that time. Sixty Black ministers voted to establish an association dedicated to the eradication of segregation throughout the South, based on a non-violent approach. The Christian principles of love and passivity had merged with the Gandhian tactic and strategy of non-violence and these men pledged to stand firm, even in the face of death if necessary. Finally, in carrying out their mission they pledged that not one hair on one white person will be harmed. After a final prayer, the ministers adjourned and headed out of the church.

I waited with Ella right outside the church for Martin to finally make his way out. After about forty-five minutes, he finally made his way over to where we stood.

"I can't thank you all enough for what you have done," he said. He shook my hand and hugged Ella. "Next month in New Orleans, we'll select all the officers and also I'm going to nominate you for the executive director," he said looking directly at me.

"I don't think that'll be a good idea," I immediately shot back. "You seem to forget that the majority of those sixty ministers are not as progressive in their thinking as you are."

"But you deserve the position," Ella added. "This never would've happened without you, Bayard."

"I am very content to do my part without a lot of attention and fanfare," I offered. "Martin, the last problem you need is a bunch of ministers attacking you for backing me for that position. They view this as a very Christian controlled and oriented association, and you know as well as I do how they would respond with a sinner in charge."

"Ella's right, this is your baby and you need to be involved in its early growth," Martin said. "I will nominate you in February for the position."

"Are you ready for your first fight?" I asked as we finally made our way down the steps and joined Coretta at the bottom. "Because it will definitely be a battle."

"You are the greatest and most qualified student of non-violence as a tactic for change in this country and we have pledged to never harm a hair on a soul, which is a pretty strong commitment to your way of thinking, and you should be out front to lead it."

Bobby pulled the car out front and Ella, Coretta and I climbed in the back seat while Martin sat up front with Bobby. As we pulled away Martin said,

"Back in 1935 Dr. Howard Thurman, the great preacher and leader for years, while in India asked Gandhi to come to America, not for white America, but to help the Negro in his fight for civil rights." King paused for a moment probably to allow us to ponder where he was going with this story. "Gandhi told Dr. Thurman that he would love to, but first he had to make good with his message in India before bringing it to this country. What is key and very prophetic was his final words. He prophesied that it might be through the Negro in America where the unadulterated message of non-violence will be delivered to the world." He finished, turned to the back, and said while looking directly at me. "You are God's choice to make Gandhi's prophesy come true."

23.

The hectic schedule of the past two days left me totally exhausted. After Martin dropped us off at the Atlanta Airport, we just did get to the gate before it closed, and the plane sat on the run way for an hour because the weather in the New York vicinity was too turbulent to allow planes to land. We arrived well after midnight and a little after one o'clock I finally opened the door to the apartment and made my way inside. For some reason Arthur failed to leave a light on for me, something he usually did when he knew I'd be getting home late. I found the switch on the wall and the ceiling light illuminated the room. For a moment, I didn't know if I should plop down in a chair and take a deep breath of relief or keep going straight to the bedroom. I decided on the second option, turned the light off and stumbled into the bedroom. Arthur lay on his side asleep. I was in no mood for romance. I got undressed and climbed into the bed.

I just wanted to sleep but suddenly Arthur had different plans for us. Without a word, he began to rub my back and my entire body just relaxed as I could feel the tension leaving my body. His hands continued to wander all down my legs, and he moved in very close and I felt the wetness of his mouth against my skin. His hands finally softly rubbed between my legs. Normally this aroused me to the point that I would turn and face him and begin kissing his lips and all over his body. But not this night. The need for rest outweighed my desire for sex. I pushed his hand just as he began caressing my erection.

"Not tonight, Arthur," I said without turning to face him.

"Are you serious," he shrieked. "What's wrong with you Bayard? You never turn me down and for that matter probably no one else laying naked in the bed with you."

"Occasionally, Arthur, the body will crave rest more so than sex," I said. "This happens to be one of those times."

Without turning to face him, I instinctively knew that he had moved away from me back on his side of the bed.

"Every once in a while, the normal, average person will need to bypass a night of sex, but not you Bayard," he said dryly. "Not you, the one gay man whose reputation precedes him. I have never known you to turn down the opportunity to enjoy someone between your legs. What is it? Were you with someone else while in Atlanta?"

I abruptly turned to face Arthur with his back to me. I grabbed him by the shoulder and forced him to turn and look at me.

"No, I wasn't with someone simply because I wouldn't have had the time, and I have no desire to engage in short one night stands any longer."

"You did in Pasadena and that was only three years ago, how do I know that those three years have made that big a difference in your life?"

"Why are you doing this?" I stared straight ahead refusing to make eye contact with Arthur. Something seriously bothered him, and this had been going on now for quite a while. He seemed determined to engage in confrontations with me regardless of the circumstances. "Is it you don't like the direction my life is going?"

"Please don't get all dramatic with me. Let's just drop it."

"No, I don't think we should just drop it," I grimaced. "Are you not happy in this relationship?" Without waiting for his answer, I got out of bed, grabbed my pants lying across a chair on my side of the bed and slipped them on. "I need to think." I refused to look back at Arthur. Instead, I grabbed my lute propped against the wall, and walked to the living room and closed the door behind me.

Davis Platt had sent me the instrument while I served my three-year prison term back in 1944. I learned to play it without ever taking a lesson. Same was true for the harpsichord in the living room. Music was therapeutic for me and right at that moment I needed some therapy. It became clearer every day that Arthur and I needed to seriously consider bringing our relationship to a close. We had drifted apart over the past year.

I began to pluck the strings on the flute and allowed the tune to develop. Bach's "Ave Maria" resonated throughout the room. Arthur's caustic reference to the Pasadena incident struck me like a sledgehammer across the body. He knew how sensitive I felt about that mistake I had made. In my most intimate moments, I had cried and shared the shame I felt about that situation. He used it as a tool to destroy my excuse for refusing his advancement. I felt betrayed and would find it very difficult to forget that transgression of our love for each other.

As the two of us continued to drift apart, I couldn't allow this failure in my personal life to interfere with the challenge I felt, as I was now an intricate part of the most historical movement in the country. Though my role relegated me to the shadows of the major leadership under Martin, my work in the background became more critical as the cause moved to the forefront of the major events in the country. I felt practically hypnotic and I knew I could probably fall asleep right there playing and enjoying Bach. I finally reached the point that I had trouble keeping my eyes open. I didn't want to go back into the bedroom for fear that Arthur was still awake. So, I placed the lute on the end table, stretched out on the couch and drifted into sleep.

"Who the hell does that country preacher think he is?" Roy Wilkins bellowed inside Mr. Randolph's Office.

I sat in the chair next to him. Mr. Randolph sat behind his desk and just listened as the head of the NAACP let off some steam.

"He pretty much told the press that legal remedies to civil rights issues had passed and the only alternative is to take to the streets in social protest."

"Come on Roy, that's not what he said," Randolph said as he leaned forward placing his outstretched arms on his desk. "He suggested that maybe it was time to explore alternative ways to defeat segregation."

"Damnit Phil, why are you always so condescending to every two-bit leader who thinks he can take over the movement?"

"That's kind of harsh, Roy," Randolph responded. "Legal remedies have certainly served us well over the past forty years. And it's because of the NAACP's excellent work that we finally were able to get the dreadful **Plessy versus Ferguson** decision overturned."

"And that's exactly why our strategy is the best," Roy said having somewhat cooled down. "What kind of man is King?" Roy asked looking at me. "You've spent some time with him so what's your assessment?"

"He is a brilliant, charismatic preacher who has the people rallying to him as no one person has done since Booker T. Washington," I suggested.

"You're not helping the cause here, Bayard," Randolph said.

"I'm sorry but this is not a time for bruised egos. Events are happening at lightning speed and all our concentration must be how we in New York can help." I caught the glimpse of displeasure aimed at me. I just didn't have the kind of tact that Mr. Randolph possessed.

"As head of the NAACP, you're going to have to work with him," Randolph said. "No one will forget all the good accomplishments the Negro has enjoyed as a result of your organization. But Roy, we must think clearly on this matter. We can't afford to show resentment towards each other, or they'll have a field day."

Roy became more adamant. "Phil, that group down there acts like it was their boycott that finally brought Montgomery to its knees and ended segregation," he said. "It wasn't that boycott or King's flowery speeches about non-violence and Christian principles, it was the United States Supreme Court ruling that segregation on the buses was unconstitutional and it was our lawyers that helped argue the case." He paused to allow his words to resonate. "But all the press and all the credit went to Dr King and his associates."

"Does it matter who gets the credit as long as we achieve our goals?" I asked.

"For money raising issues and recruitment to the organization, yes it does matter," Roy quickly replied. "And look at the damage they've done to our organization," he continued. "All of our local offices have been forced to close because the state has outlawed all organizations that exist for the purpose of eliminating segregation. And my State Representative Medgar Evers has even taken a position with the new association."

"That's not the case with the new association," I suggested, deliberately ignoring his concern for Medgar's new association with the SCLC.

"They're considered a Christian organization and therefore are protected by the First Amendment," Roy explained.

"Will you please just sit down with Dr. King here in New York and let's work out these differences," Randolph asked.

"Because of you Phil, I'll do that," Roy said. "But just because of you. I am not about to succumb to a bunch of Baptist preachers who only recently discovered there is a race problem and we need to save souls here on earth as well as for heaven."

"Bayard, can you set up the meeting here in New York at this office?" Randolph looked at me.

Bringing Martin to New York to deal with the heavy weights in the civil rights movement would be like feeding the lamb to the lions I thought. His initial exposure outside of saving souls for heaven, as Roy put it, was the bus protest and there was unanimity among all the participants. No one jockeyed for position and control. King was not at that level yet and he just might get devoured by the leadership outside of the South. Mr. Randolph was rather naïve in that he only saw the good in people. I recognized that other side to Roy and the other leaders who would be in that meeting.

"Bayard, can you do that?" Randolph repeated his request.

"When?" I asked.

"As soon as we can get Dr. King to New York? Is there something wrong? You seem rather reluctant about the idea?"

I was but I couldn't discuss it with Roy Wilkens sitting in the chair next to me. Instead I said, "Not at all. I'll call him today and find out what's good for him."

"Please don't misinterpret my position," Roy said. "I respect what Dr. King has accomplished in Montgomery, and we showed him our appreciation for his efforts when we invited him to speak at the National Convention last summer. His speech went over well, but I am not sure that our members believe protest is the right way to accomplish our goals."

"That's why we meet and discuss these issues," Randolph said.

"Exactly who should I tell him will be attending this meeting and how about his lieutenants like Abernathy, we going to invite them also?" I asked.

"Since we plan to consolidate leadership from both the North and South, I believe we should open it up for as many leaders in both the civil rights and union movements. It is imperative that we bring those groups under one accord." Randolph stood up behind his desk and Roy and I followed suit, also getting to our feet.

"Just keep in mind as we move forward, that my organization is the grandfather of all civil rights organizations, and I expect it to be treated with the proper respect as the elder in the group."

"No problem, NAACP deserves that respect although I've always had a serious problem with the manner that our great scholar and leader for years was treated," Randolph said as he now walked around his desk and stood next to us.

"Obviously, you're speaking of Dr. Du Bois," Roy said.

"He is a great man and has been mistreated by this country and by many of the new leaders," I added. "We all are beneficiaries in many ways of his hard work over the past fifty years."

"I'd be interested in knowing how some of the early pioneers in the civil rights movement, men like James Weldon Johnson and Dr. Du Bois, would view this switch from fighting for legal remedies to taking to the street in protest," Randolph quipped.

"We all know how Booker T. Washington would have viewed it," I suggested. "He'd have spoken out against what happened in Montgomery."

"Just remember there are a whole lot of Booker T. Washington's still around," Roy advised. "And we have a lot of them right in the NAACP. This is going to be a hard sell for me, but let's just see what happens moving forward."

"Dr. King has called for a second meeting of the SCLC next week in New Orleans and he has asked me to be there. I'll approach him on the idea of the meeting at that time," I said.

"Got to get back to the office," Roy said. "Please let me know the outcome, and if we plan to meet exactly when." He finished and walked out of the office.

Mr. Randolph and I remained inside his office. After Roy closed the door, he signaled for me to sit back down and he took the other chair. He reached out and took hold of my arm.

"Bayard, do you know how deep you are in as a key player in this entire movement?" he asked.

"I kind of get that feeling," I answered curious as to where he planned to go with this conversation.

"And you know I look upon you just like a son?'

"Yes." I now knew where he planned to take this conversation which probably could best be described as a miniature lecture.

"Consolidating the entire civil rights movement is now in your hands. You must bring those preachers, those outside the church and the atheists, as well as the agnostics, all together for one cause and that is the Negro cause. You cannot afford any mistakes as you made in the past. Do you understand?"

"I understand and I know the point you are making."

"Good, then I need not say anymore. Go get this job done for the country." He finished, stood back up and I followed him out of his office.

24.

Martin called the meeting to order right at nine in the morning at Reverend A. L. Davis' New Zion Baptist Church in New Orleans, Louisiana on February 14, Valentine's Day. I had caught a very early morning flight out of LaGuardia, and because of the one-hour time difference between New York and New Orleans, I arrived there right at eight o'clock, grabbed a cab and made it to the church fifteen minutes before the gathering began. Ministers, all wearing dark suits, white shirts and dark ties, from all over the South, filled the first 3 rows of the pews. That seemed to be a standard dress for Baptist Ministers when not wearing their robes.

King stood at the podium with Abernathy, Steele and Gardner Taylor behind him. Taylor was probably the only minister there not from the South. I found a seat at the back of the church. I considered my function to be an observer and nothing more. Why Martin insisted I be there I didn't know but would soon find out.

After Taylor delivered an opening prayer, Martin got right down to business.

"As I call your name, I want you to stand and be recognized. Reverend Steele who is now first vice-president." Steele stepped forward from behind Martin to be acknowledged. King continued, "Reverend Davis second vice-president, Reverend Samuel Williams from Atlanta third vice-president, Reverend Jemison from Baton Rouge, secretary, and the only non-pastor Medgar Evers from Jackson, Mississippi, assistant secretary, and Reverend Abernathy, treasurer."

Abernathy moved forward from the back and stood next to Steele. "My brothers, these are the officers for the new association and will represent us as Christian ministers in the image of Jesus Christ our Savior. God bless all these men and God bless all of you who have taken the time to come here to New Orleans to help the Southern Christian Leadership Conference get off to a great start. Let's give ourselves a good round of applause."

All the ministers stood and clapped for what seemed like five minutes.

"Our next piece of business today is to choose an Executive Director to run the day-to- day operations of this new organizations. And I have the man just perfect for the job." Martin paused for a moment to allow the others to wonder who that person might be. He then pointed to the back of the room at me. "Bayard Rustin will you please come forward."

Immediately and before I got to the front, the grumbling began. I finally reached the podium and stood next to Martin.

Martin held his arm high in the air and out of respect the grumbling stopped. "This man has done more to help our cause here in the South than any other individual. He came to Montgomery and introduced the concept of non-violence as a tactic to defeat our enemies. He has helped us to integrate our Christian principle of love with the Gandhian concept, and it worked perfectly in Montgomery. He then took on the chore of laying out a planned structure of how we can…"

"But he's a queer," someone shouted from the audience. "And we don't want him associated with this Christian organization. This would be an abomination against Christ who made it very clear that homosexuality is a sin against God."

"You're right Reverend Jones, but adultery is a sin against God also. How many of you could participate in this Christian organization if that was a rule for admission," Dr. King replied.

"Dr. King, we respect your leadership and what you've managed to do, but there is no way one hundred Baptist ministers can agree that a homosexual should run our organization," another minister shouted.

"Then I imagine many of you need to return to your churches and remove your choir directors and organists," King shot back.

Pandemonium was about to break out in the church as ministers commenced to discuss this crisis among themselves. What had begun as a unified group of men with no dissension, had now been reduced to a bunch of shouting matches, all aimed at Martin who stood there trying to defend his support for me.

Another minister in the front row held his Bible high in the air and shouted, "Martin, you need to go back and read your Bible again. I'm sure you studied the issue of homosexuality in school. Genesis 19, Leviticus 18 to 20, Romans 1: 18 to 32, Corinthians 6, 9 through 10 and Timothy 1, 8 through 10 teach us that homosexuality is an abomination and those who participate in it will never make it to heaven."

"Brother, I don't mean to get into a long debate about passages from the Bible," Martin rejoined. "But in many of those same passages from Paul, he also tells us that adultery, stealing and lying are sins. How can you equate one as being worse than the others? Now can I continue to tell you why I believe this man should be our Executive Director?"

"No," resounded throughout the sanctuary.

"Martin our association was formed as a civil rights group and homosexuality is not a civil rights issue, it's a gay rights issue, much different." A minister sitting in the second row stood and shouted. "Certainly, you can find a heterosexual Black man who can serve in that position since he will be representing all of us."

I'd had just about enough of this rhetoric with no meaning and substance. I turned to Martin and was prepared to tell him that I had no interest in representing this group or these men with such negative and ugly perceptions of a segment of our society. But before I could speak up, he responded to the man and I really liked what I heard.

"The Southern Leadership Conference was founded on the basic principle of human rights not just civil rights. Human rights have a greater dimension and encompasses all levels of human behavior of one man toward another." He paused for a response but evidently the ministers decided to let him have his say and remained reticent. "There is no difference in a gay white man being beaten and bludgeoned by the Ku Klux Klan than when it is a black man and let me assure you the Klan dislikes our gay brothers as much as they dislike us."

It was now up to me to rescue Martin from the travesty. I didn't want to be the reason for dissension in the group. They needed a consensus coming out of this meeting and I was the one who could make sure that happened. I leaned toward Martin and said.

"I don't want the job."

He turned and looked at me with a perplexed expression. "What?"

"It's much too restrictive and I can serve you in a much more expansive role, so just let it go."

"Do you want to say something to the group?"

"No, what I might say could cause trouble with me working with you going forward and we have very big challenges before us." I wanted to clear the air on this matter, because one of those challenges confronting me was to get him to New York for that critical meeting with Roy Wilkins and the others. This seemed rather miniscule in comparison.

"What are you going to do Martin?" a minister asked.

"I'm going to withdraw Bayard's name for consideration, and I suggest we look to someone within the association who might have the time, even with his pastor responsibility, to do the job."

I stepped down from the podium and hurried to the back of the room. I noticed that not one of the ministers looked in my direction as I made my way down the aisle. Guilt can haunt you like a bad dream. Their treatment toward me was unnecessary. But I chose to be a much bigger person than those one hundred men, who displayed a prejudice against a Black man who happened to be gay. To me that was a double indictment of them as ministers and Black men also. My initial inclination was to keep walking right on out and to the airport. But I promised Mr. Randolph that I would arrange the meeting between Roy and Martin, so I had to sit there and endure the insults that had been inflicted on me.

"Brothers, our next business is to discuss the fact that the President, Vice-President and Attorney General all turned down our requests for their involvement in this new and important movement in the South."

Martin's announcement caught me by surprise and tweaked my curiosity. I quickly dismissed what had just happened and tuned in on what he was about to tell the group.

"Therefore, I am suggesting that the Southern Leadership Conference take on a march on the nation's capital as our first major project. We need to gather right on the grounds of the mall in front of the Lincoln Monument and express our disappointment in the President. I believe we should call on all other concerned organizations to join us in this endeavor. After all, this issue impacts most groups that represent the poor and minorities of this country. We shall call it a Prayer Pilgrimage for Freedom. Are you all with me?"

"Yes," resounded. Martin received positive affirmation of his planned march.

With that response, I knew I did the right thing by taking my name out of consideration for the Executive Director. They would still be fighting that battle with no clear winner. Because at this point in their early growth, they needed a cause that had practically one hundred percent support, and he just got that. The meeting with Roy loomed now even more critical. To pull off this march, Martin would need the support of the NAACP, because it would be his first venture outside of the deep South and into Roy's territory, but the nature of the meeting had to be altered. I had to wait until this all ended and hopefully spend a few hours alone with Martin. He owed me that much. I'd rescued him from a battle he might easily have lost and that could have damaged his leadership with this minister laden association.

After five interviews with various reporters from both white and black newspapers, and after shaking hands with every minister who had showed up for this session, Martin finally made it to where I still sat at the back of the sanctuary. Abernathy trailed right along with him.

"Bayard, I don't quite know how to express my disappointment in the behavior of the other ministers in there this morning," Martin said.

I didn't get up while he and Abernathy remained standing. "It is what it is," I offered as a weak explanation as to how I felt about the rejection I received, from the very people who were there because of my hard work. However, the one lesson I learned well from my Quaker grandmother was to never carry a grudge. It will only weigh you down and prevent you from moving forward. "Are you in a hurry?"

"I need to get to the airport because I have a seven o'clock flight back to Montgomery, but I know we need to talk because I'm going to depend on you to help organize this prayer pilgrimage."

I didn't quite know if I should take that as a compliment or insult after what happened earlier in the day. He now wanted to suggest that I help organize an event that will make men, who had just trashed me because of my personal life, look good. But Grandma's admonishments over the years about grudge took control.

"I have a nine o'clock flight back to New York so maybe we can ride to the airport together and have the opportunity to talk," I suggested.

"That's just perfect," Martin said. "Reverend Davis has one of his cars waiting for me in front of the church. Let's head on out so we can get going."

The three of us sauntered out to the front steps of the church and met Reverend Davis. He surprisingly grabbed my hand and vigorously shook it.

"Mr. Rustin, I want you to know that we all appreciate everything you have done for us and believe me, we are very much aware of your contribution," he said.

I had a strong inclination to resist his gesture of gratitude, but then I thought of Grandma. "Thank you, Reverend Davis." While shaking his hand and listening to his words of gratitude, I looked beyond him at the long stretch of Cadillacs waiting for us. My thoughts recalled Amzie Moore in Mississippi and his comment about the ministers down there who all had big Cadillacs.

He obviously detected my lack of enthusiasm and released his grip on my hand and turned to talk with Martin. After hesitating at the top step, we all started down to the car.

"Reverend King you have now become more than just a preacher and pastor at a local southern church, you are now the leader of what can easily become the most important civil rights association in the South and maybe in the country," Reverend Davis said.

"We must always be aware that we are all about human dignity for all men and not just civil rights for a select group of minorities," Martin said.

I figured that was meant for me.

"You're exactly right Reverend and you are the right person for this job," Reverend Davis concurred. He stopped right at the front of the steps while we continued to the car.

The driver jumped out of the driver's seat, ran around to our side and opened both the driver's side door and the back door. Dr. King climbed in the front seat, and Abernathy and I took the back seat. The driver then hurried back around, got back in the car and without any further delay pulled off into the traffic.

Martin turned his body around in order to talk directly to me. "Bayard, I'm going to need the support of all the major organizations up North to participate in the pilgrimage, so I was hoping that you could set up a meeting in Washington, D. C. with the key players in the next week or so."

That fast, he just wiped out my need to get him to New York. This meeting would take precedence over all other possibilities. Now the meeting would not be with Roy and a few other New York leaders, but with as many leaders in the civil rights movement and in the unions and not in New York, but Washington, D.C.

He continued, "Roy Wilkins at the NAACP is going to be very important and it is mandatory that we get him on board right away. I'm assuming that we'll have no problem with Phil, and I don't know where James Farmer will come down on this idea. But through your good work, we'll soon find out if they're with us or not."

It now occurred to me that I had just been taken by a southern preacher almost twenty years younger than me.

"I'll be more than happy to take on this assignment," I exaggerated. "In the morning, I'll talk with Mr. Randolph who will be overjoyed that a movement on Washington, similar to his back in 1941 was really going to happen. As for Roy and the others, I'll contact them and strongly urge that they meet with you.

"Don't strongly urge," Martin shot back. "Insist."

"I'll do my best," I said as I noticed the drop off for United Airlines coming up. "I can get out right here." The young driver pulled over to the curb and as I got out, I shook Abernathy's hand and leaned forward and shook hands with Martin.

"We must work as a team, Bayard. Please put behind you what happened earlier at the church," Martin said. "I need you and will depend on your wisdom and knowledge as we get more involved in shifting the ground that we stand on."

"I'll be on top of this first thing in the morning." I finished, closed the door and headed into the terminal. It didn't quite happen the way I planned it, but I did accomplish my goal and that was a meeting between the old guard civil rights leader and the new man on the block.

25.

"I don't know if this is a good idea," Randolph said from behind his desk at the office in Harlem. I sat on the other side in the same chair I occupied only a few days earlier. "What's Martin trying to do, challenge Roy right on his turf?"

"Not at all," I said leaning forward in my chair. "In fact, he has the greatest amount of respect for Roy to the point that I believe he might feel just a little intimidated by him. Roy has all the history behind him, and Martin is new to this game."

"Why is he coming right into the man's territory? They have Clarence Mitchell working the Congress all the time and I believe he has a decent reputation with Eisenhower. And then there is Powell. I don't believe that last meeting between them went that smoothly. When you get on that man's turf it can only mean trouble."

"That's why it's important that you throw your full support behind the march and that you convince the others to also support it," I said to the very man who could make all these disparate parts fit together.

"Martin and his gang represent a generational shift in the tactics used by Negroes, different from what the majority of the people are used to." Randolph placed his hand under his chin, something he did when in deep contemplation.

"The approach must change from what's been for almost a half-century," I said while he appeared to be in deep thought. "Martin's social justice through peaceful non-violence adds a way over-due balance to the one-dimensional approach of Roy and all the lawyers, who believe progress can only come through the courts."

"Question is will that approach work outside the South and on how large a scale?" Randolph questioned. "The Montgomery experiment was restricted to only one medium- sized city with a minimal size Negro population. It did not extend beyond the boundaries of that city and they rallied around a cause that had practically one hundred percent support."

"No doubt, Martin and his group of southern ministers cannot make this happen without a great deal of help, and that help starts with you and Roy," I said with strong emphasis on Mr. Randolph.

"So, they are really prepared to flex their muscles and take on a nationwide pilgrimage to Washington?" Randolph stood and I knew he was about to end the conversation. "Yes, I'll give you all the support you need, because I do believe this will be a test of your ability to pull this off and finally build your reputation as a legitimate Negro leader."

"Once we get the momentum going on this project and schedule a press conference, I don't think Roy will want to be left out, especially if we have Farmer from CORE and the Urban League on board," I suggested. "On the other hand, his biggest challenge will come from the Negro Baptist ministers in some of the larger Northern cities. They will not look kindly on a bunch of southern ministers invading their turf and stealing their thunder."

"That could be a problem, especially with Reverend Jackson out of Chicago who, from what I understand, acts like a dictator over the National Baptist Convention. None of the ministers dare to challenge him."

"There is only one minister who bothers me and that is our friend over there in Harlem," I said. "And there is one important quality that all ministers should possess, and he doesn't and that is forgiveness."

"I'll handle Adam." Randolph strolled to the other side of his desk and stood staring down at me still in the chair. "Is this something you're up to doing?"

"As long as you're out front with the other leaders, I can do all the leg work, and with Ella and Stanley lay out a plan to make this work." I now stood up. "Back in 1941 when I first met you, I was thrilled to be working on your project to bring a half million Negroes to Washington to protest discrimination in defense factories. We never pulled that one off and now we have that opportunity." We both strolled over to the door, opened it and stepped into the lobby area. "I'm anxious to get this done for Martin, who deserves the national recognition and for you because you never did receive the same kind of recognition back then."

"And do it for yourself, Bayard. Show these bigots and hypocrites that they don't know the extent of your talents because they can't get beyond the limits of their minds."

We hugged, something we seldom did, and I headed out of the building onto the street in Harlem. I needed to get my team that had assisted in the creation of the Southern Leadership Association back together, and structure the prayer pilgrimage to Washington D.C.

It was after eight in the evening when we all assembled in Stan's office. Ella, Stan, Tom, and Rachelle sat listening as I explained the project and they winced when I also told them that Dr. King and Mr. Randolph wanted to pull this off on May 17, the same day three years earlier that the United States Supreme Court handed down the historical decision in the Brown V. Board of Education.

"We only have three months to pull this off," Stan said. "I don't know if we have enough time to make this a success, and since this is the first event outside the South for Dr. King we can't afford to fail."

"And that's why you have to find out where the money is." I smiled at Stan. No doubt he knew where to go get the money in New York and this time it was critical that he come through for us. "Ella and I will concentrate on the overall strategy and the tedious job of organizing the march. Can you imagine how difficult that's going to be with a bunch of preachers and politicians all vying for headline time?" My thoughts for just a couple seconds flashed back to Congressman Powell across the street at a bar while we nervously waited for his arrival at the Garden. "And add to potential turmoil, you going to have a bunch of southern Baptist preachers lined up against men like Powell. It's going to be interesting if nothing else."

"What can we do?" Tom finally spoke up.

"Rachelle, you're going to work closely with Ella and Tom you just stick with me and I'll have plenty of work for you," I instructed.

"Do you know how big this can be?" Ella finally spoke up. "With all the giants in the Negro movement in this country and you have one white man with a strong communist affiliation, a Black woman, a gay Black man and two college kids planning the first major march on the nation's capital in this century. If successful, how do you think they'll record it in history?"

"Can't you say the same about the formation of the Southern Christian Leadership Conference?" Stan suggested.

"Exactly," I said. "But let's not worry about how history might look on us, let's just get this done and I'm sure the historians will take care of the rest."

"Let's go make history starting early tomorrow morning," Stan said. "I'll be here by eight and welcome any early bird."

"I'll bring donuts," Ella added.

"Let's do it," I said. "Tomorrow morning at eight. Right now, I'm getting out of here and going home for some well-deserved rest."

"Anything you need me to do, I'm free to come with you?" Tom quipped.

I momentarily stared at him, ignoring the others in the room. He was still troubled and looking to me for his out. "Not tonight," I said. "Don't stress, believe me, you and I will be spending a great deal of time together in the next two months." I felt compelled to provide him with some encouragement.

We all got up and headed out of the office onto West 57th Street. I flagged down a cab and jumped in the backseat. "West Village," I instructed the driver. Contrary to what I had told the others, rest was the very last thing on my mind. I knew my relationship with Arthur was no longer certain for the future and felt compelled to visit one of the up and coming gay clubs in the village.

It had been at least six months since I'd spent an evening in Julius Bar, the go to place for the fast-growing Gay community in New York. For a while the owners had fought the transition from straight to gay and would often call the police if they detected men there just to cruise. For years, the owners forced gays to look away from the rest of the patrons for fear they would offend someone by making a pass at them. Before my relationship with Arthur, I had done some cruising and engaged in several satisfactory sexual affairs. But since my accelerating involvement in the civil rights movement and a growing relationship with Dr. King, I had refrained from that kind of activity. Pasadena was always in the back of my mind. Determined to never make that mistake again, I strolled inside the bar and down the narrow hallway through a crowd, some standing at the old wooden bar and others sitting at tables made of barrels.

"Bayard, over here."

I looked to the left at the end of the bar and smiled. I had met Harry Hay and Dale Jennings on one of my trips to Los Angeles a few years ago. They signaled me over to their table.

"Bayard, how are you my friend?" Harry asked as he and Dale both stood, and we hugged. I then took a chair at their table. "It's been a while. I haven't seen you since Pasadena."

"I'm doing really well," I said. "What brings you all to New York?"

"Let me grab you a drink," Harry got up. "What's your pleasure?"

"Scotch and soda," I said.

"Got it." He hurried over to the bar.

"You know. We share something in common besides being two gay men," Dale said. He then leaned half-way across the table. "You were arrested back in 1953 in Pasadena and I was arrested in 1952 in Los Angeles. They charged me with solicitation of an undercover policeman, but I fought the charge on the grounds of entrapment and won." He paused to let his story register with me.

"While serving my time in California, Harry came to visit me," I said. "He told me about your situation and wanted to know if I was interested in pursuing the same course of action. To be quite honest with you, I told him no."

"And that's why I planned to contact you before I left New York. I wanted to know why a fighter like you wouldn't take on the system. Why you chose to serve out your sentence, and not challenge the conviction based on entrapment?"

Harry returned to the table and placed the drinks down. He then sat in the chair. It was timely because it provided me with a few needed moments to collect my thoughts and respond to Dale. But first I took a sip from the scotch and soda.

"I can assure you that I am not ashamed of who I am, not as a Negro nor as a homosexual. But I was ashamed of the reason for going to jail.

It was definitely entrapment, but I allowed it to happen and should have been much wiser." I paused for a sip. "I admire the stance you took in California and you probably did make a difference in how the gay community is treated as opposed to the hetero. But you must realize that I was out there representing an organization and I let them down. That was not good, and I only wanted it to end as quickly as possible."

"Dale's actions led to the first attempt to organize the homosexual community in this country to fight for their civil rights also," Harry added to the conversation. "But Bayard, no one is questioning you for what you felt was right in your situation. And our entire community is proud of what you've done over the past year with Dr. King in Montgomery. It is important that we have our people involved in activities that highlight our extreme ability, to do other than just lay in the bed with another man."

"What's happening with the Mattachine Society?" I asked. "I know you two are part of the group that put the association together, so what's happening?"

"You're right, I was one of the founders but no longer associate with the group," Harry said also taking a drink from a glass filled with beer. "I didn't create the group as an assimilationist group, trying to fit in with the majority society. You see I don't believe we should spend our time, resources and energy just to adopt the cultural traits of the heterosexual world. We are out here seeking their societal acceptance, instead of viewing ourselves with a cultural identity that has a greater humanity than what we're fighting to become."

"Not quite sure I agree with you," I said. "No need for us to stay in the closet or better still underground, having affairs in the park and the backseat of cars or in theaters, places where we are perfect targets for the police."

"That's just what I don't quite understand about Negroes," Harry guffawed. "You people trying to be like the very people who been lynching and killing you for centuries, not to mention making slaves out of your ancestors. And now you down in Montgomery with Dr. King talking about wanting to sit next to some white person on a bus."

I had a great deal of respect for Harry, so his loud and boisterous behavior didn't bother me at all. He was such a strong advocate for the gay community in Los Angeles, I couldn't do anything but admire his courage. The same held true for Dale. Despite our differences on the direction the community should take, we still had a strong friendship and admiration between us.

"Harry's got a point," Dale joined back into the discussion. "Take that Brown V. Board of Education decision by the courts over three years ago and the white folks still haven't integrated the schools. You all keep begging to let you in and they're still saying hell no to you all, and to the court. Why are you struggling so hard to be a part of that?"

"You see the major difference between our two minority groups is that you all have allowed the white people to brain wash you into believing that you are not equal to them," Harry said. "And for some reason, you all have accepted that lie. We in the homosexual community will not allow them to de-humanize us at all."

"You don't think the homosexual community has been brainwashed also to believe something is wrong with them?" I didn't really want to have this discussion, but they pushed me to the point I had to respond to their assertions. "Then why don't they come out of the closet and be proud of who they are?" I asked.

"Security," Harry shot back at me with no hesitation. "We have to eat, hold down jobs and make sure we don't get beaten by every hetero out there, who feels it is his responsibility to beat the gayness out of us. You know the damage that Joe McCarthy has done with his witch hunts for communists and homosexuals. Just a few years ago a major airline made a concerted effort to determine if any of their employees were homosexuals."

I decided to bring this to a close. After all I had come to Julius to relax and not confront any issues. My last year had been nothing but confrontational and my home life was also becoming that way. I just wanted a few hours among friends whom I could relate with and not hold back. I lifted my glass high in the air.

"Let's toast to who we are," I said. "Our differences in no way measure up to our similarities."

Harry and Dale held their glasses high in the air. "Here's to be who we are and who we will be far into the future," Dale said.

We all drank from our glasses and it was Harry's turn to make a toast. He held his practically empty glass up again. "And let's toast to finishing these drinks, getting out of here and heading over to Harlem, a place where we can definitely be ourselves and have a great time at the Cotton Club."

26.

"I'm afraid we have a problem," Randolph said to me over the phone. He had called a little past six in the morning. After spending practically the entire night in Harlem with Harry and Dale, and consuming one too many scotch and sodas, I wasn't in the best of condition to entertain his opening line to me. It seemed that we always had a problem and spent most of our time putting out the fires. I could just imagine which fire it would be this time.

"What's the problem?" I asked rather sarcastically. "And when aren't we putting out problems."

"Talked with Roy last night and tried calling you, but Arthur informed me that you weren't in and he had no idea when you might be there," he said, paused for a moment and switched up on me. "Is everything okay between the two of you?" he asked.

"Why, what happened?" I asked instead of offering an answer.

"He seemed rather upset and his tone very sarcastic as though it was an unusual request to ask if you were home."

"Our situation is rather tense but nothing that can't be dealt with," I answered rather abruptly. I wasn't perturbed with Mr. Randolph for asking, because I knew if there was one person who really looked out for my best interest if was him. "But you said we have a problem."

"Yes, it's Roy Wilkins over at NAACP. I met with him late last evening to discuss the idea of a prayer pilgrimage. Told him that Dr. King wanted the northern coalitions to join him in sponsoring a march on Washington, D. C. sometime in the spring. I thought he'd buy off on the idea, but he expressed some serious reservations. He's going to be here in my office at ten, can you make it over here?"

"I'll be there."

"Good, I'll see you then and think of caveats we can offer Roy while showering or while on your way over here. See you then." He finished and hung up.

After hanging up with Mr. Randolph, I called Stanley and told him that I would be late getting to his office and that he should begin to develop a position paper justifying the prayer pilgrimage, and have Rachelle and Tom begin to organize a list of unions, religious institutions and any other liberal leaning group that might be willing to participate in the pilgrimage. I'd planned to ask Ella to begin making contacts with the NAACP branches throughout the South that she had assisted in organizing, but with the hesitancy on Roy's part I held back. I knew Stan would find some busy work for her until this problem was resolved. A little after nine I walked out of the apartment down to the street and flagged down a cab.

"135 West 125th Street." I instructed the driver, sat back and attempted to do what Mr. Randolph suggested, and that was come up with enough caveats for Roy Wilkins so that he would endorse and join in our effort to finally carry out a march on Washington.

Roy turned and looked back at me from the chair he occupied in front of Mr. Randolph's desk, just as I strolled into the office. He attacked right away.

"Bayard what are you doing, trying to make King the official black leader of America," he said in a cynical tone.

"Good morning to you, also," I said as I sat down in the other large chair in front of the desk. "Dr. King stands on his own and I have no special influence on what he decides he wants to do." I considered Roy a friend but sometimes his demeanor could be rather domineering and dogmatic. After last night, I wasn't in the mood to be condescending.

Mr. Randolph immediately intervened. "The idea of the gathering in the Nation's Capital was not Bayard's idea, but came out of the meeting of the Negro ministers in Atlanta in February. Evidently, they had sent a request to President Eisenhower asking him to make a statement about the violence in the South, and also supporting school integration. They received no response, so they decided, since he wouldn't come to them, they would go to him."

"I am not willing to concede the leadership role my organization has played for over fifty years here in the North and especially in Washington, D. C. with Clarence Mitchell, to a bunch of southern ministers who've decided to flex their muscles."

"Roy, we're not asking you to do that, just join with them and show that we have strength in numbers," Randolph offered.

"Let's face the fact," I began. "The center of gravity and the center of activity for the civil rights movement has shifted to the South, especially since the historical victory in Montgomery last December. In the future, most of the activity will be concentrated in the southern cities where the problem is the most blatant."

"However, keep in mind, there is no victory in Montgomery without the Supreme Court decision, and that was a result of Thurgood Marshall and other NAACP lawyers," Roy reminded us.

"But it's always the squeaky wheel that gets the oil, you know that Roy," Randolph said. "It's the yearlong boycott of the buses and the fact that Negroes were willing to walk rather than ride segregated buses, manned by abusive drivers that caught the attention of the media and the country. And Dr. King was the acknowledged leader of the boycott, so he got the credit. Roy, you've taken the lead for years, but now it might be someone else's turn. We need to let this play out and see what happens. If Dr. King and the southern ministers come north and fall flat on their faces, then the ball will be back in your court."

"I don't know Phil, it's a different ball game up here," Roy suggested as he changed subjects. "King's approach to mass direct action used in Montgomery was effective down there but may not work up here." He paused and looked at me. "And your non-violent approach is something we all would love to adhere to, but you go out there in Harlem and tell those Negroes that when a white man hits you turn to the other cheek or calls you a nigger, just smile and keep walking." He turned and looked at Mr. Randolph. "King and Bayard's approach could work in the South where our people are conditioned to accept the violence from white folks and not strike back. So that has a limited effectiveness and I don't believe it will work on a national scale."

Mr. Randolph stretched his arms across the table as if trying to touch both of us. "I have been in this game longer than any of you, and certainly longer than Dr. King who is still a very young man, and I believe that you all have room to merge both approaches for the benefit of our people."

"NAACP must come in as equal participants with the King association and there must be language in the platform that urges the President to push for school integration and also stresses the importance of voting rights for our people," Roy conceded.

"Bayard, can you and your team make sure that happens?"

"No doubt," I said.

"And I'd like the organizing for the march to take place at the NAACP headquarters here in New York."

"Is that doable, Bayard?" Again Mr. Randolph queried.

"No problem, we'll move our operation over there in the morning."

"And let me urge Phil, that you, Martin and I be co-chairs, will that also work?"

"Bayard?"

This time I smiled knowing darn well that was not my call. "You couldn't have a better team."

"My final request is that the march take place on May 17, the anniversary of the Supreme Court decision in the Brown case." Roy looked first straight at Mr. Randolph and then over at me. "Can you get Martin to agree to that date?" He asked me.

I smiled knowing that was the exact date we had in mind. "Sounds reasonable and will give him all the details later this afternoon when I talk with him."

"Good, then I think it is settled," Mr. Randolph said. "We are about to make history and Bayard, you and your team, better make sure all the I's are dotted and t's crossed. They will be looking for us to fail and we can't let that happen."

Roy got up from his chair and we followed his lead. "Let me get back over to the office and have the staff clear out a space for your team to work," he said. "Phil, you always have a way of getting your way. But I know how important this is to you and will offer my support and that of the NAACP. I'm doing this for you, and hopefully those southern ministers will not disappoint you."

"I appreciate that Roy, and I'm sure with our support it will be a success." Mr. Randolph strolled from behind his desk and patted Roy on his back and he led us out of his office.

True to his promise, Roy found room for us to work out of the NAACP Headquarters at 20 West 40th Street. The room was cramped, we had three telephones two typewriters and a window to look out on New York City whenever our labors got the best of us. Throughout the month of April, I found that I struggled with two different dilemmas. Our goal in the civil rights movement was to eventually become socialized into the larger majority community. We strove for the rights to not be discriminated in housing, transportation and education, very admirable goals. But I also struggled with Harry Hay's words to me in Julius that night I ran into him. He made it perfectly clear that as a homosexual, he had no desire to be socialized into the world of heterosexuals because he believed there was no value in the assimilation. Often as we constantly fought with the white establishment to do nothing more than hold a rally at the Lincoln Memorial, Harry's position took on greater relevance.

However, some of our most intense opposition came from right within the ranks of the Negro world. Just as we believed all was moving along smoothly and we entered the month of May, Tom came running into our small working space at the NAACP.

"Bayard, Thurgood Marshall has gone public in his attack of Dr. King," he shouted. "He's referred to Dr. King as a rebel rouser and troublemaker. Said that marching in the streets is not the way for Negroes to achieve their rights, and the gathering in Washington on May 17 will be a mistake."

Marshall's attacks did not come as a surprise to me. It only conjured up past experiences with him, when he blatantly opposed the Journey of Reconciliation of which I played a major role. After the Supreme Court decision in the Irene Morgan versus the Commonwealth of Virginia, that ruled state laws demanding segregation of interstate passengers on buses was unconstitutional, the Congress on Racial Equality and Fellowship of Reconciliation decided to sponsor a Journey of Reconciliation throughout the upper South in order to test compliance with the Supreme Court decision. I happened to be one of the sixteen men and women, both white and Negro, who boarded the buses and tested the ruling. Marshall vigorously opposed our two-week sojourn through Virginia, North Carolina, Tennessee and Kentucky. He warned that disobedient movements on the part of Negroes and our white allies would result in wholesale slaughter, with nothing good achieved. It didn't lead to a slaughter, but it did get me twenty-three days of work on the chain gang in North Carolina.

"Congressman Powell has already contacted President Eisenhower to let him know that he would do all in his power to stop the gathering." Tom snapped me out of my musing in the past. "Clarence Mitchell, the NAACP lobbyist on Capitol Hill, has also appealed to Roy Wilkins to pull his support out, because the protest might cause Southern senators to boycott the civil rights bill that's making its way through the Senate right now."

"Roy Wilkins can't afford to pull out now," I said, still thinking about Marshall and his opposition. "Powell is going to be Powell and so there's no need to worry about what he might do. And Thurgood will probably never support any movement that is not connected to the legal approach."

"I guess then that we're going to keep pushing forward," Ella said.

"Absolutely, we have a tremendous responsibility and cannot fail. Failure is not an option."

'What about the Southern Senators and their opposition?" Tom asked.

"Men like Strom Thurmond will never support any legislation that promises any kind of equal rights for any minority group in this country," I said. "Last year, Thurmond drafted what has come to be known as the Southern Manifesto claiming the decision in the Brown case in violation of the Tenth Amendment to the Constitution. Eighteen other Southern Senators also signed it. So, if they have the audacity to claim a decision of the Supreme Court is unconstitutional, there is no way we will ever get their support on any kind of civil rights legislation."

"We have less than a month and support has been pouring in from all over the country," Ella said. "We have religious groups, labor groups and everyday people who have signed up to attend."

"Just like we laid out the initial foundation for the Southern Christian Leadership Conference, we are also going to make this happen," Stanley added. "Let's get back to work and concentrate on putting the finishing touches on this project so Bayard can deliver it to Mr. Randolph, Dr. King and Roy Wilkins and we can claim another victory for the people."

"Well said." I finally sat at the desk, grabbed the phone and dialed Martin's number in Atlanta to provide him with an update report on just how well the project had progressed toward completion.

"This will be a Prayer Pilgrimage and not a protest march against the President," Mr. Randolph said while standing in front of a myriad of microphones from the various radio and television stations. Dr. King and Roy Wilkins stood right behind him. I stood to the right, along with Ella and Stanley. We had driven down to Washington, D.C. to hold the press conference announcing the Prayer Pilgrimage scheduled for May 17 right in front of the Lincoln Monument. "We are seeking to bring to the attention of the entire country, the deplorable conditions that the Negro has to endure in the South and that this should end immediately."

Dr. King and Roy Wilkins took to the microphone and spoke for a couple minutes, each articulating their reasons for combining forces to tackle the evil of segregation. They gave off the appearance of a united front of Negroes ready to protest and fight for equality. However, they were very careful not to project the pilgrimage as a protest against the President, and in fact, had kind words for him. To no one's surprise but to everyone's dismay, Congressman Powell showed up at the last minute, went right up to the microphone and interjected himself into the conference.

"The world is about to experience the collective force of the Negro community, and I am so proud and supportive of what these Negroes have done in putting this prayer pilgrimage together and what better day than May 17, the very day that the United Supreme Court handed down the historical decision that has brought an end to segregated schools. I want you all to know that I am one hundred percent in support of what these men and their organizations plan to accomplish and look forward to bringing a message that day, that will outline what the Congress will accomplish this year in civil rights legislation."

Just as quickly as he appeared, he finished and left the podium before we had a chance to say anything to him. My biggest fear now would be that he would attempt to steal the show, just like he did last year at Madison Square Garden. Somehow, we had to make sure that didn't happen. This was being billed as Dr. King's coming out performance, no longer restricted to the South but now active throughout the country. I knew that was exactly what Powell feared and why he pulled the stunt of showing up at the conference and getting his time at the microphone. He let us know that we had invaded his turf, which was Washington, D.C. and he would have none of it. However, this time I was determined to stop his antics.

27.

The day of the pilgrimage I showed up at the mall before seven o'clock. A chill shot smoothly through my body. I stood there staring at an empty mall. I didn't panic because it was still early, and we had gotten excellent response from various groups, associations, churches, the fraternities and sororities. They all told us they would be there. But still I had a nervous stomach and didn't dare eat or even drink a cup of coffee. I had no desire for a cigarette and that was unusual.

The groundskeepers had just finished constructing the scaffold platform and hooking up all the microphones. Dozens of portable toilets had been set in place and just as many trash bins were strategically set up where the crowd would eventually congregate. A number of Capitol Hill Police had already arrived and stood around talking with the local D. C. Police, also there. Now we only needed a crowd. I walked past the main stage, up the steps of the Lincoln Monument and into a holding room where all the dignitaries and speakers would congregate. No one had arrived and that gave me a chance to just sit and reflect on the schedule of speakers and their time slots. There would also be gospel singing, led my Mahalia Jackson who had insisted that she be on this program. With prayer, there had to be music is what she told Mr. Randolph. We didn't bother to tell her that it really wasn't a prayer pilgrimage, but served as a subterfuge for the real intent. The meaning of the gathering was to put the world and especially this country on alert, that Negroes would no longer allow the abuses they had suffered over the years to continue, and to attain equality, they would demand the right to vote. That would be the essence of the New Negro as defined through a non-militant Christian love, and implemented through a non-violent social confrontation with those who would stand in their way. We were ready to act, and I felt proud playing a small part in making it all happen.

Any fear of failure began to dissipate a little after eight o'clock as the busses pulled up to the mall and men and women, dressed like they were on their way to church began to line up along the sides of the reflecting pool. By eight-thirty, the section roped off up front with chairs for the dignitaries and special invited guests also began to fill up. I took in a deep breath and released it as I watched the crowd continue to grow.

Finally, at nine o'clock, Mr. Randolph, accompanied by Roy and Martin, strolled on to the speaker's platform and took their seat. Congressman Powell was not with them and he was scheduled to be the third speaker of the day. Hopefully, he wouldn't play games like he did at Madison Square Garden. We did everything possible to accommodate his concerns, which I knew amounted to nothing more than those of the President. He did Eisenhower's bidding. This time, however, I was determined not to play his game and if he held out, we would move forward, and he'd forfeit his chance to speak. This was much larger than him and his outrageous ego.

Since Abernathy was not scheduled to speak, we asked him to do the opening prayer. After a fifteen-minute delay, he walked up to the microphone and began this historical meeting with a prayer, followed by Mahalia Jackson. She literally rocked the crowd back on its feet with her rendition of "Precious Lord Take My Hand," and set the mood for the day as every speaker used their ten minutes to fire up the atmosphere with spell binding elocutions that alerted the country to our undeniable truth, that change was on its way.

As I stood off stage listening to Mr. Randolph open the program, then followed by Reverend Mordicai Johnson, President of Howard University, and several other speakers it became quite clear to me that this was destined to be an outstanding introduction of the New Negro and his determination to change his condition in this country. We had early on established five objectives for the pilgrimage. In order to be successful, our speakers had to demonstrate a consensus of black unity, provide an opportunity for blacks from North of the Mason/Dixon line to demonstrate their support for the movement just beginning down South, protest the violence in the South, urge passage of civil rights legislation being discussed in Congress and, in deference to Roy, speak out against the legal attacks on the NAACP in the southern states. The speakers articulated these objectives and then to close out the program, King took the stage and exceeded all expectations of what we believed he could accomplish.

He started as he usually did, with a slow, deliberate recitation of the condition Negroes found themselves in this country. His words flowed poetically, building a crescendo of enthusiasm as he touched on the controversial subject of the right to vote.

"Our most urgent request to the President of the United States and every member of Congress is to give us the right to vote. Give us the ballot," he exclaimed as only a Negro Baptist minister could do. He continued on that note for fifteen minutes intermittently repeating the phrase, "Give us the ballot," until he had the crowd shouting right on time and in unison with him, "Give us the ballot." In a stroke of genius, Martin closed out by linking Roy's interest in litigation through the courts with my emphasis on social activism through the Gandhian tactic of non-violence, as he electrified the crowd, "Give us the ballot and we will quickly and non-violently, without rancor or bitterness, implement the Supreme Court's decision of May 17, 1954."

As Martin walked off the podium to a rousing ovation, I realized then that he had a gift for saying things in a poetic way, and that he had a greater understanding of the psychology of Negroes than I did. Now I could only help him take that gift to its greatest lengths, as he could spread his wings and become the spokesperson to make the Declaration of Independence and the Constitution live up to its dictates that all men are created equal. In doing that, Martin could become the most important spokesperson for this country in its long history. I had gotten him this far, now I had to take him all the way to the top.

Part THREE
INDIA AND LONDON

28.

April 5, 1968

I arrived at LaGuardia Airport a little after seven in the morning for a scheduled flight to Memphis, Tennessee with a change of planes in Atlanta, Georgia. After checking my bag, I grabbed a cup of coffee and settled in the waiting area and concentrated on the television directly in front of me. The channel was turned to NBC and the anchor out of New York had just brought in the reporter covering the King assassination in Memphis.

"Good morning this is Hugh Downs and today all our attention is on Memphis, Tennessee, where last night at approximately seven-twenty p.m. the apostle of peace, Dr. Martin Luther King, Jr., died from a bullet wound to his neck. He was standing on the balcony to his second story room at the Lorraine Hotel, a place where Negro dignitaries stay when they visit Memphis. Memphis Police have issued an all-points bulletin for a well-dressed white man seen leaving the scene after the shooting. And the police chased and fired on a radio equipped car carrying two white men. The police also found a high-powered hunting rifle about a block and a half from the hotel. They are not certain that the rifle was used in the shooting. Mayor Henry Loeb has reinstated the dusk to dawn curfew he imposed on the city last week and Governor Buford Ellington has called out four thousand national guardsmen. Police report the murder has touched off sporadic acts of violence."

Downs had referred to Dr. King as the apostle of peace and that designation was fitting and proper. How ironic that after preaching peaceful non-violence since the Montgomery Bus Boycott over a decade ago, that he would suffer such a violent death at such a young age. As I recalled all the challenges that we undertook during those years, my legs went weak and I felt faint. I watched and listened as Downs continued his report.

"Dr. King had returned to Memphis to prove that he could lead a peaceful non-violent march in support of the garbage workers' strike for more decent wages. Here is some footage from his last speech delivered last night."

I had seen this footage earlier in the morning before leaving for the airport and wasn't sure I could handle seeing it again. Martin looked so tired and somewhat angry.

"I just want to do God's will and He's allowed me to go up to the mountain top and I've looked over and I've seen the Promised Land. I may not get there with you, but I want you to know tonight that we as a people will get to the promise land. So, I'm happy tonight, I'm not worried about anything. I'm not fearing any man. Mine eyes have seen the glory of the coming of the Lord."

Reflecting on the many speeches and sermons I'd heard this man deliver, this one seemed to have the most meaning. He knew something terrible was about to happen. He would often say to me, "Bayard, I'm not going to live a long life, but what is longevity if it has no meaning and accomplishes nothing." As I sat there and listened to the loud speaker call out different flights preparing to leave, I felt satisfied that I had done my part with him to help his life have a great deal of meaning even though it was cut short by an assassin's bullet.

"Flight 358 to Memphis, Tennessee, with a brief stop in Atlanta, Georgia is now ready for boarding at gate number 8. Please have your boarding passes ready for the attendant and enjoy your flight with us today."

Over the years I had taken many flights to places all over the world and been involved in many causes, but this was the most difficult trip I would ever take. How do you say goodbye to a man who meant so much to you over a short period of time, but seemed as though it was an eternity? As I boarded the plane and settled into my seat, I closed my eyes and continued to reflect on the enormous accomplishment, we experienced together in a twelve-year period.

29.

February 1960

As we entered a new decade, hopes soared for greater civil rights victories throughout the South. Martin had become the symbol for change and the catalyst for Negroes to stand up and be counted as dignified citizens in their communities. And among those communities were the colleges and universities. Early in February, four young Negro students from North Carolina A and T in Greensboro decided to sit at the lunch counter at Woolworths Department Store and refused to move until they were served. Within a week, students from Negro colleges in different cities and states followed the example of the Greensboro Four, and a new trend had begun in the movement.

I had just returned from an overseas trip to Ghana where I participated in that country's opposition to France testing a nuclear weapon in the Algerian Sahara. The War Resisters League for whom I had worked, suggested that I make the trip to encourage the pacifist from all over Europe to help Africa resist the nuclear testing on their continent. My trip, however, was interrupted when Mr. Randolph made it quite clear that he wanted me back in the states to help plan a major protest at both the Democrat and Republican National Conventions that summer. Soon after I arrived back home, the young Negro students began their own protest here in the United States.

I arrived back in New York on a late Friday evening and for the first time in years, headed home to an empty apartment. Prior to leaving for Ghana, my relationship with Arthur hit a very sour note. Evidently, he'd had enough of my deep involvement in all these various movements as well as his involvement in a homosexual relationship. He broke off our relationship because he'd decided to marry, and was determined to have what he considered a normal family relationship with a wife and children. At least that's the reason he gave me for the separation. I suspected it probably was much deeper than what he said, and probably had a lot to do with his future promotions in the English Department at Columbia University. How would it look for him to show up with his other half who happened to be a man and, also a Negro? Just too much for him to handle so he bailed out.

I had grown fond of Arthur. We had been together for four years, and I did feel somewhat depressed when it first happened. But I had also experienced a similar situation with David Platt right after I got out of prison back in 1946, so this time it was much easier to make the adjustment. In fact, a week after Arthur moved out Tom moved in and we engaged in a very short relationship until he left to attend college at Howard University. As I strolled into my apartment, I had no one there waiting for me except my harpsicord and lute. But I was home and ready to take on this special project that Mr. Randolph planned for the summer.

Mr. Randolph had scheduled a meeting with Martin flying in from Atlanta, Stanley, Ella and me for that Monday morning. I had the entire weekend to satisfy a need that had been building up for a very long time. It was very difficult to find male companionship in an African country and when it seemed that I had a willing partner, Pasadena nixed that idea. But now back home I knew there would be no problem finding company at Julius for the weekend. That was the purpose Julius served for us. We could find companionship for the night without a great deal of hassle. I showered, dressed and caught a cab over to the club, knowing that I would not be returning home alone.

"I believe it is absolutely necessary for us to make some noise at the two major conventions this summer," Randolph said to the group that sat around his conference table in the office in Harlem. "It's the only way we are going to inject the issue of civil rights into the presidential campaigns. Neither one of the leading candidates at this point are willing to speak out for fear of losing the southern vote."

"Will Roy Wilkins be with us?" Martin asked.

"Don't know," Mr. Randolph said. "I invited him to this meeting, but he said his schedule was such that he couldn't make it."

"That's his polite way of turning down the invitation," I surmised. "So that means he is not interested in taking on the Democratic Party and the young Massachusetts Senator, who appears to have a good chance to defeat Hubert Humphrey and Lyndon Johnson in the primary and win the nomination.

"I don't know Phil, is this something we can really pull off without the NAACP with us?" King continued his questioning.

"As you recall, he was initially reluctant to get involved in the prayer pilgrimage back in 57, but when it became clear that we would receive a great deal of press coverage he joined up," I reminded them. My comments were specifically directed at Martin because for some reason, he seemed rather intimidated by Roy. This giant of a man, whose voice roared with authority when he spoke, became passive when in the presence of leaders, especially Roy.

"Martin, there are people in the NAACP who are not going to support anything that you do for a couple reasons," Randolph said. "The primary reason is that you are making an impact on this country and the SCLC is considered a rival of the NAACP and pretty much beating them at their own game, and that is bringing about change in this country." Randolph paused evidently to allow the first reason to register with Martin. He then continued, "The second reason is tactical, and I imagine somewhat a philosophical difference how our people should act in face of the violence. They believe, and especially my good friend, Thurgood Marshall, that it all should be done through the courts and he is appalled that you would suggest that you actually go to jail and remain there. That goes against his training as an attorney. He is trained to get people out of jail, not agree they should remain inside."

I knew Martin felt rather uncomfortable because he continued to adjust his position in the chair. I sometimes wondered if he recognized the power he had in the community. And that he now had by-passed Roy, Whitney Young at Urban League and no doubt James Farmer at CORE as the pre-eminent Negro leader.

Martin turned and looked directly at me. "Bayard are you going to organize both pickets?" he asked but did not wait for an answer. "The only way I'll feel comfortable getting SCLC as well as myself involved if you are in charge of organizing it."

I didn't get a chance to answer. Mr. Randolph beat me to it. "Absolutely, no doubt," he said. "You know Bayard has been in Africa for the past two months but when I knew we might want to pull this off, I had him come back home to head up this effort. Also, he has his others; you, Stanley and Ella." He pointed to them. "This is the very best organizational team in this country," he continued. "Certainly, you still recall the job they did in organizing the SCLC and then the prayer pilgrimage."

"Are there any potential land mines?" Martin asked.

"Not that we can foresee, other than you are going to have some very unhappy presidential candidates, who the last thing want to see happen is any disunity at the convention. And this will certainly signal something is wrong." Randolph leaned halfway across his desk to make his point. "Of course, you never know what Adam's going to do. If he is one thing, he is not predictable."

"I guess I can sell it to the board at SCLC," King said. "At some point, we'll probably be able to put some money in the pot."

"We're all set and I'm sure Bayard and his team will get to work on this right away," Randolph said.

Martin glanced at his watch and started to get up. "I have a meeting over at Gardner's church," he said. "I'm in, but please remember no land mines."

"I think we can handle that," Randolph said as he accompanied Martin to the door and out of the office.

We were all set to go to work on planning the demonstrations at the national conventions but in the middle of our third workday I received a call from Martin.

"Bayard, I've been indicted by a Grand Jury in Montgomery on charges of tax evasion," he practically shouted into the phone.

Martin had finally arrived on the government radar and it all stemmed from his speech three years ago at the prayer pilgrimage. As long as he concentrated on segregating soda fountains and buses, he offered no threat to the system, but once he reached out and took on the issue of voting, something that could change the power paradigm in this country, they decided to sick the dogs on him. Not much I could say at this point. Only listen.

"You remember the trouble I was having with one of my MIA members back in '58, well he decided to testify in a Grand Jury hearing that I'd improperly taken money from both MIA and SCLC and didn't report it on my taxes in 1956 and '58. So now I'm being charged on two counts of perjury. This is all wrong Bayard, all wrong."

"Are you back in Montgomery now?" I asked.

"No, I'm in Atlanta and authorities in Montgomery are asking for extradition back there."

"Martin, listen to me closely, it is important that you go back to Montgomery and voluntarily surrender to the authorities," I urged him. "You cannot have them come after you like a common criminal on the run from the law. Make plans to go back right away."

"My God in Heaven, stories are already circulating about me that are not true," Martin scowled. "What they are accusing me of doing would betray my moral instincts and all my teachings. Stories and lies that I live in a lavish home or own a fancy car are not true." He paused to catch his breath. It was necessary for him to get this all out. I understood and was willing to listen. "I don't even wish those things were true. I own just one piece of property and that's an old 1954 Pontiac. I'm renting my home here in Montgomery. I make no pretense to absolute goodness, but if I have one virtue, it's honesty." His voice quivered, and I knew he was close to tears.

Stanley and Ella glared over at me and the looks on their faces indicated they knew something was wrong. Evidently tired of just sitting there waiting, Stanley got up and walked out of the room. Ella, obviously curious as to what was happening sat there listening.

"Martin, none of this nonsense is true so you are worrying over nothing," I said hoping to calm his nerves.

"You say it's nothing," Martin shot right back at me. "Do you know if found guilty, they can give me four to six years in prison?"

"There is no way we can let that happen," I chimed in to calm his nerves. But I also believed that of all the leaders, he was the one who had to stay out of jail for any other reasons than the civil protest.

"Bayard, you have to help me out. I need the best attorneys in this country to defend me and in order to hire them, I'll need money. Contrary to what the Fed's believe, I am not rich."

"Martin, you go on over to Montgomery and before they can lock you up good, we'll have you out on bail. And we'll put the work that needs to be done for the protest this summer on hold and go to work on your defense. Don't worry, this too shall pass."

"Bayard make this go away and I'll be in your debt for a very long time," Martin said, and I could detect some pleading in his voice.

After explaining to the others what was going on, I headed over to Mr. Randolph's office to let him know that the plans for the protest would have to be put on hold, because we all had to make a very concerted effort to raise enough funds to get Martin the very best defense money could possibly buy. Mr. Randolph agreed so we shifted our emphasis and again I took the lead in laying out the strategy.

Over the years I had developed the unique ability to take a crisis and convert it to an opportunity. That's exactly what I needed to do in this situation with Martin. Serious as the charges were, I saw this as the perfect time to place Martin and SCLC at the center of what was becoming the major movement in the country. I needed novel ways to seize the public's attention and win their support for Martin. I needed the world pulling for him against an obvious miscarriage of justice.

Since Roy refused to join in this effort, I had to move our operation back to the In-Friendship office space in Stanley's building. Fortunately, it was still available, and Ella, Tom and Rachelle joined us as we went to work. Roy and Powell both refused to join the committee I established as the foundation of this effort. Mr. Randolph took over the reins of the Committee to Defend Martin Luther King and I was designated as the Executive Director, relegated to the back room of the effort simply because bad publicity would hinder our attempts to raise the two hundred thousand dollars needed for his defense. Despite being in the shadows of the cause, it was my ideas that took hold as the committee began its work.

After settling into our new office, I shared my first goal with the others.

"We need to mobilize the celebrities around this effort because they have the capability to create the kind of public attention we need," I said to Ella and Stanley sitting in the two chairs in front of my very small wooden desk. Rachelle and Tom sat on an old worn out couch back against the wall in the office.

"Who do you have in mind?" Ella asked.

"There is this young calypso singer who is starting to make a name for himself," I said. "And I understand he has quite a social conscience."

"Harry Belafonte," Tom shouted out before I could mention his name.

"Have you heard him sing?" I asked looking to the back of the room at Tom.

"Yeah, I sure did," he responded. "At a concert in Brooklyn last year. He is going to be the best."

"We'll use him to form a cultural committee to mobilize celebrities in the entertainment industry on King's behalf," I said becoming more enthused each minute as I thought of the potential. "Not only can they raise a ton of money, but if we can get them to do a concert, that will bring the kind of attention we need right now."

"The big question mark is, will he do it?" Ella asked.

"No problem, I'll get our Chair to reign him in as well as other entertainers," I said. I then focused my attention on Stanley. "What we need right away is a strong statement to be placed as an ad in the New York Times. And I need to reach outside our little group to get it done. We need to expand our tentacles and I have the perfect person for the job."

"Who is that?" Ella again did the asking.

"She's a young playwright whose play, "Raisin in the Sun," has received all kinds of accolades from the press in their reviews."

"Lorraine Hansberry," Rachelle shouted again beating me to the draw as Tom did earlier.

"Have you seen the play?" I asked her.

"No, but I definitely plan to do so," Rachelle said.

"And how do you plan to get her to do it?" Ella again asked

"The same way as I plan to get Mr. Belafonte on board. The elder of the civil rights movements in this country, Mr. Randolph." I answered.

"You seem to have it all under control?" Tom quipped. "What are we supposed to do since we're not doing anything on the conventions until this is over?"

Before Tom could finish his question, I had gone into my desk drawer and pulled out two large size pieces of paper with names and telephone numbers listed. I got up, walked around the desk and back to where they sat. I handed one sheet to Tom and the other to Rachelle.

"You have over a hundred names and telephone numbers on these two valuable sheets of paper. Get busy," I finished and returned to my desk. "We have to raise two hundred thousand dollars and we probably can't count on the entertainers to raise it all, so we need donations from everyone on those papers." I paused while Tom and Rachelle examined the names of the paper. "When you call, don't be shy. Asked for the big dollars and let them come down if necessary. But by all means don't start off low because that's exactly what they will give."

"You think we're finished for today," Stanley asked.

"Unless you have something you want to suggest?" I said.

"Need to spend some quiet time because even though we've put the brakes on the picket this summer, I still want to work on some various approaches we might use. I want to make a distinction between what we want to see happen at the Democrat convention in Chicago and the Republicans later in the month."

I sat and watched as Stanley, Ella and Rachelle walked out of the office. Tom stayed behind. I knew what he was up to but didn't really want to accommodate him.

"I'm not heading back to Howard University until in the morning, can I stay with you tonight?" he asked.

"If I say no, where do you plan to spend the night?"

"Probably head on over to the Y.M.C.A. on 135th Street."

"You're getting pretty bold with your behavior?"

"Why not? That's the way you taught me to be. Just don't worry about what others may think and be myself, and that is a content gay man, who loves his mentor."

Tom was a young, tender, and soft lover and I did enjoy being with him. But at times, I felt rather guilty because of the age difference. After Arthur and I broke up, I did allow Tom to live with me until he decided to head off to Howard University and complete his education. That was two years ago, and we'd seen very little of each other. But our friendship was still quite solid. He and Rachelle had been with me since I returned from Montgomery four years ago and I did love them. In different ways, obviously. Tom had learned a lot about being gay, but I still considered him somewhat of a neophyte and did not want him hanging out at the Y. M. C. A.

"Let me finish up here with the calls I need to make to Mr. Randolph and then we can head over to Julius grab some food and then go home."

He smiled. "Take your time. I'll be ready when you are."

30.

By the beginning of May, fund raising efforts were in full swing. Harry Belafonte had recruited an array of stars who agreed to perform. I had talked with the 369th Regiment Armory on 142nd Street in Harlem, as the location for the gallery of stars concert. The committee debated where best to hold the concert and some preferred Madison Square Garden or Carnegie Hall, but Mr. Randolph, with my concurrence, leaned to the Armory because of its significant symbolism. It was named after the 369th Infantry Regiment, also known as the Harlem Hell Fighters, that fought in Europe during World War I. The men spent over six months in combat, the longest of any American unit in the war and suffered over 1500 casualties. They were the first American fighting unit to cross the Rhine into Germany.

When they arrived back home in February 1919, they marched in a parade that began in Greenwich Village and continued to Upper Manhattan into Harlem. The parade, led by Big Jim Europe's Band, with Bill Bojangles Robinson as regimental drum major, led the victory march right up to the armory where the men had trained to go overseas. We could have chosen no better location for us to hold a concert to raise money for Dr. King's defense. We set another symbolic date for the event, May 17, the sixth anniversary of the famous United States Supreme Court decision in the school desegregation cases. After the initial concert in New York, Belafonte planned similar events from Boston and Los Angeles. We figured the concerts should raise one-hundred thousand dollars. We needed to devise additional ways to raise the other one-hundred thousand. That would have to be accomplished through a direct appeal to the liberal public and the best medium to reach that group was the "New York Times."

Mr. Randolph and I decided to restrict that discussion between the two of us. If we included the others, King's trial might be over before we reached a consensus. We decided to discuss the matter over breakfast at Sylvia's on 125 Street. I strolled into the restaurant a little after eight and immediately saw Mr. Randolph at a table next to a window looking out on the street. He loved that place and they usually would accommodate his wishes to be seated there. I hurried over and sat in the other chair at the table.

"You order yet?" I asked

"Not breakfast but coffee. Told them to bring two cups because I knew you'd be walking through that door before he got back to the table."

"Thank you. I need a cup. Didn't get a chance to brew a pot at home."

"That's because you probably slept in right to the last minute."

I relaxed back in the chair as the waiter placed the two cups in front of us. "You all ready to order?" he asked.

"Eggs, bacon, grits and biscuits," Randolph said.

"Same for me."

The waiter wrote the order on a pad and then headed back toward the kitchen area. I opened the conversation.

"I believe we got three choices of who might write this article," I said.

"Okay, let me have it."

"We got Jimmy, we got Lorraine and I believe we might be able to convince John Killens, all good choices."

"James Baldwin is no doubt the most brilliant writer of the three, but I do believe we should ask Lorraine Hansberry to pen the appeal."

"You're thinking about the need for a Black woman's involvement. We do have Ella Baker, but she's mostly in the background." I took a sip from my cup and anticipated his answer. Mr. Randolph had always been out front on the issue of women's equality. During the great period of the Harlem Renaissance he, along with Dr. Du Bois, were often a voice in the wilderness on the issue.

"You're exactly right, we need a young, dynamic woman out front and Lorraine fits that description."

"Seems like you could have told me your decision by phone and saved me a trip uptown," I said with a smile.

"I know, but that's not the only reason I wanted this private meeting with you." Mr. Randolph now paused to sip from his cup.

"Okay, I'm listening."

"This time I don't believe Roy and the NAACP are going to be with us. I'm not sure if it's him or the board, but word is that he feels that Martin is becoming a real threat to the NAACP fund raising activities and SCLC is threatening them in terms of national appeal. Roy had no problem as long as Martin's activities were confined to the South. But now he is becoming a real force all over the country and we are trying to raise two hundred thousand dollars for his defense. I'm sure Roy feels that's money he could use for his operations."

"Quite seriously, I believe there is some truth to Roy's concerns. The problem confronting the NAACP is that its method and approach to change is becoming too conservative, and quite frankly is much too slow in getting results." I paused while the waiter placed our breakfast plates in front of us.

Mr. Randolph said a prayer and I continued before digging into my breakfast. "The NAACP is not staying up with the times and still believes they should dictate the tactics to be used. That's not the case any longer. One problem they have is that only a few individuals are involved in the action. It's a few clients who have challenged some discriminatory law and the attorneys. The rest of the race are spectators. One positive development in Montgomery is that all the people felt they were playing an equal role in the struggle and not just on lookers. This is a problem that the NAACP will not be able to overcome unless they concede that direct non-violent action is the best way to go."

"This is a battle I fought with James Weldon Johnson and Walter White when they were Secretaries to the NAACP. Back then, they won the consensus from the people that law was the best way to go. Even when I challenged President Roosevelt with the strike back in 1941, I confronted a great deal of opposition."

"What will happen if Martin's SCLC actually becomes a threat to Roy?" I asked.

"Don't know, but I do know it is to his organization's advantage if Martin is conveniently removed as his competitor?"

"You're not suggesting that Roy might prefer for him to get a prison sentence that will take him out of the picture?"

"No, not at all," Randolph shot back. "But there is one other individual who might feel challenged by Martin's considerable growth as a leader, and his office is right down the street from me."

"Congressman Powell," I suggested.

"Exactly," he smiled. "As we move forward with the plans for the protest, I believe Adam is going to put up a great deal of opposition."

"No matter what he does, we will not back down from our plans." I scooped a fork full of eggs and tossed it in my mouth.

"Not at all."

"The concert is set to be held in two weeks, Martin has a team of the best lawyers that good money can buy, and so we need to get beyond that trial and back to the main goal of confronting our politicians on the grounds at the conventions."

Mr. Randolph finished off his breakfast and swallowed the last of his coffee. "I'll talk with Lorraine today and get her to working on the article for the 'Times.'"

I also drank the last of my coffee, we paid the waiter and got up to leave.

By seven o'clock in the evening, the Armory had filled to capacity and a long line of people waited outside for entry to the concert. I felt elated with the turn-out. And the array of artists there to perform was just as impressive. I stared in awe at the level of performers with Sammy Davis Jr., who was the first star to take to the stage. Sammy was followed on the stage by the Alvin Ailey Repertory Ensemble, led by Ailey himself. They had perfected a performance titled "Revelations" and just perfect for the cause and event. Dressed in full length white dresses, women in the 32-member dance team, accompanied by men with only white pants and no top, performed a series of maneuvers that told the story of African American faith and tenacity from slavery to freedom, and set to spirituals and blues music in the background. They excited the crowd to a fever pitch and all the performers that followed them were also energized by the dance group's performance.

During the concert, I had young volunteers with tin cans, hats and bowls, working the crowd asking for donations. Even though they had paid a minimum of twenty-five dollars for admission, we still hit them up for an extra few dollars. At the end of the night, we counted eighty-thousand dollars from the ticket sales and the contributions during the concert. That was way short of our goal, but every penny counted. The next, Sunday, the article written by Lorraine Hansberry would appear in the "New York Times" laying out the need to get Martin the best defense, and the obligation for the rest of the country to support what was happening in the South.

Sunday morning, I got up early, went out and bought a newspaper. As soon as I got back in the apartment, I turned to the full-page ad that all New York and a lot of the world would be reading about Martin and our cause. Lorraine did an excellent job on the ad. I had read it earlier and gave it my approval but was anxious to see it in print. I read the ad with great delight,

"Small wonder that the Southern violators of the Constitution fear this new nonviolent brand of freedom fighter. Small wonder that they are determined to destroy the one man who more than any other, symbolizes the new spirit now sweeping the South—The Reverend Martin Luther King.

"Again, and again, the Southern violators have answered Dr. King's peaceful protest with intimidations and violence. They have bombed his home, almost killing his wife and child. They have assaulted his person. They have arrested him and now they have charged him with "perjury"—a felony under which they could imprison him for ten years. Obviously, their real purpose is to remove him physically as the leader to whom the students and millions of others look for guidance and support and thereby to intimidate all leaders who may rise in the South."

On the date of Martin's trial, we had raised over one hundred and fifty thousand dollars in New York and over fifty thousand came in from other locations. The trial began on May 25 and I followed it closely, getting reports from Martin at the end of each day. Finally, on May 28, it went to the jurors and after three-hour deliberations, they returned a not guilty verdict. Finally, that interruption was out of the way and we could get back to the business of planning the protest of the political conventions only a couple months away.

Harlem had always been the place for political and social malcontents. It was that way when I first arrived there back in the late 1930's and it had remained the same ever since. When I began to hear rumblings about this new group of malcontents, led by an ex-convict who called himself Malcolm X..I didn't give it much consideration. He was some kind of sect leader for a group out of Chicago called the Nation of Islam, headed by another man who had taken on an alternative name, Elijah Muhammad. Malcolm X asked for a meeting with Mr. Randolph and me. As I strolled into the Mr. Randolph's office early in the morning on June1, I wondered, what could this man possibly want from us. He was already there seated in one of the usual chairs in front of the desk. He rose when I walked in.

"Bayard Rustin, my brother pleasure meeting you," Malcolm X said.

"Feeling is mutual," I replied as we shook hands.

Mr. Randolph remained behind his desk and said. "You asked to meet with me, but I want you to know early on that I am not a supporter of your leader or your movement."

"That's well understood," Malcolm X said. "But we plan to become a very intricate part of what happens here in Harlem. And we plan to recruit men and women to our cause, and just want to be assured from you that you and your friends will not get in our way."

"It's a free country," Randolph retorted tersely.

"Is it true that you all are taught that the white man is the devil," I said. "I believe your leader refers to him as the 'blue eyed devil.'"

"You are right, we do view the white man as the blue-eyed devil, as taught to us by the Honorable Elijah Muhammad."

"And it's true that you don't support our efforts to bring about an integrated country," I continued.

"That is also true," Malcolm X replied. "We don't believe in the idea of joining the races because there will always be one group inferior to the other. And according to the Honorable Elijah Muhammad, we can never again accept that role. We must have our own land and our own country eventually."

"How do you plan to accomplish that?" I asked.

"The plan has not yet been revealed to the Honorable Elijah Muhammad, but in due time, Allah will give him instructions on how to proceed. In the meantime, it is my job to continue recruiting our people into the cause."

As he would usually do, Mr. Randolph now leaned half-way across his desk to make a point. "I've observed you standing outside Negro churches and berating the people who are Christians, talking about they're worshipping a blue-eyed Jesus."

"I am only trying to help them see the light and make their way out of a slave way of thinking."

"So, you believe because they believe in their God and Jesus, they think like a slave?" I asked.

"Wasn't it the slave master that gave them their religion?" Malcolm X asked.

"Obviously, you are going to run into a great deal of opposition here in Harlem and for that matter all over New York with that kind of thinking," Randolph said. "You're wasting your time if you believe our people are going to abandon their religion for a foreign, and to them, somewhat exotic religion."

The most disconcerting aspect of this man's beliefs was that he possessed a charisma that could be quite effective. But his message was all wrong and I saw nothing but trouble in the future dealing with him and his group. I believed he was here in Mr., Randolph's office for only one reason and that is to let us know they are around and will be here for a while.

"Mr. Randolph, you are only one of a few who I admire and that's why I wanted to sit with you and share our plans. I don't see any reason why we can't exist in the same space, without one trying to run the other out. It is my prayer that you share this with me."

"I have always been a man of peace and will continue for the very few years I have left on God's earth," Randolph exclaimed.

"Have you talked with Roy Wilkins at the NAACP?" I asked

"Haven't even tried," Malcolm X shot back right away. "There is so much distance between the Nation and them, my efforts, if so desired, would be in vain. But I do hope that you'll keep the door open for a visitor every once in a while."

"An exchange of ideas is always a very good thing," I said before Randolph responded. I could tell he was just about ready to explode. "I can assure you that we over here will have a very open mind, and not interfere in what you're doing and of course would expect the same respect from you."

"You'll have no problems with me or with members of the Nation," Malcolm X said.

We stood and prepared to leave as Mr. Randolph came from the other side of his desk.

"Please tell Mr. Elijah Muhammad I send greetings." Randolph patted Malcolm X on his back.

"I invite you all to visit Mosque Number 7 someday and you might then know the wonderful message we receive from the Honorable Elijah Muhammad every week."

We stood and watched as Malcolm X walked out the door into the reception area and finally out of the building.

"Now can we get back to the business at hand," Randolph said. "We only have less than a month to the first convention and still have a lot of work to do."

"Gladly," I replied and sat back down in my chair.

He returned to the other side of his desk and sat in his leather chair. "Now where are we and is there anything I need to do immediately."

I listened to Mr. Randolph, but my thoughts were still on Malcolm X. I just knew that my involvement with him had just begun.

31.

Martin and Mr. Randolph stood on the top steps of the building that housed the Pullman Porter's office in Harlem, in front of microphones and news reporters. Martin had flown up early that morning for a news conference announcing plans to picket both the Democratic and Republican National Conventions in July. Right after Martin's acquittal in the tax fraud case, we all went back to work and since I'd played such an instrumental role in organizing the boycott, they decided to make a public announcement that I would direct the actions. It was a calculated risk they were taking, since Powell opposed the protest and would possibly use any tactic possible to upset our plans. No doubt they recognized, as I did, an attack on me again because of Pasadena could cause trouble. I stood off to the right with Stanley and Ella as Mr. Randolph spoke first.

"Dr. King and I are in complete agreement that the United States Congress and the President of the United States, have moved too slowly on the important issue of meaningful legislation to once and for all put an end to this dual society, where one group of citizens are deemed superior to others. This is a moral issue of grave importance. And this country cannot profess that it is built on the belief in a God who loves all His people, and then mistreat one segment as badly as the Negro is treated in the south." As he usually did when making a profound statement, he paused to let the reporters absorb its importance.

"The time has come when the political parties of this country must feel this revolutionary mood and determination of the Negro People," he continued, now getting right to the point. "We have, therefore, wired prominent community leaders, Negro and white, in Los Angeles and Chicago, informing them that we intend to be present at both the Democratic and Republican conventions. We are asking them to cooperate with us in a massive non-violent march on the conventions. The millions of Negroes denied the right to vote in the South are appealing to the people of Los Angeles and Chicago to represent them before the conventions." He paused and placed his arm around Martin's shoulder.

"Dr. King and the Southern Christian Leadership Conference has joined this effort, and it gives me a great deal of pleasure to relinquish the microphone to him."

Martin, in his slow methodical manner, approached the mike. "The Board of Directors of the Southern Christian Leadership Conference has voted unanimously to join with Mr. A. Phillip Randolph and the other organizations, who have decided to make a stand for justice. They have decided to make a stand against hate, and they have decided to make a stand for non-violent change to how this country has operated for far too long." He looked in my direction. "With Mr. Bayard Rustin in the lead we are assured of a well-organized protest, and a non-violent assembly of God's children to tell these two political parties that they must take a stand and pass meaningful legislation, whoever is elected president?"

"The Congress passed a civil rights bill in 1957," a reporter in the front row shouted.

Martin stared over at me as if to say get up here. I hurried up to the mike. He stepped back and allowed me to take over.

"You're right, the Congress did sign a Civil Rights bill, but it was so weak after Senator Strom Thurmond filibustered for twenty-four hours and Majority Leader Lyndon Johnson made so many concessions to the Senators Eastland from Mississippi and Richard Russell of Georgia, by the time it got to President Eisenhower's desk for signature it was referred to as a bill with no real teeth. Just like quail stew with no quail."

"But it was some progress you must admit." Another reporter suggested.

"If you consider it was the first civil rights legislation passed since 1875, I guess you can call that some progress. But since its passage, Negro voting in the South has only improved by three percent. Mr. Randolph and Dr. King believe that progress is much too slow."

"Some people in this country believe that the Negro is trying to move too fast and needs to just wait and eventually equality will come?" A reporter in the back row shouted.

It was my turn to look back at Martin. I had answered the substantive inquiry regarding passage of the bill three years ago, and now this was his area of expertise. He caught the hint and walked back up to the mike. I took my place back along the side.

"Don't you think ninety-five years is a long enough time to wait?" He asked rhetorically. "Don't you think it's time to provide the Negro with all the rights and privileges that is part of being an American citizen? Well, if you don't believe it is long enough, Negroes do, and we plan to do something about it. Just like we did in Montgomery, we plan to do all over the South and into the North where necessary."

"Where in the North do you see problems?" Bill Worthy asked. I hadn't seen him since we got back from Montgomery over four years ago. He had spent years in Africa covering the struggle for independence among the African nations. I instinctively knew why he asked that question and that was to bring attention to the problems of school segregation right here in New York.

Just as if we were playing tag as speakers, Martin turned and looked at Mr. Randolph who obviously took that as a hint that he should handle this question since it dealt with the North. He hurried up to the mike and Martin moved back.

"The problems here in the North are more subtle than down South, but they do exist," he said. "In the South you have segregation by law and here in the North it's by residential living. Here in New York the entire Black population is bunched up in Harlem and that's where all the children attend school. But there are no Negroes living on Long Island, so those schools are all white. Negroes still have difficulty finding decent jobs, you know the old saying 'last hired and first fired,' is real and alive in New York and across the bridges in New Jersey and in Connecticut. Truth be told, this country has a lot of work to resolve its racial problems and we feel that the two major parties should play a larger role in getting that done. That is why we will protest outside their conventions next month. Now with that said, we thank you for coming out today and will see you all in Los Angeles first and then in Chicago later in the month."

Mr. Randolph and Martin strolled back toward the door into the building, but before they got there another reporter shouted.

"Which of the two candidates between Kennedy and Nixon are the worst on the issue of integration?"

Without returning to the podium Mr. Randolph shouted.

"They're both just as bad at this point."

"You don't support either one of them/"

"Exactly." Mr. Randolph finished, and we turned and walked back inside the building with reporters still shouting questions.

The three of us retreated into our favorite meeting place, inside Mr. Randolph's office. Stanley and Ella headed back over to our working office. Mr. Randolph sat behind his desk while Martin and I occupied the two chairs out front.

"Do you think Roy will come around?" Martin asked.

"I believe there may be two important factors that will keep him from joining us at either of the conventions," Mr. Randolph said, and I was pretty sure I knew exactly what they were. "The first factor has to do with the NAACP. It has become a victim of its own intransigence against change. They believe all conflicts belong in court and because of the victory in 1954 in the Brown school decision, they are committed to that approach. That is an organizational problem and old ways are very difficult to break." Mr. Randolph paused for a moment. He reared back in his chair and continued. "The second factor is a personal one. Roy is losing control to you Martin and I'm not sure he can handle that very well. He waited years, laboring under the leadership of Walter White and then in 1955, when he finally got the head job at NAACP, you come along and begin to challenge him as the most important Negro leader in this country."

"That is not my intention," Martin said emphatically. "I still consider the NAACP as the most important Negro organization in this country."

"You do, but not everyone else does anymore," I said. "After the Prayer Pilgrimage in 1957, you just catapulted to the top of the leadership ladder. Your speech was so dynamic that as you may recall James Hicks in the "Amsterdam News" announced you as the new legitimate spokesperson for the Negro in his article. He criticized Roy and even wrote that Mr.

Randolph was not as instrumental as you in pulling off the pilgrimage."
I looked across at Mr. Randolph for a response, but he gave none, which
was not unusual for him. "Roy was livid with the article and threatened
to get James removed as a writer for the paper. That's when the struggle
with Roy began and I don't believe he will ever take a backseat to you."

Martin adjusted his position in the chair as he appeared a little
nervous. "I have always had the utmost respect for the NAACP and would
hope that it would be reciprocal."

"Well, it isn't," Randolph said. "Martin, you have to…"

Mr. Randolph stopped in the middle of his sentence as the office door
swung open and Adam Clayton Powell bolted into the room.

"What the hell was that this morning?" He shouted.

"I believe it was a press conference," Randolph replied calmly.

"What are you Negroes trying to prove?" He asked but didn't wait
for an answer. "Do you really think that you can disrupt the two major
national conventions in this country?" He stood between Martin and me
but looked directly at Mr. Randolph as if we weren't in the room. "Phil,
you're too damn old to try to do something like this. Didn't you get your
fill of this kind of nonsense back in 41?" He turned and stared at Martin.
"And King, you need to go on back down South where your methods
can work. Negroes up here are not going to stand for no one hitting and
kicking them and not strike back."

He now turned and glared at me. "You supposed to be the leader of
this nonsense and with a damn queer leading a protest march against the
national political parties?"

Mr. Randolph sprang out of his chair. "That's enough of that kind of
talk in my office," he bellowed. "If you want to have a decent conversation
then change your tone and your words and if you can't do that, I'll ask
you to leave my office."

Powell walked right to the front of the desk. "Phil, what are you
thinking about? You can't do this. It'll weaken my position in Congress
to get things done for our people."

My inclination was to shout at this man that he never got anything
done, and his only claim to fame was driving around in fancy cars taking

long vacations in the Bahamas and showing up at events with a different woman every time he made an appearance in public. But I remained quiet and allowed Mr. Randolph to deal with him. Martin also remained quiet.

"You really do lack the manners and decency of your father," Mr. Randolph said, ignoring Powell's concerns about his position in Congress. He had awakened a sleeping giant because Mr. Randolph very seldom raised his voice or made disparaging comments about another person. He always found the good in people, but evidently Powell had crossed that threshold with him.

"You had the audacity to hold a press conference in Harlem without notifying me," Powell also raised his voice. "No one does anything down here without my involvement Phil. You should have learned that lesson years ago when I destroyed your scheme to carry out a voter registration drive."

"Adam, I've never taken an active position in opposition to your re-election, but don't push me. You're up for re-election this year and I'd rather stay out of the race, but this kind of behavior on your part must end."

"Are you threatening me Phil?"

"No, not at all but asking that you control your behavior when you're in my office. Now if you don't like what we plan to do at the conventions, then let your position be known. But don't ever come in my office again insulting my guests."

Powell backed up a few steps. "I'm warning you, if you pursue this silly idea, you all will pay dearly." He finished, turned and walked out the door, slamming it behind him.

Mr. Randolph sat back down in his chair and I could tell he was visibly shaken. We sat there not knowing exactly what to say at that point. They probably were more concerned how I would respond to his obviously disgusting referral to me. They didn't understand that kind of attack no longer affected me, because I had lived with them for so long. I needed to break the silence.

"We'll have a set of platforms demands ready by the first week in July," I said. "Platform chair for the Democrats is Congressman Chester Bowles from Connecticut. The chair for the Republican party is Thurston Morton, chair of the Republican National Committee."

"What do you think he's going to do?" King looked directly at Mr. Randolph ignoring my attempt to shift the subject.

"I don't know, but whatever it is, it won't be nice, because he is not a nice person," Randolph said.

"I don't know if we need to get into a fight with the leading Negro elected official in this country," King suggested.

"There is nothing that we can do to appease that man unless we give into his constant demands." I shifted my emphasis to the subject that seemed to most interesting to them. "I'm sure both camps have contacted him asking for his assistance to get us to cancel the protest. He is the only person who probably will be courted by both parties because he voted for Eisenhower in 56. And Kennedy is his friend and he'll probably be comfortable with either one of them as the president."

"Bayard's right Martin," Randolph said, again looking directly at Martin. "Powell will only be happy when he has you, especially, groveling at his feet."

"That seems to be par for the course," Martin quipped. "Seems as though every Negro leader is out to get me for no reason at all."

"Now they have their reasons," I quickly responded. "As long as you were down South leading marches on a small scale, you were no threat. That all has changed, and you are the man and even the white media is beginning to see that and giving you more coverage than Powell. And I can assure you that does not sit well with him."

"I'm surprised that both candidates haven't reached out to you for an endorsement," I said.

"They know my position," King replied. "I don't endorse candidates, and I understand that Nixon has already gotten the support from Jackie Robinson."

"If you disrupt their conventions, you might become persona non gratta." Randolph suggested.

"It's what we must do, and nothing can deter the fact that both parties have to be more receptive to the Negroes." King glanced at his watch.

"I need to get to the airport. You all know I'm leaving for Brazil and a national conference day after tomorrow."

"How long will you be gone?" I asked aware that I needed to share with him the platform demands.

"I'll be gone for five days."

"Good, and I'll be ready to brief both of you on what needed to be stressed to the platform chairmen from both parties."

"Let's get you to the airport," Randolph said.

We strolled out the office and the building. The driver who had brought Martin from the airport to the press conference, sat waiting in the car. He pulled up to the curb, Martin climbed in the back seat and as they drove off, I knew that Powell's threat as to what he might do still bothered him.

Just as the cab disappeared around the corner Mr. Randolph placed his arm around my shoulder. "Bayard, I want to talk to you, let's go back into the office for just a minute or two."

Curious as to why, I followed him back up the steps, into the building and to his office. I took my usual seat as he sat behind his desk. I could tell something really bothered him. He hardly ever frowned.

"This has to be very hard on you," he said, and I knew exactly what he meant. "Being gay and Negro is like being on two crosses at the same time. If whites aren't attacking you because you are a Negro, then Negroes are attacking you because you are gay. Where do you get the strength to endure?"

After all the years I had known Mr. Randolph, this was the first time he'd ever addressed me this way. I wasn't quite sure how to respond, so instead I chose to listen. My silence meant he needed to give me some indication the purpose for this discussion.

"You remind me of Wallace Thurman, a brilliant young man who came to Harlem from Los Angeles with plans to make a difference during the heyday of the 1920's. He was a genius just like you and also a homosexual, but in the end, didn't have the courage that you have. I believe his struggle within was so intense that he ultimately committed suicide by drinking himself to death. Died right here in the Harlem Hospital around 1933. The two crosses were too much for him to bear. Bayard, I don't want to see the same happen to you." He did his usual pause to allow his words to sink in.

I found it an interesting comparison. I knew of Thurman's genius and that he challenged the established leadership at that time. It seemed that I was doing the same. I had no response to Mr. Randolph's comparison.

He continued. "The Negro confrontation in this country is getting ready to blow up and at this point you are one of the most important men in that battle. You know the powers that be are going to come after you, just as Powell did earlier today. Don't let the pressure become so intense that you do as Wallace Thurman did. You need to know that I will not stand around and allow men like the congressman to attack you. But I need to know if you get to the point that you don't believe you can handle the two crosses anymore, pick the one most important to you."

I took in a deep breath and released it. He waited for a response. "I never have run from a battle and I won't now," I said. "One thing this country has is plenty of bigots who are essentially weak and insecure men. Powell, despite all his grandiose behaviors, I believe is a very weak man. I will never succumb to the pressure of men like that."

"Good, because you're like a son to me, and I am always concerned about your well-being."

Mr. Randolph stood up and came around the desk. I also stood up. We hugged and then I headed out of his office. Nothing else need be said. We understood each other.

I needed some space between me and the men I had been dealing with for the past four years. I always thought it would not be difficult to fit in where I knew I was not welcome. Aside from Mr. Randolph, all the other leaders that I interacted with, sometimes daily, were for the most part homophobic. To a certain degree, I believed Martin also harbored resentment and to a degree fears that somehow the gay community was a threat to him. To men like Powell, to be gay was all he needed to know in order to negate any credibility you may possess as a valuable participant in the fight to destroy segregation.

After leaving Mr. Randolph's office I needed to mentally cleanse myself of the filth I endured from Powell. I needed to be around my folks, at least for the afternoon. At that point, I didn't care who knew. It was something I had to do. I flagged down a cab and climbed in the back seat.

"Where to?" the driver asked as he turned his meter on.

"Twenty-eight, West Twenty-eighth Street," I said.

He glared at me through the rear-view mirror. "That's the location of the Eberhard Bathhouse?"

"I know."

32.

"We got real problems with Roy and the NAACP," Randolph said to me over the phone in a calm manner which was part of his overall demeanor. The only time I ever saw him begin to get upset was when Congressman Powell called me out of my name.

I had just arrived at our makeshift office when the call came through.

"He sent me a scathing, near hysterical letter," he continued. "Are you there Bayard?"

"Yes, I'm here," I said. "Can you read the contents of the letter?" I asked. Not that I needed to hear it but felt a need to appease Mr. Randolph.

"Hold on, let me get it." There was a moment of silence and I could hear him rustling through papers, then. "Here it is, 'Dear Phil, I am irate at the fact that you all announced at your press conference, that the NAACP will be a willing participant in the boycott of the Democrat and Republican Conventions later in this month. We submit that your statement misleads the public as to role the NAACP will assume in this project. We have never agreed to recruit or join in recruiting five thousand pickets. The NAACP cannot permit its name to be used as a sponsor of mass picketing around each convention.'"

"We miscalculated Roy's opposition," I suggested. "We knew he initially opposed the idea of the protest, but at least I believed he would come around especially after he saw the plans and that SCLC was involved."

"We have to figure a way to neutralize him," Randolph said. "If he goes public with his opposition to the protest then we are pretty much dead in the water. The press will play it up as a rivalry between the Negro leaders and it gives them a chance to pit Roy against Martin, and that could be disastrous."

"The new and effective SCLC against the old and rather conservative NAACP would make good press," I added. "You're the arbitrator in these disputes between Negro leaders. You have to talk with Roy and get him to back off or we might as well call off the protest."

"I'll call him this afternoon and do the best I can. According to the wording in this letter, I'm not sure he will be willing to listen."

"They're always willing to listen to you," I said.

"Also, I got a call from Martin down in Brazil. Left a message for me to get right back to him and that it was awfully important. I'll call him after I talk with Roy."

"We just wrapped up the demands you all need to make to the platform committees," I said. "Soon as you clear up this other matter with Roy, I'll share them with you."

"Good, let's talk later this afternoon." Randolph finished and hung up.

"Sounds like things are heating up," Stanley said as he and Ella sat in the room with me, while I talked with Mr. Randolph. What's going on or better still is Roy acting like Roy and creating a problem?"

"Nothing that can't be handled." I pulled a package of cigarettes from my pocket, took one out and lit it. I felt right then like I could smoke an entire pack all at the same time. Were things unraveling on us? "Let's go over those demands one more time." I needed to occupy my time so that I wouldn't dwell on Roy and his rather immature attitude.

Ella looked down at the paper before her and read. "Here's what we are suggesting as demands, both parties should repudiate all segregationists, declare racial discrimination to be unconstitutional, endorse the southern sit-ins as having the same validity as labor strikes, support the reduction of congressional representation in districts that deny Negroes the right to vote, uphold the Supreme Court's 1954 school desegregation decision as morally right and the law of the land, and condemn colonialism and racism in all their forms East and West."

"They're awfully strong demands," Tom said as he walked into the office with Rachelle next to him. "No way you're going to get either party to agree to them."

"That's why it's imperative that we conduct the protest outside both conventions," I said.

That's a bold move for any organization," Tom continued. "Neither of the candidates are going to take kindly with you interfering in their attempt to a smooth convention."

"That all can be avoided if they simply agree to our demands," Ella said.

"Most important is that we remain as a unified force for change," I said just as the phone rang. I grabbed it up and stiffened as I heard a rather emotional Mr. Randolph on the other end.

"Bayard, Martin wants to pull out of the protest," he shouted.

"What? You can't be serious."

"I just talked with him down in Brazil. He was practically hysterical, and it has to do with you."

"I don't understand."

"Adam Clayton Powell has threatened him with a serious rumor about the two of you."

I gripped the phone tightly. It didn't take a genius to know what rumor he would spread. "He wouldn't dare."

"Yes, he would, and Martin is running scared. Plans on pulling out of the protests."

"Why, he knows it's not true."

"Doesn't matter, that's not a hole he'd want to try to crawl out of."

"I'm going to call Martin right now and tell him he just can't do this. He can't give in to that kind of pressure."

"I think that's a good idea." I could detect the urgency in his voice. "He listens to you and might listen now." Randolph finished and we hung up.

I sat stone faced not exactly knowing how to take all this in. How deceptive and unethical could one man be? Was his venom directed at me because of my sexual preferences, or at Martin because of his successes over the past five years? Successes that tended to diminish those of Powell. This egotistical maniac would sacrifice the advancement of the entire race for his own gratification. Frederick Douglass once wrote that power concedes nothing without a struggle, never has and never will. We were in the middle of a struggle but the pathetic aspect, not against a bunch of bigots but against one of our own.

"What's going on?" Stanley broke my musing. "What happened with that call that's changed your entire behavior?"

"I need about fifteen-minute privacy if you all don't mind?" This had to be a private conversation between Martin and me.

"What's wrong, Bayard?" Tom now asked.

"Please, just give me some privacy," I scowled.

I closed my eyes so that I wouldn't be affected by the stares that came from each of them, as they got up and made their way out of the room. Rachelle closed the door behind them, and I grabbed the phone. This had to be one of the most difficult calls I had to make in my entire life.

"Martin, this is Bayard," I said as he came on the phone. "What is going on?"

There was a pause and I didn't know if he would talk to me. Finally, "Bayard, I guess Phil has filled you in by now and that's the reason for this call."

"Exactly," I said. "He also told me that you want to pull out of the protests. Is that correct?"

"This man is dangerous, and he will go to the press and tell them that he has it from a good source that we are engaged in a relationship."

"But you know it's not true."

"You know that, and I do too, but I cannot have my name associated with such a tainted kind of affair."

His words offended me. Nothing about my relationships were anymore tainted than the ones he conducted outside his marriage. "I take offense at that language Martin."

"I'm sorry, I didn't mean it in an offensive manner, but you have to know that my career would be ruined if that kind of rumor surfaced."

"The rumor is already out there about your extra marital affairs, what's the difference?"

"Society is more willing and understanding of an affair between a man and woman, but they are not tolerant of one between two men or two women. That's just where we are today, Bayard, and there's nothing we can do to change it."

"But you're willing to put everything on the line to change the prejudice against our people but not against another minority group."

278 | Williams-Denton-Zinsmeyer

"I'm sorry Bayard, but there's nothing I can do but bow out of the protest marches. My ministry, the congregation at Ebenezer and all the Negroes who believe in me would be devastated if this kind of rumor got out."

Maybe I didn't know this man after all. Maybe he just hid his homophobia better than the others. All along I believed we had a much tighter bond, one that couldn't be broken by a rumor and a lie. I took this as a personal affront, but quickly recognized that despite my personal feelings, we could not lose Martin and the SCLC on this project. We couldn't let Powell win. The sacrifice had to come from me.

"If I resign from the project and no longer serve as an advisor to you, maybe that will take the steam out of Powell's threat." I said with great reluctance.

"That just might work," King said. "If you're no longer in the picture then the issue of homosexuality goes away."

His concurrence stung deeply inside of me. I thought he might reject that idea and do as I knew Mr. Randolph would, and fight against the bigotry. But he didn't and now I had to follow through and resign from the project and disappear into obscurity. This, I knew, could end my involvement in the civil rights movement, but I also knew it was the sacrifice I had to make.

"You do understand why this has to be done," King continued. "This could be too much of a distraction for what we must accomplish."

I wanted to shout into the phone to please do not justify your cowardly behavior by trying to convince me that what you are doing is for the best. But instead, I agreed with him. "I will make my resignation known to Mr. Randolph and will also make it clear that I no longer advise you, and that you are not in any way under my influence."

Momentarily silence prevailed. I imagined Martin trying to order his words so not to offend me anymore than he had done.

"Bayard, you have to know that this is not something I want to do, but something I have to do. You have been so good to me and to our cause in the South, so that I feel something like a traitor to our friendship."

Somewhat traitorous and I wanted to tell him that, but again I exercised proper restraint. I just wanted to get off the phone and get out of this precarious position I occupied in a movement that didn't want someone like me involved. This time I vowed to step away from a movement I'd come to love, and deal with other matters that I always put on hold for the cause.

"I understand Martin." I lied. "But I'll always be available to you. I love my people very deeply and will do anything to achieve change in this country. You will lead that change Martin. Do it well my friend and hopefully we will be able to work together sometime in future."

"I hope so Bayard. Be blessed my friend."

We finished and hung up.

33.

The seething anger I felt had subsided after a week of solitude, doing nothing but playing my harpsicord, reading Ralph Ellison's Invisible Man and James Baldwin's, "Another Country" and "Giovanni's Room," all for the second time. Martin and the SCLC Board totally cut me off from any communications with them in an official capacity, and I would undoubtedly be taken off the payroll. I no longer represented them in the New York Community, and a few of the ministers even took this as an opportunity to denounce me as a sexual pervert and a sinful man. Martin didn't go to that extreme, but he never denounced those attacks. Despite his betrayal, I still believed in him, simply because I had faith that he would be the Moses of the Negro and carry the race to a promised land.

His betrayal caused a stir within the intellectual community in New York. Nat Hentoff wrote a scathing article attacking his actions. I read it with a great deal of satisfaction and viewed it also as strong support for me in a "Village Voice" article when he told the readers that, "He worked for years," speaking of me, "as the most brilliant tactician in the civil rights field." He turned his poison pen on the flamboyant congressman. "Powell's flamboyance on a platform is a poor substitute for Rustin's integrity and skill in the wings."

The leading Negro writer of the day, James Baldwin also took a swipe at Martin in an article in "Fortune Magazine." I also found great solace in his words. "King lost much moral credit in the eyes of the young, when he allowed Adam Clayton Powell to force the resignation of his extremely able organizer and lieutenant, Bayard Rustin. Rustin has a long and honorable record as a fighter for Negro rights and is one of the most penetrating and able men around. The techniques used by Powell were far from sweet; but King was faced with the choice of defending his organizer, who was also his friend, or agreeing with Powell; and he chose the latter course."

My spirits were also boosted when I received a note from Lorraine Hansberry, "Bayard, I was shocked at the Powell business and horrified. Needless to say, you are one of the most precious sons that the Negro people and this country ever produced. I appreciated the support from intellectuals of their caliber. It assured me that I did something right. I recognized that the bigots had scored a temporary victory, but knew, in the long run, they would regret turning their back on me. I was the real force behind the Civil Rights Movement and in many ways the brains behind King's successes. I knew he realized that fact and someday would reach out to me again.

Besides King's refusal to support me against the other attackers, my greatest disappointment came from Stanley Levinson. Since the formation of In Friendship back in 1956, we'd worked together on the formation of SCLC, the Prayer Pilgrimage and advising Martin on various positions he should take on different issues. Stanley and I had a standing breakfast date every Wednesday and Thursday. Right after my expulsion from representing King and the SCLC in New York, he conveniently began to find excuses not to join me in the mornings, and soon after he closed our office space in his building. To my utter dismay I soon heard that right before Martin decided to cut all ties with me, he had a conversation with Stanley. Despite that Stanley was a known Communist, he convinced Martin that my homosexuality was a larger risk to him. He led him to believe that attitudes in the country toward homosexuals were too volatile for King to deal with. The rumor that Martin and I had an affair did not go over well in the anti-gay Negro religious community, and that he needed to regain their confidence by cutting all ties with me.

Since my work with the Civil Rights Movement seemed to be over, the other members of our team also began working in other areas. Ella moved on to work with the emerging Student Non-Violent Coordinating Committee, Tom had gone on to study at Howard University and Rachelle took a job with the Workers Defense League in New York.

Mr. Randolph continued to be my closest friend and ally. He insisted that I work even closer with him on the labor issues and I began to spend most of my time, when I wasn't traveling, in his Harlem office. I began to occupy most of my time between dealing with nuclear dis-armament issues and the problems that the school union in New York had with the Board of Education and the Mayor's Office.

Even though I had been removed from any participation in the planned boycott, I followed closely its development. Powell's attempt to disrupt the protest failed. The Sunday before the beginning of the Democratic Convention, King spoke at a Kick-off Rally, but despite his efforts only 65 pickets showed up the next day. In fact, King kind of disappeared from the rallies and, according to Michael Harrington who called me every day, King spent most of his time in a hotel room, talking politics with Michael. The third day of the convention, Michael called me and shared his impression that Martin really was socialist at heart and did not believe Negroes would ever achieve economic parity under a capitalist system. That made him feel good since he happened to be one of the leading socialists in the country. Having Martin as an ally was encouraging.

Two weeks later in Chicago, the demonstration at the Republican convention was limited to a single protest rally on Tuesday, led by Martin, Mr. Randolph, and Roy Wilkins, who had finally joined them after King reached out to him. When Mr. Randolph returned to New York he made it quite clear that the effort missed my organizing skills, and they never should have allowed me to pull out of the planning stages of the event.

Despite a hunger to still be a part of the movement, I faced the reality that for now my participation ended. That's when I received a call from Ed Gottlieb, Executive Chair of the War Resister's League.

"Bayard, we want you back over here working on issues that are becoming really important," he said with no hesitation.

"In what capacity and I need to get some kind of salary now that SCLC has terminated my working relationship with them?"

"You get your old position back as Executive Secretary and salary has to be negotiated. Our budget is way below twenty thousand, but we'll squeeze something out for you. What do you say, you want to come back to your old job?"

Instead of fighting for the rights of Negroes if I took the position with War Resisters League, I'd be fighting to get rid of the nuclear arsenal. I knew for sure my passion was still with the civil rights movement, but

I had no choice I had to eat. This would be a smooth transition and instead of applying the non-violent philosophy to fighting segregation in the South, I would now apply it to fighting nuclear proliferation all over the world.

"What do you say, Bayard, you want to come back and work with us? We need you." Ed allowed just a little pleading to creep into his voice.

After what I had just been through, his words "we need you" were like music to my ears. "Yes, definitely. When can I start?"

"Tomorrow, if you're ready to go. We're still over here on 45th Street and I have office space all ready for you."

"Who is active with the group now?" I asked, not that it mattered. I was going to take the job regardless. But after the last five years of fighting men who had a hang up with my sexual preference, I wanted to make sure that wouldn't again be a problem.

"The same group of activists who were here back in 56. Your friend David McReynolds for one."

Enough said. David and I had been friends for years. He shared many of the same attributes as me, one he was gay and two he believed in the need for a redistribution of resources to equal out the country's skewed distribution of money.

"George and Lillian Willoughby are very active," Ed continued. "In fact, George serves as the Director of the Committee for Non-Violent Action and when you get here tomorrow, they want to discuss a major plan for a major protest against the nuclear proliferation that has taken over this world."

"I'll be there first thing in the morning," I said. We hung up and I called Mr. Randolph to share the news with him. I closed the harpsicord, strolled into the bedroom. It was time to come out of hiding. I decided to spend a few hours at Julius in the West Village.

"Bayard, this is a young man with a monumental goal," Ed said as I walked into the conference room of the War Resister League Office. "Brad Lytle meet the great one, Bayard Rustin."

Brad was a skinny, young kid with long stringy hair and wore horn-rimmed glasses. We shook hands and all sat at the conference table.

"Brad has a great idea, tell it to him," Ed said.

"Yes sir," Brad sat straight up in his chair and looked at me. "Me and sixteen other protestors of nuclear proliferation plan to march to Moscow and confront the Soviet government."

"Okay, how do you plan to get there?" I asked.

"Walk across the United States from San Francisco to New York, making strategic stops in Chicago, Washington, D.C. and leave out of New York by plane. We then plan to land in London and pick up our walk from there, going through France, Germany and straight north until we reach Moscow."

I first glanced over at Ed and then stared at this young man who I believed had lost his senses. "You plan to do what?"

"Some group has to take a stand against the idiocy that has control of both the government in this country and in Moscow. And how better to make that point than by walking for peace. And we want you to be a part of this effort," Brad exclaimed.

"Logistically, that would be a nightmare," I said. "There is no way you can make it all the way to Moscow by walking."

"We certainly want the support of the War Resisters League, but we plan to do it with or without your support."

"I don't know, sounds just a little too ambitious," I said.

"But I think we can offer our support if you have the young people who are willing to try," Ed intervened. "When do you plan to start out?"

"December 1," Brad replied. "I plan to fly out to San Francisco on Friday, and we will start out on that Monday."

"When you make it to London, you'll really need Bayard's assistance since he is very familiar with the rules and the dealings with the different countries you'll be entering."

I gave Ed a hard stare. Did he just volunteer my time to this effort that was certain to fail?

"I would offer his services when you take out from San Francisco, but he'll be in India with me at the annual War Resisters Conference."

Now, I really gave him a hard stare. No one had mentioned going to India before and so this was the first time I heard of it.

"We have pretty much laid out our plans for travel throughout the United States," an excited Brad continued, "we have the sixteen who will make the trip and have set up stops for evening rests. There are ten men and six women who will make the trip."

I stretched my arms out on the conference table and leaned forward in the chair. "I will do what I can to assist you all, but I want to go on record as opposing this particular project. It's much too risky and the problems you're going to confront, if you make it to Europe, are almost insurmountable. But we will help."

"Thank you, Mr. Rustin. It was important that we get your support because you are probably the most recognized leader of the non-violent protest movement in this country, after the successes you had assisting Dr. King in achieving in the civil rights movement. And now we do need your assistance in achieving similar results in resisting war and nuclear proliferation."

"We will try as best to follow your progress," Ed said as he stood, and we followed his lead. "And there should be no problem getting Bayard to London to assist in the European leg of the trip."

"I'll be in touch with you all once I get to San Francisco," Brad said.

I admired this brash, young man and certainly wanted them to succeed. It occurred to me that all protest movements at the time faced incredible odds. Martin was in the middle of the battle to eradicate a segregated country and Brad now leading a struggle to eliminate nuclear weapons in the world. I felt especially fortunate to participate in both movements, despite that my activities with Martin had come to an end.

Once Brad had made his way out of the office, I turned and looked directly at Ed.

"India, when did that come about?" I asked.

"It had always been in my plans for you to go with George Willoughby and Jeanette Rankin," Ed replied. "It's the Tenth Tercentennial Conference of the War Resisters International and for the first time it's being held outside of England. And for a very good reason."

Not bad company I thought. Willoughby was Chair of the Committee for Non-Violent Action and had a great reputation as a fighter for the elimination of all violence in society. Jeanette had been the first elected woman to the United States Congress, and voted against our entry into World War I in 1917 and against entry into World War II in 1941. She possessed an impeccable commitment to non-violence.

"A serious disagreement is brewing between Western countries and those in Asia and Africa, and you may end up being the mediator between the two."

I knew of the battle brewing between the East and the West, but never figured I'd be pulled into the middle of the fight. War Resisters had formed in Great Britain during World War I as an uncompromising voice against the violence and destruction of the war. Its goal had always been an emphasis on opposition to warfare.

Gandhi changed that emphasis as he began to use non-violence differently. He concentrated his emphasis against colonialism. As a result, all the delegates from Africa and Asia were more interested in concentrating on the injustices of colonialism, whereas, the Western countries wanted to stress opposition to nuclear war. That's why the conference was to be held in India for the very first time. Every year prior it had been held in England.

"I'm not sure I'm ready to take on that kind of responsibility," I finally spoke up. "There are over sixty-five countries represented at the conference, with a larger number of members than the United States. Surely they can find someone else to mediate this battle."

"You're right, there will be a lot of delegates there, but out of the large number, no one is as qualified to mediate and bring this possible confrontation to an amicable close as you."

"I appreciate the compliment, but I'm not quite sure that's a fact." Since Montgomery, I had been thrown in the middle of the various battles between friends and enemies of the movement, now I was about to be thrust into an international one.

"Bayard, need I list all the reasons why you are perfect fit for this role?" Ed asked.

"No, I guess not. When do we leave?"

"Tomorrow evening. I have your ticket but don't dare give it to you now. You might decide to conveniently lose it."

"Yeah, you're right. It might be more than just conveniently, but instead deliberately."

"Get out of here and go do what you have to so you can leave tomorrow," Ed instructed. "You think you made a mark in Montgomery and in Washington, that'll be minor with what you are about to accomplish internationally. On the long plane ride over there, make sure you study the issues completely." Ed handed me a folder with several different documents. "This will give you a very clear understanding of the situation even though, I believe you already understand what's going on."

I took the folder, gave him one final hard stare and headed out of the office.

34.

I stared out the window of Air India Flight 1010 as it circled Calcutta in preparation for landing, and memories of my trip here back in 1947 vividly came to me. The plane made a very smooth landing, taxied up to the terminal and we made our way off. As soon as we walked into the terminal, I saw a man holding a sign that read Mr. Rustin, Mr. Willoughby and Mrs. Rankin. He smiled when he spotted us, probably assuming we were the three he should pick up and drive the two hundred and fifty miles to Gandhigram. I had been on that plane for over fifteen hours and didn't want to sit for another five hours in a jeep. But I had no choice. I had plenty of time to read the papers included in the file Ed gave me to review.

"We are the three that you are looking for," George said. There would be no language barrier in India. They had been under the Colonial rule of England for so long, most all the people, especially those in the cities, spoke the language.

"Welcome to India, I am going to be your driver to Grandhigram," the young man said. "Please follow me and we can get your luggage from down below and be on our way."

We followed the young man down to the baggage claim area, retrieved our luggage and walked out of the airport to the curb where the young boy had the car parked illegally. I smiled knowing that the police had ignored his illegal parking, because the young man probably had slipped him a rupee. The driver piled the luggage on top of the Jeep and tied it down. George and Jeanette climbed in the back seats and I sat up front next to the driver.

As he pulled out into the traffic he said, "Get ready for a pretty bumpy ride up to Grandhigram. The roads are still underdeveloped, and we had a very heavy rain over the past week leaving a lot of holes in the road. "

When we finally arrived in this small village town named after Gandhi, a large crowd of War Resisters stood in front of the house where we would lodge for the duration of the conference. I immediately spotted

Devi Prasad, a face from the past. I first met Devi in 1946 when I made my first trip to India to study Gandhian Philosophy of non-violence. When the small car came to a stop, I jumped out and rushed over to Devi.

"My God, I never expected to see you here with the American delegation," Devi said as we hugged and shook hands. "I've been following your career in the United States and assumed you were deeply involved in the civil rights movement with Dr. Martin Luther King."

"I have been until recently," I said. "But now I'm back involved in the entire war resister movement, because of the problem we all confront with the proliferation of nuclear weapons." I didn't see the need to go into a lot of detail.

"We must have dinner and get caught up on all that has been going on in our lives," Devi said.

"Let's do that," I concurred just as Willoughby tapped me on the shoulder.

"Bayard, we need to go inside and check in. Seems as though we will share a room with two representatives from Great Britain."

I followed Willoughby inside where we stood in front a man sitting behind a desk staring at a paper with names on it. He looked up at us when we approached the desk.

"We are from the United States delegation," Willoughby said.

"Ah yes," the man said as he spotted our names on the paper. "Mr. Willoughby and Mr. Rustin, you will be sharing a room with two others. You are on the second floor. The bathroom is at the end of the hall. Please be patient because there are twenty others on that floor, and you all will be sharing the bathroom. Dinner will be at seven this evening in the main dining room straight ahead." He paused and snapped his finger. A young boy, no more than thirteen, ran up to the desk. "Take this luggage to Room 217 and be careful. You can follow him up to your room and I'll see you in a few hours for supper."

Just as we followed the young boy, I whispered to Jeanette who still stood in line for her room assignment, "See you at dinner."

She smiled and replied, "Okay."

A strong musty smell hung in the air as we entered the room. Four cots lined up along each wall, with two dressers and a couple lounge chairs. It was not the most comfortable living quarters but could be tolerated for the few days we'd be there. I grabbed the bed closest to the window and the boy put my luggage on top of it. He did the same with George's luggage and then stood there with his hand out.

I looked at George. "I don't have any converted money."

"Neither do I," George said.

"That is quite all right. I can take American money," the boy said.

I pulled out a dime and gave it to him. George gave him a nickel.

"Thank you," the boy said and rushed out of the room.

"He should do pretty good this weekend," I said as I watched him leave the room and close the door behind him. "Most of the people coming in today and tomorrow will have only the money of their country and probably the conversion to rupee is much higher and will give him a nice day's work."

George flopped down on his cot and stretched his body with his head resting on the pillow. "I could skip dinner and just sleep through to tomorrow," he said.

I also sat on the side of my bed. "I know what you mean, but you know we can't do that."

As I relaxed back on the cot and closed my eyes, the door swung open and the young boy strolled into the room followed by two men who looked to be in their early twenties. He placed the luggage on the beds and stood in the middle of the room with his hand and arm extended.

The two men pulled out coins and handed them to the boy, who then darted back out the door.

I looked over at George. "Yes, he's going to do quite well before the day is over." I then got up and extended my hand to the new arrivals. "My name is Bayard Rustin from the United States and this gentleman over here on the bed is George Willoughby, also from the United States."

"Mr. Bayard Rustin as I live and breathe," one of the men said as he shook my hand and squeezed it tightly. "Your reputation precedes you.

We knew we'd be sharing a room with two Americans, but never dreamt it would be with Mr. Rustin. My name is Mike Sinclair from Liverpool."

"Mike it's a pleasure…"

"Mr. Rustin, I'm Samuel Johnson, it is a real pleasure to share a room with you," the second young man interrupted me. "You are a hero among the Gandhian Non-Violent believers in England, because of the excellent work you have done in the United States fighting against an Apartheid government there."

I felt a little uncomfortable as the two men simply ignored George just as if he wasn't in the room. "We all have put time in for the cause in our country," I said hoping that would bring George into the conversation.

"Being from the United States and knowing how important it is that our Western nations stick together, I imagine you all will join us when the debate begins on the direction that the War Resisters League should go in the future," Mike said.

After fifteen hours on a flight and another ten hours over rough terrain, I wasn't really in the mood to tackle the assumption in his statement. But it needed a response. "I believe we may see merit in both sides of the argument, but we do look forward to a healthy discussion and an agreeable resolution to the issue."

"You know the only reason the Asian and African delegations insisted that the conference be held in India this year, is because this country was once under English rule and being a former colony will make it easier to argue their point of view," Samuel said just as if he had shared information with us that we did not know.

"You do know the days of colonial rule are quickly coming to an end," I said.

"Yes, and we do hope they can end without having to change the original mission of the War Resisters League. After all, the question of nuclear proliferation is much more important than any other issues out there today," Samuel said.

Finally, George spoke up. "One thing is certain and that is we will not solve the problem now because it is dinner time. Let's go meet other members and have an enjoyable dinner."

"Sounds like a wonderful suggestion," Mike said. "I understand the use of the toilet facilities may be much more of an issue to deal with than colonialism and nuclear proliferation since we only have one facility for all of us."

We all made our way out of the room. "Just like always, we will find an answer to all the pressing problems tomorrow during our general meeting," Samuel said.

"I agree and well spoken," George said as we sauntered down the long hallway to the dining table.

"As all the delegates to this conference know, the great Mahatma Gandhi took the idea of non-violence as a protest weapon to a new level when he aimed it against the British Colonial Rule here in India," Sri G. Ramachandran, a disciple of Gandhi and convener of the conference began his opening remarks to all of us congregated in the auditorium. "The most important issue confronting this organization is the subjugation of native populations in Africa and here in Asia. And the most pressing issue is that this subjugation come to an end as we move into the first decade of the second half of the Twentieth Century. It is important that with a new beginning comes a fresh and new outlook on life. The past World War showed the world the dangers implicit in imperialism as well as its evil nature."

He paused as the auditorium erupted in applause for his words. Some of the delegates from Africa jumped to their feet and raised their fists in the air. He signaled for them to calm down and continued.

"You cannot have an exploiting society talking about peace. You cannot evade the issue of injustice and then talk of peace. I think peace without justice will be a complete fraud."

Once he finished his remarks a man from the Dutch delegation stood to his feet and shouted. "Allow us the privilege of rebuttal."

"Are you a spokesperson for the Western nations present here today?" Ramachandran asked while still at the podium.

"Yes, the European nations expected this attack from the others and prepared for a response. I am Johannes Van Hoebeek, from the province of South Holland in the Netherlands. Our country knows the ravages of war like many other countries in Europe. We were invaded by the Nazi Army on May 10, 1940 and remained under their vicious control for five years. We suffered over two-hundred and ten thousand deaths, of which one-hundred and forty thousand were Jews who fell victim to genocide at the hands of the Nazis. We understand suffering and do recognize at sometime soon colonialism must end. But because we were no match for the Nazi army, they destroyed our country and we are still recovering. That is why we believe that eradication of extremely powerful weapons must be our first consideration at this conference. With all due respect to my brethren from Asia and Africa, we must never lose track of our first driving goal, and that is confronting the evils of nuclear proliferation." Johannes finished and returned to his seat in the auditorium.

"Any other speakers from the Western contingent," Ramchandran asked.

I watched as the young man from England stood and made his way to the podium.

"My name is Samuel Johnson from the United Kingdom. On behalf of our entire delegation of twenty participants, I want to thank Ramchandran for the outstanding job he has done bringing us altogether, but I must take exception with his claim that India is free of any commitment to become a strategically located state in our fight against communism flowing out of the Soviet Union regularly. And it appears that India may not be entirely truthful when dealing with this very touchy subject. We are aware that Prime Minister Nehru has ordered an increase in the number of weapons that the country will purchase, as the skirmish between this country and Pakistan picks up steam because they both claim rights to Kashmir. Your country is also concerned with your Chinese border and Goa and even the Portuguese. Potential conflicts in the future with these countries has forced your country to build weapon's stores." Samuel finished and sauntered back to his seat.

"Please allow me to respond to Brother Samuel Johnson's comments," Ramachandran said as he returned to the microphone. "We in the War Resisters League here in India have raised noise with the authorities regarding that problem. We have received negligent response. In the very near future, you will read of mass demonstrations in the streets of New Delhi, protesting the actions of our government."

I had been so busy wrapped up in the civil rights struggles back home that I failed to follow the problems developing between the different countries. There was no excuse at all for colonialism to continue. But the young spokesman from Great Britain did not address that issue at all. Instead he thought he'd pointed to India's duplicity but with very little favorable response. This was not, however, a win or lose situation. Without this group's support for the end of colonialism, our international following may suffer.

"Colonialism is the sin of the world," an African delegate had made it to the podium and taken the microphone. I didn't see him as he made his way to the front. I was completely absorbed in the map in front of me. "Imperialism and colonialism go hand and hand and the African continent has suffered more than any other location in the world over the past centuries. It is time for pacifists to take a strong stand against these two evil 'isms.'" He finished and hurried back to his seat.

Mike Sinclair, the other pacifists from England, practically ran up to the podium and grabbed the microphone. "The only major nuclear power here with us today is the United States and they, right now as we meet in India, have a delegation of pacifists who are walking from San Francisco to New York with plans to fly to Europe and continue their walk to Moscow. It appears that their position is one of concentrating on the proliferation of nuclear weapons as the primary problem confronting all nations."

Ramchandran hurried up and stood next to Mike. He leaned toward the microphone and said. "One of the representatives from the United States is Mr. Bayard Rustin. He can clarify the position of the country's pacifist community, if he'll come forward and address the delegation." He waved for me to come to the podium. "Please, Mr. Rustin address the delegation. We need to know the position of your country as to what is the most important issue confronting the pacifist community, nuclear proliferation or colonialism and imperialism."

Not sure what to say or how to address this imbroglio between my friends, I slowly strolled up to the podium and took control of the microphone. I knew my preference was for the movement to take on the cause of apartheid in the United States and colonialism throughout Africa and still in some parts of Asia. But it needed to be balanced because the threat of nuclear proliferation was real. And, if by chance, an all-out nuclear war happened to break out, then none of the other issues would really matter.

"You all are very much aware of the battle waging in my country for equal rights for all our citizens," I began. "That struggle is much like the one here in India, just over fifteen years ago when the great leader Mahatma Gandhi used the tactic of non-violence to finally bring down colonial rule in his country. Those of us who accept pacifism as the only sensible way for people of the world to deal with their differences, must always stay united."

I paused to collect my thoughts as I moved forward. I had to connect both the fight against colonial rule with the continuous struggle to prevent nuclear proliferation together. There was no way that this collection of peace-loving men and women should leave this place as anything other than one in unity. "Both militarism, nuclear proliferation and colonial oppression are sinful and wrong, and we must stand together against all these evils. As much as the great Negro leader Dr. Martin Luther King, Jr. hates segregation, he despises all forms of violence just as much." Again, I paused to assess the mood of the listeners. They appeared to be content on listening to my every word, so I continued. "Whether the problem be that of war, color or caste, man can be unjust to man. American to American, Indian to Indian. The problem is rooted in man's ability to be unjust; and therefore, can only be approached if we are opposed to all injustice. It is not a matter of one being more important than the other for us as a collective body. They both are important and most important is that we continue to work together for peace, freedom and equality all over the world." I finished and felt a sense of success when the entire body of delegates applauded me.

296 | Williams-Denton-Zinsmeyer

I returned to my chair and listened as all the speakers after me seemed to add to my comments of unity. When we finished, a consensus had been reached that all our struggles should be built around the Gandhian tactic of non-violence, with both the master himself and Dr. King as examples of how to be successful.

My words continued to resonate throughout the conference for the next two days and whenever possible, delegates from different countries extended invitations to me to visit them in their homeland. My schedule was so intense that I never had the opportunity to have a lunch or dinner with my old friend Devi. By noon of the third day, the same driver who had brought us out to Gandhigram also packed our bags on the same car for the trip back to Calcutta.

With Jeanette and George in the back seat, I climbed in the passenger seat. The driver was about to pull off when Devi came running up to the car.

"Bayard, my friend I am sorry we didn't get a chance to spend some time together and get caught up on what has been going on in our lives," he said.

"The conference was a whirlwind of activities and I seemed to be called to every meeting with no break," I said.

"I know you were the hero of the conference with your remarks the other day. You have set the standard for the pacifist movement as it goes forward and prepares later on for next year's conference. Hopefully, we will have it again here in Gandhigram and then maybe we will have more time to talk."

Hopefully so," I agreed. We shook hands and he moved back away from the car. The driver pulled off from the curb and we began our journey back to Calcutta.

After ten hours of traversing the rough roads, we finally arrived back in Calcutta. On our way back to the city, George and I decided to spend a day or two there visiting with our friend, Vinova Bhave, who was the original inheritor of Gandhi's philosophy on non-violence. Calcutta was one of the poorest cities in the world and we wanted to get a close-up look at the extent of its poverty, and no one better to take us through the streets of the city than Vinova.

After dropping Jeanette off at the airport, the driver took us to the home of our friend, and he greeted us at the door.

"My fine American friends I assume that you all are just coming back from the conference in Gandhigram."

"We are and decided to postpone our trip back home for a day so that we could visit with you," I said.

"Good, then come in and you shall spend the night here with me."

Taking our shoes off at the door, we followed him into his living room, where there was no furniture but a mantle with a bust of Buddha and a picture of Gandhi. The floor was lined with cushion pillows. Vinova gestured pointing at the floor. I managed to sit down and cross my long legs, not a very comfortable position for me. George seemed to struggle also to get to the floor and position himself on a pillow. Vinova, obviously had no problem at all.

"I understand that you became the center of attention at the conference this past weekend," Vinova said looking at me. "We in the pacifist movement are confronting a real and potentially destructive dilemma. If the Western World stays at odds with the emerging nations in Asia and Africa, there is no way our unity will continue, and the major super powers engaged in an insane war of weapon proliferation will eventually destroy all of us."

"And I was thrown right in the middle of that chaos," I said.

"You were the right one," Vinova suggested. "Being a Negro from the United States, you are in a unique position. Your country is one of the super powers with enough nuclear capability to destroy the entire world, so you are obliged as a pacifist to support the position of the Western nations and that is abolition of all weapons of mass destruction." He paused and shifted his position on the pillow. "You also are a Negro who has been the victim of a vicious apartheid system of oppression and, of course, you share the pain and suffering of your homeland in Africa. You recognize the dangers of these weapons in the hands of White Europeans and Americans and you also recognize the sinful nature of these same people, because of their greed to control other people's countries. It was best that you spoke to the issue and from what I have heard, did a great job of moderating between the two groups."

"I noticed coming into Calcutta young boys and girls eating out of the same garbage pile right next to the hogs," George finally intervened and joined the discussion. "I have never seen this kind of poverty before."

"Yes, you are absolutely correct. You will not see this level of poverty in too many countries, although we know it does exist all over the world, and especially, in those countries that fell prey to the exploitation of the Western countries," Vinova explained. "In Calcutta, it was called the drain of wealth and this city can stand as the best example of British arrogance and their greed." He paused to study our response. He got none and continued. "The British did not attempt to integrate into our society as other invaders in past centuries did. They never meant for the wealth to remain here, but instead took every drop of resources out of here and straight to England. The result is what you will see in the morning when we tour the city and visit a village."

Listening to Vinova explain what happened in India as a result of a one-hundred-year occupation of the country by Great Britain, I realized that my dislike and distrust of a capitalist system was well placed. As an economic system, it has served European countries quite well, but for all other people around the world it has been a nightmare. I briefly thought of Wilbur and Mae back in the Mississippi Delta. They had something in common with the people here in India, they both have been exploited and robbed of dignity by white people. All this re-enforced my firm belief that nothing in the world will change until capitalism is rejected and replaced with a socialist economic system. I knew my feelings would be vindicated in the morning when we viewed poverty in Calcutta.

36.

It was a great site looking down on New York City as our plane circled the airport and started its final descent to the ground. Over the years, I had travelled quite a bit and it always felt great when I arrived back home. This had been a relatively short trip, usually they lasted for two or three months. After leaving India, I stopped off in London to visit with my good friend April Carter one of the leading pacifists in all of England. Even though we had been together throughout the entire trip, George and I parted company as he continued to the States. But no matter how long I was gone, when I saw the Statue of Liberty and the Empire State Building, a feeling of relief came over me. I planned to stay home through the winter, and even though I had been removed from any involvement in the Civil Rights Movement, I would follow it closely. The sit-ins had escalated over the past three months and my contribution was quite visible as the students employed the non-violent tactic. I wanted to be available to them if they needed my assistance in training others, as the number of students participating continued to grow on all the Black college campuses.

After landing, I followed the passengers off the plane and down to the baggage area. It was still early Saturday evening, and I planned to spend some quality time with the men I considered my real friends and not just associates. I grabbed my luggage, hurried outside and jumped into a cab. I needed to drop my suitcase off at the apartment freshen up, then head over to Julius and have some time to myself and be who I really am. I had tried to conform to what society dictates from a gay man and it never seemed to work well for me. Even though I did exceptional work for Martin and the civil rights movement, in the end they turned their back on me. For this night, I was determined to do what makes me happy. I would not spend the night alone.

A little after ten o'clock I sauntered into Julius and an exuberant excitement shot through me as I saw Tennessee Williams sitting at a table with his partner Fred Merlo. I had met Williams one time before when a plaque honoring Eugene O'Neal was placed at the Barrett House on

Broadway. I had always admired O'Neal for his first major production, **Emperor Jones.**

Williams recognized me as he waved me over to their table, where there was one empty chair.

"Bayard Rustin, the one man who has set out to change the South, how are you?" Williams asked as I sat down and shook hands with both men.

"Frustrated because the South has to be forced to change," I replied. "You know that better than me, having come from Mississippi."

"I believe we met at the laying of the plaque in honor of Eugene O'Neal a few years ago," Williams said ignoring my response to his question. "Eugene was one of the great pioneers in confronting issues head on. He undoubtedly will go down in literary history as one of the greatest playwrights of the century."

Just as he finished, the waiter strolled up to the table. "Can I get you all another round, and how about you my friend?" he asked looking at me.

"Yes, bring the same for the two of us and also my friend's order," Williams said.

"Double Scotch and soda. Light on the soda." I said.

The waiter wrote the order and quickly walked away.

"A double, you mean to act up tonight," Williams said.

"I been out of the country for the past week in India and had no chance to imbibe," I said in defense of my order. "I don't mean to act up, but to catch up."

"How much catching up do you plan to do?" Fred asked as he joined in the discussion.

"Let's just say, I don't plan to leave this place alone tonight," I said.

"In all seriousness, the work you've done with Dr. King has been outstanding," Williams said. "I read Jimmy Baldwin's article in "**Harper's Magazine**" and agree with him. Dr. King lost a great deal of his moral authority by turning his back on you."

"I won't deny that I was hurt when he didn't turn down my resignation to represent SCLC in New York, but also relieved that I was now removed as an obstacle to the forward progress of the movement."

The waiter placed our drinks on the table in front of us. I snatched mine and took a large sip.

"Bayard, no man has a right to pick and choose what group of people in this country should or should not have what they believe to be their quality of life," Williams said as he also took a sip from his glass. "Your choice in who you spend your time with outside your professional career is no one's business and Dr. King was wrong to not stand up for you."

"He's a minister," I suggested. "He is not his own man in that capacity, he is a captive of the church and the dictates of that body. There are certain positions that he can take and there will be no repercussions from the church body, and then there are others he just cannot take. Accepting a homosexual man as part of his team was more than he could get the others to accept and, therefore, more than he could accomplish."

"This world believes that we are sub-human, filthy and immoral human beings," Williams quipped with cynicism. "Allen Grey in **Street Car Named Desire**, commits suicide after Blanche calls him disgusting because he is having an affair with an older man."

"I wondered if the charge of being disgusting was because he was having an affair or because the affair was with another man," I asked.

"Williams smiled. "Isn't that the beauty of literature, be it a novel or play, you create questions that only the reader or audience can answer, and they do so to their satisfaction."

"I've been fortunate to live in the lifetime of some of the very best playwrights. Of course, you, O'Neil and Arthur Miller are the very best this country has to offer," I said.

"You're very kind and I appreciate the compliment," Williams said. "As a writer, I look at society and then try to create stories that project a better world for all of us. But you on the other hand actually do something to make that change a reality. And for that matter, I admire your tenacity. You can never give up my friend. We need you." Williams lifted his glass up and finished off his drink. "We need to get out of here and leave you to your pursuits for the night."

He and Fred stood up. Williams dropped two twenties on the table. "Have another drink on us. This will cover my tab." We hugged and he and Fred sauntered to the front and out the door. I sat back down at the table and began to look around. The bartenders were always on the alert for men cruising but I knew that before the evening ended, I would leave with someone who could bring me the joy that I sought right at that moment.

After an exquisite night with a blond, blue-eyed beautiful man, and I let him out of my apartment sometime around four o'clock in the morning, I slept until ten. When I finally did get up and dressed, I sat at my harpsicord and began to play. The music had a soothing affect just like the love making from last night. But it was soon interrupted when the phone rang. My initial reaction was not to answer it, but on second thought, I got up and strolled over to the coffee table and picked it up.

"Bayard, thank God you are back," Ed said. "We need to talk today."

"Ed, this is Sunday, can't it wait until tomorrow."

"Afraid not, so get yourself together and get on down here to the office." He hung up allowing for no more discussion.

In defiance of this intrusion into my time, I decided he'd have to wait. I sat back down at the harpsicord and continued to play for the next half hour. I finally fixed me a small breakfast, had a cup of coffee, then shut down everything and headed for the office.

"Hopefully, you did not unpack your bags," Ed said as I walked into his office and took a seat right in front of his desk. "Because they need you in London and right away."

"What are you talking about?" I asked although I pretty much knew what this was all about.

"Brad Lytle and his marchers have made it to Chicago, and it looks like they will reach New York by the end of April. From there, they'll fly to London and continue the rest of their march through Europe into Russia." He paused to allow this information to register with me. "We were able to get the support of the Campaign for Nuclear Disarmament of which April Carter is the head. I know you just met with her for a day."

"Yes, but that was just a courteous visit. We go way back, and I wanted to make sure she was doing well."

"We were only able to get their support if you would fly over and take control of organizing the logistics for the march through Europe."

"Ed, I just got back from a tedious and tiring trip to India. And you know damn well I was opposed to that march when we first discussed it back in December."

"I know and feel really bad even asking you to take on this new burden. But the bottom line is they know you are probably the very best at logistically organizing a mass movement and could do this in your sleep. You can't turn those marchers down, not after they've already made it to Chicago. We'll cover all your expenses."

"To include continuing my salary so that I can pay my rent here in New York."

"Yes, absolutely. Now you have to know that April insists on it being you and point blank told us she wouldn't work with anyone else."

"How long will I have to be there?"

"As long as it takes to get the job done."

"And when do you want me to leave.

"As soon as you can get your business in order but no later than Tuesday. We need to get you over there."

"This is Sunday, so you're giving me just the rest of today and tomorrow to get all my business in order. And I'll probably be gone at least two months.

"Or longer."

Images of that gorgeous young man I spent the night with suddenly occupied my thoughts momentarily. I had plans to spend more time with him over the next few weeks but now that was nixed by the call to duty.

"Bayard, I know this is not what you would rather be doing. Your energy is still dedicated to the movement in the South. But remember they locked you out of any involvement with Dr. King. So please re-direct that energy to this project. Your attention to detail will assure us all of success."

"Ed, I am not happy with this at all," I said, and he could easily detect the irritation in my tone. "I know you and the other members of the organization are committed to the elimination of nuclear weapons. But you must know that I am just as committed to the elimination of segregation, lynching's and the oppression of my people."

304 | Williams-Denton-Zinsmeyer

Ed leaned forward resting his elbows on his desk. "I know that and if Dr. King were to call right now and ask that you be relieved of your responsibilities with War Resister League, I would agree. But Bayard, you know that isn't going to happen."

"Please make my reservation so that I leave early afternoon," I said and got up from the chair. "And I'd like to stay at the William Penn House in Bloomberg. It's a Quaker Inn and my grandmother always said she wanted to stay there if she went to England. She never got the chance, so I'll do it for her."

"We'll make all your reservations for your trip. And they will be ready for you by noon tomorrow." Ed also got up and strolled to the other side of his desk right next to me. "Bayard, I don't have to tell you that nuclear proliferation is the number one menace in the world, and someone has to make a stand against it."

"Tell that to the millions of Negroes who are being brutalized and humiliated in the South."

"That is important, but so is this. And right now, there is nothing you can do about the situation in the South. But there is a lot that you can do to make this happen."

"You know this entire mission could be a logistical nightmare, especially as we try to cross into the Communist countries in the East. Hopefully, you all have thought this out."

Ed placed his hand on my shoulder. "No, we haven't and that is more of the reason that we need you. Just like Dr. King hadn't thought out the logistics of the Montgomery Bus Boycott or the Prayer Pilgrimage to Washington, we haven't figured it all out. That is why all these various movements are certainly blessed to have a Bayard Rustin."

"I'll see you in the morning. I think I'm just going to spend a few hours enjoying this short interval from the world's problems, that for some reason I seem to be called upon to solve."

We shook hands, hugged and I exited the office.

37.

April met me at the airport and first drove me over to the William Penn House in Bloomberg, where I checked into the hotel and dropped off my luggage. We then drove to the office space set up for this project on Chancery Lane, right across the street from the famous Lincoln's Inn. April also had an office right next to mine, since we would be practically tied at the hip for the next few months preparing for the arrival of the marchers. Michael Randle also a staunch protester of nuclear proliferation, made up the third member of the team. Michael was an active member of the Campaign for Nuclear Disarmament and had just come off a protest march in February with Bertrand Russell. April, a tenacious advocate for disarmament anxiously got right down to business, as the two took chairs in front of my very small wooden desk.

"Our first job is to win the support of Canon John Collins of St. Paul's Cathedral," April said. "He is the leader of the anti-nuclear forces in England."

"I would have thought that Professor Russell would be the logical leader, since he has been deeply involved in the anti-war issue as far back as 1915," I said.

"We all love Bertrand Russell and he is a valuable member of what we are trying to do," Michael said. "But Professor Russell is so eclectic that no one issue can hold his attention to the point that he takes the lead. When we need him, he's always there."

"Will we have any problems with Canon Collins?" I asked.

"There might be some problems," April said. "Canon Collins strongly opposes any form of direct action and civil disobedience. What I know about your leader of the march, he is a young hot head, who believes that his way is the only way. If that's the case, I do not believe we will be able to get the support of Canon Collins."

"When do you think we can meet with Canon Collins?" I asked.

"He knows you're here and is anxious to meet with you," Michael said. "I can probably set it up for tomorrow. Is that too early for you?"

306 | Williams-Denton-Zinsmeyer

"Absolutely not. If he is available, I am also. We need all the help we can get, when those marchers arrive on this side of the Atlantic. And even if we can't get their support, we certainly need to neutralize them so they'll make no negative statements about us."

"I believe the government will remain silent on the march," April said. "They don't want to appear to be an ally with the Soviet Union and we already know they will oppose the message from the march. McMillan is a conservative and will not take a strong stand against military buildup. It just seems to be in the nature of conservatives, not to mention the amount of money industries make off war."

"The real question is what happens when we cross over into Europe?" I asked. "We need the support of the French and the Germans."

"That's why we took the liberty to schedule a gathering next week in Groningen, just North of the Netherlands for weekend meetings with European Pacifists," April exclaimed. "They will all be there arguing that the march should proceed through their country."

"First things first," I shot back. "We need to make sure the team is in order right here in London before we turn our attention to the continent. We do need to meet with Canon Collins, tomorrow."

"I believe I can make that happen," Michael said.

"Good, but now I do need to get some rest." I glanced at my watch. "Nine-thirty and I feel like it's four in the morning."

"Please forgive me," April leaned forward in her chair. "But we are just so excited to have you here and know that we will make a loud impact on nuclear proliferation, I just wanted to get going right away."

"I am just as anxious and really do appreciate all your enthusiasm. But please give me a chance to let my body get a few hours' sleep and I'll be as full of energy as you all."

"In the morning when we pick you up, I'll have our meeting with Canon Collins arranged," Michael said as we all walked out of the office and to the car.

April dropped me off right in front of the William Penn and we said our good-byes for the night. As I strolled into the hotel and by the registration desk the attendant stopped me.

"Mr. Rustin, I have a call that came in for you earlier in the evening." He held the scratch paper out and I took it curious as to who would be calling me in England, and better still how many people knew I was over here. I picked up my pace but abruptly stopped right in the middle of the hall when I opened the note and read the message.

Miss you already. If I had known you were leaving for England within the next few days would have made arrangements to possibly go with you. Enjoyed our initial evening together and want to be with you now. Please let me know if that is possible. This is your blue eyed, blond friend from the other night. You can reach me at 212-385-4481. If I don't hear from you, I do understand. But please know the other night was ecstasy. Bill

I looked back at the registration desk to see if the man who handed me the note was still standing there or better still staring at me. My concern wasn't with him. I never hide my sexual preferences and didn't plan on doing it while in London. My concern was how did Bill get this information. I reached my room, unlocked the door and hurried inside. I couldn't feel any anger toward Bill, in fact, felt comforted that he had reached out to me. But I was concerned as to how did he know where to reach me.

I stretched out on the bed and gave his suggestion some consideration. To come home to him every night, while in London would be a real treat. But I didn't need the distraction and that is exactly what he would be; a wonderful, delightful distraction. I wouldn't call him right away and especially not tonight. My eyelids began to close, and I placed the note right on my chest near my heart. What a great way to go to sleep, thinking about Bill and all the beautiful things we could and did to each other.

At nine o'clock the next morning, I sat with April and Michael on one side of an oblong, shining conference table. Our meeting with Canon Collins had been scheduled for nine, but his secretary told us he was running just a little late.

"We are starting to get some rumblings from Germany," April said. "Seems as though they're not very happy, because they weren't included in the planning of this march."

"Have the Germans ever been happy about anything, but their own country and own identity?" Michael quipped.

"Can't really be worried about that right now," I said. "But we do have some very influential Germans committed to our cause. If necessary, I can call on them at the right time."

"You know we don't hear much about the march over here," April said. "In fact, if we weren't involved in the planning, I don't think we'd know about it. Is it not getting coverage in the United States?"

"For some reason, the press has chosen to give it very little coverage," I said.

"Has President Kennedy put the muzzle on the press and asked that they not give it much coverage?" Michael asked.

"There is always that possibility," I said. "It would be in Kennedy's best interest if it had never happened. As an ostentatious liberal, it is a cause he should support. But as the President of one of the nuclear giants he can't afford to do that. I believe they plan to ask for a meeting with him when they get to Washington, D.C."

"Do you think they'll get the meeting?" April asked.

"I doubt it. Probably with a second level staff person if at all," I replied just as Canon Collins strolled into the room.

"Forgive my tardiness," he said and then took a chair at the front of the conference table and reached across to shake my hand. "You of course are Bayard Rustin. It is a pleasure to meet you. Your excellent reputation precedes you."

After shaking his hand, I leaned back in the chair and anticipated April triggering the conversation. She did just that.

"Sir, you are aware that the United States has initiated a march against nuclear proliferation, and it started in San Francisco and is now on its way to Washington, D.C. Once they arrive in New York, they plan to catch planes over here to London and continue their march through Europe and into the Soviet Union. They need your assistance."

Canon Collins folded his hands and placed them in his lap and leaned back in his chair.

"Yes, we are aware that the contingent of marchers are now travelling through the United States. But I don't believe the United States has sponsored this march," he said.

"You are correct," I said. "This march is sponsored by the Committee for Non-Violent Action."

"You do know that it is our policy not to support any activities that use civil disobedience as a tactic. Furthermore, we know that your leader of the march has made it clear that they support unilateral disarmament. That makes no sense if only one country disarms. It leaves the world at the mercy of the country that continues to possess nuclear arms. That could be devastating in the hands of the wrong country."

"Do you believe the United States is as big a threat to resort to the nuclear option as is the Soviet Union?" I felt compelled to ask.

"My friend the United States is our very close ally but let's look at the facts, the only country in the world to ever use such a bomb was your country. And not only once, but twice on a poor agrarian people," Collins answered with no hesitation. "I believe the citizens of your country function on a false premise that they are sometimes the most gifted, blessed by God in the world. And therefore, the most loving and caring, but they are some of the cruelest with their slaughtering of the Native Americans, the enslaving of your people and now today you have to fight for the right to sit where you please on a bus, and your children go to the worst schools while white children have the very best."

I never thought I would resent hearing the truth because facts speak for themselves. I knew every word Canon Collins spewed about America was true, but for some reason it rubbed me the wrong way hearing it from a person in another country. We could possibly trade barbs as to which country did the most evil. My image of the starving Indians in Calcutta and how Vinova tied that tragedy to Great Britain's greed, crossed my mind. But I was on a mission and April's glare at me to stay on course convinced me to move on.

"You make my mission here much more difficult if you and your organization refuse to support the march when it arrives in London," I said. "Is there some way we can compromise?"

310 | Williams-Denton-Zinsmeyer

"How do you compromise principle?" Canon Collins asked.

"Please let's not lose track of the larger picture here," Michael intervened.

I welcomed his comments and needed them to be in support of me. He had a lot more influence on this man than I did.

He continued. "We all share the same goal and that is the eradication of means of mass destruction. In fact, we all oppose any form of warfare."

April now leaned forward. "The nature of war has changed drastically since the use of air power. Wars were originally battles between male warriors and the casualties for the most part were suffered by the men. But now, with advanced technology, women, children and the old can be the victims. That was certainly true with the bombings we suffered at the hands of the Nazis, and they suffered in Germany from our air power. And heaven forbid the pain and suffering the Japanese people must still deal with because of the Atomic bombs dropped on them. That is the larger picture we all must deal with, not whose approach to protest is the best. All protest of such atrocities is good."

The stinging accuracy of April's words caused us all to sit momentarily in silence. As I listened to her blunt truthfulness, I recognized that I had been dragged into the two most explosive issues of the new decade.

Canon Collins broke the silence. "You are absolutely right, and I feel that we must do something short of endorsing your march to keep the solidarity alive. Let me suggest that my organization sponsor a welcoming rally on Trafalgar Square when they arrive."

My initial reaction suggested that I discern between a rally and a sponsorship. But that was of little importance. He had agreed to show solidarity. "That would certainly be a welcomed gesture from your group and serve as a catalyst to kick off the march through Europe."

"Then it's settled," April spoke up. "I will work with the members of CND to work out the logistics for the rally. And we do thank you Canon Collins for the offered support."

"As Michael said, we cannot lose focus of the larger picture and that is the very plain fact that we are on a collision course with civilization. The Bible tells us that it will be fire next time. Let's not have that next time."

In the most appropriate fashion, we allowed Canon Collins to have the last words as we all got up and made our way out of the St. Paul's Cathedral. We could now concentrate on our next major battle now that London was on the team. Getting all the various Pacifists groups on the continent to join was our next goal and that would happen in another week.

38.

"Groningen has a very interesting history," Michael said while driving into the city after a seven-hour trip from London. April sat in the back seat resting after having driven the first leg of the trip. "Archaeologists have traced signs of life there as far back as 3720 B.C. and the first major settlement here in the Third Century B.C. It has to be one of the oldest areas of inhabitants on the continent." He paused and glanced over at me. "One of the last battles of World War Two took place in Groningen and interestingly, it was fought by the Canadian Infantry. Also interesting is they refused to use artillery support for fear they might harm civilians."

"That's the exact point I made when we met with Canon Collins," April said as she leaned forward from the back seat. "I guess if you can consider a battle as a moral and ethical one that is exactly what happened in Groningen. Men who figured war should be confined to warriors and the casualties should be among them."

"Morality and war are like an oxymoron," I said.

Michael slowed down and looked for our hotel. "Our meetings will take place right in the hotel in their special conference room."

He finally pulled up in front of the hotel, and as soon he stopped three young men, dressed in hotel uniforms, rushed to the car and opened the doors. I got out, as did April, and followed Michael inside the old, gothic architectural designed hotel. April and I waited in the lounge area as Michael checked us all into our rooms.

"It would be awfully nice if the entire weekend went as smoothly as checking into this hotel seems to be going," I said.

April smiled. "No way. We are in for some real battles among the representatives. They all will want the march to go through their country."

"I'm sure you can handle it." It was my turn to smile.

Michael strolled back to the lounge area. "We're all set," he said as he handed each of us our keys to the rooms. "The bell boys will get our luggage to our rooms and why don't we meet down here for dinner."

"How about we meet back down here for breakfast," I said. "It's already after eight and by the time we get into our rooms, shower and dress it will be after nine and for me after that long ride, it will be bedtime."

"That sounds reasonable," April concurred. "I'm pretty tired also. Let's re-group in the morning."

"No problem," Michael said. "Any way, I'm tired of looking at your faces after being cooped in the car with you all for seven hours."

We all laughed and headed to our rooms.

A select group of men sat on both sides of a very long conference table in the meeting room at the hotel. I found it interesting that April, the only woman at the conference, also served as the Chair for the proceedings. At nine o'clock, she rose from her chair at the front end of the table.

"I want to thank each of you for fighting through the rather bad weather to meet with us here to discuss the proposed march through Western Europe into the East, and finally into the Soviet Union with the final stop being Moscow." She pointed at me. "I am so pleased to have one of the leading organizers, the man responsible for the successful Montgomery Bus Boycott in the South in the United States, Bayard Rustin, to help facilitate the movement of the American marchers through Europe."

I felt a little strange and uncomfortable receiving credit for a boycott that was the effort of thousands of determined Negroes and the leadership of Martin.

She continued, "Let me recognize the dedicated peace lovers here with us today." I was surprised that she knew all of them and called out their names. "Accompanying me from England is Michael Randle. From Germany we have two representatives, Gerhart Schmidt and Ernst Werner; from France, Baptiste Alaire; Belgium, Maurice Lambert; and from Switzerland a man who has just returned from the conference in India, Johannes Van Hoebeek; finally, from Finland we have Aaron Nieminen."

Johannes nodded at me as we had both been at the conference in India, and here we were now in Europe discussing, for the most part, a similar situation.

"The main issue to be discussed here today, and the reason for this meeting, is to decide the route the marchers will take once they arrive on the European Continent," April continued.

"There is no question that the route must be through Germany," Gerhart Schmidt spoke up. "It is critical that we pass through West into East Germany for symbolic reasons. It will stress the importance of German re-unification."

"It is important that Germany seek re-unification," I said. "But let's keep our eyes on the mission, and that is to make a strong statement against nuclear proliferation. We can't have the concentration deviate from that objective."

"Bayard is right," April said. "We cannot lose focus of our objective, but I also agree with Gerhart that at some point we all must be concerned for the re-unification of a country that should have never been split up because of nasty politics."

"My country might have some problems with a pacifists group passing through France at this critical period," Baptiste Alaire spoke up. "Our leaders, as well as most of the country, are concerned with the escalating violence in Algeria. There is one faction that favors giving Algeria their independence just to cut down on the killings, then there is the more conservative group that believes the revolt must be put down with all the military might the country can muster. Of course, they would be opposed to any march for peace. De Gaulle will probably oppose allowing the marchers in France because of the crackdown on political dissent."

"There is also the fact that France has just recently tested a nuclear bomb in Africa near the Algerian border," I said. "That is reason for the march to cross through France, if we can get the approval from President De Gaulle."

"DE Gaulle is in favor of releasing Algeria to its own independent rule," Baptiste said. "Although he does believe in France's nuclear capability, but independent from the United States or Soviet Union, more the reason why he would oppose the marchers."

April now turned to Johannes Van Hoebeek. "What position will your country take?" she asked.

"Neutral. We take a neutral position in the cold war battle between the two major powers, and probably would not express an opinion on the march one way or another."

"How about Finland?" April turned and looked directly at Aaron Nieminen.

"We are in the same position as the Netherlands. We will remain neutral, and our biggest fear is if the marchers are turned away at the East European border states, that will cause a disturbance. Something we do not want to see happen."

"That pretty much leaves Belgium," April said and now turned to Maurice Lambert.

"Our country will support the marchers and they will be welcomed to enter as a pathway to the Soviet Union," Maurice exclaimed.

April looked at me and I nodded in agreement. "Okay, then I believe our first issue is resolved. When the marchers leave England, they will enter the continent through Belgium, then into Germany, East Germany, Poland and finally the Soviet Union. Do we all agree?"

All of us nodded in agreement to the logistics of the march, but then turned to the political message. As they discussed it, I knew it would clash with Brad's message he was importing from the United States. Michael led the discussion.

"It's been mentioned that as the marchers traverse the United States that at each stop, they protest in front of a military facility. We cannot have that here. Only at select places will they be able to protest, and we will choose those locations."

"That will definitely be necessary when going through West Germany, and I'm sure the authorities in East Germany, Poland and the Soviet Union, if we are fortunate to get into these countries, will also designate places they can protest," Gerhart again spoke up.

"The placards and signs they are carrying must also be changed," Michael continued. "They read 'Refuse to Serve in the Armed Forces,' and another 'Refuse to Work in Military Industries,' and finally, 'Refuse to Pay Taxes for War.' There is no way the marchers will be allowed to carry those signs through Eastern Europe and into Soviet Union. You need to make that clear with them immediately." Michael looked at me and I nodded in agreement.

"Your Americans will have to realize when they cross over into less democratic countries, their job is not to bring freedom of speech or democratic principles to those countries," Gerhert went into a semi lecture that I didn't particularly appreciate, but since we were getting our way on most requests, I tolerated it.

April joined in. "Bayard, I understand that the leader of the march, Brad Lyttle, might be a problem once he gets over here. I am hoping that you will be able to handle him so that we will not have any problems."

"That's why I'm here," I said tersely. "I will make sure that the marchers from America understand and comply with the rules on this side of the ocean. I don't believe Brad will do anything to jeopardize the success of the march." I said, but not quite positive that he would not try to have his way.

This was easier than what I thought it would be. But I shouldn't' have been surprised, after all, everyone there believed in peace and opposed nuclear proliferation. I listened as the men talked about the peace movements in their countries and was pleased that everyone added the non-violent component to their discussion. Gandhi may have initiated the first major non-violent peace movement in India, but it had grown leaps and bounds because of the implementation in Montgomery, and then as part of the prayer pilgrimage in Washington, D.C.

It had now spread to Europe, and ultimately, would have an impact in the Soviet Union, where it is just possible that Nakita Khrushchev will see the political advantage to at least considering its value.

"I imagine we have pretty much wrapped up our business for the day," April said. "We are about to take part in history when the marchers reach London, then into Belgium and finally into Moscow with a message of peace. Let us all return to our places and do everything within our power to make this a success."

We all concurred with her, got up from our places at the table, shook hands or hugged or did both and pledged our support for the people who, about now, were making their way into Washington, D.C. After one night in Groningen, we were anxious to hit the road and get back to London early in the morning.

"White and Negro students defy the southern laws and ride buses into the heart of segregated cities in the South," read the lead story in the London Times. I lay stretched out on the bed in my room at the William Penn late in the morning after we arrived back from Groningen. I felt exhausted from the drive up there, the very intense meeting and then the long drive back to London, left me somewhat hyped and I knew I wouldn't get much sleep. When I strolled into the hotel, I grabbed the newspaper with the intent to catch up on the happenings back home. "Congress of Racial Equality, under the leadership of James Farmer, has organized bus trips usually leaving out of Washington, D.C. and traversing the South with Negroes and whites sitting next to each other in both the front and back of the buses. They pledge to continue the integrated bus trips until the segregated facilities at the Bus Depots and the seating on the buses comes to an end."

As I read the article, I felt a tinge of envy simply because I was so far removed from the civil rights struggle back home, and because James had gotten the idea from me to integrate the buses by having Negroes and whites sit next to each other, as far back as 1947 when we first challenged segregated laws in Virginia and North Carolina. James had emerged as a civil rights leader and here I was stuck in England when I should have been back in the states involved with Martin and the SCLC. I appreciated what the War Resisters League did for me. Without their willingness to bring me on, I probably would still be struggling to make ends meet. But I didn't like the role I had to play as fellow traveler first to India and now to England, when I really wanted to be right in the middle of what was happening back home.

I folded the newspaper and placed it on the nightstand. I strolled over to the small desk in the room and grabbed pen and paper. I couldn't stand this isolation. I would write to Martin and reach out to him. I wanted back in as soon as I returned to the states. The eradication of segregation, through the utilization of the Gandhaian non-violence philosophy, would be my legacy to the world. I began that journey with Martin and planned to finish it with him. Ministers and bigots be damned, I would not allow them to stand in my way.

39.

"You have to talk with Brad Lyttle," April said as I climbed into the backseat of the car. "He is being unreasonable." She pulled out into the street and headed to the place where the marchers were staying after arriving in London from New York.

"He is being quite the brat," Michael joined in the conversation. "Claims that the marchers will use the same placards they had in the United States. Also, in order to save money, wants his people to stay in hostels and not travel by car while in the city."

Fifteen marchers, to include seventy-six-year-old A. J. Muste, had flown to London after finishing the walk in the United States, at the United Nations Building in New York City. They flew in last night and this would be our first time greeting them. Michael's contacts on the other side of the ocean had alerted him that Brad was coming to Europe with a chip on his shoulder. Seems as though he got wind that we held our meeting in Groningen and made decisions that affect the marchers without his in-put. I knew it was my job to bring him down from that ego trip and understand this was about more than him. Now I understood why April and the others insisted that I be here. They knew there might be problems from the American group, and I was the right person to play peace maker. I had to respond.

"Brad is a little difficult," I said. "When he first introduced this project, I was opposed to it because of all the problems we'd have trying to walk across Europe. At our initial meeting, he insisted it could be done so I gave in. Now I'm not sure that was a good idea."

"Please let him understand that this is not the United States, but London and soon for them it will be the entire continent of Europe," April said as we pulled up to the hostel where they'd checked in late last night when they arrived.

The first person I embraced when we met them in a small conference room that the owners of the hostel allowed us to use, was A. J. Muste. I had pretty much gotten over the hurt he caused me back in 1953. He hadn't walked across the United States, but at the very last minute decided he wanted to give it a try across Europe. As we embraced, I whispered, "We have to contain Brad, or this might be the end of the road."

He pulled back from me and gave the look that he understood. We all sat down around the conference table and April took charge.

"We are delighted to have you all in London and our leader, Canon Collins, has organized a rally for you all in Trafalgar Square for tomorrow afternoon. Hope you are up for it."

"It's been a long journey, but we are only halfway to our destination," Brad said. He then looked right at me. "Bayard so glad you could make it over here. We're anxious to hear what your plans are for us getting into Europe and up to Moscow."

"We've laid out a route for you all that we feel will be most advantageous. April will go over the logistics, and then we must discuss our behavior as we proceed through each country and especially the Communist controlled ones," I said then relaxed back in my chair.

"We are not concerned about either politics or ideology," Brad snapped. "Our only goal is to deliver a message of no more war and stop the insane race to nuclear destruction of the world. That's the message we delivered in our country, which of course is a democracy, and that is the message we plan to deliver in the Communist countries."

"It's the message that we all want to deliver," April said. "But if you want that message to reach the people, then you have to modify your approach according to the particular government's approval which you will need."

"When you begin to make concessions you ultimately lose the message you are trying to get across," Brad said. "The same message we delivered in the United States has to be what we use here and on the continent."

"Then I can assure you that you will not make it across Europe, because you will probably not gain entry into any of the countries," Michael spoke up.

I glanced over at A. J. hoping that he would catch the hint to intervene. He was the senior in the group and as such Brad would be compelled to listen to him. His long record as President of Fellowship of Reconciliation in New York earned him the respect of everyone in the room.

"I thought you'd cleared this up," Brad said and looked at me.

I refused to engage him in this brash unnecessary exchange. "It's not our decision to make," I said instead. "Either you agree to go along with the requirements for entering each new country, or you go back home. The choice is yours."

"No, it's not," A. J. finally spoke up. "Brad, we all appreciate your leadership in this matter, but this is not a one-man decision. I believe that we need to go along with Bayard's recommendation that we jettison the use of our signs from the United States, and use the ones developed over here in England. Who agrees with me?"

For a moment, none of the other thirteen members of the group raised their hands and then slowly each one of them lifted their arm up in support of A. J.'s suggestion. Evidently, Brad felt the pressure of the majority and also lifted his arm. With that issue resolved, I now felt confident to take on the other of Brad's poor decisions.

"Mr. Muste should be complimented for his courage at his age to attempt this walk for peace," I started. "But he also should have the convenience of spending the night in a much more comfortable facility than this hostel. I plan to make arrangements for him to stay at the William Penn Hotel where I presently reside during my stay in England. I invite any of the others to also join us there."

Brad jumped to his feet. "We can't afford to stay there, it's a question of finances."

"I understand that you do have sufficient resources to stay at a place better than this. You all are about to undertake a very treacherous walk across some tough terrain in Europe, all the way to Moscow if you are fortunate to make it there. You have only two more nights to be in London, do yourself a favor and enjoy that time by staying in a decent hotel."

"And if you don't have the money, our organization will cover the difference," April interjected. "You are our guests and we want you to be as comfortable as possible. Will you accept our invitation?"

"Yes," resonated a resounding approval from everybody around the table, except Brad. I guess he was only willing to make so many concessions.

"Good this is all settled," April said as she took back control of the meeting. "I believe you all took cabs here from the airport, but we have arranged for you to be driven around London while you are here."

I expected Brad's opposition because he didn't want them to be driven but to walk wherever they went. But he said nothing. Evidently, he wasn't prepared for a third defeat.

We will have the drivers here to take you over to the William Penn within the next hour, and we'll see you for dinner this evening and finally the big rally tomorrow," April said as she got up and prepared to leave. "Welcome to London and God bless you on your continued journey to make our country safer for everyone."

The next few days were whirlwind busy. I joined the walkers in all their activities and because of the importance of their mission the number had grown to thirty, with fifteen from England joining in. I had considered joining them on the march but decided not to for two reasons. The other day when I read the article about the freedom riders for equality underway in the South back home, I wanted to get back to the states and again be involved in the struggle there. Granted the struggle to end nuclear proliferation was important, but my heart just wasn't' there.

I had also encountered passport problems even in England. European countries were reluctant to issue passports to individuals considered dissidents, and my reputation preceded me. For that reason, I decided not to attempt the walk. But, along with nearly ten thousand British dissidents, who supported the efforts of the now fifty walkers, I accompanied them out of London and to the boat that would take them up the river to Belgium, where they were scheduled to enter the continent.

The day after they left England, I packed my bags and April and Michael drove me to the airport for my return home.

"We did our part and we did it quite well," she said as we neared the entrance to the airport. "Now you can go back to the United States and do the same for your people because they need you."

"You went practically a month without being hassled at all," Michael said.

I knew exactly his point. In every venture that called for my involvement in the states, my sexuality became an issue. Not once did anyone allude to or mention the subject. I never kept it a secret, and I'm sure they all knew about my haunting experience in Pasadena. It led me to appreciate the British more than I had in the past.

April pulled into the airport drop off area. I grabbed my bags.

"I'm going to miss you all," I said as I leaned back in the car on the passenger side. "It was just great working with you. And we all will go down in history because of what we have done here."

"We'll be following what you do in the states because we know there are many great accomplishments awaiting you," Michael said as we shook hands.

"We love you Bayard and always just be you, because that is such a great person to be," April said.

"Let me get out of here before you all make me blush." I smiled threw a kiss April's way, then turned and walked into the terminal on my way home to whatever great adventures awaited me there.

PART FOUR
The Greatest March in History

40.

April 5, 1968

I strolled into the Atlanta Airport for a change of planes to continue on to Memphis, Tennessee. I had an hour wait, just enough time to grab a coffee and a bagel. I stopped at the marquee to get my gate number, then continued down the corridor until I came to a coffee shop. As I sat there sipping on the coffee, I reflected on a number of crisis issues burning at me. Our country was in turmoil. Only five years ago, they assassinated President Kennedy, murdered Medgar Evers and three years ago they killed Malcolm X and now Martin. All these killings in less than one decade.

Coupled with the domestic slaughters all around us, the carnage in Vietnam continued at a rapidly growing rate. Violence dominated a decade that had gotten off to such a great start with the election of Kennedy, and the idea that America would enjoy a kind of Camelot. But it was all falling apart. I glanced at the television mounted in the corner on the wall. The picture was depressing. Riots had begun to break out. A mob of Blacks was rushing down streets, breaking windows and looting stores, then setting them on fire. The police seemed to be outnumbered. The commentator said, "Chicago is out of control as the angry mob takes out their frustration, and seeks revenge for the murder of Dr. Martin Luther King, Jr. by terrorizing the community. We just heard that Mayor Richard Daley has given the order to shoot to kill anyone carrying a Molotov cocktail, and shoot to wound all others."

We had just suffered through three years of riots and now the killing would continue. When will it all end? I finished my coffee and headed for the gate. It was time to board.

The plane taxied out to the runway for takeoff. I had strapped in well, and listened as the stewardess went through the usual instructions given to the passengers. I relaxed back in my seat as the engines exploded with the full jet power and before I was aware, we were flying above the clouds.

"Our flight time over to Memphis is one hour and fifteen minutes," the captain came on the loudspeaker and announced. "Please keep your seat belt fastened if not out of your seat. Weather conditions are good for a smooth ride so sit back, relax and enjoy the flight."

As the plane cleared the clouds and the blue sky and sunshine became very visible, I thought how unpredictable life can be and as a matter of fact is. Staring out at the sun as it still rose in the East, I silently acknowledged the existence of a powerful source and it didn't matter if referred to as God, Allah or Yahweh, the presence was real. Because of his enormous existence in our lives, it was futile and a waste of time to question His decisions.

"You're on your way to Memphis?" the middle aged, very attractive white lady sitting next to me in the middle seat asked.

"Yes, I am," I replied.

"It's shameful what happened there yesterday," she said. "Dr. King was a wonderful, Christian man. I certainly hope they catch the killer and real soon."

"I feel the same," I said.

"Did you have the pleasure of ever meeting Dr. King?"

"On a couple occasions, yes I did."

"What a blessing that you actually met him. I would've loved to have met him or heard him preach a sermon."

"He was quite a speaker," I said.

"And the fact that he brought the entire idea of Mahatma Gandhi's concept of non-violence to this country, and then established the Southern Christian Leadership Conference and of course what he did in that great march on Washington, is a tribute to his greatness and his legacy. I just loved his I have a dream speech."

"Yes, he was a great man. It is a great loss to this country." I remained very humble in the conversation.

"Attention this is your captain. We have been instructed to turn around and go to Washington, D. C. Evidently there is an important person on this plane, and the President of the United States has instructed us to get him to the White House due to the crisis in relation to the killing of Dr. Martin Luther King, Jr. yesterday. I apologize for the inconvenience, but we must follow the instructions of FAA and the President."

Just as he finished the stewardess approached my seat on the plane and said.

"Mr. Rustin, the President of the United States wants you at the White House and will have a limousine waiting for you when we land."

I was probably as shocked as every passenger on the plane and especially the lady sitting next to me, who stared at me with a look of astonishment all over her face.

"You must be someone very important that the President has interfered with the flight to get you back to Washington, D. C. And I've just been rambling on and here I am next to an important leader. What do you do and who are?"

"Name is Bayard Rustin and I am simply a servant of the people and a person who truly loved Dr. King with all my energy." I said and closed my eyes, and tried to imagine why the President had decided I needed to be there with him while he dealt with this crisis.

41.

October 1962

"Students and faculty, press and friends, I am pleased to introduce the two dynamic debaters who will debate two different perspectives regarding the Negroes place in American society," Professor Gregory Jackson, from the School of Journalism at Howard University, announced to a packed house for the debate. "We have with us this afternoon Mr. Bayard Rustin, veteran civil rights worker and advocate for the inclusion of Negroes into the mainstream of the country. To argue the opposing view, we have Malcolm X, member of the Nation of Islam, to argue why the Negro should not seek admission into the larger society but look for ways to create a separate nation."

I stood at the podium with a microphone to the right of the moderator, Malcolm X was to the left. Staring out into the crowd I smiled at Tom who had arranged this debate between the two of us. Now in his last year at Howard University, he had become very active in the civil rights issues and had influenced Stokely Carmichael, who viewed me as the champion of the movement. Malcolm had wanted to speak on the campus, but was denied permission by the administration because they deemed him to be too militant. After much cajoling by Tom and other Black activists, they finally agreed as long as his appearance was in a debate. Tom jumped on the opportunity to contact me in New York and argued strongly that I was the most competent to debate the firebrand Malcolm X. In fact, I was probably the only Negro with some involvement in the movement, willing to take him on.

When I arrived back in the United States after my short stay in England, the issue of civil rights had exploded, and there were groups trying to get out in front and take the lead. The Student Non-Violent Coordinating Committee had organized after a turbulent gathering at Shaw University in Raleigh, North Carolina. SCLC had also organized demonstrations based on the success of Montgomery. The NAACP still protested all the other organizations now involved in the movement, from the assumption that they should be the only one representing the Negro in his struggles for equality. And the Nation of Islam had gained a great deal of respect, because of their militant stance against any form of integration into the fabric of American society. I hadn't quite made it back into the mainstream of the movement, but this was a good start.

"My first question will be directed at both of you and calls for a definitive answer," Professor Jackson began the debate. "You both have very different approaches to solving the problem of the Negro in this country, why do you think the masses should accept your approach? By coin flip earlier, Malcom X goes first."

"In the past two years, the Honorable Elijah Muhammad has become the most talked about Black man in America because he is having such miraculous success in getting his program over among the so-called Negro masses," Malcom X began. "In 1959, Time magazine wrote he has eliminated from among his followers, alcohol, dope addiction, profanity, all of which stems from disrespect for self. He has successfully eliminated stealing and crime among his followers. The Time article also pointed out that he has eliminated adultery and fornication, and prostitution, making Black men respect their women, something that has been characteristically absent among our men. Time also pointed out that Muslim followers of the Honorable Elijah Muhammad have eliminated juvenile delinquency. If he has shown such success among his followers, it only makes sense that his teachings be extended to the entire race which ultimately would eliminate all the vices that now plague my people."

Malcom X finished and all attention turned to me. From the anticipatory stares the audience directed at me, I knew Malcolm had scored well with his answer. Now I had to match his success.

"No one can question the good that Elijah Muhammad has done with a very small segment of the Negroes in the United Sates. He has gone into the prisons and provided many who see no hope for their future, with a new way of looking at life," I exclaimed. "In fact, I believe he was able to do the same for you." I looked directly at Malcolm X. "But let's keep

330 | Williams-Denton-Zinsmeyer

focus of what we are supposed to respond to and that is how do we solve the problem of the Negro in this country. I do not believe the moderator was looking for an answer about all the good one group has done within the race, but how to end the oppression and segregation we face. To that end, I believe with the success in Montgomery, Alabama we have come up with a method that encompasses the Gandhian philosophy of non-violence to counter evil, and is exactly what our people should utilize."

Malcolm was prepared to respond but the moderator intervened with another question.

"The Nation of Islam believes in a separation of races but Mr. Rustin you are one of the strongest supporters of an assimilationist approach. Who is correct? Mr. Rustin, you can go first.

From the disdainful glare on Malcolm X's face I don't believe he was too satisfied not being able to respond to my answer to the previous question. Hopefully, that was not an indication of a rigged debate to favor me, since Malcolm X was not a favorite among the educated and middle-class bourgeoisie overly represented in the faculty at the University. I didn't need their help to win this debate and didn't want it.

"What the Negro wants is to become full-fledged citizens," I said. "Their ancestors have toiled in this country, contributing greatly to it. The United States belongs to no particular people, and in my view the great majority of Negroes and their leaders take integration as their key word, which means right or wrong, they seek to become an integral part of the United States. We have, I believe much work yet to do, both politically and through the courts. I believe we have reached the point where most Negroes, from a sense of dignity and pride, have organized themselves to demand to become an integral part of all the institutions of the country. We believe justice for all people can be achieved." I finished, turned and looked at Malcolm X.

"We believe integration is hypocrisy," he began with a degree of indignation in his tone. "If the government has to pass laws to let us into their educational system, if they must pass laws to get the white man to accept us in better housing in their neighborhoods, that is the equivalent of holding a gun to their head, and that is hypocrisy. If the white man were to accept us, without laws being passed, then we would go for it. Any…"

"Go ahead Brother Malcolm, straighten them out," someone in the audience shouted.

"Please refrain from commenting. These gentlemen do not need cheering sections," Professor Jackson scowled.

Malcolm continued, "As any intelligent person can see, the white man is not going to share his wealth with his ex-slaves. But God has taught us that the only solution for the ex-slaves and the slave master is separation."

"One more question before we take a five-minute break and then finish up with three more questions. "There has been a great deal of criticism that the Honorable Elijah Muhammad teaches a form of hate against our Jewish community. Is there any truth to that? Let's go with Mr. Rustin first and then close with Malcolm X."

Now, with this question I was convinced that the debate had been rigged by the administration, and I wanted to just walk off in protest. What did this question have to do with the state of Negroes and their progress toward equality? But unless I did walk off, I had to give an answer.

"This I don't believe is one that I should have to respond to because I am not in the Nation of Islam, but I'll answer it as best I can with that in mind." I felt compelled to let the moderator and the administration know that this was not a fair debate and instead of doing this, they should have just denied Malcolm X access to the college. However, if they had continued to deny him access the charges of denial of First Amendment Rights would have raised its ugly head. I had to answer.

"I have been given to believe that Elijah Muhamad has stated that one of the reasons that Negroes are so oppressed is that the Jews are exploiting them, and the Jews are also attempting to exploit the Arab world and stir up difficulties in the Middle East." I finished without addressing the question of hate. I believed it was much too strong a word.

All eyes turned to Malcolm X as he paused probably to get his thoughts together on how to respond to this rather egregious attack. He finally began. "If you have read what the Honorable Elijah Muhammad has written, and he has written much," he scowled. "I don't think you can find an article where he has ever pointed out the Jew as an exploiter of the Black man. He speaks of the exploiter, period. He doesn't break it down in terms of Frenchmen, Englishmen, Jew or German. He speaks of the exploiter and sometimes the man who is the guiltiest of exploitation will think you are pointing the finger at him and put out the propaganda that you're anti-this or anti-that. We make no distinction between exploitation and exploiter." He ended, abruptly turned and walked off the stage and huddled with his supporters in the corner.

I had to confront Dr. Jefferson. I hurried over to the opposite corner where Malcolm X stood. He was evidently going over his questions for the next set, but looked up when he saw me nearing him.

"Why are you skewing the debate in my favor?" I asked.

"We didn't want this hater on our campus, but the students insisted on it. We did the next best thing possible to try to direct the debate in your favor so that he won't appear to be a hero to our students."

I couldn't do anything but smile it was so ridiculous. "Why did you think I needed to cheat to win the debate," I asked.

"Just a little assurance to make sure you won," Jackson said now with a frown as if to let me know he did not appreciate this confrontation.

"Please do not do that in the next round of questions." I turned to walk away but stopped suddenly.

"You, Bayard, I probably dislike more than Malcolm and the Nation," he scowled. "They are at least men, and they are less tolerant of your sick behavior than I am. And I am intolerant of men who sleep together. You do considerable damage to our race that is already under attack as moral degenerates. But I'm only doing what I was instructed to do."

I turned and said, "That makes you worse than either Malcolm or me. At least we are honest brokers while you do the dirty work for others." I hurried over to where Tom and some of the others stood.

I exuded very little enthusiasm for the next round of questions and was relieved when it ended. Malcolm and I shook hands after it ended, and I assured him that he was not the only one under attack. He gave me a somewhat quizzical look and then left the auditorium with his followers. In an utter display of disdain, I did not bother to shake hands with Jackson, and I'm sure that did not go unnoticed. Standing outside the auditorium waiting for a cab to take me to the airport so I could get back to New York, Tom brought up the subject.

"Reason why you didn't shake hands with Professor Jackson after the debate ended?" he asked.

"I have my reasons," I said.

"He was a plant by the administration to make sure you beat Malcolm X so that he would not look good in front of us," Tom said. "We complained when we found out he was going to moderate, but it was him or nothing. We thought maybe he could possibly get through the series of questions without making his bias too noticeable. But it was clearly visible."

"When I confronted him, he made an unnecessary comment about me and that's the main reason I didn't shake his hand at the end. Bigots, be they racist or homophobes, I don't like and as I grow older find it very difficult to tolerate."

"You know most of the activist students here on campus admire you and consider you the person they want to follow," Tom said. "They think that you have the best analytical mind, the coolest demeanor and support your militant, non-violent approach to eradicating segregation and war. As draft age students, we all are a little concerned with what President Kennedy is doing over there in Vietnam. We're afraid that could escalate. We will look to you to be the voice of opposition."

"This country could be in for some very difficult days ahead with the young raising hell about the draft and Negroes raising hell about racism," I said as the cab pulled to the curb. "Heaven help this country if all the voices of dissent unite against the evils of our government." I finished and jumped into the cab.

The plane set down at La Guardia at seven-thirty. I followed the passengers out to the lobby and down to the baggage claim area. However, since I had no luggage, I sauntered outside and the older man in control of cab service, waved the next waiting driver up to where I stood. I jumped in the back seat and said.

"159 W, 10th Street in the West Village."

"You got it," the driver replied, turned on his meter and headed out into the traffic.

I relaxed back in the seat, closed my eyes for a minute and thought of that sensuous man waiting for me at Julius.

42.

Time seemed to be pushing forward at an astronomical speed as we now were in the last week of December and the year 1963 knocked anxiously on the door to enter and reveal the many secrets waiting for us. I had enjoyed a reprieve from serious issues for over a month and found time to nurture what could be a budding relationship with my new lover. Our love making was so intense at times, that it almost frightened me. But after almost two months of hedonistic behavior it was time to come back to reality, and return to solving the problems of the world. With that on my mind, I sauntered through a light winter snow up the steps and into Mr. Randolph's office.

"Come on in," he said from behind his desk.

"Looks like we're in for a winter snow before New Year's Eve," I said as I took my usual seat in his office. The delicious aroma of a freshly brewed pot of coffee tickled my senses. He kept the coffee pot right behind his desk on a credenza.

"I know you want coffee," Randolph said. "It's ready."

That's all I needed to hear. I jumped up, hurried back to the coffee pot and poured a steaming hot cup. After adding cream and sugar, I hurried back to my seat with cup in hand. I took a sip waiting for him to initiate the conversation.

"Something's been weighing heavy on my mind for the past two weeks," he began.

"What's that?" I asked.

"The march that never happened back in 1941."

"That's a long time ago. Why are you dwelling on that right now?"

"Because we never got everything promised to us."

"You got Executive Order 8802 from the President. Isn't that what you wanted to happen?" I took another sip of coffee, then set the cup on the front of Mr. Randolph's desk, pulled out a Pall Mall and lit it.

"Evidently that was not enough," Randolph scowled. "It needed congressional teeth to make sure it was implemented and obeyed by the war industry during the time. It was really more window dressing. We never got the number of jobs that we needed to make a difference in our condition."

"But it did work. The President challenged you to make him do something about discrimination in the factories, you did, and he signed the order. That was progress." I couldn't believe I was justifying that act because at the time, I was so angry that he called off the march, I didn't speak with him for months.

"The success was not permanent and now we've lost all the ground we made."

"Maybe we need another march and this time follow through on it," I suggested.

Mr. Randolph leaned forward on his desk, a sign he liked my suggestion. "I'm not opposed to that idea," he said. "In fact, it's way overdue."

Now it was my turn to lean forward in my chair as I took another long drag on the cigarette. "1963 is the Centennial Year for the Emancipation Proclamation, maybe we build the march around that celebration and have it on the mall in front of the Lincoln Monument. That would be symbolic.

"We'll need support from the labor unions. In fact, I'll talk to my group, The Negro Labor Council about being the primary sponsor. How's that sound?"

"Just like something we need to get moving on right away," I said. "We'll need at least eight to nine months of planning, and before it gets cold next year."

"Bayard, I'll need for you to draw up a blueprint for the march." He now relaxed back in his chair. "Yes sir, we are going to do it and it will be next year." He smiled. "A massive march on Washington will bring attention to the unfulfilled social and economic promises never fulfilled in a hundred years."

"What about Martin?" I asked. "You know a march of this magnitude, he has to be included. He is the voice of civil rights and his support is mandatory."

"Along with Roy at the NAACP and Whitney at the Urban League, and of course Dorothy Height at the Negro Women's Council," Mr. Randolph added. "But first we need Martin because with him on board and with the march's potentially national recognition, Roy and Whitney will come along kicking and screaming, but nevertheless, they will come along."

"Martin will insist on a different theme." My thoughts momentarily reverted back to Montgomery in 1956 when I tried to convince him that economic issues were the most important that should be resolved. He rejected the idea back then and chances were awfully strong he would do it again. "He is going to want to build the march around essentially civil rights issues, voting and segregation."

"Let's get him on board and then we can fight out the details."

"Are you going to make that call?" I asked but already knew the answer.

"You can't, not yet," he shot back. "Why don't you go to work and get me that blueprint, we're wasting time." He smiled. "And time is not on my side."

I got up to leave. "I'll get my old working team together, obviously however without Stanley."

"We never talked about that," Randolph said. "Why did he turn against you in such an ugly way?"

"I don't know and probably will never know."

"You all worked so closely on the SCLC project."

"Probably he didn't want to share Martin with me. He saw me as a threat to his relationship to him."

"If he is still advising Martin, what will he have to say about this project, especially with you so closely involved?"

"Once again, my answer is the same. I don't know."

"Someday, Martin will come to realize that he made an awful error cutting ties with you and keeping Stanley on board. This country is probably more fearful of a communist than a gay fellow."

"I'd better get busy if you want to pull this off before the cold weather sets in next fall," I said and sauntered over to the door, opened it, but before leaving turned and said. "This is where I want to be, and nothing will stand in the way of making this the grandest participatory event of the people." I closed the door, exited his building and headed back over to my office still at the War Resisters League. I had to call Tom and Rachelle to get them back on board.

It seemed rather strange to be working on a major project without Stanley and Ella involved. We spent so much time back in the middle fifties working together, but not this time. I did manage to recruit a young, bright man out of Chicago and a dedicated member of the Socialist Party, Norm Hill. He was based in New York on the staff of CORE. Farmer agreed to lend him to me just for the drafting of the plan. Tom was home from Howard University on winter break, so we had to get this done within a three-week period. Due to other commitments, Rachelle couldn't work on it around the clock. Her job called for her to be there during the day, but she did show up at night.

After a solid week of working day and night, we finally drew up a blueprint for action and called it; "A March for Economic and Social Equality." The entire team met with Mr. Randolph and presented it to him.

Sitting behind his desk, he read the main points. The March will call for two consecutive days of non-violent direct action, culminating in a great rally at the Lincoln Memorial, where the Emancipation Program will be presented to the Nation. The marchers will visit Capitol Hill and demand that the Congress pass legislation to address the economic disparities in this country. If Congressmen and women fail to visit with the marchers, then they will conduct a sit-in. This will all occur on Friday. The march would take place on Saturday.

"I don't need to read all the fine print, but I commend you all on a great job." Mr. Randolph looked up and said. "Now we just have to go to work and get as many organizations as possible to join us."

The four of us shook hands for a job well done.

"Step one is now done," I said. "But tomorrow we begin Step Two which is to contact all the relevant organizations and convince them to join the effort."

"We have a lot of work in front of us," Randolph spoke up. "I appreciate this great beginning but in the future our efforts will have to double. So why don't you all go home and rest for the next step that will begin tomorrow. Bayard, I need you to stay."

The three again shook my hand and then strolled out of the room, closing the door behind themselves. I again took my seat in front of the desk.

"I presented the idea of the march to both James Farmer and John Lewis. They both are on board with their organizations. I've also talked to Dorothy Height over at the National Council of Negro Women in D. C. She thinks it's time for such a march and agrees that Negro women should be at the forefront. Now it's time to reach out to Martin. He's coming into town tomorrow for a noon meeting here in my office." He paused to let this register with me.

I hadn't seen Martin since the confrontation. I had written him a couple times but never received a response.

"I want you here for the meeting. Are you comfortable with that?'

"You shouldn't ask that of me," I said. "Martin broke off his communication and working relationship with me because of his concerns about the homosexual issue. I didn't walk away from him. The real question is will he be comfortable with me?"

"I'm fully aware of what happened," Randolph shot back. "Still, my question is will you be comfortable in the meeting."

"And if I tell you no, do I have a choice?"

"You don't. I expect you to be here by noon or earlier."

"What if he insists on changing the theme of the march, are you comfortable with that?" I asked shifting the burden to him.

"There is only one way to respond, we need Martin to make this an absolute and total success."

I wasn't thrilled about the manner that Mr. Randolph had corralled me into participating in the meeting, but I had no choice but to comply. I got up and stood behind the chair.

"Guess I'd better do like the others and go get some relaxation and a little rest."

"See you tomorrow," Randolph said.

I turned and walked out of the office.

The night was sweet as honey with Bill next to my side. I had met him at our usual rendezvous place, Julius, and hurried back to my apartment. We could hardly take time to get our clothes off before being all over each other. Once we had exhausted ourselves, he found a second burst of energy and told me he had to go and couldn't spend the night. This was becoming a common occurrence and I began to suspect that he must have someone else.

Since I had gotten back from England, he'd managed to spend only one full night with me. When we were together, ecstasy reigned in that bedroom. I had never experienced a lover quite as passionate and satisfying as I found him. But just like the mysterious note I received in England from him, his need to leave after the love making made me wonder really who is this man? Soon, I would find out.

After Bill left and I got back in bed I couldn't sleep. The meeting for tomorrow overwhelmed me with anxiety. It would be my first meeting with Martin since the telephone conversation over two years ago. I had managed to follow his movement throughout the South, noting that he did have some victories, but Albany Georgia was a nightmare for him. He needed victories over the next few months and his close friend, Fred Shuttlesworth, told him success was waiting in Birmingham. Bull Connor was just waiting to bust some Negro heads. But if the march was done correctly and Martin joins in, it could be the biggest victory for him of his young career.

My eyelids finally felt heavy and I drifted out of the conscious thought of Martin into a sub-conscious dream of Bill.

Strolling into Mr. Randolph's reception area, I didn't know how I would respond once inside his office, being there with Martin. Just as important, how would he receive me after this period of separation? I was about to find out as I swung the office door open. He turned and looked back at me. Communication between us was instantaneous. His eyes told his feelings and I know he regretted the actions he took against me. And hopefully, he could detect the forgiveness in my demeanor as I hurried over to him.

"Martin, I often wondered if I would ever see you again, and of course I no longer have to wonder," I said as we shook hands and hugged.

"It was a mistake and a cowardly act for me to turn my back on you," he said.

"We have a much more important issue confronting us, and let's leave the past behind and move forward." I sat in my usual chair in Mr. Randolph's office and Martin sat back down in the one right next to me.

Mr. Randolph had his usual place behind the desk. He took the lead. "Martin, I know you have to catch a plane this afternoon over to Birmingham, so let me get right to the point."

"I know, my time is short. Fred Shuttlesworth believes our next campaign should be in Birmingham. He promises that what happened in Albany won't happen there. You all know Police Chief Pritchard didn't take the bait. He was determined to keep the Fed's out of Albany, and the best way to do that was not to respond to the peaceful non-violent demonstrations. When we couldn't get his policemen out of their calm demeanor, then we knew the battle was lost there. But Fred claims we'll have no problem getting Bull Connors to respond violently. We'll plan for the marches to begin when the weather breaks. But that's not why you have me here."

"Martin, we need to make a major statement to the world that since the Emancipation Proclamation was passed in 1863, our progress has been almost non-existent in this country," Randolph' exclaimed. "Economically, we lag way behind most other groups and certainly way behind white America. Our challenge, then, is to conduct a major march in Washington, D.C. during the centennial anniversary of the Proclamation, and to make our demands in front of the Lincoln Monument. I need your support for this enormously important effort."

"I agree we need to do something on a national scale during 1963, but I'm just not sure what that something should be," King said. "What do you plan to be the theme behind the march?"

"Economic equality," I said, joining in the conversation.

"It won't happen with SCLC if the theme is not based on civil rights," Martin said. "We are in the middle of a war down South, fighting essentially for civil rights for the Negro. For us to change direction and join in a march that stresses economics would not look good to our followers. I know economics eventually will drive this movement, but right now we have to get the right for Negroes to enjoy the same freedoms as every other American."

"Let's synthesize the two," I said. "We can make it about jobs and freedom."

"That's it," Mr. Randolph practically shouted. "Jobs and Freedom is our theme and our slogan going forward. Will that work for you?" He looked at Martin.

"I believe I can sell that to my board," he said.

"You don't have to sell anything to your board, all you have to do is tell them of the plan," Mr. Randolph said with a smile. We all got a chuckle from his comment.

"How about the other civil rights organizations," King asked. "Are they on board, both Roy and Whitney?"

"Not yet, but they will be when they find out you've joined in," Mr. Randolph said.

"You give me more credit than I deserve," King said.

"I'm not sure neither Roy nor Whitney like you yet, but I do know they respect you," Mr. Randolph said. "They will not want to be excluded from a popular initiative, and it will become very popular when the people find out you're a part of it."

"This will be one of the crowning achievements of your long and distinguished career," King added. "You've been a leader for a long time, and I want to help make this happen for you."

Mr. Randolph leaned forward on his desk, a habit he had when making a point. "This will be a crowning achievement for the Negro race. They will tell the world that this country must change, and it has to happen real soon."

"What's our next move?" Martin asked.

"To name an executive director who will be the point man to the press," Randolph suggested. "I believe it should be Bayard."

Martin turned and looked directly at me, putting his hand on my arm. "I don't mean no harm and I hope you know, your past causes no problems for me, but you might have some difficulty with the others."

"We'll cross that bridge when we get to it," Randolph interjected. "Now with you on board, we can get started with the planning and that's where Bayard comes in. We need his skills to get it done the right way. Having him involved or not involved is like having caviar or hot dogs."

"I'll go with the caviar but let's find out what the others think," Martin said. He stood up. "Since we're finished here, I want to go by and visit with Reverend Jackson before heading out to Birmingham."

"Good enough, and we'll get moving right away on this project." Mr. Randolph also got up and came around his desk.

We followed Martin out to the front where a cab waited for him. He climbed in the back. We watched as the driver pulled out into the traffic heading up 125th Street.

43.

It didn't take long for Roy and the NAACP, as well as Whitney over at the Urban League, to join the bandwagon and become an official partner in the planned march. There were serious concessions associated with their support. Mr. Randolph and I met with them in his office and considered their demands. Roy expressed his concerns.

"Phil, you know the NAAACP does not condone street protest," Roy started. "We do not condone civil disobedience. Change comes only through the courts."

"Not quite true," Randolph said. "The Montgomery Bus Boycott achieved change as a result of social disobedience."

"Not true at all," Roy shot back. "You know damn well those rednecks did not concede an inch throughout that entire year and as an aside the boycott got a whole lot of good people fired from their jobs. What good is riding in the front of the bus if you don't have a job and cannot feed your family?"

I knew what Roy was insinuating, and he was correct in his position.

Roy continued, "The Supreme Court ruled that segregated seating in the buses in the city of Montgomery was unconstitutional. Immediately following that decision, the city ordered the segregated sections be eliminated. The NAACP won that case that led to the desegregated system."

I couldn't allow Roy to dismiss all the hard work that thousands of regular citizens put in to break the back of bus segregation in Montgomery. I had a visual of that old woman, walking to work, looking tired and beat. She wasn't a lawyer but a warrior. Her victory didn't come in the courtroom but on the streets. I had to speak up.

"You're right Roy, the court decision finally broke the back of the segregated system," I said. "But you must keep in mind that the bus company and the city were looking for ways to concede to the demonstrators, and still save face. The Court offered them that opportunity. The decision to desegregate had been made, they just needed an easy out."

"Gentlemen, we don't need to get into a pissing match as to who did what to achieve the goal of desegregation." Randolph intervened. "It was a victory and you all can share in the success. Now let's get back to the fact that we will need both the NAACP and the Urban League involvement to pull this off."

"I'm with Roy on this matter," Whitney Young said. "The Urban League is traditionally a social service organization and not a protest group. We cannot do anything to jeopardize our tax-exempt status."

"No problem there," I said. "Practically all the organizations that will participate are tax-exempt. The government won't dare try to take away their exemption."

"I can bring the NAACP in under one condition," Roy said. "It cannot be billed as a civil disobedience march and all plans to sit-in or picket the Congress or the White House must be jettisoned."

"I don't like that concession and I'll probably lose a lot of my young people who are always up for a fight," Randolph said. "But Roy we need your numbers as well as your financial support, so the change will be made." Randolph paused before turning his attention to Whitney.

"What's it going to take to get the Urban League support?" he asked.

"Here's what my board is going to insist on in order for the League to join," Whitney exclaimed. "We have to be fully involved in the planning of the event. We cannot be linked with a program of civil disobedience, especially in the nation's capital and on the new President's watch. We want an equal say in the selection of the executive director of the march and finally, we need assurances that the demonstration will be inter-racial and non-violent."

Mr. Randolph glanced over at me, and I could pretty much read his thoughts. The Urban League wanted to be assured of some control and Roy wanted to curb potential emphasis on Martin at the expense of the others. We had no choice. There was no meaningful march without the two most recognized civil rights organizations.

"I think we can work it out," Randolph said. "Can we now count on you?"

"You can count on the support not only in numbers but in finances also," Roy replied.

"I need only run this by my board and with all the requirements you agreed to, I think I have enough influence with them to get it done. So yes, you can count on the Urban League."

I sat there somewhat in disbelief. We were really going to be able to pull this off with all the organizational support we would need. Labor unions, civil rights organizations and churches were all on board, and now I had to go out and make it work. But first I had to face another challenge.

"Who do you propose for the executive director of the march, the person that will meet with the press, the congressional delegation and possibly the president?" Roy asked while looking directly at me.

Mr. Randolph and I knew the reasons for the question. Roy didn't want the job to come to me because of what he considered a sordid past. Once again, it appeared that my glory would be taken away from me.

"We can take that up in a subsequent meeting," Randolph responded trying to divert the issue.

"That's fine, just as long as it's understood that Bayard cannot do the job," Roy said and even looked directly at me. "Nothing against you, my friend, but you do come with some heavy baggage, and if brought out into the open could hurt the cause."

"Let's table that until I can canvass all the others on the management team," Randolph said with a slight amount of irritation in his tone.

"Don't wait too long," Whitney joined the discussion. "We have no time to waste on who should run this thing. There are a whole lot of issues that have to be dealt with."

"This is Wednesday, and I'll have an answer for you by Friday."

"That's good with me," Roy said.

"And me," Whitney agreed.

Mr. Randolph stood up and we followed.

"This is going to be an earth-shattering event, gentlemen, and I'm pleased that you are now aboard. We can resolve this one issue and really get going. Bayard has a great team that he's assembling."

"That's fine, but remember we still have to vote on the executive director, and I'll expect to hear from you on Friday," Roy said, shook hands with me and Mr. Randolph then hurried out of the office. Whitney did the same and was right behind Roy.

"Wouldn't life be a lot simpler for you if you could find a way not to be gay?" Randolph surprisingly asked, as we stood in the reception area of his office.

"I find life rather easy for me and I love being gay because it's who I am. Like many others who claimed to be heterosexual, I enjoy being a homosexual and wouldn't trade this body for no one else."

"If you had your choice of being straight and white rather than what you are, would you make the change?"

"No, not at all," my answer was immediate and concise, as I felt compelled to bring this discussion to an end.

"You can't do that," Tom shrieked as he, along with Norman and Rachelle sat in my small office at War Resisters League, preparing to continue our work on the planned march. "If you abandon civil disobedience as part of the march, you lose half of the young people who planned to participate."

"You're just doing that to appease the NAACP and Urban League," Rachelle gasped. "This is an incredible sell out on your part."

Rachelle's accusation hit me like a sledgehammer driving against a solid wall. She had never doubted me in the past and never said a disrespectful word to me.

"We had no choice," I pleaded my case. "Without the financial support as well as the enormous number of people the NAACP can bring to the event, our chances of success will diminish. You know I will always be committed to civil disobedience through non-violent tactics, but sometimes you have to take a step backward in order to take three forward."

348 | Williams-Denton-Zinsmeyer

"John Lewis and SNCC will never accept this, and you will probably lose a great deal of respect from them because of the change," Norman added. "Stokely Carmichael and that whole crew had a great deal of confidence in you because of what you stand for. Do you really want to take the chance of losing them?"

Frustration, more than irritation, began to set in. "You have to understand that I did not make this decision, but Mr. Randolph had no other choice. Do you want to see us make a major statement against segregation and to some extent capitalism and especially imperialism, then settle down, accept the change and let's get to work?"

I divided up the responsibilities between them and we began the early work necessary for the march to be a success. Just when I thought the matter was resolved, the phone rang.

"Bayard, what the hell did you all do?" James Farmer asked. He didn't wait for an answer. "Just when I had convinced my members that the march was something we had to be in, I find out that you all have changed the game totally to appease the NAACP and Roy Wilkins. What kind of hold does he have over you and Dr. King? You all seem to just jump to his tune."

"You know that's not true at all, but do we need to appease him to pull this off?" I shot back at him. "Yes, we do. Why, because his organization has all the resources, both bodies and money to make this a success."

"I guess the Friday visits to Capitol Hill and the White House are now out?" Farmer asked rather rhetorically. He knew they were out.

"They are out, and it'll just be the march on Saturday," I assured him.

"That changes the entire game for us. You know we are driven based on the whole concept of non-violent civil disobedience."

I could detect the irritation and anger on the other end.

"That's what all the freedom rides have been about. Causing the other guy to look bad and we have been quite successful. Now you're asking us to change our game plan."

"James, this will be much bigger than anything we have attempted in the past, including the freedom rides," I said. "It is absolutely imperative that we all be of one accord and we all participate. We cannot afford to lose your support. Please just go along with this minor change for the sake of the movement."

"Minor," James shouted so that the others in the room could hear him. "This is a major shift in operation just to appease one organization and one man."

"Not quite just one," I said. "National Urban League also rejected the Friday program. In fact, Whitney assured us that his board would never approve the march, if civil disobedience was a possibility. Something about he might lose his tax-exempt status."

"Who cares about a bunch of conservative Negroes and a board full of conservative white folks, whose only mission in life is to train Negroes the proper way to act when they come up North to live?"

He had a point. The Urban League did very little other than serve as a conduit to the white folks who wanted just good, behaving Negroes to migrate from the South. But still, they had a very good reputation and, regardless of how James and I felt about them, they were considered one of the leading civil rights organizations.

"How does Dr. King feel about this change?" James asked, having cooled off. "His whole existence is predicated on the foundation of protest and street disturbances using non-violence. Has he accepted this change in plans?"

"Yes, he has." James' tone irritated me. "He realizes that sometimes it's necessary to make sacrifices for the greater good." I wasn't quite sure if that was Martin's position, because Mr. Randolph had yet to talk with him about the change. But I surmised that he would go along with it. He had made the commitment and as an honorable man would honor it.

"All right Bayard, we'll accept the change. But please know we are not happy with it."

"I think you've made that quite clear."

"I understand there is to be a meeting on Monday to decide who will be executive director and Roy Wilkins is opposing you for that position. Do you plan to cave in on that also?"

"That's my understanding," I said, ignoring the second part of his question.

"Roy won't be with you, but how about Dr. King?" he asked, but didn't wait for an answer. "You know he abandoned you before in a rather cowardly way. Do you think he'll do it again?"

"We'll know Monday," I replied rather non-committal. I didn't appreciate the attack on Martin, even though it was true.

"Please note that you have one unhappy and discontented participant." He hung up.

"I guess someone else agrees with our position," Tom said as I placed the phone down. "This is appearing to be not a coalition, but a march led by the NAACP with a whole lot of followers."

"Don't be so harsh," I scowled just a little tired of all the opposition I was receiving that day. "We did what was necessary to make this march a success. And now it is your job to do your part." I pulled a cigarette out of the pack resting on my desk and lit it. "Let's get to work."

After another night of intense love making, again Bill got up and dressed to leave. I watched him from the bed. Usually, I would stay put and he would let himself out, but not this time. I had to get to the bottom of this. I rose in the bed and rested against the back of the frame.

"What is it with you?" I asked.

"What do you mean," Bill replied rather sheepishly.

"You know what I mean. You come over, we make some serious love and then you get up and leave," I described exactly what he knew as true. "The first night we were together is the only night you stayed over, so what is it?"

"Can we not talk about it right now? Can it just wait a little longer?"

I slid and sat on the side of the bed. This man was hiding something from me, and I needed to know exactly what it was. Flashbacks of Arthur crossed my mind, as I recalled he broke off our relationship because he wanted to get married and have a family. To me, that represented the worst of the gay community. If Bill was married with a family, but unhappy because he could only be satisfied with another man, I needed to know. Because in that situation, I didn't care to be the other man.

Bill, are you living a double life?" I bluntly asked. "Because if you are, I have a right to know. Not that I'm looking for a long-term relationship with you or I'm falling in love. Just I always want to know what's happening in my relationships."

"You saying you couldn't fall in love with me?

"I'm saying I don't want to fall in love with you. I enjoy your company and you are a fantastic lover. But it's no more than that."

"I'm going to leave now." He scrambled to the bedroom door and opened it.

"That's fine with me, but please do not plan to come back until you can explain what's going on in your life."

Bill walked out of the bedroom and closed the door behind him. I lay there trying to figure out what was going on with this relationship. It bothered me and just like a sudden flash of light, I realized what this might be about. Pasadena 1953 all over again. It had to be a set-up. But Bill hadn't solicited any information from me as of yet. I thought back on England and the note from him. Of course, the FBI would know where I was. But why? What were they looking for from me? I no longer had my close connection with Martin, and I was no longer friends with Stanley. Had I been that careless, especially after the embarrassing and very destructive incident over ten years ago?

I thought back on Roy Wilkins comments that my lifestyle was much too reckless for me to serve as Executive Director of the march. I would compromise the goal, and he might be right considering that very evening after the meeting with him, I ended up in the bed with someone who very well could be a plant from the FBI. I lay back down and pulled the covers over my head, ashamed of just how reckless I might have been.

44.

By the first of June the march had taken on a momentum of its own. Most all liberal leaning groups had signed on and the leadership had been identified. Again, Roy had his way and I was not chosen to be Executive Director. That position went to Mr. Randolph, but once named, he immediately assigned me the title of Deputy Director. Roy told him that he might live to regret that decision, but recognized there was nothing he could do about it. On paper, Mr. Randolph was the head man, but for all intense and purposes I had the job.

The banner that hung from outside the building of our headquarters at 170 West 130th Street, right in the heart of Harlem, read, "March for Jobs and Freedom." The volunteers kept pouring in by large numbers so that we had over two hundred in the office every day stuffing envelopes, making telephone calls and any mundane but essential job that needed to be done.

Much of the growth occurred due to the battles being fought in Birmingham by the protestors and the police. Just as Fred Shuttlesworth had predicted, Bull Connor practically lost his mind when men, women and children crowded the streets everyday with signs calling for the end of discrimination and segregation. Every night, millions of people sat at their televisions and watched the sight of water hoses and dogs let loose on women and children. One particular picture of a large white policemen with his knee in the throat of a Negro woman and the dog growling at her, caught the attention of the country. It sickened me to look at it.

What Martin had failed to accomplish in Albany, thanks to Fred, he did in Birmingham. The attacks were so egregious that President Kennedy, finally took to the air waves and delivered an address to the nation on June 11. I sat at home, alone, and listened to his words.

"We face a moral crisis as a country and as a people," he said. "We face massive demonstrations for equality in the streets of Birmingham and other places in the South. And it cannot be met by repressive police actions. It cannot be left to increased demonstrations in the streets. It cannot be quieted by token moves or talk. It is time to act. Those who do nothing are inviting shame as well as violence. Those who act boldly are recognizing right as well as reality."

He finally got around to what I patiently waited to hear.

"I will send to the United States Congress, a comprehensive civil rights bill calling for the eradication of all forms of segregation and discrimination. It is imperative that the Congress act immediately on this legislation for the sake of our country, and all that is decent and good. God bless America." He ended and walked back down the long hall out of the East Room.

The next morning at the headquarters we celebrated. Finally, the federal government was doing what it should have done long ago. Maybe, just maybe, the threat of comprehensive civil rights legislation would force the South to do right. But then on that afternoon, word came to me that a man I knew and admired for his courage in the face of extreme danger, Medgar Evers, had been shot and killed in the driveway of his home in Jackson, Mississippi. He was field secretary of the NAACP in Jackson and his work on part of getting the right for Negroes in Mississippi to vote led to his assassination, and temporarily halted our work until after his funeral. And the proceedings for his home going service practically ended the cooperative relationship between Roy and Martin. Word got back to me that there was an ugly scene in the church, instigated primarily by Roy.

When King arrived at the church for the service, ushers escorted him up to the podium where all dignitaries sat. We all knew that Roy did not respect SCLC, nor did he respect CORE or SNCC. He felt these upstart new organizations survived on the back of the NAACP and, as such, should always take a back seat to them. Given all the publicity that King had received over the past five years, Wilkins couldn't stand for him to receive special treatment at an event of the NAACP. He went right up to the podium and told King, he could not sit up there and had to move down to one of the pews. Not wanting to make a scene he complied, but all in attendance took note and assumed because of that embarrassment,

King would pull out of the march. He did not and plans continued to take final shape, as we moved through the month of June.

Since the beginning of the Civil Rights Movement back in 1956, there had never been an occasion where all the major organizations joined together under one roof for one particular project. I began to feel the pressure of what I was called on to do. It really took hold when on June 15 the primary organizers, the Big Six, their designated title, gathered at the Harlem headquarters and faced a crowd of newsmen and a bevy of television cameras.

Mr. Randolph stood at the microphone, with Martin, Roy, Whitney, John Lewis and James Farmer right behind him and Dorothy Height off to his left. As usual, I remained off to the left.

"Today is an historical one because for the very first time all the major Negro civil rights organizations have come together to announce a march on Washington, D. C. to address our grievances, both a social and economic protest." He paused for a moment evidently to allow the magnitude of his words to register with all the reporters. "I am honored to stand here with great leaders of their organizations and tell the country that we are very serious about the age-old denial of civil and economic rights to not just Negroes, but all people who are outside the mainstream of this country. The date for this momentous event has been set for August 28, and it will take place on the Capitol Mall at the steps of the Lincoln Monument. It is only appropriate that we make a statement there because he made a statement when he signed the Emancipation Proclamation back in 1863. We look forward to working with the press as the weeks pass and we grow closer to the actual day of the event, and even afterwards. Thank you for showing up for this most important announcement."

"Mr. Randolph how does the President feel about this event and is this a slap in his face holding it right in his backyard," a reporter shouted.

The six men ignored the question and continued to walk up the steps of the monument. They had agreed before the announcement to not take questions.

"Mr. Rustin, how will you deal with the Southern delegation when they find out that this march is really aimed at them?"

They finally reached the top of the steps, turned and made their way back where I stood and out of sight of the reporters.

"It's official now gentlemen," Mr. Randolph said once they were out of the reporters' sight. "There is no turning back." He turned and looked at me. "You and your team have to make this happen; we need a flawless, clean event for the entire world to see."

I nodded my head in agreement. What was there to say? We did need a strong showing. It would be the very first time that the Negro organizations, the liberal white groups, the unions and many churches joined together to make a statement that we'd had enough. It was time to make this democracy work.

On the flight back to New York, Mr. Randolph and I had a chance to discuss some of the more pressing problems still confronting the new coalition of organizations. After the press conference, King flew back to Birmingham where the street demonstrations still remained the center of national attention. Roy and Whitney stayed behind in Washington, D. C. where they had planned meetings with their Washington lobbyists. John Lewis also stayed in the Nation's Capital to meet with Stokely Carmichael and some of the other members of SNCC at Howard University.

"I'm not sure Martin will ever get the respect from Roy," Randolph said.

"It's just a case of sheer envy, especially now that Martin is getting a lot of the civil rights money coming out of New York. That also is a threat to Wilkins and the NAACP coffers."

"It's more than the envy," Randolph replied. "It's a changing of the guard from the old to the new. Roy and the NAACP are the old and Martin and the SCLC are the new. You see, the paradigm has changed, and you are as responsible for that as anyone in this country."

I appreciated the compliment, especially coming from Mr. Randolph, but I wasn't sure I deserved it. "Why do you say that?" I asked.

"Initially in Montgomery, all Martin had was a protest but no real technique behind it," Mr. Randolph, sitting in the window seat turned to look directly at me. I was in the aisle seat and the middle one remained empty. "Not until you went down there and introduced Gandhi's philosophy of non-violence, it was a boycott looking for a foundation. You gave them the best possible. And to show you how effective it was, we are observing it at work in Birmingham and making Martin look good and Bull Connor look evil."

I never viewed it from that perspective, in fact, I never considered myself that important. But as I listened to Mr. Randolph, I began to assess my involvement in a number of movements over the past ten years. There was the prayer pilgrimage, India and the issue of what position should the international pacifist take, and then England and the long march across the United States and the continent of Europe ending in Moscow.

"One unfortunate problem that is going to haunt us for the next two months until this march is over, and that is Wilkins resentment toward Martin," Mr. Randolph continued. "It's not going to go away and as this march begins to get a lot more publicity, reporters are going to gradually turn to Martin for information."

"But you're the executive director, we have to make sure they gravitate to you," I said. "You are the glue that will keep this march together. The others may fight among themselves, but they will not challenge you or take you on."

"All that's true but we can't control what reporters will be prone to do, and they're going to go to the person where they get the most bang for their buck. These days it is Martin."

I pondered briefly his words and then said. "You know, you're right. That's exactly what's going to happen."

Our plane began its descent into New York after the short trip from Washington, D. C. I leaned back and closed my eyes. A new battle may have been born, and this time not against the white bigots of the country but among the jealous members of our coalition.

I shared a taxi from the airport with Mr. Randolph and after the driver dropped him off first, I decided to go home instead over to Julius in the Village. I wanted to avoid Bill at all cost and figured he might be there looking for me. I had nothing positive that he was some kind of plant trying to solicit damaging information about Martin or even Mr.

Randolph, but I didn't want to take the chance. And a night of solitude, alone with my thoughts was something I really needed.

Once settled into the comfortable lounge chair in my apartment, I opened one of my cherished books, **Leaves of Grass.** Walt Whitman had always been my favorite poet as he was to the rest of the country. I turned to his poem "Song of Myself," and began to read the stanzas that addressed love making. Unlike novels or other forms of writing, poetry could not be read quietly but called for the reader to be vocal, so I began, **"I mind how once we lay such a transparent summer morning. How you settled your head athwart my lips and gently turned over on me, and parted my shirt from my bosom-bone, and plunged your tongue to my bare-stripped heart and reached till you felt my beard and reached till you held my feet. It may be you transpire from the breasts of young men, it may be. I had known then I would have loved them."**

I paused to consider my ambivalent feeling toward this great manipulator of words. He was gentle and beautiful in his verse and that was the side I loved about him. But then on the other side I couldn't ignore as much as I wanted to, he was a bigot, a prejudice man who spoke out against my people, once freed from the chains of slavery, ever having the privilege to vote in this country. How could this man who possessed such an innate ability to express the beauty of nature as well as the sensibilities of the human spirit, also think of other human beings as less than equals to whites. That troubled me, especially given the fact that he was also a homosexual, and judged as less than equal to others because of that designation.

I wondered would he have accepted me as a lover or dismissed me as a Negro. As I continued to read his verses, I felt conflicted. I read from the works of a man whom I really admired but knew the feelings would not be reciprocal.

I continued to read because that was my mood at that moment. No Martin, no Mr. Randolph, no civil rights issues or non-violent philosophy, no march to Moscow, but just me as a man and as a homosexual. **"Winds who soft and tickling genitals rub against me it shall be you. Broad muscular fields, branches of live oak, loving lounger in my winding paths, it shall be** you. Hands I taken, face I have kissed, mortal I have ever touched, it shall be you."

This was time for reflection. My thoughts traveled back in time and a vision of Jean Cessna, a young French boy who happened to be my best friend in high school came to me. He lived with his aunt, who would not allow me to their house. We would meet in the public library and always read Whitman's poetry together. I'm not sure we really understood a lot of the meaning behind his verse, but it seemed to fit us. We both knew who we were but never pursued it between us. I would have preferred my first relationship to have been with him, instead of the man it happened with one night while visiting my mother. Because of cramped quarters, I was forced to sleep with this older man who teased me all night long to the point it drove me wild, and finally he consummated the pleasure by slowly gently massaging me to an erection and bringing me to a climax. It was a pure, sexual act but I still would have preferred the first time to be between Jean and me. After high school I never saw him again. I believe he returned to France, where obviously freedom to express oneself is respected. From that time forward I knew my sexual preference and have never wavered since then.

I got up and walked over to my shelf of books and placed the Whitman back, then sat down at the harpsicord. My thoughts again returned to West Chester and I recalled my short friendship with Samuel Barber, a musician two grades ahead of me, but we both were students of Floyd Hart the music teacher at the school. Barber went onto the Curtis Institute of Music in Philadelphia and became a renowned composer. I loved to play one of his most famous, "Adagio for Strings." I played it a number of times and finally began to tire. After a good two hours on the harpsicord, my eyes became heavy. I finally got up and sauntered into the bedroom and fell across the bed. Laying there I felt pleased and disappointed that I hadn't heard from Bill. Only minutes later, the world disappeared from me in a deep sleep.

45.

"President Kennedy wants us at the White House this afternoon for a meeting," Randolph said as his call had awakened me.

"When?" I asked.

"Today, this afternoon at three o'clock."

"When you say he wants us, who is us? I reached over to the nightstand and pulled a Pall Mall out of the pack and lit it.

"I know he wants the six who were on the podium at the announcement and I want you to be there also. Martin is at the airport in Birmingham boarding a plane right now. The President wanted the meeting earlier, but we couldn't accommodate him, because Martin's flight would take a couple hours."

"You know you're asking for trouble, inviting me."

"At this point, I have no patience to quibble with Roy about who should and should not be in a meeting. You are responsible for organizing this event, so you need to be there to hear what the President has to say."

"He's going to complain when I show up with you at the White House, but by then it might be too late to do anything."

"I am not Martin and he doesn't intimidate me at all. If he'd done to me what he did to Martin at Medgar Evers funeral, I wouldn't have gone quietly. Now I already have your ticket. Just meet me at LaGuardia by noon. We have a one o'clock flight."

I had never been in the Oval Office before and I felt the importance of that room when a butler escorted us inside. Roy did have a shocked look on his face, and gave Mr. Randolph a hard stare when I walked in with him. He and Whitney, along with James and John, were seated on one of the couches. Dorothy and Martin sat on the other couch. They were talking with Attorney General Bobby Kennedy and Vice-President Lyndon Johnson when we strolled inside and found two empty chairs near the President's desk. After a few minutes, the side door swung open and President Kennedy, accompanied by his special assistant, Theodore Sorenson, hurried into the room. The President took his place behind the desk and Sorenson sat near me. All the administration's heavy weights were there, I assumed to support whatever Kennedy planned to say to us. He got right to the point.

"Gentlemen, this announcement of a massive march on Washington, D. C. is a bad idea right at this time, especially since I just sent a civil rights bill to the Congress for their consideration." He paused, I guess to gauge our response. We all remained stone faced so the President continued. "Here is the problem, you know Strom Thurmond and his boys over there are going to oppose my bill, without any additional ammunition. But this march will give them the kind of boost they need." He leaned forward on the desk. "Phil, Roy and Whitney, you all are the old hands at this, and you know how this game plays out. Please don't tie my hands and make this much more difficult for us over here."

"Mr. President, that is not our intention," Roy spoke up first. I wasn't surprised, after all he supported Kennedy strongly through the primaries and the general election. One of his concerns was that we do nothing to hurt him, and maybe the march should not be into Washington. The others all disagreed with him and that idea was put to rest.

"We need the march to bring attention to this Congress's failure to do something about the terrible violence in the South," Randolph said. I also noticed that he placed the emphasis on the Congress and not the President. It appeared that everyone planned to be extremely cooperative and cordial with Kennedy.

Still, Kennedy appeared unimpressed. "We want success in Congress, not just a big show on Capitol Hill. Some of these people are looking for an excuse to be against us. I don't want any of them to say, 'Yes, I'm for the bill, but I'm damned if I will vote for it at the point of a gun.'"

Bobby Kennedy spoke up. "It just seems to be a great mistake to announce a march on Washington before the bill is even in committee. The only effect is to create an atmosphere of intimidation, and this may give some members of Congress an out."

"Mr. President, we don't mean to offend you in any way," Martin said. "But the march could serve as a means through which people with legitimate discontents can channel their grievances under disciplined, non-violent leadership."

Finally, the word I waited patiently to hear, non-violent. I knew Martin would bring it up. But I don't know just how much impact it had.

The Vice-President finally said. "The entire civil rights initiative hinges on twenty-five swing votes. To get those votes we must be careful not to do anything that would give those who are privately opposed to it, a public excuse to appear as martyrs."

I put very little credibility in Johnson's words. He was the Majority Leader who, only two years ago, pushed through the Congress a weak civil rights bill that had no teeth at all. And as a former Southern Senator from Texas what could we possibly expect from him.

"We have already made tremendous sacrifices," John Lewis exclaimed sounding not at all condescending. "The plan was to have sit-ins in the Congress on Friday and at the White House if necessary. But because some of our team opposed that idea, we backed off. Now you are asking us not to do anything. Well, Negroes are tired of doing nothing just for the sake of keeping the peace."

I knew he really wanted to say, "Just for the sake of keeping white people happy." It didn't surprise me that the angry tone came right after the Vice President spoke. No one in the movement seemed to like him.

"We never seriously considered sit-ins against you, Mr. President," Roy cleaned it up.

"Sit-ins were on the drawing board, though," James Farmer interjected as a way to support John's comments against those of Roy.

Please, I thought, do not let this become a disagreement among the six leaders. That would be a disaster. Mr. Randolph must have read my thoughts because he chimed in.

"Mr. President, we plan only to make a statement not a scene. So, you can rest assured there will be no demonstrations aimed at embarrassing you or your administration. We can only hope that the Congress will be receptive to our message. Otherwise, I can't assure you that the next demonstration won't be drastically different."

"What I think I hear you all saying is that the march will go forward, regardless of the President's opposition," Bobby scowled. "Do you think that is wise?"

"Mr. President, we mean you no harm and I will guarantee you that every speech will be scrutinized by Bayard for suitability," Martin said.

All eyes now looked over at me. I had remained silent through the entire ordeal, probably the first time that had ever happened. But I had to be careful not to speak up and remind Roy that I was not one of the leaders and, therefore, shouldn't be there. I smiled and remained silent.

The President wouldn't let my silence rule. "What do you think Mr. Rustin, do you think you can keep this whole endeavor under control? We understand that Mr. Randolph is the director of the program, but you are really the muscle and brains behind the planning and implementation."

"I believe this group of outstanding leaders will make sure that will happen." I took the diplomatic route. "It is our plan to have a very peaceful but effective gathering here at the Lincoln Monument, in honor of him for the work he did freeing our ancestors." More diplomacy. "This is not meant to complain but to complement."

"Excellent answer," Theodore Sorenson said.

The President leaned back in his chair, a strong indication that the meeting would soon end. The side door swung open and Pierre Salinger, his communications director, said, "Mr. President, we need to get you over to the meeting with the foreign correspondents. They are still quite awe struck with how you handled Kruchev last year and the Cuban Missile Crisis."

"Gentlemen and Mrs. Height, thank you for coming on such short notice. It seems to me that you are determined to have this march," President Kennedy said.

'Yes, Mr. President the march will go forward," Randolph said with great finality. "It may seem ill-timed, but frankly I have never participated in any demonstration or March that did not seem ill-timed.

"That is exactly what we hear as we go into different cities in the South with our protest," Martin added. "To those determined to maintain the status quo the timing is never good."

A smile crossed the President's face, "It seems to me that you all should be grateful to Bull Connors down there in Birmingham. After all, he's done more to advance the cause of civil rights than any other one individual."

We laughed with the President and at the point the meeting was over.

We huddled right outside the White House gate and an angry Roy let us know of his displeasure.

"In the future, can we keep meetings at this level reserved for only the six leaders?"

I looked away so as not to be pulled into that conversation. I had to allow Mr. Randolph to handle Roy's curt and biting comment. It had absolutely nothing to do with the meeting, but I knew that was his nature.

"I believe the President will ultimately support the march," Randolph said, ignoring Roy's comment.

"The smile at the conclusion of the meeting was a good sign," Martin added, also ignoring Roy. "But now that Phil has told the President the march will go forward, there is no way any of us can break ranks. We are in this together."

Martin's comment, I thought, was a perfect comeback at Roy without directly confronting him. No one else challenged Mr. Randolph's decision to invite me. The matter was over.

"Let's all put on our big boy britches, stop any bickering and move forward. Bayard is the man who can make this happen. I told you before that I only accepted the executive director position if he could be my deputy. Now it's time to get out of the way and allow him to work his magic. Because it is magic that will be needed to make this happen. There is no one, and I stress no one, in this country more suited and prepared to do this than him."

"I'm going to need Clarence Mitchell's assistance in putting together all the logistics as we get closer to the day," I turned, looked directly at

Roy and said. It was to some degree a compromising gesture but also a truth. Clarence Mitchell was the venerable NAACP lobbyist on Capitol Hill, often referred to as the one-hundred-and-first Senator. He had the respect of all Capitol Hill, even known racists like Thurmond.

"You'll have his support," Roy said. Evidently, he accepted my slight concession. "He can identify all the potholes in the city and who to look out for and who is your friend."

"I have to get to the airport and get back to Birmingham," King glanced at his watch. "Right now, Bull Connors is quiet, but no telling when he'll start his nonsense again."

"I'll keep you informed as the parts begin to fall in to place," I said.

King smiled and hugged me. "Good to have you back."

"Thank you."

The policeman on duty in front of the White House had already flagged down four cabs, one for Martin, one for Roy and Whitney, then Mr. Randolph and me, all going to the airport. Dorothy' staff was parked out front waiting for her. The fourth cab was for John and James, heading back over to Howard University campus. We all said our good-byes and headed back to Birmingham, New York and the campus.

Earlier in the day I had arranged to have dinner with Lorraine Hansberry. Her play, A Raisin in the Sun had been a big hit for the past four years and she was a heroine to the lesbian community in New York as well as the Negro literary groups. Her play had opened at the Ethel Barrymore Theater in March 1959, making her the first Black playwright and youngest American to win the New York Critic's Award. She'd been one of the many people who had criticized Martin when he removed me from SCLC back in 1960, and I never had the opportunity to thank her personally. This provided me the opportunity to do just that. We planned to meet at seven o'clock at Sylvia's Restaurant in Harlem. But when we landed at LaGuardia and caught a cab, my first stop had to be at the headquarters for the march. I knew the staff would be anxious to hear what happened with the President. I wasn't wrong.

How'd it go?" Rachelle confronted me as soon as I walked through the door. "Is all our work in vain and have you all called off the march?"

"Was Wilkins pissed off because Mr. Randolph brought you along?" Tom asked.

"Did anyone walk out on the meeting?" Norman asked.

"Hey, let me get in the office before you start firing all these questions," I said as I made my way to my small office and sat behind the desk. They all followed me inside.

"Did Roy Wilkins and Dr. King get into it?" Rachelle stood right up close to the desk. "You know Wilkins don't like Dr. King?"

"I wouldn't' quite say he doesn't like him," I said. "It's more that he is jealous of him and concerned that SCLC is draining funds and people from the NAACP. That's his real concern and everything went just fine. We didn't get the President's support, but he didn't necessarily oppose the march."

"That's a qualifying answer," Tom shot back at me.

I knew he would not let me get away with that answer.

"Did the two have words?"

"No, they didn't, and I want you all to quit anticipating problems," I said. "Now I have to get out of here real soon for a dinner date, so Tom give me a report of the day." Tom had become my right-hand man and secretary. He was very thorough and efficient.

"It's incredible the number of calls we are getting from people wanting more information on the march, and it has really increased since you all held the press conference the other day," Tom said. "If we're not careful we're going to have a logistical nightmare. You need to schedule a meeting with the Washington D. C. Police and the Capitol Hill and Park Police and come up with a plan to handle the traffic."

"You get that done," I said, looking directly at Rachelle.

"We are also getting a ton of requests for special seating from elected officials from all over the country," Norman chimed in. "Everyone wants to join in on the band wagon. You are going to have one hell of a successful event"

"I hope so," I said. "We'll only have a limited number of seats up front, so don't commit to anyone. We must be very selective. Each organization is going to insist on special treatment and that could turn out to be a nightmare."

"I hope this time you get the credit you deserve," Tom said, evidently alluding to what happened back in 1960.

"We don't need to worry about who gets credit or covered most by the press," I replied. "We leave that kind of nonsense for Roy and his friends. We only worry about getting things done." I pulled out a Pall Mall and lit it. "We only have less than two months to make this happen. I can't stress enough the importance of staying on top of your assignment."

"When do the others plan to send some help here to New York?" Norman changed the nature of the conversation. I was grateful to him.

"Remind me to call Mr. Randolph in the morning so he can call the others, especially Roy."

"You all seem to lean heavily on the NAACP and Wilkins," Norman said.

"They have the most money and the bodies. That's why he feels he can flex his muscles," I replied.

"Yeah, he alone changed the entire scope of the march," Tom said, a reminder that many of the young people were still not happy when we eliminated the demonstrations for Friday.

"The message is more important than the method," I said. "On Saturday we will be able to deliver the message worldwide and that's exactly what counts. Now let's get back to work. We have no time to waste and quibble over methods and tactics."

They all scattered out of my office and back to their stations.

Sylvia Brown met me at the door with a smile. She had opened Sylvia's Soul Food Restaurant on Lennox Avenue in the heart of Harlem just a year ago, and business was booming for her. Lorraine suggested that we eat there for two reasons, the food was excellent, and she insisted on supporting a Negro woman in business. I had no problems with either of her reasons.

"Mr. Rustin, thank you for coming," she said. "Ms. Hansberry and Mr. Baldwin are both waiting for you in the other room."

Jimmy Baldwin, I thought. That was a surprise. I didn't know Jimmy planned to join us. In fact, I didn't even know he was in the country. But it made sense. Only a few months ago they had released his essays titled **Fire Next Time**, under I believe Dell Publications. I was slightly embarrassed because I had been so busy, I still hadn't read them. I had begun to read them when they first came out years ago in **Commentary Magazine**. I did know they had caught fire and became the talk of the country. I anticipated a great discussion with two of my favorite people.

"Jimmy, Lorraine, what a treat," I said as I sat in the one empty seat obviously, they had set up for me. "I feel like I'm in the company of artistic genius, two of the outstanding writers in this country. How are you both?"

"Good seeing you Bayard," Baldwin said.

"How you been doing with your busy schedule?" Lorraine asked.

"I have to admit I'm working overtime and making no money, but getting fantastic gratification for what might be accomplished in the next two months."

"I'm quite intrigued with the march you all plan for August," Baldwin said. "I imagine this is the extension of the one that Phillip Randolph did not get a chance to pull off back in 1941."

"Not really, but again yes in a very interesting way," I said.

The waiter approached our table and asked, "Are you all ready to order?"

"Not yet," Lorraine answered. "Give us a few minutes."

He turned and walked away.

"You really have gotten back in with that church crowd after what they did to you a few years ago?" Baldwin asked.

"If you're alluding to Dr. King's involvement in the march, I guess the answer is yes.

"How can you possibly believe in those preachers?" Baldwin asked.

"I don't necessarily believe in them, but in the cause."

"But to get to the cause you have to deal with them."

The waiter finally brought glasses of water to the table. "Are you ready now?" He asked.

"Why don't you just come back in fifteen minutes and we'll be ready." Lorraine again took the lead.

Again, he turned and walked away.

"Word has it that they refused to allow you to be director of this march, even though you are doing all the work that a director does," Baldwin continued relentlessly on this subject. "Again, they're running from who you are. As a homosexual man, you're in the wrong business, because you're dealing with men who are homophobic, and I bet it was King who rejected you for director."

"As a matter of fact, Martin supported me. It was your good friend, Roy Wilkins who adamantly opposed me. He…"

"My friend, you know you're kidding," Baldwin interrupted me. "That man is worse than the preachers in his bigotry. And the irony is that he is head of the most prestigious and largest civil rights organization in the country."

"I really do find it ironic that Negroes are prejudiced against gay men and lesbians," Lorraine finally chimed in.

"They proudly claim their bigotry by quoting from the Bible," Baldwin said.

"What I try to get across to them is that the Negro will never be free if there is any group in this country still oppressed," I took out a Pall Mall and offered one to both Jimmy and Lorraine. They accepted and we lit up.

"Problem is that our people are so naïve and subject to their rhetoric, they believe what comes out of pulpits every Sunday," Lorraine said. "What they don't realize if they keep doing what they get away with now, someday Christianity will become irrelevant."

"Yes, that's excellent," Baldwin exclaimed. "That's why you created that scene in your play when Beneatha, the daughter, questions the existence of God."

"And Mama slaps her and tells her to repeat after me 'In my house God exists,' or something to that effect," I added.

Lorraine smiled, evidently pleased that we knew that part of the play.

"I was attempting to make a point that church folks better take heed to," she said.

"What do you plan to accomplish with this march next month?" Baldwin picked up the glass and sipped on the water. He had just put the cigarette to his mouth, took a deep inhale of the smoke and it caused him to cough.

"It is to alert the world that Negroes no longer will settle for a bigoted society with segregated facilities, unequal pay, and unemployment," I said.

"You might manage to do that, but what you're definitely going to do is piss off a bunch of rednecks who are going to spill our people's blood," Baldwin claimed. "I just hope your accomplishment is not outweighed by the blood flowing in the waters."

Lorraine signaled for the waiter to return to the table. "Let's eat because we are not going to solve the problems of this country tonight."

"Will you two come on August 28 and sit in one of the reserved areas?" I asked.

"Just for you, I'll change my schedule to make sure I'm there," Baldwin said

"No doubt this will be a history making event and I want to be there," Lorraine agreed.

The waiter made his way to the table, took our order and hurried off to the kitchen.

46.

Operating out of our Harlem headquarters we had put together an impressive team with the top leaders assigned specific jobs, and I expected each one of them to carry out their responsibility in an exemplary manner. No complaints, no fussing and no arguing among all the players. We had gotten enough of that from the outside as the interest to the march increased daily. By August we figured the goal of one hundred thousand had been met, and all additions after the beginning of the month would be frosting on the cake.

Complements of my organizing skills began to appear in editorial pages of the major newspapers, and the more they wrote about me, the more it appeared I was in charge. And that led to the first major confrontation about me and it came from Capitol Hill. Mr. Randolph called me at the headquarters.

"We got problems," he started, not even a greeting.

"Don't we always have problems," I replied rather cynically. "What is it this time?"

"Let me read briefly from a speech on the Senate Floor by Strom Thurmond that has now been picked up by major newspapers. "The Negroes are planning what they consider a march on Washington, D.C. for August 28 to express their concern of this country to fully integrate them, both socially and economically, into this country. But how serious can they possibly be when they have someone who is of questionable character in charge of organizing the event. The person is Bayard Rustin and he is no one who should even be allowed on the steps of the Lincoln Memorial. First, he is a known draft dodger and had to be thrown in jail for refusing to serve his country during World War II. Second, he has belonged to the Communist Party in the past and is known to still have close friends who are card-carrying members of the Party here in the United States. And if that is not enough, he served time in jail back in 1953 on a moral charge in Pasadena, California. He was caught engaging in disgusting immoral acts with two other men in the back seat of a car. Now how can this man possibly represent the values of the marchers and the values of this country?'" Mr. Randolph paused momentarily. Assuming that he had my attention, he continued. "'Something must be done to stop this man from making a mockery of our democracy,'" he ended.

I couldn't believe that my past had come back to haunt me again. But once I got beyond that fact, my thoughts slipped back to the summer of 1960. Difference was this time the attack came from a white southern politician, and not a northern Negro as in the past. I had a strong inclination to scream in frustration from this recurring nightmare, where my enemies would not allow me to live in peace.

"Bayard, are you there?" Randolph asked.

"Yes, I'm here. What do we do next?"

"I've already heard from Roy and he is rather calm if you can believe that?"

"I imagine he took the opportunity to remind you that if this backfired, that is allowing you to keep me on as your deputy director, it was all on you."

"No, not at all. As a matter of fact, he was relatively calm and only suggested that we have a meeting of the leaders, as soon as possible, in order to respond to this attack. You know we're going to have to do that because I'm sure the newspapers will be jumping all over this story."

No doubt he was right. How long would I continue to be fodder for their sensationalism? This kind of attack never happened in England or Europe. I had been in both places many times, and never was my past the subject of their newspapers. Why did I care for this country so much that I kept returning to these abuses? Jimmy had criticized Richard Wright for never coming back, but maybe he was the only wise one among us.

"Bayard, I'm going to have to call a meeting of the leadership to figure out how to counter this attack. But rest assured, the leadership will back you this time. We will not have a repeat of 1960. I haven't talked with Martin yet, but I'm sure he'll be on board. He won't make the same mistake again. Keep your head up high and continue the planning. I'll let you know when something is decided. I'm trying to get the meeting for tomorrow, so we can put this to bed before it lingers too long and becomes more than what it is."

"Again, I find you having to come to my defense. I know the press is going to be outside my door this morning, but I will deflect any questions about Thurmond's comments to you and the others."

"Be strong, my son," Randolph finished and we both hung up.

I got up and strolled to the door, opened it and looked out at all the young people busy carrying out their duties with one thought in mind, and that was to make August 28 a success. Most of them knew nothing about my private life, my years as a Communist, and the three years I spent in prison labeled a draft dodger and of course my preference of men for lovers. The latter always seemed to be the most damaging. But these were young men and women with idealist dreams and goals. It was their Camelot and, despite my past, they would continue to allow me inside. I sighed as Rachelle ran up to me.

"There's a ton of reporters out front wanting to get a statement from you," she practically screamed. "What's going on Bayard, what's happened? Are we going to call off the march?"

I hadn't noticed him coming up next to me. But Tom also exclaimed. "Thurmond's attack on you has hit the streets and every newspaper reporter in the city is looking for blood. There like a bunch of vultures and you have to go out there and confront them."

"I know, and I will, but keep your voice down and don't appear so damn concerned. We don't want everyone else to get involved."

Most of the workers had stopped what they were doing and stared over at us. I needed to address them before going outside.

"Please, everything is all right. We just have a little problem and I'm going to take care of it right now. Remember we have a deadline approaching and if we plan to make this the greatest protest event in this country's history, keep working."

I looked directly at Tom. "You stay in here and by all means keep them busy, so they don't come outside to see what's going on."

"Can I come with you?" Rachelle asked

"Don't you need to get an accurate account on the number of buses committed to the march, and weren't you having some problems with the Mississippi delegation's attempts to rent the buses from the company down there?"

"Yeah," she said meekly because she knew the reason I asked.

"Then get to work and let me handle this." I didn't mean to be harsh, but my mood had changed because I was forced to deal with nonsense. I needed some release. I made my way to the door, opened it, and walked outside.

"Mr. Rustin, I know you've read the comments by Senator Strom Thurmond on the Senate floor yesterday and appearing in the **Congressional Record** today. What is your response?" a reporter, standing closest to me, shouted.

"I'm pleased that you all have showed up this morning for an update on the progress of the march. Well it's…."

"That's not why we're here this morning," another reporter interrupted me. "Strom Thurmond essentially said you are a disgrace to your country because you are a draft dodger, a communist and you're gay. How do you plan to respond to those charges?"

"We've had some problems getting some southern bus companies to rent buses to Negroes for the trip up here," I deflected. "We are calling on the President and the members of Congress from those respective states to help us out."

"Mr. Rustin, it is rather disingenuous of you not to answer our questions about the comments Senator Thurmond has directed at you. We are only here to give you a chance to respond to them," a third reporter in the back shouted out over the others.

"Because I haven't had the opportunity to read his comments and before I respond I should at least read them." I did deflect.

"Here, I have the comments from the Congressional Record." an additional reporter held the "**Congressional Record**" up for me to see.

"I appreciate your gesture, but I have a march to plan, and this is already the second week in August. We have buses to organize and concerns as simple as to how many outhouses should we order and where should they strategically be placed. Do you think I have time to read and concentrate on some comments a Senator I know does not like me, made in the "Congressional Record?" I was angry but needed to be careful how I responded. "Now, if there are any questions on the march itself, I'll entertain them, otherwise I plan to go back inside and get to work."

"Yes, one final question," a Negro reporter I knew wrote for **Jet Magazine** said. "Do you fear that Mr. Randolph and the other leaders will remove you from your position at this time?"

"I can't speak for them," I shot back. "But I believe they will be holding an emergency meeting sometime tomorrow. At that time, they will decide how they want to proceed. I am sure they will have a press conference to express their position on this matter. Thank you all for coming but I must get back to work." I ended, turned and went back up the steps and into the office. Just as I walked in, the workers all made a dash back to their work areas.

I strolled through their work areas back to my office, went in and closed the door. Before I was seated, Tom walked in along with Rachelle.

"Some man said his name is Bill, gave me this note and said you needed to call him," Tom said as he handed me a piece of paper.

"Do you know this guy?" he asked.

"Doesn't matter," I shot back. I opened the paper and read the note with the telephone number. "Can you excuse me for a minute?"

They both stared at me with the expression we need to be in here when you make this call. I knew they deserved to be, but I chose to deal with this in private. When I didn't relent, they got up and walked out closing the door behind them.

I dialed the number and waited for Bill to answer. After three rings, he did.

"Bayard, how are you?"

"Doing fine, real busy and I know you didn't call to check on my mental and physical being. What can I do for you and why the emergency?"

"Can't talk to you about it over the phone."

"What is this surreptitious nonsense," I shot back at him. My disdain for him still lingered and I'm sure he picked it up in my cold demeanor.

"I know we parted company on anything but friendly terms," he said. "But this is bigger than our relationship. I can't discuss it over the phone so can we meet somewhere this evening."

"I can meet you at Julius about six?"

"No, too many eyes and ears from the bureau hang out there."

Mention of the bureau caught my attention. "Does this have to do with the FBI?"

"Can I possibly come by your place, say about eight?"

"I'm expecting company at nine, so can we finish whatever it is you want to discuss or share with me in an hour?" I didn't have any plans for later that evening, but just wanted him to understand there would be no hit and miss affair that night.

"I hear you loud and clear and yes it won't take an hour."

"See you at eight and no need to bring any libations. I won't be in the mood."

"Again, I get your message loud and clear because it is not subtle at all. See you then." He finished and we both hung up.

As soon as I hung up the phone, Tom hurried inside. Rachelle was right behind him, but he waved her off and closed the door so just the two of us were inside my office. I sat back down in my chair at the desk. He stood.

"What did he want?" Tom asked with a sound of urgency in his tone.

"I don't know. Said he couldn't tell me over the phone. I agreed to meet with him this evening at the apartment."

"Bayard be careful. I did some checking around and found out he does undercover work for the FBI. He's a plant and hangs out at gay bars and restaurants collecting information on both gays and lesbians to give to the director." He paused to allow his information to sink in with me. "Have you been carrying on with this guy?"

"Never mind, how'd you get this information?"

"Don't doubt me Bayard, just believe me. If he's coming over tonight, I want to be there."

"I appreciate your offer, but I do believe I can handle myself."

"Not when it comes the blond blue-eyed good-looking guys," Tom exclaimed. "You got a weakness for them and before you know what's happening, he'll have you back in that bed pumping you for information."

Tom had always been brash and self-assured of himself. However, he'd overstepped his bounds. He meant well but I didn't need this youngster to baby sit me.

"At fifty-one years of age, I believe I can handle myself, so no I don't need you to be there," I said emphatically.

"Bayard, you got too many people counting on you and too much in the balance for you to mess up now," he insisted. "Let's face it, I know you better than anyone and know your weaknesses. Sure you won't change your mind?"

I could only chuckle at his cockiness. "Tell you what if I begin to feel weak in the knees and can no longer fight the temptation, I'll call you to get right over and rescue me. How's that sound?"

"This is no joking matter, but if you insist on seeing him alone, just remember I'll be at Julius's and can get over there right away."

"Thank you for the encouragement. Now you need to get back out there and manage the volunteers before they begin to wonder what's going on. I promise you, I'll be all right."

Tom stood staring at me and finally strolled up and put his arms around me. I hugged him and then we broke from the embrace and he sauntered back out of my office to the work area. Just as I sat back down and put my elbows on the desk with my head leaning forward nestled between my hands, the phone rang.

"Now what," I muttered as I picked up the receiver and brought it up to my ear.

"Bayard, the meeting is set for eleven o'clock in the morning over here at my office," Mr. Randolph said. "I need you to be here."

"Wait, you're not suggesting that I should be in that meeting?"

"Absolutely, it's about you."

God, I thought, how many embarrassing situations did he think I could take? I was sure Roy would get his licks in on me. "I don't know if that is a good idea," I said. "If they planned to remove me, I didn't want to be there to witness it.

"Please, Bayard, this is not open for discussion. Please be here tomorrow at eleven so we can put this issue to bed and move on with the march."

"I'll be there." I conceded. I had no choice.

"Good, see you then. We'll need your input." Mr. Randolph said and then hung up.

I sat a comfortable distance away from Bill in the living room of the apartment. He sat in the big leather lounge chair and I reared back on the couch. I felt no attraction, and only wanted this to be over. Tom's admonishment about my weaknesses had disturbed me and I needed to prove him wrong. I began the conversation.

"The times we spent together, you never did tell me who you worked for," I said. "Not that it was important then but now I am curious."

"That's why I'm here," Bill said as he moved up to the front of the lounge chair. "This is going to sound rather bizarre to you, but I was recruited by J. Edgar Hoover's agents to spy on you and, right after you began to get so much publicity as a leader of the march coming up later in the month, to get you in a compromising situation."

I glared at this man while my emotions ran wild and all kinds of thoughts crossed my mind, Pasadena in 1953 being the dominant one. But why the confession now. I had to ask, even though my primary inclination was to tell him to get the hell out of my apartment. Instead I asked.

"Why me and why did you agree to do this dastardly act?

"You got to know that Mr. Hoover hates homosexuals as much as he hates Negroes. But if you get one person who is both homosexual and Negro, his hatred is overwhelming. He wants to destroy you, embarrass you and make you hate yourself for who you are."

He was letting it all out and suddenly he broke down crying. Despite what he had done, I began to feel sorry for him. I didn't understand how he could allow himself to get caught in such an ugly trap. But at this point, I could not concede to his emotions. I wanted him to finish and get out.

"What kind of human being are you?" I asked.

"A desperate human being who was out on his luck and the bureau gave me a way to get back on my feet. The money was good."

"Am I to assume that suddenly you got a conscience?"

"No, I began to believe in you, and I developed strong feelings for you."

"If the money is so good, why didn't you continue?"

"Setting you up for failure was too much for even me." Tears flowed freely down Bill's face.

"I guess I can assume that your real name is not Bill?"

"You assume right, and I cannot afford to give you my real name."

"I understand, so what happens to you, now?"

"I told them no, so I'm out. Probably go somewhere else to live even though I love New York."

I could feel my sympathy for him slowly creeping in and surpassing my utter disdain. I needed to end this and get him out of my apartment.

"Then it was the FBI that gave you my address in London?" I asked. I needed to know the full extent of his involvement to destroy me before I threw him out.

"Yes, if you had responded they were willing to get me over there to keep an eye on you and if possible, get you in a compromising situation so the English would kick you out."

"What if I had responded, would you have carried out their plan?"

He didn't answer immediately but just stared at me with the tears still flowing. He finally stood up. "Yes, at that point I probably would have because of the sum of money they offered. But you have to know as I've followed you now with the march, there was no way I was willing to get involved."

I stood also, hurried over to the door and opened it. "I don't know if I should be angry with you or feel sorry for you. Either way, I want you out and if you happen to see me anywhere in town, please act like you don't know me."

He stumbled up to the door, stopped right in front of me. I turned my face away while I continued to hold the door open. Evidently, he got the message and continued out into the hallway. I quickly slammed the door behind him and felt like I needed to take a bath to wash the filth of that man off me.

47.

"I speak for the combined Negro leadership in voicing my complete confidence in Bayard Rustin's character. I am dismayed that there are in this country men who, wrapping themselves in the mantle of Christian morality, would mutilate the most elementary conceptions of human decency, privacy and humility in order to persecute other men." Mr. Randolph stood on the steps of his office building, confronting a series of reporters from the media. A slew of cameras clicked on when he began his press conference on behalf of the leadership for the march. Reporters began taking notes and sticking their individual microphones in the air to catch his every word.

In the meeting he insisted that I attend there was unanimous support for me, to include Roy, and his support was most heartening because of the negative comments he had made in the past. They agreed unanimously, with the strongest support from James and John Lewis, that I continue as the organizer of the march, and that any future attacks on my personal past would be shunned and opposed by the leadership.

Finally, my organizational skills far outweighed what happened in the past and these men made that quite clear during the meeting. For once they all agreed on something, and that something happened to be me. My cup runneth over and my chest stuck out, but I remained humbled by their support and once the press conference ended, I rushed back to the headquarters and got back to work. But just for one moment while in my office, my thoughts raced back to the confrontation with the man called Bill. I owed him a certain amount of gratitude. If he hadn't come to his senses and recognized that what Hoover wanted him to do was not only unethical, but to a certain degree immoral, I may have weakened to my sexual desires and fell into the trap. Now that I knew I was under the radar of the FBI chief, there was no way I would even consider any kind of sexual activity for the next two weeks, and after that I'd be very careful when selecting partners. No more picking up men at Julius.

Now that we had entered the last few days before the march, the number of supporters constantly grew, and various groups or organizations joined us every day. Although George Meany refused to endorse the march, his individual unions did. Walter Reuther of the United Auto Workers was one of the main spokesmen and became a part of the leadership team. The Steelworkers Union, Ladies Garment Workers, Packing House Workers and Electrical Workers, all unions committed to the march.

The leadership also expanded from the Big Six to the Big Ten. Randolph convinced the others to add Walter Reuther, Matthew Ahman, a Catholic; Eugene Carson Blake, a Protestant; and Rabbi Joahcim Prinz, a Jew to the leadership team. It was no longer all Negroes, but a good mixture of race and religion, out front in the message we planned to deliver on August 28.

We also continued to debate what should be the main focus of the march. I pushed for economic issues, Martin for desegregation and voting rights for Negroes in the South. But the theme that won was support for President Kennedy's civil rights bill. Roy and Whitney made strong arguments that, in order to get the President's support for the march, we needed to show unity with him on his prize piece of legislation. It turned out to be a smart move. By the middle of August, the President announced his support for the march and that meant total support from all the resources we would need in Washington, D. C. to make this happen.

Some of our most active support came from Hollywood. Randolph called me on the Saturday after our press conference and exclaimed.

"I just received a call from Harry Belafonte. He has gotten the support from an array of entertainers that reads like a who's who list of greats."

My excitement grew instantaneously. "You have the list?" I asked

"Sure do."

"You ready for this?" he asked but did not wait for an answer. "We have Burt Lancaster, Sidney Portier, Charlton Heston, Sammy Davis, Jr., Lena Horne, and Marlon Brando. Is that enough?" He asked, knowing darn well the answer.

"That's more than enough," I replied. "What a…"

"Let me continue," Mr. Randolph cut me off. "There is also Paul Newman, Joanne Woodward, Eartha Kitt and Joan Baez, and many of them not only want to march but want to entertain before we march over to the Lincoln Memorial. So, you need to plan a musical salute for early in the morning."

"I believe we are about to pull off the most monumental event, save the Presidential Inaugurations, ever done in the Nation's Capital," I proudly proclaimed.

"Only because of your organizational skills, my son," Randolph said. "I knew what I was doing when I insisted that you be the second in charge when really you should have been the first."

"Doesn't matter, we're going to get this done. I got a great team working with me. But I need to get back to work. We are less than two weeks to the march and there are a ton of loose ends that have to be closed. I'll be at your office by nine in the morning with an update." I finished and we both hung up.

Just as I settled back in my chair and closed my eyes for a much-needed moments reflection on all that was happening, Tom burst into the room and tossed a couple newspapers on the desk.

"The haters are now crawling out of the woodwork and expressing their racist attitudes," he said as he pointed to the top paper,

It was a copy of the **Wall Street Journal**. I didn't bother to pick it up but stared down at the article Tom pointed to. "A recent poll indicates that two-thirds of the American people are opposed to the march to take place in Washington, D.C. by civil rights organizations and other supporting groups on August 28."

I grimaced at the statistics but then read an article in the **New York Times** that Tom now held in the air since I refused to pick the papers up myself. It was an editorial from a local clergyman. He wrote, "Tempers are bound to flare in the heat of the Washington summer. There is danger that people will be injured, and property destroyed."

I looked up at Tom trying to figure out the point he was trying to make, but before I could say anything, he thrust a copy of the **New York Herald Tribune** at me. An editorial by management read, "If Negro leaders persist in their announced plans to march one-hundred-thousand strong on the capitol, they will jeopardize their cause. The ugly part of this particular mass protest is its implication of uncontained violence if Congress doesn't deliver." I knew the reference was to the civil rights bill that had just been submitted to committee in the House of Representatives for consideration.

The last paper he held up was from Charleston, South Carolina. William Jennings Bryant, a representative from that state, had quoted the following statement to the paper, "This attempt to force Congress to bow to demands is a dangerous precedent, and could someday lead to the overthrow of free government and destroy the liberties of our people"

"Enough," I said just in case he might find an additional paper with ridiculous quotes, like the one from Bryant. "What are you trying to prove?" I asked even though I knew the answer.

"That all isn't as rosy as we might think, because so many groups and people have joined in the march, we can't afford to let our guard down. Our enemies are out there."

"I know that," I shot back. "And I don't plan for that to happen, but for this Congressman to suggest that a peaceful march could, in any way possible, be a threat to our liberties is just plain insane."

"Bayard, one thing I have always loved and admired about you is your optimistic nature about human behavior," Tom said. "But I think it has gotten you into trouble in the past and often led to many disappointments. I just want us to be careful that we don't let our guard down."

"I appreciate your concern, but can I please get back to work."

Right after Tom closed the door behind him, it reopened and this time it was Rachelle with a problem that had to be corrected.

"Bayard, Ms. Hedgeman is outside and insists on talking with you," she said.

Anna Arnold Hedgeman had been quite active in New York politics for years, and I had met her back in 1954 when she was the first African American woman to serve in a Mayor's Cabinet. Mayor Wagner put her out front on many of the issues confronting Negroes in New York.

I stood behind my small desk and said. "Please bring her in."

Rachelle went back out of the office and returned with this middle-aged Negro woman who exuded nothing but class. I had very little dealings with her over the years, but always did admire her tenacity on behalf of Negro women. She was a woman in the class with Dorothy Height.

She strolled into the room and I came from behind my desk and met her. She extended her hand and we shook, something many women wouldn't dare do for fear it would compromise their womanhood.

"Bayard, we have a real problem with the program you've proposed for the march at the Lincoln Memorial," she said.

My first thought was how did she know about the program since it hadn't been printed yet. "I'm not quite sure what you're driving at Anna, the program hasn't yet been finalized nor has it been printed."

"My dear friend, I am sure you have not considered a woman speaker for your program. Please don't deceive me, am I correct?"

She scolded not to try deceiving her. I answered honestly. "You are absolutely correct. The program at this point consisted of only male speakers," I said.

"What is wrong with you men? Don't you think Negro women are affected by prejudice and bigotry? When you were down there in Montgomery, Alabama, tell me who was doing most of the walking to their jobs?" She paused as if to allow me to answer, but then continued. "You know it was the women and now in Birmingham, did you see the picture of the woman with the racist policeman's knee in her throat and the vicious dog growling over her?"

"Yes, on all your questions," I said.

"Well, what do you plan to do about it?"

"I'm going to contact Mr. Randolph as soon as you leave and bring it to his attention and correct our error. I can assure you that we will find a spot for a woman speaker. Who would you recommend?"

"Myrlie Evers, the widow of Medgar Evers who was just shot two months ago, right in his driveway. She is a very strong woman and no doubt would do a wonderful job representing us."

"I will make that recommendation to Mr. Randolph, who will then share it with the other leaders and if she is available, I'll have a spot for her at the microphone on August 28."

"Speaking of leaders, you didn't even respect Dorothy enough to schedule her to speak. That is shameful." She abruptly got up and headed for the door.

I met her there and opened it.

"I'll await your word that this has been taken care of."

"You will hear from me no later than tomorrow."

"Good day Bayard and I admire the tremendous job you are doing in putting this whole affair together, for the Negro people of this country. I certainly hope you get the credit you deserve."

"Thank you, Ana," I bowed my head as a gesture of respect. She walked out, and I closed the door.

I contacted Mr. Randolph who immediately got in touch with the leadership team and before the day was over, they approved Myrlie Evers to speak. The problem turned out that she wouldn't be available, so we substituted Daisy Bates, a real fighter who had been President of the Arkansas NAACP and on the National Board, to speak. That pleased Roy because that meant, along with him, the NAACP had two speakers while all other organizations had only one.

With all visible problems solved I was ready to move our operation from New York to Washington, D.C., the actual location of the march. The night before we changed cities, Harry Belafonte had planned a pre-victorious march concert at the Apollo Theater right up the street on 125th in Harlem. A little after seven when we finished packing, and sent the New York volunteers home with a party at the office.

Tom, Rachelle, Norman and I then walked the three blocks to the Apollo. There was a long line up 125th Street of men and women of all ages waiting to get inside the theater for the show. Belafonte had a star-studded line-up of entertainers to perform. We strolled to the front of the line and security let us in. We then made our way down to the front row where Mr. Randolph, Roy and his wife, Whitney also with his wife were already seated. I looked back behind us and there appeared to be no empty seats on the main floor or up in the balcony. I thought of all those poor folks waiting outside to get in. There just was no way. If we let them all in, the fire marshal would surely close the theater down for violation of capacity seating.

After another fifteen minutes, they dimmed the lights and Harry Belafonte strolled onto the stage and up to the microphone.

"Good evening and welcome to the Apollo Theater for a special tribute to the men and women, who have put in an enormous effort to assure that next week's national march on the Nation's Capital for jobs and freedom will be a success. Sitting in the front row are the men and women to whom we owe a huge debt of gratitude. Would you all please stand."

We rose to our feet and the audience began to applaud. It lasted for all of two minutes, and in order to bring it to a close Mr. Randolph signaled for all of us to sit back down.

"Now sit back and relax and enjoy the show. We have an array of entertainers that will light up the theater. So, let's welcome to the stage Quincy Jones to get the show started."

For the next two hours, we listened and reacted to the music from not only Quincy Jones, but Thelonious Monk, Tony Bennett, Herbie Mann, Carmen McRae. The elder statesman of entertainers, Billy Eckstein, closed out the show. We were thoroughly entertained and energized for our trip down to Washington, D. C. in the morning, for the final preparations for what we now knew would be one excellent event.

48

"Here are the latest figures on the participation in the march tomorrow," I began addressing eight of the ten leaders. Martin and James were not there yet. Martin would get in later that afternoon from Birmingham, where he was still in serious negotiations with the mayor to integrate the facilities in that city. We got word earlier that morning that James had been arrested and jailed in Plaquemine, Louisiana for leading a civil rights demonstration.

"We have fifteen hundred buses, twenty-one special trains and three privately chartered airliners, not to include the number of automobiles something we just couldn't account for," I said. "Our first estimation had been for one-hundred thousand, but we now know we will far exceed that number. I am predicting at least two-hundred and fifty thousand tomorrow."

They all had stunned expressions as they struggled with the magnitude of what we might accomplish tomorrow. Dorothy was the first to raise a concern that I knew they all shared.

"Are you sure we have planned sufficiently to accommodate that large a number of people in this city?"

"I can assure that our plan is as thorough as humanly possible," I replied.

"That's not good enough, it needs to go beyond what is humanly possible," she said with a smile.

I also smiled. "We've done our best to cover all aspects of the march from the number of portable toilets and where they should be located, to installing public telephones, compliments of the local telephone company. We even have stations with bottled water for the walk from the Washington Monument to the Lincoln Memorial."

"My God, that's only a few short blocks," Roy quipped.

"I know," I shot back, "but that's just how thorough we have been. We have first aid stations set up so that we are prepared for any possible emergency."

"How about the possibility of violence?" Rabbi Joachim Prinz asked. "You know there is an entire element of people who want to see this fail, just pulling for some violence. In fact, I wouldn't doubt they are laying plans to try to disrupt tomorrow's events."

I anticipated that question. It had to come because all the emphasis we placed on a peaceful non-violent march. Just as I knew it was coming, I'd prepared for it. "We have an elaborate plan to assure no violence occurs before, during and after the march," I began. "We have organized our own police force as you well know. We have volunteers from major jurisdictions along the east coast they are already here."

"From what cities?" Reuther interrupted and asked.

"Let's see, Boston, New York, Philadelphia, Newark, Wilmington, Baltimore and Richmond," I answered and continued. "We've divided our forces into two groups, one consisting of white officers and the other blacks. The white police force will deal with any white troublemakers, if indeed we have any and the black force, of course with Negroes. In other words, we don't want any possibility of any racial friction, where a white person is arresting someone black or where a black is arresting a white." I paused to allow the leaders to take in my scheme for averting racial tensions. "Finally, anyone making trouble outside the circle of our march will be handled by the local Washington, D.C. police, but again white handling white and black handling black."

"And the local police force as well as the feds, I assume, have agreed to this plan." Roy now asked the question.

"It took some effort, but we got it done. Actually, over the past two months, we've met with the various police forces on numerous occasions to work out the plan. We are sure this will work just fine tomorrow."

"What's the order of the program once we get to the monument?" Mr. Randolph asked although he knew because I designed it with him, but he asked just to inform the others.

"We have entertainment early in the morning at the Washington Monument, then about ten o'clock we will march over to the Lincoln Monument, we'll have the National Anthem, and Marion Anderson, who is already here, will sing it, then the convocation, then remarks by each of you, except the woman who will be speaking is Daisy Bates since Mylie Evers was not available."

"Make sure I don't follow Martin." Roy was the first to make that request.

The others made the same request. No one wanted to follow Dr. King because they all knew of the power he delivered with his speeches, and figured tomorrow he'd probably be exceptionally dynamic. They seemed to recall his "Give me the ballot" speech, now six years ago during the Prayer Pilgrimages here in Washington.

"You do have Mahalia Jackson on the program?" Dorothy asked. I was surprised through all of this she never insisted that she should be on the program. I believe that's what made her such an outstanding leader. She was always willing to share the glory.

"Yes, Ms. Jackson is already here and excited about participating," I said. "But let's get back to this problem of having to follow Dr. King to the microphone. The only way to resolve that is to have him go last. Is that acceptable with everyone?"

I received a unanimous yes from all the leaders. "If there are no other questions, then I believe we are finished here. Please be at the Washington Monument at nine o'clock in the morning, and of course you all are invited to attend the musical show at eight." I finished, sat down and Mr. Randolph took control.

While Mr. Randolph was tying up some loose ends with the leadership team, Tom opened the door, "Excuse me," he said then hurried over to me. He leaned down and whispered, "You better come to the front of the hotel, Malcolm X has just arrived and a whole bunch of reporters are right behind him. Someone said he is about to hold a press conference denouncing the march."

I got up and started for the door.

"What's the problem?" Randolph asked. He knew something must be wrong for Tom to crash the meeting, whisper to me and then I get up to leave.

"Malcolm X is out front, and he has a whole bunch of reporters following behind him," I said. "This could cause some problems for us."

"What are you going to tell him?" Randolph asked.

"Try to convince him not to make any negative statements about tomorrow's march."

"To hell with him," Roy scowled. "We don't condone anything the Nation of Islam does and sure are not going to bow to him."

"It's not bowing to him," Randolph shot back. "Bayard bring him back here, so we can talk to him. We need no disturbance going into tomorrow."

I followed Tom out into the lobby of the hotel. Standing off to the right surrounded by what appeared to be reporters, Malcolm X saw me as I approached. Instantly two of his bodyguards, stepped in front of me with hands folded and menacing stares. He stopped talking to the reporters, waved his bodyguards aside and reached out to shake my hand.

"Brother Bayard, it's good seeing you again," he said as we shook hands. "I haven't seen you since I had the honor to debate you at Howard University."

We released our grip and I wasted no time. "Brother Malcolm, can we see you back in the conference room?"

"And just who is we?"

"The leadership for the march tomorrow. We've just wrapped up our final meeting before the big day and heard you were out here. They asked me to invite you back to talk with them."

"What business do they have with me?"

I placed my arm around his shoulder and one his bodyguards made a move toward me. Malcolm waved him off. I led him down the hall to the room, opened the door and we strolled inside followed by his bodyguards.

Mr. Randolph stood to welcome him as did John, the only two who did.

"Brother Malcolm," Randolph said. "We understand that you plan to hold a press conference this evening for the express reason of denouncing the march tomorrow, is that correct?"

"I believe you are making a grave mistake when you join with our enemies in a display of unity, when it is known that they never do intend to unite with us on an equal basis," Malcolm X exclaimed. "You are betraying the trust that the Negro people put in you all as leaders when you make this false display of coming together for their cause."

"You and Elijah Muhammad may feel that way, but the entire Negro community of leaders and organizations have united behind this march." Randolph retorted. "Tomorrow we had hoped to show, for the first time since I can remember in my long history of being involved in racial issues in this country, that the entire Negro community stands as one. Don't spoil it for us by going out there and slamming what we want to accomplish. You can harbor your personal feelings about me, Bayard and the rest of these men and women in this room, but for this one day, keep them to yourself. You will be a better man for it."

Of all the people in that room, I knew that Malcolm respected Mr. Randolph more than the rest of them. A year ago, when Mr. Randolph called all the leaders in Harlem together to form a coalition for economic independence within the community, based on the Black Wall Street of Tulsa in 1921, he included Malcolm X in the fold. It was one of the first times he'd been welcomed by other leaders in Harlem. For that reason, while Malcolm considered Mr. Randolph's words, I knew he would probably concede on this one issue. He owed it to him.

"Only through tomorrow, but come Thursday, you and the others are fair game," Malcolm said. "I respect you and for that reason I will not hold the press conference, but I strongly feel this is a major mistake on the part of all you gentlemen and Ms. Heights." He finished, turned and walked back out of the room.

Once he closed the door, I believe every person at that table breathed a sigh of relief knowing just how devastating Malcolm could be in his attacks. I was especially relieved. That possibly could be the final fire that had to be put out. Within the next few hours, I would find out differently.

I settled into my suite on the fifteenth floor with a double shot of scotch, pulled out a Pall Mall, lit it and prepared for a couple hours of solitude. It lasted only ten minutes. I had just turned on Walter Cronkite and the CBS Evening News when the phone rang.

"Bayard, Bobby Kennedy just called me, and we have a problem with John Lewis' speech for tomorrow," Randolph practically shouted into the phone.

"What's the problem with his speech?" I naturally asked not having read it yet. I planned to review all the speeches later that evening, but right now just needed to relax.

"Here is part of it, 'The time will come when we will not confine our marching to Washington. We will march through the South through the heart of Dixie, the way Sherman did. We shall pursue our own scorched earth policy and burn Jim Crow to the ground non-violently.' That's what's wrong with it."

"That's actually part of his speech?" I asked not knowing what else I could possibly say after hearing what he read.

"That is actually part of his speech and it has the White House up in arms. And Archbishop Patrick O'Boyle has threatened not to deliver the opening prayer tomorrow, if he doesn't change it."

"Some of it actually sounded pretty good, burning Jim Crow to the ground non-violently is something I could support," I quipped.

"Get serious Bayard, this has to be changed," Mr. Randolph said.

"I'll be downstairs in the meeting room in five minutes, can you meet me there?

"Yes, I'm already here."

I'd just gotten inside the room when Mr. Randolph thrust a copy of John's speech at me. I took it and sat down and began to read. Once I finished, I placed it on the table.

"He calls Kennedy's civil rights bill too little too late, and that will play right into the hands of those in Congress who already oppose it. I can hear them now down on the Senate floor, 'even the Nigras oppose this bill,'" I said jokingly. "You know they can't say Negro because all their life they referred to us as Niggers, but when they get here that's not appropriate, so they compromise as Nigras."

"Okay, now that you've given us a short lesson on why southerners say Nigras instead of Negro, can you get back to this young man's speech?"

392 | Williams-Denton-Zinsmeyer

"I'll say it's consistent with the direction the SNCC group seems to be going. They are unwilling to accept the status quo and don't believe in the system. I imagine some of their better writers drafted this for John."

"As a matter of fact, it was your young friend Tom Kahn that drafted it," Randolph said. "Why is he so angry, he's white."

My inclination was to say and he's also a homosexual and that puts him in the same category with the Negro, and that is why he's angry, but instead I said, "I'll go talk with John and see if he will consider changing some of the inflammatory language."

"No, not if he will consider, but that he must," Reuther who had just walked into the room said.

I snatched the paper off the table and walked out of the room. Since I had made the room assignments for leadership, I knew John's room number. I knocked on the door and waited for an answer.

"Yeah, who is it?" John asked

"It's Bayard Rustin and I need to talk with you."

"Okay, wait a minute."

I could hear him scrambling around inside and then the door swung open. "What's the problem?" he asked and waved me into the room.

I strolled inside and stood next to the bed. "John, you have to change your speech," I got right to the point. "You have everyone up in arms with some of your more inflammatory lines."

John sat down on the bed and looked up at me. "Like what?" he asked

"Like burning Jim Crow and creating your own scorched earth and of course going through the South like Sherman, alluding to burning everything from Atlanta all the way to the ocean during the civil war."

"My Board decided that we had to take a hard line, because we knew all the other speeches would be weak and written to accommodate the President and the unions. We don't plan to change what needs to be said."

"John, it's the wrong time and the wrong place for that kind of rhetoric," I entreated. "We just can't let you read this particular speech. Now I can get Tom to help you draft an alternative tonight. What do you say?"

"I say no, can't do it."

"You do know the Justice Department will have the cut-off switch and cut you off in an instant and if that happens, then the smooth operation of the march will be over. You don't want that on your conscience, do you?"

John got back up from the bed. "No, I don't, but that probably won't happen. They wouldn't dare enforce that kind of censorship."

"Let's not test them," I shot back. "Keep in mind that they control the Mall and can do pretty much whatever they want to."

"Like I said, I'll take my chances."

"That's final?"

"Pretty much so."

"Then I'll see you at the Washington Monument at nine in the morning." I turned and walked out of his room. I had to go downstairs and tell the others that John Lewis refused to compromise and then wait until the morning to determine how this will finally play out.

49.

Anxiety throughout my entire being ruled the morning, as I met Rachelle in front of the Washington Monument at a little after six. It wasn't the fact that I still had to deal with the Lewis dilemma, but that no one had arrived on the mall but for a very few young people. Had we overestimated the potential turnout for the march and was it possible we might have less than one hundred thousand, which in that case it would be considered a failure. We stood at the foot of the Washington Monument and stared out across the mall. I spoke first.

"We might be in for a complete disaster today." I said as I turned and looked at her.

"It's still early and unless a whole lot of people were lying to me, I know the buses will start rolling in any minute," Rachelle said reassuring. "May I suggest that you concentrate more on the problem with John Lewis than if a crowd is going to show up today. They will be here."

"We put in a whole lot of work and took a great deal of abuse for this not to be a success," I said feeling rather dejected. My thoughts returned to the attacks I endured from Senator Thurmond and the balancing act we had to do with the President, who finally did come around. But there was a strong possibility that he would withdraw his support if John didn't change the content of his speech. I knew that the President had the Justice Department ready to pull the plug on the microphones, if they got word that John refused to make adjustments. That could possibly bring the entire march to a close because chances are good, if they pull the plug, they won't bother to turn the speakers back on. That could be just as big a disaster if there is not a sufficient turnout. I had to wonder why I took on all these burdens. Those were my thoughts as I watched two reporters from the **Washington Post** trotting over to me.

"Mr. Rustin, it's almost seven o'clock. Where is your crowd? You promised that there would be over one hundred thousand here this morning, there can't be no more than two- hundred right now." He pointed to the few gathering on the mall. "Do you think you're going to get one-hundred thousand by noon?"

I had to deflect his negativity. I reached in my pocket and pulled out a paper, glanced at it and then stuck it back in my pocket. "Everything is going just as planned and the marchers will be here," I said. "I can assure you that we are on schedule and the buses will begin to arrive any minute

"There you go, a bus," Rachelle shrieked in a very excited voice. "And another one right behind the first. They are beginning to show up."

I gave the reporter a very confident expression and he turned and walked away.

"There was absolutely nothing on that piece of paper," Rachelle said. "I saw it."

"I know," I smiled,

The two buses showed up just in time and I took that as a good sign. I wanted them to just keep coming, don't slow down and don't stop. Looking out over the mall, I recognized there was a lot of ground to cover, and we had predicted it would be filled from one end to the other. I watched as Tom hurried toward us.

"They are coming in droves," he said just as excited as Rachelle. "The streets are packed with cars and droves of people are walking down Massachusetts Avenue from the train station. It is going to happen Bayard; it is going to happen."

He surprised me with a hug. Then hugged Rachelle and I began to relax somewhat. It was still a long way from the number we needed to reach, but at least it was a good sign. We stood and watched as the crowd began to grow. A warm and good feeling came over me, as I watched the mixture of races and men as well as women, and many families with their children lining up in front of the Washington Monument.

The sun, now beating down in full splendor, indicated that it would be a very hot August day in the Capitol. Fortunately, we anticipated that possibility and had provided bottles of water along the march route from the Washington Monument over to the Lincoln Memorial.

I turned my attention from the crowd, to a car that pulled up in the open access road to the Monument and watched as Joan Baez and Quincy Jones got out and headed over to where we stood. Harry Belafonte approached them and directed both to the area where they would perform prior to the march. A young man with drums, along with a woman who had what appeared to be a guitar, made their way to where the others stood.

The early morning entertainment would soon begin. A number of artists recruited, by Harry, would perform right up to the time that we began the march to the Lincoln Memorial. It was now beginning to take shape and I knew I could turn my attention to John, who would soon show up for the march. However, I still recognized that it could all be for naught if we could not convince John to change the context of his speech.

The young men and women of the movement were determined to flex their muscle and be heard by the entire nation. And unfortunately, their muscle flexing seemed to be leading them from the non-violent approach that defined the movement for the past seven years since the Montgomery Boycott, to a more radical position. I admired the courage of these folks but knew they lacked the political savvy as to how you change a nation. You just couldn't do it through confrontation, especially when you are so outnumbered, but instead through compromise and cooperation among the parties. This march was a critical component to our strategy, because the Negro could not do it alone. If John made that speech, we would lose our religious, union and governmental support, all of which we desperately needed. John had to come to his senses and recognize just how much he had to lose if he continued down that road of militancy.

For the next four hours, the crowd continued to grow so that the entire mall became covered with bodies of people. As I looked out from the base of the Washington monument, my earlier anxiety dissipated. Rachelle, Tom, Norman and I smiled at each other as we began to realize that we would exceed our wildest expectations. Our celebration would be among ourselves, because once the world recognized the magnitude of what we accomplished the credit would go to the ten leaders. No one would accept that a select few had worked diligently to make this happen. We were the no names and knew it would probably remain that way tomorrow and into the future. But I still had the John dilemma to resolve.

Right at nine o'clock, Joan Baez began the entertainment at the Monument.

"The world is one great battlefield
With forces all arrayed
If in my heart I do not yield
I'll overcome someday."

She sang for a good fifteen minutes and was followed by Odette, Bob Dylan, Leon Bibb, Josh White and by eleven o'clock Peter Paul and Mary closed out the musical.

I stood right to the left of the entertainment and welcomed all the leaders along with many dignitaries, who would march in the front with us. Josephine Baker showed up first and was followed by Marlon Brando, Jimmy Baldwin who had promised me he would be there. Fifteen minutes later, Ossie and Ruby Davis strolled up to the front and greeted Mr. Randolph and the other leaders. Then Lena Horne, Burt Lancaster, Jackie Robinson, Sidney Portier and the last person to arrive at the front was Charlton Heston. It was near noon and time for us to march to the Lincoln Memorial. Just as we began the walk, John Lewis showed up and joined us at the front.

"John, have you changed your mind, and will you make the changes?" I asked as we walked across the mall to the Memorial.

"No," he said in a defiant voice.

"Mr. Randolph will need to talk to you when we get to the Memorial. There is a room behind the Lincoln statues. Meet us there before we begin the program."

He said nothing, but I knew he would be there. It was Mr. Randolph and out of respect no one turned down his request.

By twelve-thirty a sea of people stood on the mall carrying approved signs that read, "Equal Rights NOW," "Jobs for all NOW," "Integrated Schools NOW," "Voting Rights NOW," Freedom Rights NOW." Suddenly the marchers nearest to the Memorial steps began to sing,

"Mine eyes have seen the glory of the coming of the Lord,
He is trampling out the vintage where the grapes of wrath are stored
He has loosed the faithful lightening of His terrible swift sword
His truth is marching on.

398 | Williams-Denton-Zinsmeyer

Glory, glory Hallelujah
Glory, glory Hallelujah
Glory, glory Hallelujah
His truth is marching on."

While listening to the singing, Bishop Patrick O'Neal walked over and stood next to Mr. Randolph and me.

"Here is how I and some of the other religious leaders feel and I believe Mr. Reuther will join us. If Mr. Lewis begins to read that inflammatory speech, we will all get up and walk off the stage. Now, Phil please talk to that hot head and convince him that he is spoiling something you have waited over twenty years to see happen." He finished and walked back over where the other clergy stood.

Mr. Randolph abruptly walked over to John standing by himself away from all the others. "John, please come with me. Bayard, you come too."

We followed him into a room and sat at chairs there for people to rest or just wait their turn to speak.

"John, it has been a long time coming, but I have waited for this day for over twenty years. You were only a baby, if born at all, when I organized the first march on Washington to protest the lack of Negroes in defense jobs when we could go over to Europe and fight a war for this country." He paused and placed his hand on top of John's, something he would often do if trying to convince someone of something, especially if it were important to him.

John sat quietly listening as Mr. Randolph continued.

"Do you feel it is right for you and your younger bucks to deny me this day and not only me, the entire Negro race because you want to prove to the world that you all are not willing to take anything off white people any more. Let me assure you, that you all are not the first wave of young Negroes to take that position. We did it in the twenties, thirties and even the forties" He paused and put his hand now on my shoulder. "This man has been doing it all his life and now we reached the pinnacle of our attempts to make a strong statement and you want to spoil it."

"We don't want to spoil it for you Mr. Randolph or for Mr. Rustin," he said.

"In that case, get with your people and change your speech. We still have some time and we can move you down further in the order. But just do this for me. I believe I've earned it as has Bayard."

John continued to sit quietly, I'm sure contemplating Mr. Randolph's words.

"I can get Tom in here to help you," I said. "I know he helped write the original draft because his footprints are all over it."

"It may not set well with some of the others in SNCC, but right now it's not setting well that I may be responsible for spoiling something so important to you." John looked directly at me. "If you can get Tom in here and if you think we have time, I'll remove the more offensive parts of the speech."

I relaxed in my chair because now the final obstacle to what would undoubtedly be an outstanding civil rights event had cleared its final hurdle.

"Gentlemen, we had better get out front, it's time to get this underway," I said, and we got up and returned to the stage, looking out at what had to be way above two hundred thousand men, women and children. "What a glorious day," I whispered.

I walked over to the right side of the stage out of view of the crowd, but still able to see each of the speakers. Mr. Randolph escorted the great Marion Anderson down the steps to the microphone. There was a degree of irony surrounding the first performance of the day, and that was Ms. Anderson returning to the very same place where she sang before over seventy-five thousand on-lookers on Easter Sunday in 1939, just after being denied the right to perform at Constitution Hall before an integrated audience by the Daughters of the American Revolution. Ms. Anderson performing the national anthem would be symbolic of what we represented with the march. I felt very warm inside as she performed in that strong contralto voice, her rendition of the anthem.

She was followed on the stage by Bishop Patrick O'Neal with the invocation. Mr. Randolph then strolled up to the microphone to deliver the keynote address, to be followed by a series of speeches all restricted to ten minutes.

"Let the nation and the world know the meaning of our numbers," he began. "We are not an organization or a group of organizations. We are not a mob. We are the advance guard of a massive moral revolution for jobs and freedom. The revolution reverberates throughout the land, touching every city, every town, every village where Negroes are segregated, oppressed and exploited..." He went on to speak for another ten minutes ending with, "Those who deplore our militancy, who exhort patience in the name of a false peace, are in fact supporting segregation and exploitation. They would have social peace at the expense of social and racial justice. They are more concerned with easing racial tensions than enforcing racial democracy."

It occurred to me as I listened to him that he had counseled John against the danger of militancy in his words, whereas his were borderline militant. Being in his early seventies, he could get away with it, and not a twenty-three-year old. For the next two hours, leaders took their turn at the microphone, with Floyd McKissick standing in for James Farmer, still locked up in Louisiana and Daisy Bates filling in for Myrlie Evers.

By four-thirty, the heat had tired out the crowd and the speeches became rather redundant. I began to worry that our march might lose its electricity unless someone stepped to the mike and lit a fire. Mahalia Jackson had been placed right before Martin, who stood next to me waiting to be introduced by Mr. Randolph and close out the program.

"She's going to liven that crowd out there," he said.

I looked at him and replied, "I know."

Mahalia had picked an old spiritual, a song she felt most appropriate for the occasion. She began,

"I've been buked, And I've been scorned,

"Yes, I've been buked. And I've been scorned, children

"Tryin' to make this journey all alone."

Jesus died to make me free. Jesus died to make me free.

Nailed to the cross on Calvary"

Her tempo continued to rise, and I could detect a stirring in the crowd. She finally brought them to a crescendo of joy with her final stanza.

"I'm going to tell my Lord when I get home. I'm going to tell my Lord when I get home.

I've been mistreated for oh so long."

The crowd broke out in a joyous roar of approval. She had touched a nerve and they just couldn't hold it in any longer. Men and women flung their arms in the air and some began to dance right in place. The energy had returned just like Martin said it would. She finished and now it was Martin's turn to take it on home.

"At this time, I have the honor to present to you the moral leader of our nation," Randolph exclaimed from the microphone. "I have the pleasure to present to you Dr. Martin Luther King, Jr.

"This is your time to shine," I said to him as Mr. Randolph finished the introduction and Martin strolled up to the microphone.

This was the moment everyone had been waiting for and I thought back on the request of all the other speakers to not have to follow him.

"I am happy to join with you today in what will go down in history as the greatest demonstration for freedom in the history of our nation. Five score years ago a great American in whose symbolic shadow we stand today signed the Emancipation Proclamation," he began. "This momentous decree came as a great beacon light of hope for millions of Negro slaves who had been seared in the flames of withering injustice…"

I glared back behind him at the magnificent statue of Lincoln and the writing right below.

In this Temple
As in the Hearts of the People
For Whom He Saved the Union
The Memory of Abraham Lincoln
Is Enshrined Forever

As Martin continued, I could hear his words, but they did not register with me as I slipped back in time and recalled the many battles we fought together. The time back in 1956 when I was forced to leave Montgomery, but he brought me back one night exhorting me to not give up and just how important I would be going forward in the civil rights movement.

The time he first came to New York and Powell attempted to drive a wedge between us because of my homosexuality, and the fact that he finally succeeded in 1960.

"Now is the time to make real the promises of democracy. Now is the time to rise from the dark and desolate valley of segregation to the sunlit paths of racial justice…"

His cadence picked up and I knew soon he would hypnotize the people with his magical use of words in a southern preacher style. But I still wasn't concentrating on his words but on our past. I thought back on the evening we stopped by Rosa Parks' house, and how impressed I was with her courage and determination to make a difference. I also recalled her words, "How can one race of people hate another as much as they do us?"

"We must conduct our struggle on the high plains of dignity," Martin bellowed out to the crowd. "We must not allow our creative protest to degenerate into physical violence…"

I don't believe I ever felt so satisfied and fulfilled in one of my life's accomplishments as I did at that moment as Martin uttered those words. I recalled the evening I walked into his home and saw the gun in the chair and knew then I must teach him not only non-violence as a tactic but as a way of life; a philosophy. He never deviated after our discussion and as he told over two-hundred and fifty thousand people that violence is not an alternative, I knew that indirectly I had touched all those people through him.

His cadence was working overtime and his energy touched everyone around him, including me.

"We will not be satisfied until justice rolls down like waters. And righteousness like a mighty stream…"

But that justice and righteousness must be for all people I pondered. Did he include the homosexual community, or did he even consider the injustices they suffered in this country just as Negroes did? Once Negroes gained victories, would they include my friends, my lovers and all the children who will be born gay, in his call for justice to roll down like water, or would he, as many Negro ministers, be exclusive in his inclusion. Was

Martin's words, spoken so eloquently, meant for only racial oppression or in his mind did it include the other side of me?

Martin exceeded his ten minutes and just when I assumed he was wrapping up his speech, he took off in a different direction.

"Even though we have difficult times ahead of us today and tomorrow, I still have a dream. It is a dream deeply rooted in the American dream. I have a dream that one day this nation will rise up and live out the true meaning of its creed we hold these truths to be self-evident that all men are created equal...."

I could appreciate the strength of these words, but I still struggled with their extension beyond just my race but also my sexual orientation. I deliberately remained outside the fight for gay rights, because all along I wanted to believe that as the race progressed toward equality, it would take the homosexual community along with it. I began to have my doubts when Martin jettisoned me for expediency years ago. I could only hope that now, as he made these proclamations about equality and rights, he meant to include every minority and oppressed group.

"I have a dream that my four little children will one day live in a nation where they will not be judged by the color of their skin but the content of their character...."

The crowd that earlier had become rather reticent was now fired up. As I stared out into the thousands of faces, I wondered how many out there shared my dilemma. They were here for two purposes but could only reveal one for fear of rejection. King had it right, we all should be judged by the content of our character and every homosexual man and every lesbian in that crowd should feel no shame about who they are. I caught a glimpse of Jimmy and Lorraine sitting in the third row out front, and you couldn't find two finer individuals representing this race and had proven their worth through their works. The content of their character was exquisite and sexual preferences only secondary.

Finally, I could detect that Martin was about to bring his speech to an end because he now had that Baptist Preacher's rhythm to his words.

"Let freedom ring and when this happens when we allow freedom to ring we will be able to speed up that day when all God's children, black men and white men, Jews and Gentiles, Protestants and Catholics will be able to join hands and sing in the words of the old Negro spiritual, free at last, free at last. Thank God Almighty we are free at last."

The deafening roar of the applause from the jubilant crowd shattered what had been the stillness of the afternoon as Martin finished, turned and walked back into the crowd standing behind him.

Once Reverend Benjamin Mays gave the closing prayer and the crowd, still excited by Martin's peroration of I have a dream, began to depart and sing,

"We shall overcome. We shall overcome someday. Deep in my heart, I do believe we shall overcome someday..."

I stood there, watched and listened. Two hundred and fifty thousand men, women, children, from all races and denominations and sexual preferences had just made the greatest statement for freedom and equality ever witnessed in one setting in this country.

"We'll walk hand in hand. We'll walk hand in hand. We'll walk hand in hand someday," they continued to sing as they made their way back to their buses, cars, trains and for some airplanes. "We are not afraid. We are not afraid. We are not afraid today. Oh, deep in my heart I do believe we shall overcome someday."

I continued to listen as their voices slowly faded. Without a doubt, all other speeches had faded away, and the only one that ring true for these spiritually endowed marchers was that of Dr. King when he told them of his dream. I knew his vision would resonate far into the future and years from now still be remembered. He secured his place in history, and I felt good knowing that I helped him reach that pinnacle of greatness from the time I first sat down in his home years ago, to the minute before he walked onto this magnificent stage and delivered, what I believed, would become his greatest speech ever, and one that would far exceed all of us in life. The Civil Rights Movement had its greatest day and despite the fact of my disappointment that my total being was not included, I still felt good. Successes could only get better from that day forward.

I finally made my way back to where the leaders and other dignitaries stood shaking hands and congratulating each other on a magnificent day.

"Bayard, congratulations," Roy said as he approached me and shook my hand.

Suddenly they all began to applaud.

"Without Bayard Rustin this day would have never happened," Randolph said as he placed his arm around my shoulder. "The country and the world owe a debt of gratitude. And knowing you, my friend, you probably wouldn't accept it."

He was right. All my life I rejected platitudes. "Thank you," the only words that came to me. My sight blurred from the tears that filled my eyes.

Martin grabbed and hugged me, something I know he wouldn't do ten years ago because of the stigma that most Negroes believed about homosexuals. Now it didn't matter, and I guess that is progress.

"Bayard, you have no idea how indebted I am to you," he said as his voice choked. "You have taught me all that I know about the importance that whatever I do be based on a philosophy of non-violence. I love you my friend."

"I love you too Martin, and you will always be one of my heroes. Of course, Mr. Randolph remains forever my number one hero."

"As long as you live and as long as I live, I will always acknowledge that the gains we have made in the Civil Rights Movement is due to you, and someday you will get the credit you deserve." Martin finished and moved back away.

"Gentlemen," Theodore Sorensen said as he hurried into the room, "President Kennedy would like to visit with you all in the Oval Office. Can you come with me now?"

"I believe Bayard should come with us," Roy suggested.

"No," I shot back. "The President wants to talk with the leaders and not the workers. Maybe at another time."

I stood there as they all left the room and out into the dawn of the day. I remained behind and watched as Tom, Rachelle and Norman came inside. This day really belonged to these three and the hundreds of workers dedicated to the success of the march, and they deserved all the accolades but only history someday would record what they did to make this happen for the entire world.

Epilogue

April 5, 1968
The White House

As the plane circled Dulles Airport, I could see the smoke rising to the sky from the fires burning in Washington, D. C. It had been nearly five years since that great afternoon the world witnessed in this same city, and where the now deceased Dr. King made the majestic speech sharing his dream of a country of peace and tranquility. Now, as I glanced out the window, I recalled Malcolm X response to the dream with the comment, it is more of a nightmare for Negroes in this country. But as they burned their neighborhoods and invited violence in order to restore order, it was the Negro creating the nightmare.

"Oh, my Lord, what are we doing to our country?" the lady sitting next to me remarked. "What a tragedy that the very man who preached peace and love, his memory is being tainted with turbulence and hatred."

I looked at her but had no comment. She was correct. The Negro at that very moment became his own worst enemy. Since the march in 1963, this country experienced the bombing of the Sixteenth Street Baptist Church in Birmingham, Alabama, where four little innocent girls were killed while attending Sunday school. Two months later President Kenned was assassinated in Dallas, Texas. Malcolm X fell to an assassin's bullet in February 1965, and now Dr. King and the only way his followers knew to respond was through more violence. This would mark four straight years, beginning with the Watts Riot in August 1965 that violence reigned in our streets. And who suffered the most were the very people perpetuating the destruction.

The struggle for a non-violent revolution in this country was lost when we failed to control the rhetoric coming from Stokely Carmichael and the young radicals, who had taken over control of SNCC from John Lewis. I am sure his shouting black power intoxicated a lot of young people, but what they never realized it had no promise of victory. Just like the pillaging and burning in the streets of Washington, D.C. on this day had no future for those participating.

"Good luck with the President," the lady said snapping me out of my musing.

The plane landed and came to a complete stop. We exited and as I made my way out of the terminal, a man holding a sign "Bayard Rustin" caught my attention. I hurried over to him.

"I am Bayard Rustin," I said.

"Good, we need to get you to the White House immediately. The President is waiting for you and other Negro leaders. Get in and we'll use the sirens to get through traffic which is backed up." The man grabbed the brief case I had carried on the plane. And as I slid into the backseat I asked. "What about my checked baggage?"

"All taken care of. It'll follow you wherever you go," the man said. "If the President has you stay over, it'll be delivered to your hotel. But if you leave after the meeting, it will be placed on the plane to wherever you are going. Now let's get you to the White House."

The driver pulled out of the airport onto the highway and turned on his siren. He got in the fast lane and soared by most of the traffic. I lay back, closed my eyes, and thought how ironic to be going to a meeting with President Lyndon Johnson instead of John Kennedy, who would have been in the final year of his presidency if not assassinated and reelected. History's twist during the past five years was that Johnson probably accomplished more for the Negro than what Kennedy could have done. We got the Civil Rights Bill, originally introduced by Kennedy but orchestrated through Congress by Johnson. And the next year in 1965, the President twisted enough arms to get the Voting Rights Act passed. Johnson, a Southerner, had turned out to be a great president for the Negro, and I was proud to support him back in 64. Actually, we had no choice. What Negro in their right mind would have supported Goldwater?

Just a year ago, I criticized my friend Martin for his ill-timed speech at Riverside Church in New York against the Vietnam War. I still believe that we just couldn't afford to alienate the President in that manner, because we needed him as we moved forward from protest to politics. It was necessary to play the game because more than anything else, the Negro needed economic security. The president was the key to gaining that security and just as he had made it possible through the Voting Rights Act for millions of Negroes to vote, he would do the same through his Great Society Programs for economic gain. After the speech at the Riverside Church, I do believe that Martin jeopardized those programs, and we once again parted company.

As the driver pulled into the front of the White House, I just wish I could have been more positive about his plans to conduct a Poor People's March on Washington, like the one we did in 1963. For some reason, he just couldn't break away from what he perceived as a need for protest by marching. I told him, and it was our very last conversation, that what worked in Montgomery in 1956 just wouldn't work again in Washington, D. C. in 1968. I was devastated when I received that call yesterday because I didn't have a chance to rectify our differences before he died. I knew that would haunt me for the rest of my life.

As I strolled into the Cabinet Conference Room in the West Wing of the White House, I was struck by the large number of leaders, both white and black, sitting around the table. Most notable was Thurgood Marshall, recently appointed to the United Supreme Court. He had never agreed with Dr. King's confrontational approach to desegregation and often in the past had criticized him. Now he sat at the table as an admirer of the man. Roy Wilkins sat on one side of the President and Clarence Mitchell on the other. Early on, Roy had very little respect for Martin but grew to admire him as a natural leader, and did accept Martin as the head person in the Civil Rights Movement after his speech in 1963. I found a place on the other side of the conference table between Dorothy Height and Washington, D.C. Mayor Walter Washington.

"We are going to show a unified front this afternoon as we pay tribute to a very great man who symbolized the best that this country has to offer," President Johnson began. "I have to admit that for the past few years, especially since his shift from domestic to international issues, our relationship faltered a great deal."

Yes, it did, I thought. He went from being Martin Luther King to being Martin Luther Coon.

"They are waiting for us over at the National Cathedral where they have a memorial service planned. Then we'll come back to the Fish Room where I'll say a few words to the country, and finally we'll get back here for a session on how to curb the violence that has taken over our cities."

We closely followed the President's plans for the day and at a little past four o'clock our meeting ended. The driver who picked me up at Dulles also drove me back out there and explained that my luggage would be waiting for me when I landed in Memphis. They held a plane's departure for me, and I finally lifted off at six-thirty.

As the plane climbed up toward the clouds, I looked back down at the city with the smoke and fire. I then stared up at the blue sky that was still radiant before the darkness. I could only hope that after this brief skirmish with violence ended, the radiance of the movement would return. We owed it to Dr. Martin Luther King, Jr. whose life I now went to glorify as the greatest apostle of non-violence the world has ever known.

CPSIA information can be obtained
at www.ICGtesting.com
Printed in the USA
BVHW072039090820
585854BV00001B/6

9 780997 655223